I0818173

CINDER
VALE
CAROLINE
PECKHAM
SUSANNE
VALENTI

FANTASY ROMANCE SERIES BY CAROLINE PECKHAM & SUSANNE VALENTI

Ruthless Boys of the Zodiac

Dark Fae

Savage Fae

Vicious Fae

Broken Fae

Warrior Fae

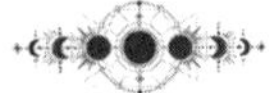

Zodiac Academy

Origins (Novella)

The Awakening

Ruthless Fae

The Reckoning

Shadow Princess

Cursed Fates

The Big A.S.S. Party (Novella)

Fated Throne

Heartless Sky

Sorrow and Starlight

Beyond The Veil (Novella)

Restless Stars

The Awakening: As Told by The Boys (Alternate POV)

Live and Let Lionel (Alternate POV)

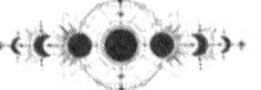

Darkmore Penitentiary

Caged Wolf

Alpha Wolf

Feral Wolf

Wild Wolf

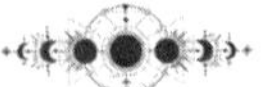

Sins of the Zodiac

Never Keep

Echo Fort

Cinder Vale

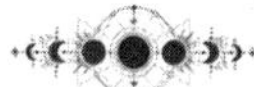

Crown of Hearts and Chaos

Hollow

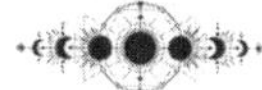

A Game of Malice and Greed

A Kingdom of Gods and Ruin

A Game of Malice and Greed

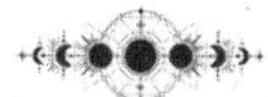

Age of Vampires

Eternal Reign

Immortal Prince

Infernal Creatures

Wrathful Mortals

Forsaken Relic

Ravaged Souls

Devious Gods

First published in the UK in 2026 by King's Hollow LLP
This edition first published in the US in 2026 by King's Hollow LLP
20 Eversley Road, Bexhill-On-Sea, East Sussex, UK, TN40 1HE
Distributed by Simon & Schuster

www.kingshollow.co.uk

Copyright © 2026 Caroline Peckham & Susanne Valenti

Interior formatting & design by Wild Elegance Formatting
Map design by Fred Kroner
Cover design by Caroline Peckham
Stock photos from DepositPhoto
All rights reserved.

No part of this publication may be reproduced or transmitted by any means, electronic, mechanical, photocopying or otherwise, without the prior permission of the copyright owner.

The moral right of the authors have been asserted.

Without in any way limiting the author's, Caroline Peckham and Susanne Valenti's, and the publisher's exclusive rights under copyright, any use of this publication to "train" generative artificial intelligence (AI) technologies to generate any works/images/text/videos is expressly prohibited. The authors reserve all rights to license uses of this work for generative AI training and development of machine learning language models.

ISBN: 978-1-916926-35-6

1 3 5 7 9 10 8 6 4 2

This book is typeset in Times New Roman & Assassin

Printed and bound in the US

This book is dedicated to the readers who love nothing more than to steal away into lands of soul-bursting fantasy, where dark Fae rule, Dragons scorch the earth with their almighty fire, and where love is found in its rawest form. Right here, and in the other lands contained upon your bookshelf, you can sink into a world where your heart burns for the characters between the pages and you'll soon remember you are right where you belong.

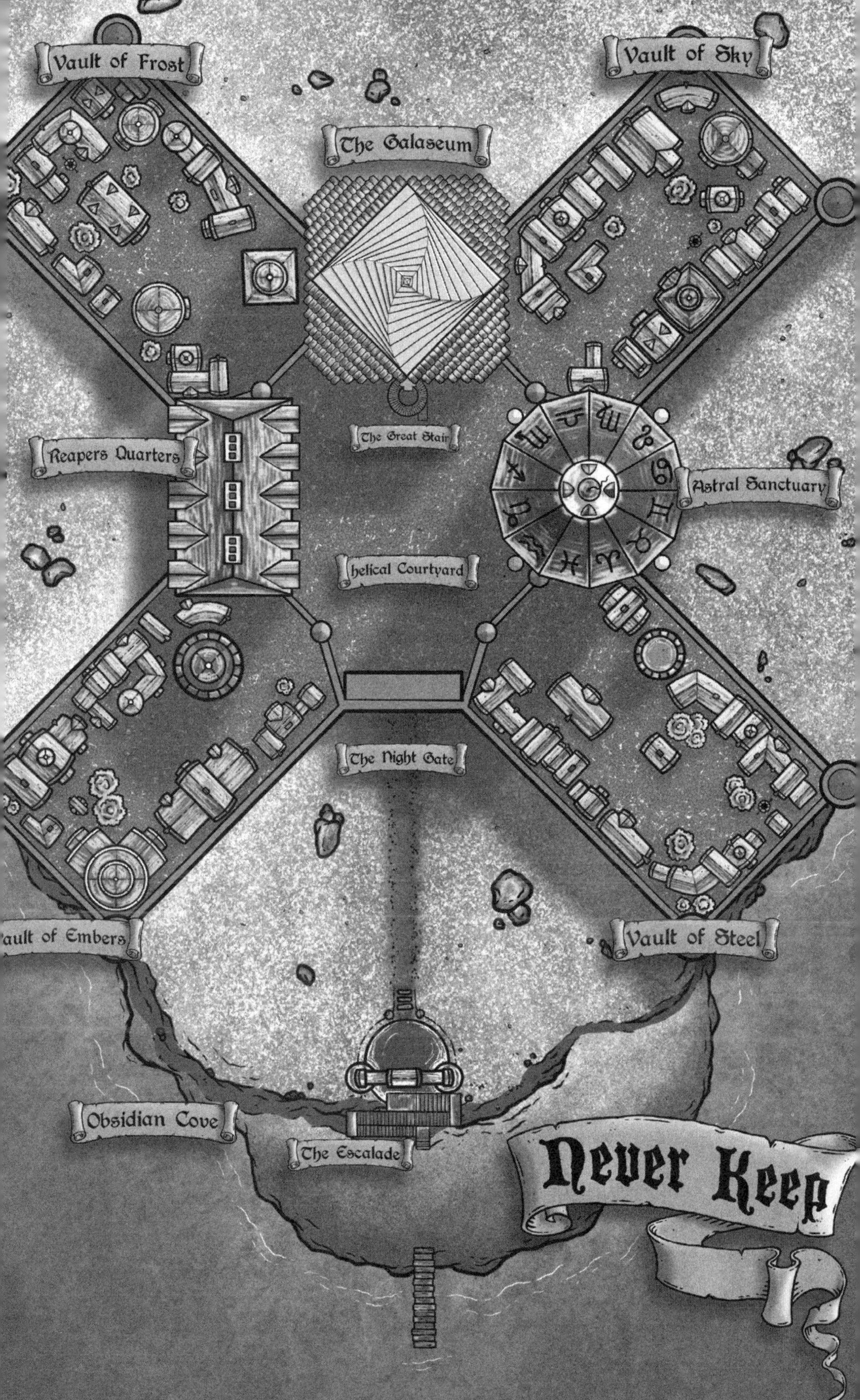
Vault of Frost
Vault of Sky
The Galaseum
The Great Stair
Reapers Quarters
Astral Sanctuary
helical Courtyard
The Night Gate
ault of Embers
Vault of Steel
Obsidian Cove
The Escalade
Never Keep

The Enclave
Neverkeep
Grimvale Passage
Helle Fort
Collingsgate
Altian Sea
Rackmere
Tower of Nor
Pomair
Echo Fort
Ironwraith
Leegaith
Hagard
Osciron
Wentos
Rifarn
Blackthorn Peak
Zenhyr Peninsula
Cinder-Vale
Pyros
Wandershire
Brinlass Lagoon
Crathguard
Valinsale
Cascada
Reefgale Port

Cavern of Lost Souls

Wrathbane

Steelhold

Lothsmere

Singer's Crest

Hargonville

Valborn Plains

Windy Bottom

Axethorn

Stormfell

Tempana

Avanis

Ramdale

Hallow Heath

Slateforge

Mount Hevast

Mount Tilor

Ravensview

Coalmere

The Crux

Raglith / Stone Castle

Castlelorain

Here There Be Vampires

Brissale Beach

Undashine Shore

Sunken Isles

Marellin

The Waning Lands

Coralia Falls

KAISER

CHAPTER ONE

A pitchy howl cut through the fog in my mind and my lips twisted at the corner. A smile.

It felt strange upon my lips, the accompanying warmth in my chest akin to the fires that burned so deeply in the heart of the volcanoes north of Cinder Vale.

My body was cold in contrast to that burn. I could name that sensation easily enough. Fire and ice were clear cut, two opposing forces that countered each other. This smile was harder to understand. I had to lay out the facts in my mind to even guess at what it meant.

The first, that I was bleeding out on a battlefield.

The second, that my people had lost the fight and our city had fallen to the hands of the Stonebreakers of Avanis.

The third, that I had been stabbed by Everest Arcadia just after she had returned all emotion to me, her Void cutting through some unknown power that had held me hostage. Then she'd left me there to die. But somehow, I still lived, my fingers tight around the dagger that was buried beneath my ribs.

Lastly, a familiar howl was calling to me across a field of ruin, speaking to me in a way I had long ago learned to understand.

North was coming. There; perhaps that was the reason for my smile.

It wasn't long before the wet nose of a Wolf pressed to my cheek and my gaze found my brother's. He was the largest Werewolf I knew, his beastly grey and white form towering over the largest of war horses.

"You came," I said, my voice roughened and dry. The shimmering blue form of Calcifiend landed on North's muzzle, clicking his tongue at me and I reached up to graze my thumb across the Sayer Dragon's brow.

North lowered to the ground and pushed his head into the crook of my arm with a low whine. I fisted my hand in his fur, letting him help me roll over and climb onto his back. My wounds jarred, my fist slipping on the hilt of the dagger and blood spilled forth, staining North's pelt. The pain was molten and my vision darkened but I determinedly held onto consciousness.

My brother rose up onto his mighty paws and took off across the darkened field, carrying me away from our enemies.

The colossal ships of Cascada were retreating fast, already shrinking away into the horizon along the canal; behind us, the Avanis machines that had ripped the earth apart were still causing a raucous sound that made the ground shudder.

The Skyforgers were leaving, abandoning the wreckage of Echo Fort which had fallen from their hovering island, and many of their winged warriors raced after their floating isle to escape.

In the crater where our proud city of Cinder Vale stood, the warriors of Avanis were celebrating their victory, their cheers following us into the gloom. My teeth ground together, my mind trying to work through the logic of our next steps, but it was difficult to ignore the ragged labouring of my heart in my chest. The weight of our failure perhaps causing the hardship.

There was no choice for us now but to follow the evacuation trains and flee the scene of our defeat. Our home.

That, of all things, seemed to make my heart thunder hardest.

Calcifiend flew ahead of North, marking a path of safety to lead us away from our enemies towards the tunnel where the trains had fled.

My eyelids grew heavy, drooping until darkness seized me and I willed my body to hold on before I disappeared into the black. But there was no knowing if I would wake. And between the flickers of consciousness and nothingness, I had visions of one Fae in my confused state. A girl with wild hair and eyes that burned with accusation.

Her Void had freed me. From what exactly, I wasn't certain yet. And she had also broken the bond of the Fearsire, shattering magic that should have been indestructible. I no longer felt the connection to her and somehow the emptiness her absence left behind had become a great chasm. Where was she now? Rejoicing my death?

Well, I still draw breath, silka la vin. And I believe the stars are not done tangling our fates yet.

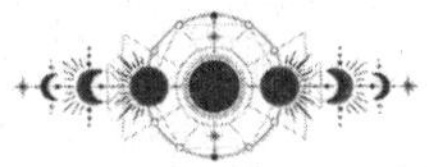

Fire. Roaring, searing, blazing fire scorched a mark on my chest and I lurched upright, a bellow leaving me, my muscles tensed and fists swinging. A wild tempest rushed through my body when I found soft flesh, my fists pummelling as I took on the group of Fae closing in around me. I punched and shoved and burned them with magic until a familiar face came into view between them.

"Stop," Mirelle commanded. She was still dirty from battle, blood flecks on her cheeks and fingers blackened by ash, her braided hair falling loose of its ties. "That's enough, love. You're safe. You're with your family now."

I blinked, slow to adjust to the heat in my veins, the adrenaline urging me to keep fighting, but Mirelle's eyes told me not to. And she had always guided me along the right path.

My breaths came heavily while the Fae I'd attacked scrambled to their feet, some of them holding poultice jars, and one gripping a heated lance which was still glowing hot from where it had touched me. I looked down at the wound beneath my ribs, now cauterized, the tissue glaringly red. With a wound so deep, they must have had to stitch it first and use a mixture of poultices to help the healing process.

Aries only knew if I would make it now. An infection might yet brew or the bleeding might not have been stopped properly on the inside. But I had looked death in the eye many times before and it hadn't taken me yet.

The floor was tremoring beneath my feet and from the dark red furnishings surrounding me and the vague shadow of the mountains moving beyond the windows, I surmised I had made it onto one of the evacuation trains.

"Kai?"

I turned to find North, his brow lined as he looked at me with some bright emotion in his green eyes. I took a step toward him and realised the extent of my injuries as my right leg gave out and I crashed to the floor, the adrenaline subsiding and leaving me raw with the pain of it all. I took stock of my ailments. There was a terrible pain in my right foot, but whether it was badly bruised or broken I wasn't sure, and there was certainly some deeper ligament damage that ran through my thigh.

North took hold of my arm, hauling me upright and guiding me back to the sofa I must have been lying on before. I limped with his help, a growl in my throat. The restriction of my injuries was a burden that made the heat in my flesh rise, but as I sat down and looked at North, the knotted lump in my chest gave way to something lighter.

His dark brown hair was sticking up in all directions, his face smeared with muck. The clothes he wore must have been given to him by someone half his size because he was nearly bursting out of them.

"You look like shit," I commented and his eyebrows lifted.

A bubble rose in my chest filled with light and it burst in my throat, creating a rumbling laugh.

North looked wildly back at our mother and Mirelle stepped forward, staring at me like I'd just grown a second head.

"What's wrong with him?" North demanded and my laughter grew louder. It felt uncontrollable, these bellowing, powerful waves of noise pouring from me – only coming more forcefully at the sight of everyone's strange expressions. I couldn't for the life of me understand what they were feeling, but I liked the way *I* was feeling at least.

"Has he been poisoned?" North begged as Mirelle kneeled down and gazed at me unblinkingly.

"No, I don't think it's that," she breathed, a tear falling from her eyes. Then another.

My laughter slowly hollowed out until the world was all too quiet. I touched Mirelle's face, catching her tears but not understanding the meaning of them. She was smiling, and I was fairly sure that tears meant she was unhappy. But weren't smiles the opposite?

"What happened to you when the Void halted everyone's magic?" she asked, her fingers knotting around my wrist and squeezing.

Memories ticked through my head and I saw it all through a sharper lens, the unusual sensations in my body cycling as I reviewed each moment.

"I was trying to reclaim the Void. I lost her during the battle. There were too many warriors seeking to capture her."

As Everest's face came to mind, a thick and potent force arose in my chest, like her hand was gripping my heart and squeezing it close to bursting.

Murmurs broke out around us like a drone of wild hornets in my ears and a snarl pulled at my mouth.

"Shut the fuck up!" I barked, the sharpness of the feeling taking me by surprise.

Mirelle squeezed my wrist to draw my focus back to her and the raking sensation in my chest lessened. "Go on," she urged.

"I was close when Everest used the Void. She wielded it to break the magic of the Fearsire."

"Impossible," Mirelle gasped.

"Apparently not," I said and a smile drew my lips wider, the rapid swing of my feelings taking me by surprise. I had no idea how to control them or if I should even try.

Mirelle took in a shaky breath, another tear escaping her, then she tightened her expression, looked to the Fae in the carriage and shouted, "Out! All of you leave, immediately."

They ran to escape the cabin, but North stayed, stepping closer to me.

"You too, North," Mirelle insisted.

"I'm done being kept out of the loop," he growled as Calcifiend landed on his shoulder. "I'm staying."

"North–" she started, but I cut over her.

"He stays," I said in a low voice and she looked back at me with widening eyes. "He stays or you can say no more."

North had been there for me my whole life. He was a constant companion and now that my mind was bright with feeling, I was seeing it all the clearer. The time he'd spent watching over me, the care he'd taken to ensure I acted appropriately. He could have abandoned me. He'd gotten nothing back from me in return for it, and I didn't understand why he'd looked after me at all, but I did know that I wanted him here now. That I felt only warmth toward him.

Mirelle nodded stiffly then rose to her feet, chin lifting as she gazed at North. My brother looked back at her and I sensed some power play was passing between them before he walked over and sat right next to me.

"Well?" Mirelle asked, her dark eyes piercing through me.

"Everest did something else to me. She woke me up. She broke some magic upon my mind, shattering it until it was gone. And in doing so, she released my soul from the nothingness." My lips tilted up again and I felt North's eyes on my face.

"He's smiling again," he breathed, looking from me to Mirelle. "Fucking smiling. But it doesn't make any sense. Why would the Void give him the ability to smile?"

Mirelle's throat bobbed and her jaw ticked before she turned abruptly away from us and stared out the window opposite. Trees swept past outside, a landscape of forest and hills shadowed by the thickening night.

"You know something," I said, the certainty filling me. I tried to get to my feet, a heated, frantic energy rising in my body. I wanted to grab Mirelle, shake her until she told me everything she knew, but North caught my arm to hold me back and the jarring of my injuries reminded me I wouldn't have gotten far anyway.

"It was never meant to be this way," Mirelle whispered as if the words were just for herself. "I only wanted to help you. To take away the pain."

"What did you do to him?" North demanded. "What the hell is going on?"

Mirelle turned to face me, her expression tight, creases by her eyes. "When I found you all those years ago, being attacked by those ice dogs, I loved you instantly. In that moment, you were mine to protect. I vowed to do all I could for you. It wasn't your injuries that hurt you most though. In the weeks after I took you in, you grieved. You grieved so deeply for your family, Kaiser. I did all I could. I soothed you. I housed you with North, knowing his Wolf nature would ensure he looked after you. But you never let go of the pain, love. You were hurting. You wouldn't eat. You were growing so thin..." More tears fell from her eyes and North laid a hand on my arm, the heat of his touch making me look his way. I felt a stirring in my chest, something coiled and barbed that wound around my heart.

North nuzzled me, his fingers brushing lightly over my arm. "I remember meeting you. I didn't have any other pups to play with who were my age and you looked about as broken as I felt back then. You were my brother the day Mirelle brought you to me. That was all there was to it."

"Then you remember his agony," Mirelle said, her voice heavy and hard.

North slowly nodded, his eyes still pinned on me. "You couldn't sleep through the night. You'd dream of your family. You'd call their names and I'd climb into your bed with you to hold you in my arms, but nothing helped. You told me you wanted to be with them. That you wanted to find them in the afterlife. I thought you might really do it. I feared you'd take your life. But then one day it just…stopped."

I frowned, remembering that time through the haze in my mind. Yes, I could recall it now. That pain.

Agony tore through me at the memory of my mama's face and I rose to my feet with a ragged gasp only to crash back to my seat when my leg gave out. My gaze fell on Mirelle and a strange fog fell over me as I tried to piece together what she had done.

My breaths came heavily; my chest wouldn't expand enough to let them pass easier.

"I'm so sorry, love," Mirelle rasped, stepping closer with a blaze in her eyes. "I didn't know it would take so much of you."

"You didn't know *what* would take so much?" I demanded, clinging to my true mama's face.

"What did you do?" North pressed.

"I went to the Reapers. I gave you a sleeping draft and carried you with me when I flew to the Astral Sanctuary in Osciron. I offered them any price to take away your pain." Her face paled as North cursed her and she didn't even reprimand him for it.

"And what did you pay?" North barked, shifting closer to me on the sofa.

"They said they would consult with the stars and ask what payment they wanted from me." Her jaw flexed again. "I would have done anything for you. You were mine. The stars had brought you to me and I couldn't let you down. I had to give them what they wanted."

She took a breath. "When the Reapers returned, they asked if I would undergo something they called the Excrucior. A tormented slumber. A sleep that would last one night only but would feel like a hundred years to me. It forced me to live through the most excruciating deaths of my ancestors, year after year, their most painful moments of body and soul relived through my mind. I experienced it as if I was them, forgetting myself at times and–" Her shoulders tremored and her lips closed tight. "Well, as hoped, the stars accepted my offering and the Reapers placed a spell upon you to supress your grief, Kaiser. At first, I was so happy that you could sleep again. That you would eat when I asked you to. But you were too quiet. Too placid. Too…empty. It seemed they hadn't just supressed your grief but all of your emotions. I took you back to them more than once. I begged for them to undo what they had done, but they said it was impossible. The spell had been cast. It was unbreakable."

"Until the Void," I said darkly, my brow lowering as this news crashed through me, all of it piecing together through the memories of a feelingless life.

"So all this time, you were under some spell," North said, gazing at me while Calcifiend chirruped quietly as if he understood what was being said. "And now…"

"Now he can feel again," Mirelle finished for him, a glint of joy in her eyes. "All thanks to the Void. She freed you."

"Well fuck a duck," North exhaled under his breath and I glanced at him, the look on his face combined with that image bringing another laugh to my lips.

"Yes, fuck all the ducks," I laughed harder, then shoved to my feet, hobbling my way toward Mirelle, the laughter turning to something wickeder in a flash. I grabbed a lamp from the closest table and hurled it at the wall beyond her head, my mirth turning to a roar.

"Kaiser," she implored, reaching for me but I smacked her hand away.

"You did this to me," I snarled, grabbing her by the throat, fingers digging in tight and cutting off her air.

"Kai!" North yelled, closing in behind me and trying to pull me back but my blood was burning again and I couldn't control the tide of liquid fire racing through me. This had to be *rage*.

Mirelle didn't fight me, her lips forming around another apology as I choked her, another tear falling down her cheek. A woman of war crumbling beneath me, showing me her only vulnerability. Me. And all of her children. This Fae who had taken us in from the streets, left ragged and lonely from the brutality of war. She had given us a home. A chance. A life. When no one else would.

Something cracked in my chest and I shoved her away. She fell into an armchair panting, her hand touching the red marks that my fingers had left on her skin.

I wheeled around, knocking North aside and grabbing a table, hurling the whole thing at the wall. I limped over to a desk and shoved it to the ground hard enough to snap it in two then flung my fist into the wall. The fire was blinding this time. My head a mess of thoughts, all tangled with jagged emotions I couldn't put a label to. Some squeezed, some jabbed, some cut, but all of them fucking hurt.

I threw my fist into the wood again and again until North wrestled me away from the wall, my knuckles split and bleeding. He jammed his knee into my bad leg and I shouted out as pain splintered through me and he dragged me back to the sofa, pushing me onto it with a firm glare.

"Stay," he ordered, pointing a finger at my face, then he whirled to look at Mirelle. "He has no idea how to control himself. He's a child in the body of a warrior. Do you know what you've done?"

"He'll learn," Mirelle whispered, her fingers still brushing the bruises which were forming on her throat. Her eyes hardened, her tears now dry and that fierce look back on her face as she made some decision. "He's now your ward, North. Teach him the ways of his emotions so he can control himself. Teach him well and teach him fast." She got to her feet, giving me a lingering look before exiting the carriage and leaving me with my brother.

North's brow lowered as he moved closer to me. "Do I even know who you are?" he whispered, almost to himself. "If all these years you've felt nothing, then how can you be who I know you to be?"

"If it helps, I don't know myself either," I gritted out.

His throat rose and fell as he considered that, his eyes dark. "We're only an hour or so from Ravensview. Do you think you can learn not to choke anyone when you get angry in that time?"

My brows lowered and I looked to my hands, flexing the fingers that had tried to strangle my mother. A heavy weight pulled at my chest and North rested a hand on my shoulder.

"That tugging sensation is guilt. You feel bad for hurting her."

"Yes, perhaps it's that," I agreed. "What am I meant to do now?"

"Apologise. Then don't do it again." He smiled then pushed a hand into my hair, restyling it to one side.

"I'm lost, North," I muttered and he met my gaze.

"No, Kai. I've got you. We'll figure this out together."

I nodded, unsure if such a thing was possible, or if I was too far gone to be saved.

"Wait here, I'll fetch us a drink. Sagittarius knows we need one tonight of all nights."

North headed from the carriage, leaving me with Calcifiend who flew onto my hand, licking a jagged scratch he found there.

I petted his head, holding him higher to study him. The glimmer of his blue scales was more captivating than they had ever been to me before. I remembered the day I'd found him out in the wilds, living off scraps with an injured wing that had caused him trouble flying.

North had insisted he would make a good pet and told me I was to look after him. As soon as Mirelle realised his power, she'd encouraged Calcifiend's bond to me. His kind usually imprinted upon Fae or others of their kind upon hatching, but it had happened late for him. Perhaps he had not known another soul until I'd come along and made his acquaintance. It felt… warm, light and good to know he'd survived the battle.

"Hello, fiend," I murmured and he released a purring chirrup. "I have a job for you."

He lifted his head, keen as always to do as I bid and I pressed my will into him to tell him what I wanted. Claws around my heart spoke of a desire that quickly devoured all other sensations. A desire that was entirely born of *her*.

"Go find Everest Arcadia. Don't let her out of your sight. And don't let her see you. You will watch her in every waking moment you can. And when the time is right, you will lead me right to her. Because she might not be my Fearsire anymore, but she and I have unfinished business that neither the stars nor the war will keep me from finishing."

VESPER

CHAPTER TWO

The hallways of the sprawling palace I was supposed to call home echoed hollowly as I strode through them. The stone felt colder than the last time I was here. The empty space more oppressive. Wrathbane Palace wasn't a place anyone might describe as homely but it had been the only one I'd ever known. Now, I felt a sharper rejection in the icy embrace of its passageways than even my Crossborn status had provided me. Though whether it was aimed *at* me or came *from* me was hard to tell.

Fae bowed as I passed. They didn't mutter anymore, though I supposed they did when I was far from earshot. What was it they whispered among themselves? Did they praise me for capturing a Dragon for our kingdom? Or did they curse me for finding a way into the position they'd always been so desperate to deny me?

They claimed I'd risen from the dead. Just another legend to add to my epitaph. And now I strode through echoing halls, living out the dream I'd worked so hard for, had sought to share so desperately with my sisters, but I found I didn't want it anymore.

"Who'd have thought I'd gladly exchange this life for just another day of your bickering and sniping?" I mused to nothing and no one, the vial of blood hanging from my neck warming against my skin.

I liked to think they still stalked me in the dark, flanking me as always. Dalia and Moraine, my sisters in arms and all other aspects too. But when I turned, there was no one there. No hint of amusement in dark eyes or the start of a smile on a hardened mouth.

Alone as always.

No, not always.

A flash of steel-grey scales and eyes shot through with silver pressed into my mind and I swallowed against the intrusive thoughts that tried to follow.

There were far worse places a Dragon might find himself than in a tower of Stormfell, I reminded myself. He even had a view of the sky. It was no dank cave at least.

I kept walking, moving through the palace and heading for the ballroom, the clip of my boots on the polished floor echoing loudly until I felt like the sound itself was closing in around me.

Right, left, right, left.

The stairs loomed before me, the swish of my brocade skirt skimming around my thighs and adding a faint rustle to the racket of my steps.

Right, left, right, left.

I could make out the polite chatter and feigned laughter of the courtiers now, all of them prancing and parading, congratulating themselves on their mere existence. Who would I exchange knowing smiles with in mockery of their bullshit? Who would I creep away to a corner with so that we might drink too much of their expensive wine and ridicule everything about them from their boots to their hairstyles?

I'd been jealous of those courtiers once. Deep down, beneath our mockery and sneering, I'd known that was the root of it. We weren't them and it rankled to be reminded of it so forcefully. No matter how fully we proved ourselves in all the ways that should have counted, we were never going to be the same as those people. Me most of all. But we had been the same as one another. We'd had that comradery and nothing else had mattered besides it in comparison. Of course that was when there was a *we* and not simply an *I*. An 'I' shared everything with no one and nothing with everyone. And so it seemed I would remain.

The grand doors appeared ahead of me, guards posted on either side, ready to announce me and welcome me in as if I really was one of them, the lies painting themselves on top of one another so thickly that they almost appeared as truth. At least until the paint cracked and gave sight of my monstrosity beneath. Then they'd see me as they always had and I would stand alone as I surveyed them in kind…

My breaths came more shallowly. My pulse pounded wildly in my ears and suddenly I wasn't striding for those doors anymore but turning, vaulting a low window and escaping into the relative silence of the decorative courtyard beyond it.

Relief rushed through me at my escape, the momentary reprieve a treasured thing. Just a moment to hide from the pressure of it all, just a moment to admit to myself that this place was even emptier than my heart which was a desolate and lonely thing indeed.

I pressed my back to the cold stone of the wall and angled my chin towards the heavens above, my fingers coiling around the vial which hung at my throat as I reached for them in every way I could, my heart twisting and splintering with their loss. The backs of my eyes burned, my throat thickened and every doubt which clung to me grew claws and dug them in so tightly that I could scarcely breathe at all–

"Well, well, if it isn't my brother's prize plaything," a low voice crooned and I stiffened, my moment of solitude shattered as my head snapped around and I found myself looking into the dark eyes of Evard Aquila.

Dragor's youngest brother had always been the one of his siblings I was most wary of. Evard was cunning, prone to knowing secrets he had no business in discovering and often finding ways to win the king's favour despite commanding the smallest of the four siblings' armies.

He looked a lot like his brother, all three of the male heirs sharing that pale hair and those light blue eyes – though where Dragor was striking in his beauty, Evard had a roughness to his appearance, his jaw stronger, stubble clinging to it always, his eyes full of dark schemes which could only spell trouble for me.

My hand fell from the vial of blood I wore at my throat in a move I fought to make seem casual while the ghosts of my failures retreated into the shadows at my back where they so often lingered.

"I didn't mean to disturb you, my prince," I said swiftly, finding the well-practiced court manners I only employed for royalty. My voice scraped roughly over the grief in my throat but Evard didn't know me well enough to notice it.

I quickly nodded my head into a bow before making to turn away. But of course it wasn't going to be that easy.

Evard caught my wrist and I stiffened as I turned to face him once more, his muscular body looming over mine in that way so many men enjoyed, like his bulk gave him some kind of power over me. This was a dance I knew the steps to all too well, though kicking a prince in his manhood might just get me hanged so I couldn't play it in the way I most preferred. Instead, I turned to my more natural talents.

I smiled sweetly, like a preening courtier flattered by his attention and he snorted in amusement.

"I've watched you play this game before," he said, releasing his hold on me. "Pretty smiles and dangerous eyes. If I'm not mistaken, you're very much enjoying a little fantasy about my death while wearing that seductive look for me."

"I spend all of my free time fantasising about death," I assured him, my voice dripping with allure. "So don't take it personally."

Evard chuckled, moving closer instead of backing away. He was either very brave or very stupid. Or likely the arrogance born with his birthright made both the answer.

"Batting her eyelashes doesn't work so she switches to threats. Let me think, what would follow on next?" He ran his fingers over his chin as if pondering then snapped them in my face and pointed at me. "Got it. This has two different plays. If I was pretty much anyone else you'd switch to insults and likely draw a weapon, maybe embarrass me in front of my peers or challenge me to a brawl to scare me off."

My lips twitched at his assessment. "But as you're not anyone else?" I purred, reaching out to taste his desires and finding them difficult to discern. He wanted something from me but this wasn't lust or violence. There was ambition to it but that was no surprise within the royal family. All of the Aquila heirs were locked in a never ending fight for supremacy until their father declared an heir to his crown outright.

Evard smirked at me. "As I'm too important to kill and one of the only Fae here who you have no choice but to accept as your superior, you'll fall into the perfect play of the ideal courtier. You'll say all the right things, bow your head low, smile and simper but all with that blazing look in your eyes which says your deference and respect isn't something you're truly giving. That's why Laurena hates you so much, you know? She can see your contempt blazing in your eyes but our big brother shields you from reproach so she can't do shit about it."

"Princess Laurena is a–"

"Bitch," he cut in before I could spew some bullshit line about how devoted I was to the entire royal family. I had to force my lips not to twitch into any semblance of a smile. Even agreeing with him on that could see me whipped. But disagreeing would mean challenging the word of a prince which could result in the same, so my only winning move was silence.

Prince Evard sighed when I failed to rise to the bait. I wouldn't agree and wouldn't contradict him either. He was right. I knew the rules to this game inside out and we could play it all evening if he insisted.

"What did my brother do to earn such unending loyalty from you?" he asked curiously.

A burning knot formed in my stomach at his words, a sense of guilt tying around my insides which I struggled to place before realising that the cause of it was that his accusation wasn't true anymore. My loyalty to Prince Dragor wasn't the thing it had once been. But I would never voice that aloud.

"I am loyal to all of the Aquila line and the great land of Stormfell. I only happen to serve Prince Dragor because it was his army to which I was assigned when I joined the battlefield for the first time. He earned my respect and loyalty in person through every act of courage and valour I witnessed and–"

Prince Evard waved my words aside like the rehearsed blathering we both knew them to be. “Alright, forget my brother. Let’s focus on the point of this little tête-à-tête, hmm?”

“Please,” I agreed and his smirk deepened.

“Until now, my siblings and I have been on a fairly level standing so far as my father is concerned. Until now, it was rather difficult for anyone to accurately guess which of us he might select for the crown.”

“Until the Dragon?” I surmised, cutting to the point because I was already late enough for the ball and I wanted this conversation done.

“Until the Dragon,” Evard echoed, his fingers flicking and a silencing shield forming around us to conceal the rest of our conversation from the potential of any prying ears. “Do you want to visit him?” he offered, tone casual, eyes gleaming.

I blinked, having expected some demands over where I’d found Bastian and how I’d captured him, perhaps an interrogation into whether there might be more of his kind out there or at least a show of his hand, but that question had thrown me.

“The Dragon?” I clarified, glancing out of the courtyard towards the tall eastern tower where I knew Bastian was being held.

“He spits your name like a curse,” Evard supplied. “There is something between you which has harboured deep hatred. And yes, I’m certain he isn’t thrilled to have been captured but it feels... personal when it comes to you.”

“We travelled alone for weeks. I think he had hoped I might not truly deliver him to this fate. But my loyalty to Stormfell is–”

“Yes, yes, Stormfell is of course the greatest love any of us will ever know. But I think we might be able to help each other.”

“How?” I asked sceptically.

“Dragor might have brought the Dragon here but he can’t get him to cooperate, or talk or even eat, so far as it stands. But you…well you not only know the Dragon more intimately than the rest of us but you have an insight into his desires. Tell me what it is he wants and perhaps I can do something for you in turn."

"Like?" I asked.

Prince Evard looked me over with that piercing stare of his, probing for my secrets and hunting for the perfect one to tempt me. I knew his style, I could feel his desire to gain my allegiance and I supposed I should have been flattered to find myself worthy of the attention of a man as powerful as him. With two princes vying for my favour it was clear that I was in a far more prominent position within the court than I'd ever been before but that didn't fill me with the satisfaction it once would have.

"You aren't married. I could secure you a good match?" he tried but I snorted.

"I want a man even less than I want to continue this conversation," I muttered and his smile sharpened, noting the lack of formality.

I didn't know this prince and it wouldn't serve me to get on the wrong side of him so I tried to soften my words with a shrug. "My only love is Stormfe–"

"Love isn't what we're discussing."

"Fine. But there isn't going to be a match made for me any time soon. I'm Crossborn. Not even the capture of a Dragon can change that." I gilded my words and refused to feel the burn of them as they simmered in my gut. This was the way it had to be.

"Ah – then perhaps I should spoil the surprise? My dear brother plans to re-name you this very night. You won't be Crossborn any longer. After tonight you'll be an air-named warrior with a house and title all of your own. Lady Vesper Dragonsbane, first of your name and head of your line. He's very pleased with himself over that one, I might add. Though I think it's a little on the nose."

My tongue stuck to the roof of my mouth, the joy, the excitement, the sense of worth that should have come at such an unthinkable gift completely absent as I took it in. I blinked dumbly and Evard's smile widened.

"So, a match?" he pushed but my ears were still ringing with his last declaration.

I started to shake my head.

"Not even one to an Aquila?"

I blinked at him again, taking far too long to realise what he was offering and I snorted.

"You think I'd make a good match for *you?*" The words hadn't meant to come out scathing but somehow they did and his eyes flashed in warning.

"Not really," he admitted. "But I think you'd be a powerful one. In truth, I have no interest in taking a wife or a husband or partaking in any of the physical pursuits your kind is famed for. But I can appreciate what you are far better than I think my dear brother does. You're a symbol of both hope and despair. You strike fear into the hearts of our enemies and show even the lowest of our people how far they might rise should their dedication be true enough. No doubt you could bear us heirs when the time comes too but I won't waste your time on practicing the endeavour. You could take lovers if you wished so long as you were subtle about it. And best of all, our union would make my big brother sick with rage."

I couldn't help but release a breath of laughter, shaking my head as I looked back towards that darkened tower.

"Your father would never favour you if you took me for a bride,"

I pointed out but Evard just scoffed.

"My father doesn't give a shit about bloodlines. He was the sixth born and looked nothing like his siblings. It was an open secret that my grandmother was fucking her personal guard and I know for a fact that her lover had ice white hair and pale blue eyes. So no, the bastard-born king won't give a fuck that you were sired in another land. He won't care that the people might hate you for it either. He has only ever cared about one thing and that is power. That's why the Sinfair exist after all. You are given the chance to reclaim power for yourselves despite the shame that has fallen upon you. And *you*, Vesper Dragonsbane, are the epitome of that goal."

"Well, I can see what's in it for me, but you're offering an awful lot for very little if all you expect me to give you in turn are insights into the Dragon's motivations," I said carefully because there wasn't going to be an easy way to say no to his offer. And it surprised me how certainly I knew I wanted to say no. He was offering me more than I'd ever dreamed of claiming in this place. He might have even been offering me the chance to become queen. But…I didn't want it anymore.

"I never said that was all," Evard purred.

"And I never said yes," I returned. "But let's leave it at maybe and I'll offer you this – all that Bastian ever desired whilst in my company was one thing and it's the one thing you cannot offer him."

"Yes?"

"Freedom."

Evard released a frustrated breath but stepped back to allow me to leave.

I dropped into a curtsey, smiling through the contempt in my eyes and he grinned as he watched me play my part.

I turned and vaulted the low wall which deposited me back into the corridor I'd attempted to escape once already then raised my chin and strode straight towards the double doors which led into the ballroom. If the guards standing there had noticed my detour or had any thoughts on it they kept them to themselves as I swept past them without a glance.

Courtiers paraded and swirled before me as I entered the brightly lit room, the huge statues of the three zodiac symbols which were devoted to air magic all seeming to stare at me as I entered.

I looked the part, I played the part, and yet standing among these Fae only ever made it clearer to me how far apart from them I truly was. I'd never be an aristocrat no matter the name they called me by and Sky Witch was far more honest than Lady Dragonsbane could ever hope to be.

The king sat in the centre of the long table which watched over the festivities, Prince Roarson and Princess Laurena at their places to his right. But Dragor wasn't with them.

I scanned the crowd, reaching out with my gifts and finding his desire to locate me and chastise me for my lateness within the throng.

I strode through the crowd, not caring that I moved across the dancefloor and made several of the Fae there stumble their steps to avoid me.

Prince Dragor was a tall man and easily recognisable once I made it past the heart of the crowd. He spotted me too, probably in part because one woman looked my way then shrieked a desperate plea of devotion to me before ripping her dress down and revealing her breasts to the room at large.

Some of her friends managed to contain themselves and haul her away but others called out more lewd and desperate promises to me.

I hardly even noticed them in crowds like this anymore. It was as if they were background noise; they might have been the rain or the wind instead of a man crying out for me to suck his toes while another begged me to choke him and call him a little bitch.

Prince Dragor barked commands at the guards who lingered in the shadows and they dragged the most vocal of my admirers away.

"You're late," the prince said as he strode towards me, taking hold of my arm and guiding me out of the crowd towards the tall doors which led out onto the balcony.

"I didn't realise my attendance was so important," I replied, though he had made it more than clear to me that he'd wanted me here on time.

Dragor's fingers bit into my arm as he tugged me outside but as the cold air struck us he released a deep breath and relaxed his grip once more.

"Remind me, dear Vesper, who is it you have sworn yourself to?"

"Do I really have to say it so often?" I asked, shifting aside so that he had no choice but to release me and I leaned against the rail at the edge of the balcony, looking out over the sprawling view of the city below us.

"I mean to honour you tonight," he began but I turned to him, my chin held high as I met his cool gaze.

"I don't require any honour. I only want what you promised me. I captured your Dragon and brought him to you. Now let me hunt the man who killed my sisters."

Dragor considered me for a long moment and I knew he was expecting me to lower my eyes but I wasn't the same woman I'd been before losing them and I would never back down from this. I'd made them a promise and I'd put it off for too long already.

"Do you remember the words of the oath you swore to me? The ones you bound yourself to on penalty of the stars themselves?" he asked slowly.

"Yes," I growled. "And I upheld my end."

"Did you? Because if I recall correctly, I specified that I would only grant you leave to hunt the man who pretended to be Cayde Avior while spying upon our kingdom once I was satisfied that your loyalty to me was without question. Do I appear satisfied to you?" he asked curiously, his eyes flashing with triumph while my gut plummeted in turn.

"I…you can't truly be questioning my loyalty after all this time?" I spluttered, my words tripping over themselves in their haste to exit my mouth.

"Can't I?" He stepped closer to me, diminishing me within his shadow and moving to place his hands on the rails either side of me so that my back was to the drop behind us.

I swallowed down the vitriol I so desperately wanted to spit at him because if I lost myself to fury now I might never claw back control.

"I have proven myself to you time and again," I hissed, unable to fully keep the bitterness from my voice.

"So it appears. But I need more proof still, I'm afraid."

"Like what?" I asked in desperation, the backs of my eyes burning with the pure injustice of it. I'd done everything he'd asked of me, I'd delivered him his Dragon despite what it had cost me to do so and yet still he denied me the only thing I'd ever asked of him.

"The Void," he growled, reaching into his jacket pocket and taking a piece of paper from his breast pocket. "Is a Fae. One who I believe trained with you at Never Keep."

"What?" I asked, shaking my head, the change in direction leaving my thoughts tumbling over themselves.

"She was one of the Cascadian Neophytes. Perhaps you took note of her while there?" He thrust the piece of parchment at me and I took it, unfolding it while his eyes bored into my face. I blinked dumbly at the woman who stared back at me from the sketch which was revealed within.

They'd gotten her eyes wrong, though the ferocious glint in them wasn't without accuracy. Her hair was a mane worthy of a lion instead of the wild tangles I'd grown so familiar with and the shape of her mouth wasn't entirely right, but I knew her all the same. In one glance I knew her. My kitty cat.

"Who is this?" I asked and he growled in frustration, snatching the parchment away from me and stuffing it back into his pocket.

"She is the only thing that matters at the moment. She is the one who caused our people to tumble from the sky and break upon the battlefield we had been so close to claiming. That woman is the Void. And she is the only thing any of us will be concentrating on until we wrestle her from the grasp of the Cascadians and force her beneath the heel of our great kingdom."

"I thought the Void was a weapon or a…monster," I said, my eyes on his embroidered jacket, my mind spinning with what he was claiming. "How do you know it's this woman?"

"The information I have on this is undeniable. Whatever rumours or expectations we might have once had of the Void...they are all null and nothing now. She is what we have all been seeking for so long. So if I decide to utilise you in any kind of hunt it will be for her. Not for some bastard who broke your pathetic heart and taught you the meaning of betrayal. Perhaps it was a lesson you were in dire need of learning – you fell for his lies easily enough after all."

I swung for him before I could think better of it and either because it had come so fast or because in that moment I really was better than him, I didn't know, but my fist collided with his jaw and sent him staggering back.

Dragor threw his hand out and I had the sense to stop myself from resisting him as the force of his air magic ripped me off my feet and hoisted me into the air over the drop from the balcony. He straightened, his hand caressing his jaw where I could already see a bruise forming and to my surprise he barked a laugh.

"With loyalty like that, who needs enemies?" he sneered.

I swallowed thickly, glancing down at the drop below me while the wind tore strands of pink hair from their ties and made them lash against my cheeks. He could hold me in the grasp of his power and dash me to pieces on the cobbles far below or hurl me all the way out into the city and break my body in the middle of the market square.

"I need vengeance," I choked out, my heart cracking open before him and he considered that for a long moment before nodding and lowering me back to the balcony in front of him.

"And you can have it. But not until I say. And not before we claim the Void or destroy it failing that. Now come, you're about to be honoured before the entire court – I'm sure my brother thoroughly enjoyed ruining the surprise for you on that one."

"You knew?" I asked, shaking my hands out as he released me from the hold of his power.

"Of course I knew. And if you plan on working to win my favour you'll agree to whatever schemes he has planned for you while reporting them all back to me."

"He offered me his hand," I said darkly.

Dragor released a surprised laugh. "Then perhaps I'll have you marry him and report back to me on his shortcomings in the marital bed. The stars know I've never found a Fae willing to sell me scandals from his bedroom before."

"I don't believe he holds much interest in the bedroom," I said, but I wouldn't be finding out regardless. Dragor might have been able to order me to do a lot of things, but marriage had never been on the cards.

"Then I'll have to set you on the trail of his other secrets. It's time my father picked an heir and we all need to stop pretending it won't be me. Once that has been made clear I will be able to put my siblings to work in my court in far more productive ways than their current scheming for my place allows."

I said nothing. It was treason to speculate after all and though I doubted Dragor would lose his head for such words, I certainly might.

I followed him back into the ballroom, ready to accept my new name and title and all the bullshit that went with it while inside, my heart was racing and my thoughts were tangling themselves into knots.

I *would* find a way to hunt Cayde down. And I was going to figure out what the hell the truth was about Everest too. And Bastian… well, Bastian was a mess of emotions I refused to even look at within myself but I was going to have to face what I'd done there as well.

I glanced at Dragor as he led me through the throng of Fae who hated what I was and all I'd ever been. I hadn't told him that I knew the one he hunted. I hadn't said a word about her to him. Which meant he really was right to doubt my loyalty. Because I'd just chosen to shield a girl from Cascada from his wrath instead of spilling my secrets to him the way any truly devoted subject should.

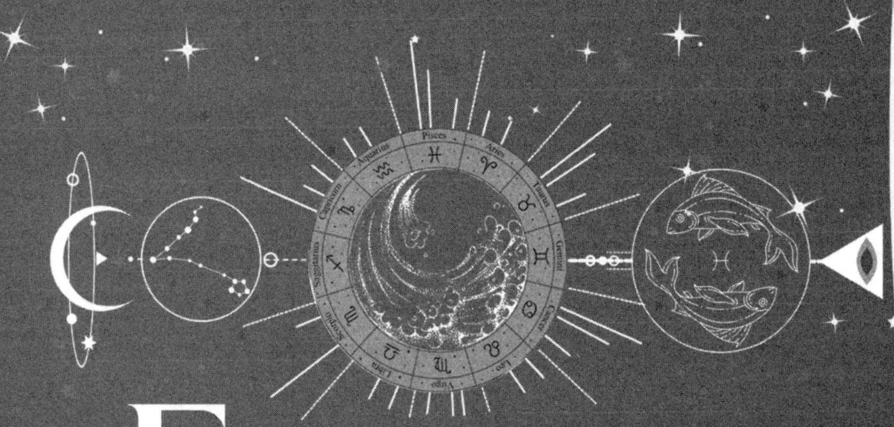

EVEREST

CHAPTER THREE

I could have the world.

Any want fulfilled.

But I still wasn't content.

"There are only two things I desire right now and you're denying me both," I growled at my father.

"I will give you both in time if only you would be patient," he insisted for the hundredth time. He was dressed in linens again, no sign of his armour, no glint of a sword. It was as if he had no intention to return to battle at all.

The heat of the day only intensified my ire. They'd given me material to make a dress at least and in my boredom, stuck here in this luxurious handwoven tent on Undashine Shore, I'd stitched the blue silk into a thing of beauty. It flowed down my body, clinging to my curves, revealing the dip of my cleavage and the sheen of my legs between the slivers of material. Yes, I looked fucking radiant but I was frustrated beyond belief.

"Did I tell you to stop dancing?" I clipped at Alina Seaman who I'd requested as my jester for the journey to Crathguard. Oh how she danced for me, her lips clamped tightly shut on the words she wouldn't dare to utter. But by the sun, the moon and the stars, she hated me. I could see it in the depths of her angry, angry eyes. Simmering there, bubbling, boiling deep and burning her from within.

She wore a grey dress with a long donkey's tail that paired with the mask and the large ears that were weaved into her hair. My choice, of course. I'd made them for her, presented them on a silver platter and watched her jaw tick whilst she pulled on her costume. Through a tight grin that had looked achingly painful, she had thanked me too.

Now, she danced for me, shaking her ass and ee-ooring like I'd requested. But not even that was enough to make me smile. The first time had been hilarious, the second amusing, but this time… it was just another disappointment.

The half-naked men who had been assigned to hand-feed me all kinds of succulent fruit from across our land shared a snigger at Alina's expense, but I couldn't summon a wisp of a smile.

I stepped closer to father, my brows drawing together. "If we can't go to war then give me Mavus Angelico at least. Your spies must have located him by now."

"Like I told you before, we are yet to find him. But I assure you, we'll bring him straight to you once he's located. Now rest, daughter. The White Mare is almost ready to sail. The whole of Cascada is waiting to come and lay blessings at our feet."

"I'm done being paraded around. What is the point of my power if it isn't used to cease the war? We could have peace in a week if we march now."

Father rested a hand on my shoulder, squeezing and leaning down to lay a kiss upon my cheek. I felt that kiss in my chest, the way it charmed my heart like a snake, luring me into the promise of his affection. I might just be loved by him now. He was yet to say the words though. Holding me ransom by withholding the last piece of the puzzle which could complete me.

"Not yet, my child. Let the people celebrate first. It will bolster the hearts of the warriors and give them time to recuperate before we head to war again."

"At least take me to the Magistrine," I insisted, thinking of the monster at Never Keep and the vow I'd made to see it destroyed. "Let's head there first."

"I will only take you there once we have defeated our enemies. Imagine the celebrations we will be greeted with in Marella when we arrive with the news of Cascada's victory?"

"But you don't understand," I implored. "The Reapers are up to something. I need to speak with our rulers."

"Yes, yes, all in good time," he said, waving a hand, clearly not having listened to what I'd said. "Go spend some time on the beach. Relax before we head for Crathguard. You have earned it, my child." He steered me toward the exit and I gritted my teeth as he manoeuvred me outside, already wincing before the cheers and laments went up.

Father nudged me toward the crowd, shouting out for all to hear, "My daughter, the great Void, has come to celebrate among her people!"

I was grabbed by eager hands, pulling me into the crowd. Many complimented my dress, others brushed their fingers over my arms and thanked the stars for my existence, while some even wept at the sight of my face.

The more they touched me, the more my heart raced and all I could think of was the way I'd nearly been crushed on the battlefield by the tide of warriors who had wanted to claim me for themselves. The clawing hands, the fingernails raking at my skin, the hungry eyes and the wetting of lips. I was the answer to the problems of the masses. I was the key to end the war. The promise made through prophecy. Here I was for the world to claim. I should have delighted in their praise, found worthiness in their love, but it wasn't what I felt at all.

I shoved my way out of them, the panic slicing into me, the claustrophobia of it all making my gut twist.

Somehow, I made it back to the tent, sensing Father's disappointed gaze following me all the way.

"Out!" I shouted at the fruit-feeders, kicking over a tray of strawberries and they scurried through the tent flaps, leaving me with Alina. She offered me a feeble ee-oor and I sighed.

"You too," I insisted.

She hesitated, glancing at the exit then back to me. "I can dance better." She started shaking her ass again, getting down on all fours and putting in some real effort to look like a jiving donkey. But not even that lightened my mood.

"I don't want you to dance. Just go," I huffed.

"Have I displeased you?" she asked nervously, knowing the power I held now. I could probably have her rank stripped. I likely even had the power to execute her. But all I wanted was for her to leave.

"You never cared about displeasing me before," I said bitterly.

"That was before I knew you were important." She bit her lip, clearly regretting the words as her cheeks turned bright pink. "I mean, not that you weren't before, it's just I didn't know you weren't, you know?"

"Just go," I growled and she finally left me alone, squeaking an apology as she went.

I sank down onto the soft green cushions laid out for me, hugging my knees to my chest and burying my face against them.

The moment my eyes closed, I saw *him*.

Twisted on that cliff with my dagger under his ribs and I squeezed my eyes shut even harder, trying to push the memory away. I should have been elated by his death. Perhaps I was, in ways. But whenever his face came to my mind, I felt something more painful too. An emotion I couldn't put a name to.

He was the reason for my mother's death and the scar upon my palm.

He was the tarnish on my soul and the reason for my eternal anguish.

He was gone and never coming back.

There it was. That hurt again. A note of regret, maybe. A longing for answers I'd never receive. I didn't know where this yearning came from, but instead of peace in the wake of his death I only found more torment.

My own father had been responsible for the death of his family. I'd seen it for myself. Yes, I'd known Abraham Rake was a ruthless soul, but I'd never considered his brutality extended to children. I was torn, my heart desiring his love and yet there were fractured, confused pieces of me resisting it too. I couldn't quiet these feelings no matter how much I tried. I simply knew too much and couldn't un-know it.

"Sorry, er, Everest?"

I looked up, finding Ransom there in a light blue shirt and white trousers, his sword strapped to his hip. At least he was one percent more ready for war than Father.

"Yes?" I said tightly, venom seeping into the word.

My half-brother kept visiting me and I had a feeling Father was ordering him to. He always brought a gift too, but I didn't think he was trying to make up for what he'd done to me. I was pretty damn sure he'd been told to bring one.

He stood stiffly in the entrance, the white curtains that made the door fluttering in the wind and ruffling his brown hair. He had a seashell in his grip, a conch bigger than his head that sparkled like rhinestones.

"For you," he muttered, then tossed it on a pillow.

I pursed my lips. "Anything else?"

He kicked his bare feet in the sand at the edge of the entranceway, looking awkward before he stepped onto the rug and moved to sit on one of the cushions. The silence stretched. The quiet pressing in until I couldn't bear it any longer.

"What do you want, Ransom?" I demanded.

"I think you're right," he blurted. "We should be marching on the other lands, not heading to Crathguard for more celebrations. We're wasting time here. You said we could have peace, right?"

"Right," I replied, narrowing my gaze. "But Father won't listen to me."

"He *has* to listen to you," he whispered, shooting a wary glance at the exit as if he was worried he might be overheard. "You can do anything you want now. It doesn't even need to be a battle. We can walk into enemy lands; you can Void them all and they'll have to surrender. No bloodshed."

"You think they'll just lay down their weapons and give up their lands?" I scoffed. "The warriors will fight, magic or not."

"But we can subdue them with our power," Ransom said quickly. "We won't *have* to kill anyone."

I nodded slowly, considering his point. "Have you mentioned this idea to Father?"

"No," he admitted. "I thought it would be better coming from, you know, the almighty Void." His tone was dry but not bitter.

I breathed a laugh and he smiled at me like we were actually normal siblings. But my laughter quickly soured and I scowled at him.

I thought of Harlon, how much easier this would have been if he was here by my side. He wouldn't look at me like I was some untouchable deity. He'd see me as *me*. But I didn't even know where he was. He'd chosen the Reapers, he'd turned his back on me and broken his promise that he would never pick them over me. It hurt. And what hurt more was that Mavus had said Harlon would do this in the end. And I hated that that snake of a trader had been right all along.

Mavus had sold me out and left me fighting for my life and as soon as he was brought to me, I'd cut his head off. I couldn't believe I'd started to trust him. I'd been a damn fool to think he was making a friend of me for anything more than personal gain.

It surely wouldn't be much longer before they found him. Then he'd meet with the sharp end of my sword.

"They're calling you Kysharna, you know?" Ransom said with a smirk. "Our saviour."

My chin lifted at that. This was what I'd wanted, what I'd raved about for years. I was the revered warrior I had always hoped to be. So why did I feel like I was drowning in a cloud of darkness? Why did I think of Kaiser's death with a knot in my chest? Why did I ache for the easy company of a warrior of Stormfell? What had happened to the girl who knew she was destined to lead Cascada to victory?

I scored a hand over my face.

"I thought you'd smile at that, runt," Ransom commented, assessing my reaction to the use of that word. But it felt good not to be on the receiving end of more fake fawning.

"You wanted to be a legend, now here you are," he added.

"How would you know what I want, pishalé?" I tsked.

"Oh come on, you never shut up about it," he taunted. "You talk loudly as well. A lot. It's no wonder you have no friends."

Again, he assessed my reaction, the jibe only making me relax further. Ransom's dislike of me was a strange kind of comfort. A normality in a sea of change.

"You're not going to lick my ass anymore then?" I questioned. "Didn't you call me your favourite sister the other day?"

Ransom pursed his lips. "Father's been telling me to do a lot of things, but I know you're not buying it."

"No, I'm not," I agreed. "Don't bullshit me like the rest of them. At least let our hatred for each other be something real that I can hang onto in this new life."

"I don't hate you," he said, his eyebrows lifting. "I mean, I don't like you. But hate? Nah, I'm not going to waste my energy on that."

"Well I hate you enough for the both of us, I suppose," I mused and he grinned, almost making me do so in return. But fuck him.

"So? Will you have a word with Father?"

"I've tried everything. He ignores my requests."

"Why is the great Void requesting anything?" Ransom asked, a glint of mischief in his eyes. "I say she could demand whatever she likes or all hell might just break loose." He rose to his feet. "You want this war to end, Everest. So make it end. You don't have to answer to anyone anymore."

He left me with that thought and I frowned after him, finding the fruit men peering back inside hopefully.

"Oh come on then," I relented, waving them in and reclining myself on the pillows as they surrounded me, flexing their muscles as they started feeding me grapes.

I chewed them blandly, trying to enjoy the experience, but I couldn't really get into it. When one of them brushed my arm and gave me a seductive look, I realised I could probably lose myself in the heat of their muscles if I wanted. But my thoughts turned elsewhere, to the keen press of a hard body, to the feel of an enemy mouth against my own, to the burning wetness I'd felt between my thighs when I'd rocked my hips over the hardness of his cock.

I clapped a hand over my eyes, a stream of curses leaving my lips in fury at myself. I was only quieted by the touch of a strawberry to my mouth and I gave in and chewed the delicious thing until it was mush.

These thoughts had to be some sort of fucked up taboo fantasy because they deserved no place in the real world. They needed to be cut out and burned. He was dead, rotting on a battlefield and all these strange thoughts of him needed to follow suit.

"Silka la vin." His voice was a rough echo in my mind that made my heart thunder. Killer of mine. That was the meaning of those words. But it only left me with more riddles than answers. How had he known I would be his end?

"Kaské, that's it." I shoved to my feet, knocking some blueberries flying and sending the men scrambling to pick them up in my wake. I strode outside to another raucous round of cheers, but I had eyes for only one person.

I made for my Father who was standing on the shore, looking out to where the White Mare was anchored in the cerulean sea and talking with a few of his men. The ship was a beastly thing, casting a shadow that dominated the shoreline, the mare at its helm dazzling under the bright sun.

A flash of blue caught my eye, dancing across the waves and I frowned, trying to see it clearer, thinking of my traitorous companion Calcifiend. But it must have been the light because I found nothing as I hunted for him.

"Father," I called and he turned, his eyes brightening at the sight of me.

"Ah, Everest, I was just regaling the moment your Void swept through enemy armies and–"

"And it shall do so again this very night," I said firmly. "We're not going to sail around Cascada on some victory parade. Not yet. Not until we win this war. Then we'll visit them with the news of our triumph."

My mind turned to the Reapers' monster at Never Keep again, but surely this was the most urgent task. We could deal with that as soon as Cascada had secured peace. The Magistrine would handle it then.

Father's lips firmed into a tight line. "Like I said, we have a plan that–"

"*You* have a plan and I am denying it. Because I am the Void and I am in charge. I will not do this at all otherwise. So we march on Pyros. That's an order."

His mouth opened and closed while his friends shared uncomfortable looks.

Father's fists curled and I remembered the strike of them as a child, my instinct to back up rioting in my flesh. But I didn't. I stood firm, staring him in the eye and reminding him of who was really in control here. If he wanted the Void, then he had better do as I say.

He wetted his lips, considering me for several seconds then he painted on a smile for his friends, slid an arm around my shoulders and marched me away from them.

"We need time to rest and send for reinforcements," he reasoned in a low mutter.

"A week then."

"You do not understand what is needed for the preparation of battle. Our warriors need to recuperate. Strategies must be laid."

"And they shall be." I pulled away from him, raising my chin and forcing him to face the decision in my eyes. "How quickly can our forces be ready?"

I looked to the ocean of people around us and the many soldiers who were basking in the sunlight. They'd already eaten many nourishing meals and they had that spark in their eyes again that told of a thirst for bloodshed.

Cascadians didn't need long between battles. We were born and bred for this life. Father just wanted us to boast about our newfound advantage over our enemies. But we'd be fools to give them time to lay their own preparations of our next strike. If we did this swiftly, we could have peace in mere weeks. Once the rest of The Waning Lands felt the power of the Void, they would bow to us.

"A couple of months perhaps," he said firmly.

"Bullshit," I growled and his jaw ticked as if he might punish me for that retort. He certainly would have done once. But he saw me as I was now. The truth of my strength.

"They could be on the road in two weeks and you know it," I hissed and I felt the Void rising in answer to my ire. How easily I wielded it now. Like a door had been thrown wide inside my head and unleashed the beast within.

His throat worked as he felt the touch of my power, the kiss of the threat. A reminder of who he was denying.

"They might be on the road in two weeks but they would be ill-prepared. In six weeks I will have them marching back to war," he said quickly, shuddering at the lost connection to his magic.

"Four and you have a deal," I said in compromise.

Father took a slow breath as I withdrew the Void from him and he gave me a stiff nod.

He touched his fingers to his throat to amplify his voice across the crowd. "Warriors, we have a change of plan. We sail for Pyros in four weeks. Rest up, for we will soon return to war to seize our first victory!"

A bellow of assent went up and a chant of 'Kysharna, Kysharna, Kysharna,' followed, making me feel all-powerful. Ransom had been right. I wasn't Father's pawn after all.

"Let's talk tactics then," I rounded on Father again. "I think we can do this without bloodshed, or at least minimal bloodshed. If we're attacked then of course we'll counter, but I think we can force our enemies to surrender with the mere power of the Void."

Father laid a hand on my back, leaning down to speak in my ear and sending a shiver along my spine at his words. "You don't know true war yet, my child. We may march on your order this time, but my warriors will play to my rules out there. You might be the crown in this game of war, but while I have you, that makes me the king."

"Key words, Father: while you have me," I warned and his eyes flickered dangerously.

"You're either with me or you're against me, child. I'm your flesh and blood. Deny that and you deny your family and everything you were bred to be. Is that what you wish for? To be alone in this war with no experience of battle strategy. I am your ally and your greatest tool in the victory you seek for Cascada. So what will it be? Do it together or do it alone?"

My chest burned as I stared at him, the truth of his words all too sharp.

"Together," I breathed because he was right; I didn't have the knowledge to wage this war alone. And the thought of doing so left me suddenly uncertain. I had no one else in the world since I'd taken my father's hand on that battlefield. Harlon had chosen the Reapers. And I'd chosen this path over a crazed plan with the Sky Witch. But with Father's hand lifting to rest on my shoulder, I felt the full weight of that choice. And for a fleeting moment, I wondered if I'd made the wrong one.

BASTIAN

CHAPTER FOUR

This cage was nicer than my last, its walls cleaner and the window an addition I might have appreciated had I only just left my last place of captivity. But it had nothing on real freedom.

I paced the large space, my fingers roaming over the manacles which bound my wrists and closed me off from my magic as I tried to force them free for what must have been the thousandth time. It did nothing other than mark my skin with cuts and bruises but I couldn't bring myself to stop trying. Just as I couldn't bring myself to stop hurling my weight at the door or throwing whatever pieces of furniture I could lift at the window. Because if I ceased my futile rebellion, I'd be giving in. I'd be accepting this cage, these chains, this end to my too-brief freedom.

My room was at the top of one of the palace's towers, the ceilings high and space large enough to accommodate my Dragon form were

I to shift, but there was no chance of that while the green gemstone remained lodged in my skin.

Air magic sealed it in place, my fingernails biting into it whenever I thought to try and claw the stone free of my flesh. But it never wavered once. The prince had cast it there just as he had cast his magic around this entire room, sealing me in and making all attempts at escape impossible. Not that it would stop me from trying.

My turbulent thoughts turned to the maker of my captivity, just as they did all too often. Of her achingly beautiful face set with resolve, those grey eyes so hard as they gazed at me.

It had been two weeks and she still hadn't shown her face.

I was starting to think she never would. But if she did, I planned on calling in her debt to me and taking her death for my own.

I snarled as anger bit and clawed within me, its presence as dominating as the beast I shifted into, the Dragon locked inside my Fae body hungry for blood in payment for this betrayal. But of course she was only a puppet in this play. A puppet I might never lay eyes on again despite my fervent desire to repay her for this incarceration. But I was certain I would be faced with the one who had been pulling her strings.

I glared at the bed I'd slept in, despising its silk sheets and soft mattress even more than I had despised that fucking cave. This place was nothing more than a lie and I was overdue a discussion with the one telling it.

As if in answer to the demands of my thoughts, the door banged open behind me and I turned from glaring at the broken furniture which was scattered around the room in pieces to take in the Fae who had arrived to disturb me. Until now it had always been a servant bearing food, fresh linens, clothes or hot water to fill my bath. Luxuries I'd once dreamed of but now withstood with nothing but contempt. I'd had no choice but to accept them; magic forcing me against a wall while my room was cleaned and the broken furniture exchanged for new. Over and over again, like a sick reset on a game I'd never agreed to play. Like they expected me to simply give in to this place one day, stop fighting against it and learn to live here willingly.

The worst thing was, I knew they were right. No matter how long I spent destroying what they brought me I'd also been giving in. I'd started drinking the water first. Less than two days had gone by before I'd been forced to accept that. It had been quickly followed by food on day four. And I'd stopped pissing on the walls like a dog by day six because truthfully, I was the only one who suffered through refusal to use the latrine.

Day seven, I'd given up hurling water on the fires they set for me in the grate because this place was fucking freezing and I was sick of feeling the bite of the snow which clung to the window frame and reminded me that I was too far north for my liking.

Day nine, I'd made use of the bath and slept in the bed because it had become clear that it was also me who suffered the indignity and discomfort of the cold floor and the stench of stale sweat on my skin.

So now I was sleeping in their bed, eating and drinking what they offered and bathing too. The only thing left for me to give in to was the destruction of their furnishings and how many more days did I intend to start by hurling side tables at walls and burning the books they brought me?

I eyed the man who stepped into my room, hating that I thought of this place as mine already.

"Bastian Carderrin?" Prince Dragor said, turning my name over on his tongue and spitting it out like he didn't much like the taste of it. "I know many of the great names of the houses of Avanis but yours took some time to research."

I bared my teeth, wanting to stride straight for this bastard and snap his fucking neck but I had felt the air shield he'd placed between us and knew I wouldn't get within five feet of him.

"Is your name some kind of homage to times past or do you truly believe yourself to be several hundred years old?" he mused.

A growl rolled up the back of my throat, smoke coiling between my teeth.

"You know I refer to the end of the Carderrin line, yes? That is where you chose to steal your name from? Though it intrigues me that you chose to coin yourself after the sole heir who ran from battle as a coward and was never seen again."

"That's a sack of horse shit," I spat. "I was taken against my will. No Fae who ever met me would have believed I was a coward who chose to run from war. My family were the greatest pillar of strength Avanis had ever seen and I–"

"Truly believe yourself to be hundreds of years old," Prince Dragor finished for me, his lips lilting with amusement. "Tell me, *Bastian,*" he said my name like it was a joke we were both in on and I growled again. "Were you born with such a tendency to fanciful delusions or was it simply that your mind cracked open after years spent beneath the ground the way my general found you?"

"General?" I asked, knowing he had to be referring to Vesper but she had never told me she ranked so highly in his army.

"Newly appointed," he admitted. "In fact, there are a lot of new things about her since she returned to her rightful place at my heel. She was gifted a new name as well as a highborn title and her new rank in my army. General Vesper Dragonsbane – it has quite the ring to it. My brother has even gotten it into his head to make a wife of her and elevate her further. All because of you."

A bellow tore from me, my flesh burning with the fire of my Dragon as it fought to escape the confines of the twisted magic which held me trapped in my Fae body. I doubled over, dropping to one knee as I fought the urgent need to shift, the loss of control making my heart race to a frantic, blazing rhythm that threatened to make it burst straight out of my chest.

Dragor watched me with a cold collection that only made my fury grow, the beast within me thrashing to be let free. After spending so many years in my Dragon form, it was more natural to me to give in to the beast than it was to try and contain it. I'd spent so long stuck in the body of a monster that I had never considered how difficult it would be to become trapped in the flesh of a man without access to the creature within.

"She's good, isn't she?" Dragor taunted. "Did you think you saw something in her? Did you give in to the temptation of her and fall for her allure? Don't tell me she had you fooled into thinking she actually cared for a brute such as you?" The breath of laughter that escaped him had me seeing red and I threw myself at him with a feral roar, colliding with his air shield with enough force to send cracks spiderwebbing across it.

Dragor straightened, his smile slipping away as he took a step back, raising a hand to throw more magic into his shield and stop me from advancing.

"You'd better pray to the stars that your magic holds, Duster," I growled at him.

"Duster?" he questioned, trying to regain his composure though I could still see the tension in his limbs as he fought to hold his magic in place to restrain me. "By the stars, maybe you really are as old as you claim."

"You came here for a reason so why don't you stop baiting me and just come out and say it," I demanded, thumping his shield again and causing more cracks to race across it.

"Alright," he said stiffly. "I came to offer you a bargain."

"As if I'd make a deal with a devil such as you," I sneered.

"I think you will," he countered. "Let's say you truly are as old as you say. That must mean you have no one left waiting for you back in Avanis?"

I said nothing but my silence was confirmation enough.

"And if what my pet tells me is true then you had no children either? No great grandbabies to think of as kin. No kin whatsoever in fact – I checked."

"Checked how?" I demanded.

"Your entire bloodline was wiped out after you…well, history says that you ran from war like a snivelling coward but for argument's sake let's say that I believe you, that you were captured and held against your will."

"You know precisely how I was held for such an impossible amount of time and what caused me to remain the way I'd been, un-aging and unchanging for those endless years." I indicated the green gemstone his witch had driven into my skin and he gave me a tight smile.

"I had the luxury of exploring the cavern you escaped from and made a few educated guesses. Turns out I was right about that crystal being able to control you, even if I wasn't entirely certain until the thing was done."

"So you sent Vesper to pierce my skin with it without even knowing if it would work?" I asked. "If it had failed she'd be dead right now."

"No sacrifice would have been too great in aid of your capture," he said with a shrug. "But luckily it worked out just fine."

"Lucky for *you*," I muttered.

"The point is, we are where we are. And even if we weren't you'd have nowhere to go. No one knows your history, no one misses you aside from whoever it was who had been holding you, I suppose, but they aren't being forthcoming with their claim."

"It was Reapers," I said, though why I was admitting any part of my history to him, I didn't know.

"Was it now?" he purred, his cold eyes lighting with that admission and I wished I could take it back. But what did it really matter anyway? "Well, whoever it may have been, that is the past and I'm here to offer you a future. I need a Dragon to help me win this war. Especially now that the Void has come into play on the side of one of my enemies."

"I would never fight for you."

"So, what? You just plan to fester in this room eternally? I can offer you riches – your kind are fond of those, yes?"

The suggestion of treasure had me glancing up at him with a longing which was all too clear in my damn expression, but I couldn't help it. It had been so long since I'd had a hoard of my own and Dragons needed treasure the way a Pegasus craved a rainbow or a Sphynx desired books.

Dragor pressed on with his gilded speech and I knew I shouldn't be listening to any of it but it wasn't like I had anything else to do.

"I could give you a title. Lands of your own – one of the biggest provinces in the whole of Stormfell. I happen to have one going spare thanks to a traitor losing his head and it runs the length of the Valbaren Plains – right across the border from Avanis where the mountain ranges are so very similar I can only imagine it would feel a lot like your old home. You could take a wife or a dozen wives of your choosing. I assure you plenty would be willing to bed a Dragon in hopes of breeding more of your majestic kind."

"I don't want–"

"You'd be so very close to free," he interrupted me. "Just sworn in service to me."

"And what, pray tell would that entail?" I sneered.

"I wish for you to fight in my battles for me. Better yet, I wish to ride you into war myself and watch my enemies burn in your flames."

"In what fucked-up delusion do you really believe that could ever come to pass?" I scoffed, shoving off of his air shield and striding away from him so that I could lean against the far wall with my arms folded over my chest.

"But you haven't heard the best part yet," Dragor purred like a cat about to spring a trap upon a mouse and I didn't much like being positioned as his mouse.

He moved to the door and opened it again, beckoning someone to join him from outside the room.

I arched a brow at the woman who stepped in, her hood drawn low so that it shadowed her face but the gleam of her eyes pierced the darkness beneath the cowl as she looked at me.

Dragor smirked as he made his final pitch and my heart lurched at the offer he was making, my eyes moving to the window and the impossible freedom which lurked beyond it.

"So, Dragon," Prince Dragor asked finally. "What's it to be?"

KAISER

CHAPTER FIVE

"Now, you remember what I said about not breaking stuff?" North sighed as I hurled my breakfast plate across the room. It smashed against the exposed rock wall opposite my bed, the shattered pieces scattering across the floor.

North pouted at me. "How am I supposed to let you out of here when you've already broken five of my rules?"

"I didn't break five," I griped, stalking to the wooden doors and sliding them open to reveal the stone balcony beyond.

There wasn't any sunlight in the chasm it looked over, but fires burned in braziers that flanked the balconies of the rooms which were cut into the rock of the giant cavern. The sheer walls rose up to a dark ceiling of shimmering stalagmites and the black sheen of the Hushed Pool sat below us, every drop of water that slipped from the sharp minerals above echoing keenly through the cave.

There were many balconies above and below, thousands

of quarters here housing the people of Pyros.

More arrived by the day, or so North told me. I had yet to see a single Fae since my entry to this room. It must have been close to a month since our train had brought us here through an underground tunnel.

Supposedly, a great stairway led to the apex of the mountain that the city of Ravensview hid within, rising up to concealed walkways and lookouts where the Talons could keep watch – with some help from The Matriarch's magpies.

Ravensview was a refuge. A place which had lain dormant for many a year, only kept habitable by a handful of Flamebringers for the event of an evacuation. It was so large that it could house every Fae in Pyros, and that was Mirelle's plan now. To summon them all here, hidden like moles in the earth. The bitterness that stirred in me was difficult to name.

When I'd arrived, I'd spent plenty of time recovering from my injuries, daily salves and potions sent to my room to encourage my healing. But it had been slow and I could still feel an ache in my leg when I moved it the wrong way. The deep slice into my chest had taken the longest to improve though. The scar from the cauterisation would remain, but the redness was finally fading and it no longer hurt to touch.

I paced back and forth, relishing the cool air as the fiery energy in my limbs increased.

North followed me to the balcony, casually resting his elbows on the stone wall at its edge and peering down at the Hushed Pool.

"First; you punched me when I told you it was omelette for breakfast again, second; you refused to wear clothes while you ate, third; you called me a cunt and nearly broke my finger when I brushed your hair and caught a snaggle, fourth; you laughed when

I told you Bigole Dick had fallen off his balcony after drinking too much ale last night–

I barked a laugh. "Bigole Dick."

North cut me a glare. "He was a retired warrior with one leg, Kai. He was always the life of the party. He loved to dance."

I laughed harder at that image and North snorted before quickly flattening his expression. I never really understood why he sometimes showed half a feeling and then quickly hid it away. I had no idea how to do that, even though he tried to teach me.

"What was the fifth rule break?" I asked, moving to stand next to him and gaze out over the chasm. I felt that swirling sensation in my stomach that I liked. North said it was something to do with the danger of falling. Some instinct against hurling myself into the abyss. But oh how tempting it was to lean into it sometimes.

I enjoyed the way it danced in my chest and made my heart thump. For some reason, it reminded me of Everest. I rested a hand on my shirt in the place the stab wound had been cauterised. That was two scars she'd given me now. And this one I liked the roughness of.

"The fifth was the plate," he deadpanned. "Tell me why you threw it and name the emotion."

"You said I might not be able to leave the room today. And then I felt hot and powerful and full of flames. That's anger."

"Your favourite." He smiled then moved closer and flicked me in the ear.

I cocked my head, putting my finger and thumb together then flicking him between the eyes. His smile widened and some of the rage inside me ebbed away.

He shook his head at me. "Mother wants you to attend the war council. I don't want her to lock you up again, so you can do this, right? You're ready, aren't you? Just don't punch anyone and you'll be good."

My lips parted, the offering of freedom filling me with a light sensation. "I can do that."

North grabbed me by the back of the neck, pulling me forward and kissing me on the forehead.

"Good boy," he said in that way I was pretty sure was affection. "I love you, freyin."

I stared back at him, warmed by those words and he gazed at me with a glimmer in his eyes I couldn't read. The silence stretched on and his brow dipped, the glow in his gaze dimming before he walked inside, leaving me pondering what he was feeling.

I followed him, letting him brush my hair before he made me put on a fine black jacket over my shirt. He took his time inspecting me before eventually giving a nod and leading me to the door.

My heart began to beat faster, quickening to the drumming pace of war. The moment North unlocked it, I was past him, through the door and racing for freedom. A wild laugh escaped me as I ran down the corridor and North called after me, "Fucking hell – wait!"

I ran faster, glancing back over my shoulder, spurred on to flee when my brother sprinted after me.

I found a stairway, the thing cut right into the stone, stretching out over a towering abyss and climbing up in a twisting zigzag. I sprinted up it, knocking into some Fae and making them cry out and all the while my laughter grew louder.

"Kaiser!" North bellowed, somewhere behind me, but not near enough to catch me.

I took the steps two at a time, hearing a few gasped words from the people I passed.

"Was that him?"

"It's the strange one."

"I've never heard him laugh before."

I made it to the top of the stairs, rounding onto a vast terrace where tables were laid out beside a bistro and beyond them was a thundering waterfall that cut through the rock. The sun blazed through the hole in the cave roof and I needed to reach it, a roaring desire inside me blocking out all else. I ran through the sea of tables, my gaze set on the rocky wall beside the waterfall and before I knew it, I was climbing it, clawing my way up and kicking my shoes off as I went to make the ascent easier. The old injury in my right leg protested at the movement, but I was fuelled by adrenaline and there was no stopping me now.

Yells called out behind me but the loudest of all came from North.

"Get down!"

"Climb up!" I shouted back, scaling it faster, almost losing my grip on a slippery rock and grinning when I caught myself a beat before I fell.

"Kai!" North yelled, a note of some emotion in his voice. I ran through them all in my head, trying to place it, always so foggy when I tried to remember them all at once. Fear? No, not quite right. Panic? Closer. But that still wasn't it.

I made it to the top of the waterfall, pulling myself over the edge, spray wetting me through. The air up here was crisp and fresh, the sky above me so blue it was like the wide open stare of a cerulean eye. And there was the sun, beating down upon me, warming my face and promising summer on the horizon.

I could feel the kiss of magic up here, no doubt silencing shields and layers of concealment spells were hiding this place well.

It crackled against my skin and warned me to retreat.

I pulled my jacket and shirt off to feel the sun better, opening my arms wide and closing my eyes to let the wind and heated rays bring my skin to life. I had never felt life like this. In all its sharpness. All its sweet everything.

I inhaled the air and relished the rush in my lungs, then I opened my mouth and howled just as I'd heard North do so many times. I knew why he did it now. I understood the call in his soul because I could feel it too at last. And there within all this feeling, was her. The girl who had offered me this. My enemy, my saviour. Silka la vin.

A flurry of magpies came at me, wings clashing with my face and silencing the howl on my lips. I batted them away but they didn't fully disperse until a woman landed before me, her black and white wings outstretched and a look of war about her. A flurry of magpies gathered above her in the sky, circling higher and higher.

"Kaiser," Mirelle gasped. "What are you doing up here?"

"Howling to the sun, I suppose."

A smile broke across her lips. "It's so good to see you at last." She swept forward, wrapping her arms around me and I found my head tilting low to press to hers.

"Are you sure you're ready to be out of your room?" she asked as we parted, glancing down at my bare chest, my shoeless feet then back to my face.

A huffing noise sounded as North hauled himself up onto the ridge beside the waterfall. "I told him to come up here," he blurted and my brow lowered.

"No you didn't," I said blankly.

"*Kai*," he said through his teeth.

"North," Mirelle said a little sharply. "What's going on?"

“He just wanted some fresh air on the way to the war council,” North said quickly.

Mirelle stepped closer to North, lowering her voice to a whisper. “How is he?”

“He’s fine, aren’t you freyin?” North looked to me and I nodded. “And he has something to say to you, Mother.”

“I do?” I questioned and North nodded encouragingly, winking one eye then trying to mouth something to me.

“I cannot hear you,” I said with my brows lowering.

“Remember the thing you wanted to say to Mirelle?” North hissed. “You know.” He cupped his hand around his mouth and mouthed, *“The apology.”*

I looked to Mirelle in understanding. “I’m sorry for choking you. I won’t do it again. I feel regret.”

Mirelle’s features softened. “I forgive you, love. Do you forgive me yet for the Reapers’ spell?”

I glanced at North, the sensation of barbed wire rolling around my chest rendering me silent.

“How would forgiveness feel?” I asked him through gritted teeth, my hands knotting into fists at my sides.

“Soft,” he said. “Like a release.”

“I do not feel that,” I growled, narrowing my eyes at Mirelle as the sensation grew thicker. My teeth ground together and the desire to choke her again almost pushed me to the brink of violence. North leapt toward me, placing a hand on my chest and looking me in the eye.

“Calm,” he said firmly. “Take a breath, Kai.”

I did so, my shoulders rising and falling as I worked to hold back the immediate desire to hurt Mirelle.

North turned to face our mother. "See how good he's doing? He can control himself now."

Mirelle's lips twitched but she said nothing more on the subject, flexing her wings in preparation of flight. "The council will begin shortly. Head to the northern haven."

She took off, leaving us there alone and North released a slow breath.

"That was close," he jabbed me in the ribs. "Keep it together, Kai." He looked around. "I think there's a walkway beyond that boulder." He set off across the mossy ground, picking his way higher toward the mountain's peak and passing the large boulder. We found the wooden boardwalk beyond it, winding along the mountainside with concealment spells making it barely visible to any Skyforgers or enemy flying Orders who might pass by overhead.

I felt them shrouding us the moment we were out in the open, keeping us blended in with the background. There were runes marked into the boulders too, the power that hid Ravensview almost as ancient as this mountain itself.

There were wooden buildings set along the path at various intervals, hidden beneath rockfaces or within caverns and I met the gaze of the Talons inside who were keeping watch undercover.

We finally reached a cave that sat in the shadow of the jagged peak of Ravensview mountain, stepping inside to reveal the truth beyond the concealment spells that shrouded this place.

An oval table made entirely of white quartz awaited us inside and Mirelle sat at its head in a seat of the same material that was fashioned into the shape of a raven's skull. A few magpies were perched on the arms and Mirelle stroked one of them, the bird crooning softly at her touch.

Many of her most esteemed Talons sat around her including several of my adopted siblings and all of them looked our way at our arrival. Kayla caught my gaze, her short blonde hair swept away from her face and rings under her eyes telling of a bad night's sleep. A small crease between her eyes telling of an emotion I couldn't name. She looked ready to rise from her seat but North moved ahead of me and hushed the questions rising on my siblings' lips.

Two seats sat empty, awaiting us I supposed and Mirelle gestured for us to take them, her eyes stitched to my face.

"Well? Who would like to start today?" Mirelle asked, her voice harsh.

"I will speak, ma'am." Gavrin Simmer said, raising a hand to gain her attention. He was a stocky man, well-seasoned in battle and his wide moustache had been in place for as long as I could remember. He ruled a portion of the eastern territory of Pyros, his gang known for the insignia of a salamander, one he wore proudly in ink across his neck. "I believe the last few councils have been unproductive chatter about our predicament but few solutions have been offered. I believe I am about to suggest what a few of us have been thinking."

"Which is?" Mirelle demanded.

Gavrin cleared his throat. "We offer an alliance to Stormfell and Avanis."

A clamour of loud voices broke out and North slammed his hand down on the table, offering his own thoughts on the idea. "Ally with the earth fuckers who took Cinder Vale? Or those piece of shit Skyforgers? Are you out of your mind?"

"I'll never stand beside them," Kayla growled beside me and the voices grew even louder, a few chiming in to back up Gavrin while the others hurled abuse at them.

Mirelle said nothing, closing her eyes and taking a long breath before she opened them again.

"Enough," she snapped and the room fell silent under her dominion. "I will not hear another word of allying with Stormfell or Avanis. I will not subject our people to standing at the sides of Fae who have slaughtered their own."

"But Cascada is going to destroy us all if we do nothing." Gavrin leapt to his feet, his face growing red and sweat rising on his temple. "Ma'am you must see reason."

"Reason?" Mirelle hissed. "Your definition of reason is my definition of madness. I will not shake the hand of a Stormfell king. I will not pander to the folly of an Avanis Earl. I may have called a retreat but I have not called a surrender."

"Then what will we do?" Gavrin begged, clutching at the collar of his shirt. "Cascada could be tracking a path through Pyros already. The Void could be at our door by sundown. Are we just supposed to sit here and wait for death to come to us?"

"We wait for no such fate," Mirelle growled. "Ravensview lays on no map. They will not find us here."

"Then what do we do?" Lydia Ashworth spoke up, one of my mother's dearest friends and a ruler in her own right. She headed the gang that resided in Wentos called the Brass Hope and she had always been a loyal, unwavering ally to Mirelle. Her black hair was coiled into a tight braid and her body was clad in armour as if she were ready for war at any hour. "I cannot stand the waiting. We must take action."

"Yes, but not in the form of war, Lydia," Mirelle said with no room for negotiation.

"What then?" Gavrin demanded. "Because I fear we will all be guttered of magic in the night when the Cascadians come to take us.

I've heard of the vile things they do to their prisoners of war. They'll eat the flesh from my bones, they'll plunder me through the night."

"No one wants to plunder you, Gavrin," North sniggered. Kayla joined in and I noticed I was grinning too, drawing some eyes my way.

"What's the situation with him?" Lydia murmured under her breath to Mirelle, but I caught it all the same.

I felt more gazes turn on me and Mirelle straightened in her chair. "Kaiser is going through a transformation thanks to the Void. He is learning the ways of new emotions, so your patience with him is greatly appreciated."

"The Vooooiiiid," Donna Kandaflame warbled, speaking for the first time, looking like she had aged several years since our defeat at Cinder Vale – and she had been plenty grey before then. She was one of the longest standing gang leaders in Pyros, her domain over the Red Skulls spreading from Blackthorn Peak right out to the western border. "Beware the Vooooooiiiid."

"What do you mean a transformation?" Lydia whispered to Mirelle as Donna started picking at her nailbeds which already looked raw. I'd never seen her act this way, something in her eyes speaking of a darkness I couldn't read well enough to understand.

"We have more important matters to discuss," my mother clipped.

"Yes we do," Gavrin piped up again. "And I know you do not wish to hear it ma'am, but allying with our enemies may be our only hope. It must be considered if you do not wish for our people to be annihilated."

"Nonsense," Zayad Raith spoke out, pushing a hand through his golden hair. The gang leader of Leergaith and its neighbouring lands was known for his fondness for the pleasure houses of his region. Mirelle had voiced on more than one occasion that she would prefer his focus turned more to war strategy than his favourite sins. He was a man to show up when it counted though, which was perhaps why Mirelle had never taken the matter into her own hands. "I will not stand at the side of a damned Raincarver. Let alone a Skyforger or stars forbid a Stonebreaker. I wouldn't even pump my cock over the most alluring of their kind. I'd sooner cut it off!"

"Ha!" Mirelle barked a dry laugh. "That is a shameful lie. Your gang is not so loyal if you thought your secret of allowing the Sky Witch to fool you would not reach my ears. You had her in your whore house and she tricked you into thinking you had bedded her. You wanted her."

Many laughed and Zayad's cheeks turned pink. I had to say I'd never seen him look so humiliated.

"I didn't know what she was. I would never have desired her if I'd known she was a Skyforger," he said fiercely.

"You're a fool, Zayad," Mirelle drawled.

"What other choice do we have but to ally with our enemies now?" Gavrin steered the conversation back on track and a few more called out to back him up.

A heated debate broke out again, a clamour of noise colliding in my skull and making my pulse thunder. Mirelle said nothing more, scowling at the ruckus and seeming no more inclined to agree to an alliance than she had been before.

When the noise had grown to a crescendo and I felt close to breaking something again, Mirelle stood abruptly from her seat. "Kaiser, you knew the Void. She was your Fearsire. You must know something about her we can use to our advantage, some weakness she has that can be used to subdue her."

Quiet reigned and everyone looked to me for an answer.

I closed my eyes, reaching out to connect my mind to Calcifiend, my secret view of Everest. He was nestled up in the rigging of a ship, peering down upon her where she stood at the prow, watching the river swirl beneath her father's vessel. I couldn't see her face, her curls fluttering out behind her in the wind, but I would know her anywhere. I could sense her in my bones and in the heavy thudding of my heart. She was in my flesh now, like a sin woven there with silk. But for all the want I had for her, there was darkness in it too. Coiling, writhing emotions that were as volatile as vipers. I didn't know if I would destroy or claim her when I found her. But I did know I would find her either way. And that day was drawing close, a plot shifting into place in my mind and solidifying itself into an unshakeable decision.

Calcifiend looked beyond the river to the warm land of Cascada. I couldn't tell which direction she was heading, the land too unfamiliar to my eyes, but I knew at least for the coming days, she was too far away to be a threat to my family.

I opened my eyes, the muscle of my heart working furiously in my chest as I met my mother's gaze. I felt like a traitor when I kept my lips sealed. But that information was mine and mine alone for now. No one would force it from my lips. I would alert my family if the Cascadian army ever drew close, but in the meantime, I would keep Calcifiend's link to the Void secret.

"So? How can we destroy her?" Gavrin asked keenly.

I got to my feet with a snarl on my lips, turning my gaze on Gavrin and prowling up to him.

"Kai," North called after me but I was locked in, my anger sharp, my desire singular.

I caught Gavrin by the back of his neck, dragging him from his seat then throwing him against the stone wall and pinning the asshole there by his chest. "Seek to destroy her and I will destroy you first. I will peel the flesh from your bones and feed it to the Matriarch's birds. Speak one more word against her and you will witness my wrath upon your worthless soul. If her death is written then I shall wield the quill, none other."

"Kaiser! Release him this instant," Mirelle commanded and I glanced over my shoulder at her while Gavrin wriggled and cursed.

"That goes for you too, Mirelle. You want forgiveness? Then you'll cast no stones against Everest Arcadia." I threw Gavrin to the floor and stalked out of the cave, leaving them to their pointless debate. They would have plenty to talk about in the face of my declaration, no doubt. But I had no care for their opinion on it.

The truth was, Pyros was done for. We were rats stuck in a drain waiting for the rain to fall. There was only one chance for us now and Mirelle knew it as well as I did. So stars help us when our people learned of the choice I knew my mother had already made.

VESPER

CHAPTER SIX

The weeping greeted me even before the warmth of the fire could wrap itself around my bones. I didn't tense at the sound, too used to the morbid sonnets which echoed around the Cavern of Lost Souls to pay them much mind. Another offering to the dark, another sacrifice to the ether. Whoever it was who found themselves awaiting their end in this place, I was confident they were deserving of it. The most corrupt souls were the most potent after all. Mine would be worthy indeed.

I stepped into the large cavern at the heart of this place, the wide firepit burning with a well-stocked fire which warmed the air so thoroughly that I could feel it baking my skin even at this distance.

I was dressed appropriately for the cavern today, the thin, taupe dress I wore leaving far more of my figure on show than would ever be practical for war but in this place I'd never once felt vulnerable to the weapons of Fae. Here, only the ether might claim me and that was a fate no armour could protect against.

I looked up at the three figures who hung by their feet above the fire, coils of air magic keeping them in place. The woman to the right was the one weeping, low murmurs and pleas for mercy passing between her ragged cries. The man to her right was dead, his throat cut and blood still pooling in a bronze bowl which was suspended between him and the flames, the red liquid bubbling as it boiled within.

The third woman was staring stoically at the wall, stowed away within the confines of her mind and perhaps succeeding in losing herself to her memories. It was likely the best course of action available to any who found themselves in her place.

A cry for mercy drew my attention to the far right of the space, beyond the crowd of Sages who danced and writhed to the solitary beat of a drum, their bodies smeared with the blood of their sacrifice. Around ten more Fae awaited their fate there, bound and bruised, the cut of their clothes betraying them all as citizens of Pyros.

Tifon pranced by me, his arms waving in the air, shirt removed and the ridges of many scars revealed across his withered chest, each one an intentional cut made in sacrifice by his own hand.

"Good pickings today, Sky Witch!" he called merrily, prancing away again to circle the fire, euphoria clinging to him as he lost all sense of himself to the blood magic.

Perhaps today had been a poor choice on my part. But I'd been riddled with a plague of my own regrets in that palace and Moya was the closest thing I had to family, or even a friend, in the whole of Stormfell right now. I hadn't thought to ask whether the Sages had been gifted any prisoners of war upon our return. An excess of sacrifices like these would keep them in this wild state of ecstasy for weeks as they feasted on blood magic with gluttonous abandon. I'd be lucky to get an ounce of sense out of any of them.

"Please," a man called from the group to the rear of the room and I found his eyes on me. I didn't need to get any closer to ask what he was begging me for, his desires reaching out to envelop me whole. He wanted nothing more than a swift death at the hands of a warrior in place of the slow end he knew he would face in this chamber of horrors.

Something twisted in my gut and I moved faster through the exuberant Sages, my bare feet warm on the stone floor beneath me, the thin dress slipping over my legs in ragged lengths.

The group of Flamebringers stirred as I approached, some cursing and backing away, others crying out for the mercy of a quick death just as the first had done.

"Let me meet Aries at the hands of a warrior," the man begged as I made it to them. "Even a witch might understand the right for that mercy."

"The right?" I mused, my gaze roaming over these Fae who flinched and cowered in the face of their demise. I couldn't blame them. This place was all the best kinds of terrifying. "Tell me then, in full honesty, what was it you were doing when you were captured and brought here?"

"We were simply fighting in the war as any guardian of their citizens would do. Just as you do for Stormfell. But our people would never subject you to this," a woman accused, glaring out at the jubilant Sages and I followed her gaze. She had a point. I'd never heard of blood magic being celebrated or encouraged in any of the other lands the way it was here, but that didn't mean I hadn't felt her desire to hide the whole truth from me within her pretty words.

"Hmm…" I took the draining dagger from the sheath strapped around my upper thigh and inspected the runes carved into its hilt. I wasn't allowed to carry any weapons in this place aside from this one blade and its purpose was blood magic, not fighting.

"A quick end," another man begged, seeing my action as indecision.

"The whole truth or it's no deal," I purred, a wicked smile forming on my lips which made the group cower and cringe. "And just to be clear – I can feel it when you lie or try to conceal details from me. Your desire to hide the full extent of your crimes has been noted already and I'm inclined to abandon you to this fate."

"Fine," a brute of a man with a broken nose spat, his eyes blazing with defiance as he met my steely gaze. "We were a raiding party. We'd won the fight with the warriors defending the town and were claiming the bounty of our victory when your people accosted and corralled us. We were doing nothing more or less than you have done in our lands, Sky Witch."

"And did you enjoy that part of the raiding?" I asked, stepping closer to him, my gifts coiling around him and tying him in my thrall.

His throat bobbed, his bloody nose wheezing a soft whistle of doom as I reached out to place my fingers against the stubble on his jaw and gave a sharp tug with my gifts.

A flash of desire hit me with a vision of his memory too, the sick pleasure he took from 'claiming bounty' as he called it. Murdering civilians, butchering the old and the young alike. This group had been very fond of doing that.

"How long did you spend haunting the villages of my land?" I asked and my hold over him tugged on his desire to boast despite the fact that he really should have known better than to give in to it. But this bastard *wanted* to boast, he was proud of what he'd done and in the hold of my gifts he wasn't able to think better of doing so.

"We were here for the battle of Armond almost a year past. When the rest of our people retreated after the victory, we…stayed on to further celebrate our dominion over the sky rats we hate so very dearly. You really should do a better job of protecting your farmlands you know – it was so fucking easy to carve our way through them and kill every dirty, rotten Skyforger we fou–"

My fist connected with his broken nose and he screamed so loud the sound echoed off of the roof of the cavern and out into its darkest corners.

The Sages all paused in their merriment, turning to look at us before cheering and laughing and moving back to their morbid festivities.

"That's the funny thing about blood magic," I said as I backed away from the doomed Flamebringers, offering them a dark smile as I went. "It works best when the sacrifice is deserving of their fate. Don't worry – you'll have plenty of time to come to that conclusion too. Some of you will be here for months awaiting your end, watching your comrades as they're carved apart piece by piece. Those bastards up there–" I pointed to the three sacrifices hanging over the fire, the first to have been selected for this voracious display. "They're the lucky ones. They'll all be dead within the week and this revelry will calm. The Sages will have had their blood orgy and then they'll save the rest of you to use in rites for weeks and months, bit by bit by bit. The best you can hope for is that they'll be in need of another death to pay for some big magic because if they don't, your suffering will go on and on and on."

I turned my back on their cries for mercy, not feeling the least bit of guilt over their destiny. Some Fae were wholly deserving of their fates and this place would at least make them pay for the crimes they'd committed even if it would do nothing to return those they'd killed from death.

A hand snatched me into the throng of revelling Sages and I gasped as Moya tugged me into a twirl around the fire, her wild red hair flying about her smiling face, blood painted in dark lines down her chin and throat.

"Have you been listening?" she called, spinning me beneath her arm and I let myself be turned around, the flames blurring in my vision before I was back in her arms again, navigating the cavern.

"I have," I agreed and she smiled widely. She was missing a tooth at the edge of her grin, one of her molars gone in favour of a dark hole.

"Been offering up pieces of yourself to the dark again?" I asked, bobbing my chin at it and she shrugged.

"Always figured I had too many teeth anyway. Hasn't made much difference to the way I chew – only the way I grin."

I snorted, letting her spin me again but as she caught hold of me, she jarred us to a halt, the other Sages dancing on around us as she peered into my eyes for several achingly long seconds before clucking her tongue and striding away.

I swallowed thickly, not wanting to ask what she'd just seen in the dark corners of my soul and following her through the crowd to the curving slope which led up to her living chambers.

Moya moved quickly, her bare feet silent on the cool stone and I was almost running to catch up to her by the time we entered the packed confines of her chambers.

"You followed the call," she said without preamble, snatching a fistful of oregano from where it hung above her well-worn dining table and hurrying through to the Close Space.

I moved behind her into the tight patch of darkness she favoured so much, supressing the shudder which ran down my spine as I entered the dim cave.

The dark pressed in on us and I was careful to stay near to the wall before dropping down to sit cross legged opposite her, not wanting to get too close to the small hole in the centre of the floor which led down to the eternal nothingness below.

Moya hummed beneath her breath as she crumbled the oregano into dust in her fist before scattering it on the stone beside the hole and painting runes into the mess she'd made.

My eyes were slowly adjusting to the gloom and I sighed as she beckoned for me to offer up my hand.

"Must I?"

"You tell me," she retorted and I gave in, knowing I wanted to hear whatever it was she had to say, however damning it might be. I'd known when I'd chosen to come here that this would come up.

Moya took my hand, slicing the tip of my finger open with the sharp point of her thumbnail and I grumbled half-heartedly as she squeezed a few drops of my blood onto the herbs and runes before shoving it all into the small hole and letting it fall away into the dark.

Something rumbled in the depths of the mountain in reply to that offering, the sensation rolling through my core and making the hairs on the back of my neck prickle to attention.

That roiling sensation of doom and foreboding ate into me as Moya leaned down towards the hole as if listening to some whisper I couldn't hear.

"A heart so torn and twisted, it has no home to claim, a soul so bruised and broken, it desires naught but pain," she said, raising a brow at me in accusation.

"Spit it out – clearly," I said though her words had already permeated my skin with their meaning and we both knew I'd understood perfectly. She was accusing me of something which I didn't want to admit to.

Moya sighed, leaning back and tapping her fingers on her bare knees, drawing my attention to the bruises she sported there.

"You were always destined for the empty path, Vesper. But you're the one who keeps choosing to walk it alone. The wind won't stop howling all the time you keep kicking up a hurricane."

"I said to speak clearly," I grumbled.

"Fine." Moya shoved to her feet suddenly and I craned my neck to look up at her in the gloom. "The Dragon was your offer of salvation. You fucked up."

She turned and strode from the Close Space, leaving me with my face burning and shame eating into my insides.

"There is no salvation for the likes of me," I called, scrambling after her, all too glad to leave the ominous presence in the Close Space behind me.

"Not now there isn't," she scoffed and my skin burned even hotter.

"You think I don't understand the weight of what I did?" I demanded, harrying her out into the chamber which held the drying herbs and scarred table.

Moya shrugged. "Not yet you don't, no matter how certainly you believe you do when pining away in loneliness in the dead of night. Scorning all who offer you kindness won't bring back the ones you've lost. And if you're going to cut your own nose off to spite that pretty face of yours then at least let me have it to offer up in sacrifice next time."

I dropped onto the three-legged stool beside the table, releasing a choked noise which was half laugh, half sob. I was a fucking mess so who knew what it was, but it felt apt.

Moya pursed her lips as she assessed me, plucking a few bones from a glass jar on a cluttered shelf and tossing them onto the table before me so that I could see the runes carved into their yellowed edges.

"Thieves' fingers?" I asked, not practiced enough in her arts to be able to read the meaning behind the way they'd been cast.

"Indeed," she crooned, petting one of the bones like it was a beloved pet. "He stole a small fortune along with the heart of his brother's wife. Quite the potent acquisition."

"Indeed," I echoed drolly, eyeing the bones with distaste. I supposed she may have left the man living without his fingers and maybe it had taught him a lesson in honour. Likely not though.

Moya waved a hand at the bones like she expected me to read them for her but I shrugged.

"You know I can't–"

"Can and can't are the chains which bind us all too often when really what we should be saying is will or won't."

When she put it that way she made my refusal sound like the petulance of a child so I bit down on my snarky retort and looked at the bones again, willing them to tell me something I didn't already know.

"They're…happy? No – pleased. Forget it, that's insane–"

"Insanity is often where the greatest truths are found. You were right, they are pleased, or rather the ether is."

"Ether isn't sentient."

"I never said it was."

I held myself back against the temptation to argue over word choices with her. Moya grinned at me proudly as if remembering all the times I'd come here in my youth only to rant and scream about the nonsensical way she spoke of the magic she wielded. Moya was nothing if not full of contradictions but somehow her rambling always made sense if you sat with it long enough.

"The ley line?" I asked finally and she nodded.

"Keystone too."

"I haven't told you about any of this yet," I protested and she shrugged.

"You don't always have to tell me everything with words, you know?"

More nonsense, but fine. That saved me the hassle of explaining what I'd done.

"Okay, so I followed the call like you told me to and fixed a kink in the ley line. Problem solved."

"Is it?" she mused and I huffed my irritation.

"Surely the ether can call on someone else if there is more work to be done on this? I have my own priorities."

"The universe likes to distract us with personal dilemmas, they're of little consequence–" Moya placed a hand out to stop my outburst at those words before it could begin, her eyes softening as she looked at me and moved around the table to caress my cheek. "Please don't mistake my words on the ether for a lack of compassion for your pain, Vesper. You know one thing does not beget the other."

I nodded once but my throat was thick with emotion again and it took me several heartbeats to regain enough control to be able to speak clearly.

"I just want to uphold the vow I made to them. They're the only true thing I've ever had and–"

"Listen to me, you need to stop with that bullshit and be honest with yourself. You aren't lacking in love because you lost them. You're hiding from it like a wolf among dogs and I'll tell you now that the pelt doesn't fit you. You want good things in this world then it's up to you to claim them. And don't come moping to me when you fuck them up for yourself instead. I've never been one to stand by that tendency for self-destruction in you. I never let you listen to those fools in fine armour who claimed to be better than you and I won't stand here and watch you convince yourself that the choices you've made were the only ones available to you. Own your shit. And don't come back here until you have. Your energy is tainting my walls."

"Bitch," I muttered with a soft smile as I pushed to my feet and she curtsied in her ragged dress at the compliment.

"The dark still whispers your name, Vesper Crossborn," Moya called as I headed for the exit.

"It's General Vesper Dragonsbane now, haven't you heard?" I sneered and she snorted like that was the biggest joke she'd heard all year.

"Like fuck it is. You are and forever will be Crossborn, my girl. And don't ever let them believe there's anything but power in the truth of it."

I nodded, uncertain why I was smiling over those words but she wasn't done with me yet.

"Listen to the dark – it's no more done with you than you are with it. Blood runs downhill!" she warned.

"You told me that before."

"And you have a job to do whether you want to admit it or not. So maybe this time, you'll listen."

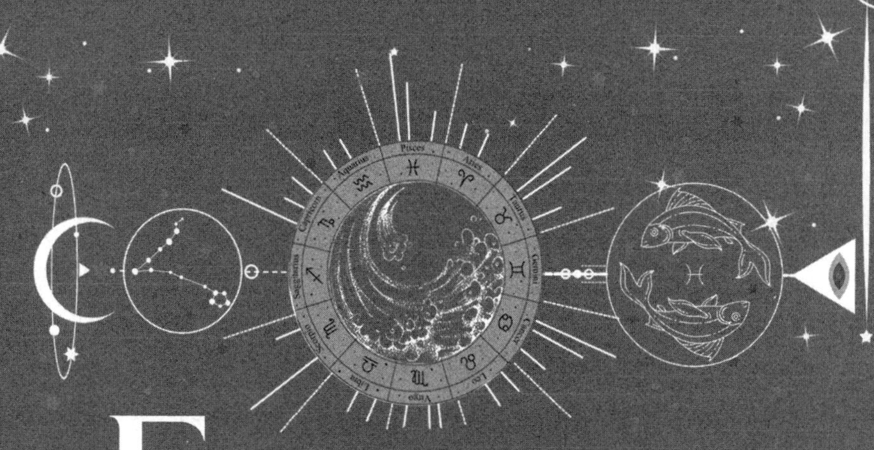

EVEREST

CHAPTER SEVEN

The magical barrier that divided Cascada from Pyros loomed ahead of us, stretching across the Undashine River in the heart of a green valley. The sun beat down on me, the thick warmth of my land a balm against my soul. I'd missed the beauty of Cascada, from her shining golden shores to her sun kissed hills, but here, standing on the deck of the White Mare, I couldn't help but feel that something was missing.

Harlon had been a constant in this land and now he was gone and my life looked nothing like it had before. But how could I resent it when this was what I'd longed for? To be honoured and recognised, to finally feel I was worth something to my people. Maybe that feeling would come once the war was over.

I set my gaze on the shimmering barrier ahead, looking to the very same river beyond it which wound away through the wilds like a snake. It was dangerous out there, monsters awaited us and I finally felt a thrill break through the monotony of my days.

I was about to flex my magic and fight a true fight at last. Father had stolen a few more days than the four weeks we'd agreed, setting anchor here on the river for several of them until the entirety of his fleet had joined the entourage. He'd summoned the cavalry too, but they would catch up to us after they'd assembled in Castelorain.

The White Mare slowed before the barrier, its halt aided by the Raincarvers who wielded the water beneath us. A few deer were startled away from the edge of the river, racing back into the thorny brush further up the hill.

The gangplanks were laid and I hurried to be the first to disembark, finding my father dressed for war at last, taking the lead as he disembarked. His armour glinted in the sunlight, the thick plates of darkest blue marked with the sea serpent Typhon and the crest of Cascada. His arms held only shoulder plates, but the rest were bare, ready to unleash his inner Merrow and coat himself in the armour of his kind. When I walked down the gangplank to meet him, he offered me his hand to step off the end as if I was some princess from Stormfell. I wore my own armour, newly crafted in the weeks building up to this moment. I'd been gifted the most beautiful metal Cascada had to offer and I'd forged a breast plate and leg guards from it which were deepest green. The clasps on my shoulders holding the plates together were decorated with the finest iridescent seashells of the Sunken Isles. It was still a work-in-progress. There were plenty of experimental lacquers I wanted to add to improve its strength and magical resistance but for now at least, it was a beautiful start.

"I'm a warrior, Father, not a delicate flower," I said firmly but he caught my arm, drawing me close.

"You're precious, Everest. I have to look after you, that's all."

He tucked a lock of hair behind my ear and my inner child melted, aching for more fatherly affection.

I knew what this man was. I knew he was ruthless, cold. I'd seen what he'd done to people and yet this pathetic part of me still ached for these crumbs of tenderness. It was a shackle I couldn't break and maybe I didn't want to. I didn't know what other home I had now. But sometimes in the dead of night, I dreamed of the Sky Witch or worse…of him. The one with the obsidian eyes. And he was far from dead within my dreams. His mouth found mine, his roughened fingers coursing over my bare skin. I'd wake breathless, shamed, and heart aching. There was no one I could voice this wicked secret to to better understand it.

Ransom descended the ship in his own fine armour and several of Father's warriors followed. There were plenty of Fae disembarking from the ships in the White Mare's wake and some of them raced off up the hills on either side of the river to scout the area.

Father nodded to the Fae gathering around us then took off along the riverbank toward the barrier. The warriors closed in around me, flanking me on all sides with Ransom close on my left as we followed.

"A little air would be nice," I clipped at them, but they didn't back up. Some unsheathed weapons and others shifted, a man to my right taking his Minotaur form with a large bull's head and huge, curved horns protruding from his brow.

Ahead of me, two warriors had shifted into Nemean Lions far bigger than any horse, their golden pelts blocking most of my view of the barrier. Even Ransom had the scales of his Merrow Order showing on his arms, the iridescent blue plates glittering with strength.

"Scared of a few beasties, Ransom?" I taunted, noting the tension lining his posture.

"I'm not scared," he scoffed.

"Then why are you walking like you stuffed a few rocks up your ass this morning?" I asked sweetly.

"Shut it, runt," he tossed back, though it was without the malice he usually aimed at me. "Or I'll make your day a living hell."

"Is that what you told the rocks before you made them face their fate, pishalé?"

Ransom cracked a smile and I rolled my eyes at it, turning to look at the Nemean Lions instead.

"You shouldn't talk to her that way," a woman hissed. A real fierce-looking woman in fact. She looked like she could crush my skull with her bare hands, and there was something distinctly root vegetable-like about her face.

"I can do what I like, Agatha," Ransom drawled. "Perks of being the commander's son."

"You think he still gives a damn about you?" Agatha cackled a laugh. "He only has eyes for his daughter now."

I smirked at Ransom, mostly just to enjoy how it made his right eye twitch with rage.

"Guess I'm his number one these days. So that makes you a number two. Which suits you better, all things considered," I jibed.

Ransom's teeth ground together. "That's not true."

"Oh it is," I purred. "You're replaceable, brother. I always said it, but your head was too big to hear it. But no one can replace the Void."

"Yeah? Well the only reason he tolerates you is because of that power. At least he actually likes me," Ransom tossed back and I couldn't deny it hurt. It wasn't like I was a fool. I knew why Father showered me with attention. It wasn't my winning personality, that was for sure.

"At least I'm respected now," I muttered, my fingernails biting into the flesh of my palm. That was all I'd wanted anyway. Notoriety. Letting go of everything else was the price of it.

Harlon.

Vesper.

My anger towards Father.

The pieces of me which were rooted in the past.

My enemy whose death I'd finally claimed.

Caterpillars had to transform and shed layers to fulfil their true destiny. Wasn't that what I was doing?

So why does it feel so fucking bad?

"You're obsessed with being admired," Ransom bit at me, earning another scowl from Agatha and a few wary looks from the other warriors. Apparently the rest of them didn't feel brave enough to speak out against my brother.

"Well, try being marginalised your whole life, Ransom. Then maybe you'd get it."

"Oh boo fucking hoo. Cry me a river, Everest," he sneered. "You loved being an outcast. You never tried to fit in. From your clothes to your weird habits. You always stood out and did your own thing, and honestly? I fucking envied that sometimes. Do you know how much pressure there is to keep up the pretence that–" he cut himself off then barrelled on, clearly changing direction. "All I'm saying is that it's not always fun being the most popular Fae in town."

I gave him a dry stare at that comment, wondering what he'd actually been going to say, but he was shooting furtive glances at the other warriors, his chest puffing up as he went into full peacock mode. Or just cock mode, more like.

"Hold!" Father's voice boomed out across the army with the

assistance of magic. He gestured for me to step forward and the warriors parted around me, fanning out in a wide semi-circle that ran right up to the boundary either side of us.

I walked up to Father who smiled warmly and placed a hand on my shoulder. "Like we discussed, daughter."

I nodded, enjoying the squeeze he gave me before letting me pass and I approached the powerful boundary with nerves warring inside me. I'd been practising with the Void, able to wield it on command since the battle in Pyros, but I hadn't yet attempted it on a huge scale the way I had back then.

This barrier had been cast by the hands of hundreds of Fae. The magic in it was ancient and legend told that the power of the great warrior Levenna Cascine was contained within it.

I raised a hand, recalling the time Ransom had pushed me through this very barrier further to the east at the highest peak in Castelorain. I would have died had my magic been Awakened. My hatred for him spiked at the memory, and the pain that had found me that day pressed keenly in upon me. I closed my eyes, almost feeling my mama's spirit lingering nearby, whispering her parting words to me.

Never rest, Everest.

I'd done what she'd asked. Kaiser Brimtheon lay dead in payment for her end. Was she at peace at last? Or was she just dust now with no cares to draw her from the grave?

I took in a deep breath, the sense of her presence leaving me and I feared it had been an illusion after all.

My gaze steadied on the barrier as I drew upon the Void, the power awakening quickly like a dog summoned to its master. Somehow during that battle, I had tamed it and it answered only to me.

The Void twisted through my limbs, serpentine and hungry as

I let it pour from me, the power invisible to the naked eye, but I could sense where it was headed. It brushed against the crackling energy of the invisible boundary and I gasped at the magnitude of the power contained within it. This forcefield equalled death. One step into its embrace and not even the stars could save you.

The Void latched onto all that magic and tugged on it, shutting it down piece by piece. I wielded it like a giant sword, carving a large arc over the river and down to the grassy bank beyond us. Within that space, the magic was dragged into the Void until it shivered out of existence before our eyes, leaving a wide hole for our ships to sail through. As simple and as powerful as that.

A smile drew my lips wide at what I'd achieved, relief filling me for truly managing it.

"Goshart," Father barked, pointing at a stout man who was all muscle with little height to even out his broadness. "Head on through that gap."

"M-me?" Goshart stammered.

"Yes, you. Off you go." Father waved him toward the hole I'd carved and Goshart released a murmur of fear as he passed by our group.

He stopped right before the gap I'd made, glancing back as if hoping Commander Rake might have changed his mind about sending him through first.

"Keep going," Father called and Goshart hesitantly tip-toed toward the gap.

Ever-so-slowly, he held a hand out, sticking it through the hole in the barrier and waving it a little to test it. He dabbed at the sweat on his forehead then started walking through the hole, leaning as far back as he could as if he was going under a limbo stick so his head went through last.

He stood upright on the other side, turning to face us with a bright smile on his face. “It’s okay! It’s safe to come through – it’s completely sa – ahhhh!”

“Eské,” I gasped in horror at the sudden violence.

A beast that looked part bear, part goat, part machine slammed into Goshart, its large teeth clamping around his whole body before racing away with him across the cracked ground of the wasteland. Its curled horns were pure metal, rising above its head into deadly points and the guttering whir in its throat spoke of some deadly contraption within.

“Goshart!” Agatha cried as her friend’s screams carried back to us on the wind. But there was no chance of going after him because ten more beasts came hurtling around a large cluster of rocks and charged right across the river to meet us.

With adrenaline burning through my chest, I unsheathed the sword at my hip, my latest creation a thing of true beauty. She was blue at the hilt, rising to a silver tip on the blade in a gradient and the metal I’d used could cut through bone with one swipe.

I ran to meet the first beast alongside my Father, Ransom and several of the other warriors, its face like a hawk’s, but its body was that of a giant cat with metallic plates of armour welded to its form. I swung my sword for its throat, but Father pushed me back, knocking me into Ransom and lunging for the beast with his blade. The beast took two strikes to the head and four more to the neck before Father managed to fell it.

“Hey!” I barked at that kill being taken from me.

Father didn’t look back, whistling sharply at his warriors and the group who had been flanking me closed in tight around me once more.

A crocodilian beast lunged from the depths of the river and caught a man by the leg, hauling him back toward the water and a bloody grave. He clawed at the ground with screams of terror but none of the warriors around me moved to help him, only pushing me further away from the chaos.

I saw a gap between Agatha and Ransom and darted for it, breaking through and sprinting toward the man who was a few seconds from being dragged beneath the river's surface. I leapt over him, driving my sword down with a punishing force and plunging it right into the beast's eye.

It released its victim at once, thrashing and letting out a guttering roar, a giant, serpent-like tail whipping out of the water and slamming into my side.

I was knocked off balance, rolling and regaining my feet fast as it lunged for me, bloody teeth snapping. But I darted to one side and jabbed my blade into its other eye, blinding it fully. The beast's tail whipped out of the water again and I leapt over it as it swept across the river bank, slicing my sword down and cutting it clean off.

The beast screeched in horror, thrashing madly and I was knocked onto my knees as it whipped around to bite me.

I splashed backwards through the water to avoid the strike, terror sinking into my chest as I saw my death coming for me. I raised my sword, trying to gain my feet and slipping on the wet rocks.

The beast caught my weapon between its teeth, ripping it from my grip and tossing it onto the river bank. I raised my hand, freezing the water that coated its scaly skin, turning it to shards. The crocodile-like monster roared in agony but it kept coming. Ever hungry, ever determined to destroy me.

With a cry of effort, I forced the ice deeper into its scales, and it staggered at last, slamming down into the water and dying with a guttural sound.

I scrambled out of the river, taking deep breaths as I snatched my sword from the ground and bathed in the adrenaline following my victory.

Father was wielding the river to drown two of the beasts and a group of his warriors were working to overwhelm the others.

My veins buzzed with excitement, the thrill of the kill setting me ablaze. I locked eyes with another monster headed my way, its body skeletal and horse-like while its boar's head was covered in metal plates.

I ran to meet it, my teeth bared and heart thundering out the call of war. For the first time in weeks, I felt alive. Like I'd finally found the place I belonged. But as I swung my blade for a second kill, Agatha grabbed hold of me, yanking me back and pushing me between a throng of bodies. Three warriors collided with the beast, fighting madly with it in a fray of bloodshed and determination. They finally cut it down, seizing my victory from me while a group of warriors held me back.

"Let me go!" I demanded, throwing elbows and jamming my heels into their feet, but they only tightened around me.

Ransom was among them, knotting his fingers around my arm and I snarled at him, lunging like a feral cat and aiming a swipe for his face. He knocked me back before I could scratch him, so I jammed my knee up between his legs instead. He croaked and fell to the ground like a sack of mouldy potatoes, standing tall one second then fallen the next. He curled in on himself at my feet and satisfaction filled me as he clutched his balls in his hands. But I still had several more warriors to fight off.

Father called out in victory and I looked up, pausing my fist which was readying to punch Agatha in her turnip of a face and finding the final monsters dead and the warriors retreating.

"Return to the ships!" Father called out, his voice amplified and echoing across the hills.

My bloody sword hung from my fingers in disappointment. I elbowed past Agatha and she let me go at last, my scowl fixed permanently on my face. I stalked back to the White Mare, heading up the gangplank and waiting for Father there.

He was one of the last to board and the ship sailed smoothly forward the moment he stood beside me and the gangplank was pulled up.

"Good job," he commended me. "Now go rest, my child. We will be at Coalmere by sundown. Then you will have more work to do."

I grabbed his arm before he could leave and he glanced at me with a flicker of irritation in his eyes, but then it was gone. "Call off your warriors. I won't be corralled like that. I'm born to fight. I killed one of those beasts single-handedly and I could have done more."

"You think I would risk some rogue monster killing you? I will protect you at all costs."

Warmth spread through my chest, but a sing-song canary in my head told me I was a delusional idiot to fall so easily for his pretty words.

"I appreciate that, but I want to fight. I'm capable of looking after myself," I insisted.

"Of course you are." He patted me on the arm. "And you will have your chance in a true battle. There was no need for you to get caught up in that skirmish."

I relaxed a little, relieved I would get my chance. Of course the plan was seeking surrender in enemy lands, but it would come to a fight here and there. I had no doubt our enemies were laying plots to attack us soon enough.

"Onward!" Father called, heading away from me as the White Mare sailed through the hole I'd made in the barrier. I could see the corners of the gap already reigniting and I imagined the boundary would heal itself soon enough, but the Void had secured our passage. From here, we could travel all the way to the barrier at the verges of Pyros and then we would make our way to the first city to conquer.

It was going to be a beautiful victory. A thing of legend. A marker of our coming dominion.

And I would be remembered as the sole reason for it all.

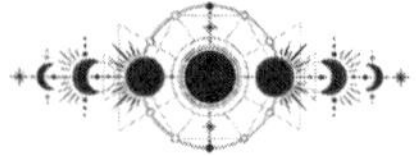

Coalmere was a ghost town.

Not a single Flamebringer to be found.

At first, we had suspected a trap, that they would lurch out from the grey stone buildings and launch fire at us from all angles. But the attack never came.

Our army spread out to search the city, from the empty streets even right down to the sewers, but no one was here.

"They're on the run," Father decided, a satisfied smile pulling at his mouth.

We stood in the town square where a large iron brazier at its centre lay dormant, the ash cold. Plenty of the warriors had turned to pillaging, stacking up piles of any valuables they found but there was very little to claim. The people who had fled this place had taken almost everything with them. A few of our people had used water magic to blast apart some buildings, but it was all a little pointless considering this city was ours for the taking. No resistance.

"Where are they?" I breathed as my shirtless fruit-feeders appeared from the direction of the river with a grand litter to carry me on. They kept bringing that thing out, hoping I might give in to it. And okay, occasionally I did, enjoying the ride for a little while before growing bored. I ended up feeling like a prize meal being paraded about for people to feast on. No, I definitely preferred walking.

Snake Abs was carrying a flag of Cascada – I couldn't remember their names, but he had a snake tattoo running across his stomach that was hard to miss. My father snatched it from him and drove the pole into the ground.

"I declare Coalmere belongs to Cascada!"

Cheers went up but they died out fairly quickly, the whole thing feeling a bit pointless.

"Pyros is hiding from us!" Father continued which roused some excitement. "We're a wolf on the tail of a rabbit and we will chase it further north. Tonight, we celebrate our first victory here in our newly-claimed city and at dawn we take the river up through their fertile land, seizing it for our own!"

At talks of celebration, a clamour broke out and it wasn't long before someone fetched a drum and a mandolin from one of the ships to play music. Ale barrels were rolled out from a nearby tavern and merriment spread through our people. But I didn't feel any of it in my heart.

I propped myself against the stone railing that ringed the brazier, watching the party around me in discontent. Shouldn't we have been more concerned about where an entire city had run to? Kaské, wasn't it worrying that not a single Flamebringer awaited us here? What if they were laying traps this very moment? What if they were waiting for us to drink until we were inebriated then attack us from every direction?

No one seemed in the least bit concerned about that possibility besides me. I noted that no one handed me a drink, perhaps laying their faith in the power of the Void to protect them if all hell broke loose.

Although a ring of warriors sat around me, none of them spoke to me. There were plenty of hushed whispers though, people pointing, staring.

Was this the life that legends lived? It was a lonelier one than I'd expected.

A flash of blue in the corner of my eye made me turn my head and a scaly tail disappeared behind the stone railing.

I lowered to a crouch, my pulse rioting as I crept toward the creature, certain I wasn't going insane. I'd seen flashes of blue in the corner of my eye far too often lately. And now that tail…

I leapt around the railing, my hand slapping down on the tiny lizard and making him screech as I squashed him to the ground.

"I knew it," I growled, locking my fingers around the small beast and picking him up. "*Calcifiend.*"

The Sayer Dragon chirruped guiltily, his big eyes blinking in that cute way of his.

"Why the hell are you following me?" I hissed, dropping to the floor and tucking him against my lap so no one else would see him.

Calcifiend clicked his tongue in answer, but it wasn't one I could decipher and I frowned at the pathetic look he gave me.

"Your master is dead," I said, my brows drawing lower.

I swear the little thing nodded, releasing a sad, mournful noise that pulled at my heartstrings. "And now you have no one."

He trilled softly, nuzzling into my hand as if to say 'I have you'.

And damn, I wanted to keep him. Was there really any harm? Kaiser was gone. It wasn't like the Sayer Dragon could betray me to him anymore. And were these creatures even capable of choices outside their master's command? Maybe he wasn't purposefully a traitor. And maybe he might take to a new master.

I ran a finger up his back and he grunted happily at my touch. "Kaské, it's sort of nice to see a friendly face. I mean as friendly as a little traitorous lizard can be. You're not all bad, are you?"

He chirruped in what seemed to be agreement and I smiled. "You're not mad at me for what I did?"

He chirruped again and I subtly cast a silencing shield around us to hide what I was going to say next in case anyone was eavesdropping.

"Maybe he wasn't such a good master to you anyway. That emotionless lump of stacked muscle couldn't have been the friendliest companion. But I am sorry. Not for killing him. I mean..." I leaned in close to whisper just to him. "Sometimes I feel strange about it. Not regret exactly but…I don't know. He was so broken. There are things about him I didn't understand, but I wish I could now. My mind can't put it to rest if I'm honest. Sometimes I dream of him. Sometimes he feels so close I can almost smell the cinders on his skin. Sometimes I wish I could smell that scent again for real. But that's just for you to know." I pressed a finger to my lips and Calcifiend rolled over in my palm, licking my thumb then sitting like a tiny dog and gazing up at me patiently as if waiting for me to continue talking. I supposed whatever I said couldn't be repeated anyway.

I gazed across the sea of warriors, finding myself exactly where I had chosen to be, yet feeling like I didn't belong. "I guess nothing in this world is as black and white as I thought it was."

SEPTA

CHAPTER EIGHT

The underbeast hummed with latent magic as it powered along beneath the ground through the enormous tunnel which had been carved so deep into the ground that no Fae other than one blessed with the magic of earth might ever hope to find it.

I tried to appear relaxed in the plush chair I rode in, this beast having been decked out for the upper echelon to use as transport and was far more lavishly embellished than those which had transported our armies to the battlefield.

I had felt like I'd been holding my breath for the entire duration of the battle that Earl Tarlord had entered into with Pyros, leaping from my seat every time a messenger brought news from the field to the horned table, sagging with relief every time the tidings were good.

My husband had seemed even more on edge than I had, professing tirelessly that he should have been out there, swinging his own sword on the field. But his curse and the potential value of the information which remained locked inside his mind had meant that he'd been forbidden from entering the fight, much to his chagrin and mine.

The match between us had been for my name and his prowess in battle. What use was he to me all the time he could offer nothing more than empty promises of vital information and countless nights of whimpering over his endlessly flaccid cock?

All of the fantasies I had once dreamed up about the man who now claimed me as his wife were being dashed to pieces day after day and though there were many reasons I could find for the failure of my fantasies to have become reality, I chose to favour one. The Sky Witch. After all it was far easier to make her a target for my ire than it was to start making a tally of Alestro's failings.

And it appeared that despite the victory Earl Tarlord had won in Pyros, her death still eluded her.

The underbeast titled skyward and I suppressed a gasp as I was pressed back into my cushioned seat, my fingers curling around the handhold which was bolted to the wall.

"Nervous?" August hissed, leaning forward in his seat behind mine so that he could speak into my ear, a string of his greasy hair falling around the edge of my headrest.

"Not at all," I replied calmly. "Just excited to see what our Earl has achieved."

"Yes, yes, it will all be very impressive," Alestro grunted from his place beside me, his words those of a petulant child. The boils and crusted scabs which covered his skin looked as angry as ever even though he had made no attempt to speak of his secrets in the last few days.

I glanced at the other Fae who rode the underbeast with us and clenched my jaw. Didn't he know we were on parade? Didn't he understand how hard I had worked to earn us a place on this machine? He hadn't once praised me for the lofty position he found our standing in society to be. I had the ear of the Earl himself and yet Alestro caterwauled like an infant denied the finest treats.

"We have been so anxious to see the new province, haven't we my dear?" I crooned, giving Alestro a sharp look and placing my hand on his thigh so that I could give his skin a hard squeeze in warning.

Alestro huffed irritably and pushed himself upright.

"I would recommend you return to your seat," August called after him. "The incline will increase sharply soon and–"

"I am well aware of how this mode of transportation functions, thank you," Alestro clipped, striding to the front of the underbeast where its metal panels would open like jaws to allow us to exit at our destination.

"Come and sit, husband," I urged but Alestro ignored me, clasping his hands at the base of his spine and staring at the exit as if expecting it to open for him at any given moment. My cheeks pinked at the public dismissal before I forced myself to breathe a laugh and mutter a light comment about the stubbornness of men which thankfully received a few titters in agreement.

"Earl Tarlord's victory at Cinder Vale will be the talk of The Waning Lands," I said, turning towards Lady Sharma who sat rigidly in the seat across the aisle from me.

"Indeed," she agreed primly, though she offered me a warm smile. Thankfully the court seemed to have landed on pitying me and my husband for now instead of scorning us and though I'd have preferred respect and reverence I would take it. Pity was an emotion I could build a friendship upon, scorn was far harder to overcome.

"I heard a whisper that our Earl demolished the entire palace already – he intends to rebuild it as a Stonebreaker haven, entirely void of the Flamebringer taint."

I smiled proudly at that. Our Earl was a man to be feared and respected throughout all of The Waning Lands.

The underbeast veered sharply upward, Alestro crying out in panic as our ascent became almost vertical and he was hurled through the central aisle at speed, smacking into every chair on his way before finally slamming into the luggage which had been strapped into place at the rear of the machine and falling down within it.

He groaned in confirmation that he still lived and I stared in wide-eyed horror at the one booted foot I could still see of his form.

August chuckled behind me and I shot him a glare which he only shrugged at.

"We both warned him," he said innocently and despite my grave dislike for the man, I had to agree with him for once. Alestro had gotten what he deserved but that didn't detract from the blow it had given my reputation to see him spinning through the air like a fool.

The underbeast sped towards the surface and there was no way for Alestro to return to his seat with the steepness of the incline, so he remained cursing by the back wall amid the heaped luggage until finally we erupted from the ground and the pale light of day spilled through the toughened glass before us.

The underbeast levelled out on a plain of black lava stone, dawn cresting the horizon to our right and excitement burning through me along with more than a little trepidation.

I got to my feet, smoothing the skirt of deepest russet which hung to my ankles and tapping my fingers lightly across the boning in my corset. My hips had been aching from sitting still in one position for so long but I resisted the urge to stamp my feet and bring full feeling back to my limbs.

The front of the underbeast lifted with a deep groan, the warm, dry air rushing in to greet us, bringing the unfamiliar scent of a distant land with it. But I refused to balk at the foreign nation as I stepped out onto it, raising a hand to shield my eyes from the early rays of dawn.

"Lady Septa," a low voice rumbled in greeting and I turned to the unfamiliar man with surprise. "The Earl has provided a litter for your arrival in the city – are you ready to embark?"

I looked beyond him to the litter which had been built with a wooden frame, carpeted with twisted vines which had been crafted using earth magic to create a seat at its heart beneath a canopy of stunning wild flowers. More litters awaited the rest of Earl Tarlord's closest attendants but the one the man urged me toward was somehow more vibrant, more full of life. The red and orange flowers which bloomed across the top of it opened and closed their petals like the movements of a flickering flame, a jest at the expense of the Flamebringers whose land we had conquered.

Alestro strode from the underbeast as I was climbing onto the litter, muttering curses about the Flamebringers, and making claims of what he might have achieved in this battle had he been present for it.

I sat carefully in the cushioned seat at the heart of the litter, positioning myself in a way that allowed my muscles to relax at last. I silently thanked whoever had decided to provide this method of transport for us as I looked across the uneven lava field which separated us from the deep bowl which contained the city.

I settled into the shade beneath the repeatedly blooming flowers, running over my plans and strategies in my mind, thinking about all the ideas I'd had for this place and trying to take in everything I could about it to see if any of them might have true merit. I was determined to prove my worth here, to offer up insights and ideas which our Earl would be able to take into consideration and perhaps even implement.

Just as I was letting myself drift into the daydream of the position I might be able to secure for myself, the litter jolted and I blinked in surprise as Alestro clambered onto it.

"My Lord? The litters are only meant to carry one. We were told the warriors would approach the city on foot. The litters are intended for the advisors," a guard tried unsuccessfully but Alestro ignored him, planting his ass on the chair meant for me alone and shunting me sideways as he did so.

I hissed between my teeth as a bolt of pain ran down my leg from the impact with his hip but he didn't seem to notice.

"I could get used to this," he said with a grin that made one of the boils on his cheek stretch to the point of bursting.

I fought the urge to recoil, trying to look past the pustules which the curse had afflicted him with to the attractive man I had once dreamed of claiming as my husband beneath them. But it was as if the boils had become a representation of the tainted soul which resided at the heart of him. His crude jokes and vulgar attitude towards life rankled me, and the nights I spent listening to him curse and cry over his flaccid cock while he pathetically slapped it against my inner thighs in hopes of stirring it to action were only making my animosity towards him grow.

It wasn't his fault. I told myself that again and again, trying to force my aggravation onto the woman who had caused this curse upon him. But as he shifted his ass to get comfortable in *my* seat, I found myself grinding my jaw against the words which wanted to pour free.

The guard gave up on attempting to make Alestro vacate the litter and with a surge of magic, a hundred vines sprung from the sides of it like the legs of a millipede, lifting us into the air before starting out across the lava field.

The litter pitched to the right, Alestro's weight unbalancing it and making what appeared to be a steady, buoyant-looking ride on the other litters into a cumbersome, loping journey which jolted my bones time and again.

I was well practiced in hiding my discomforts but I bit down on the insides of my cheeks to stop myself from flinching every time Alestro's elbow or hip smacked into my side.

Tunnels led us beneath the ground and when we emerged at the heart of Cinder Vale it was to find a ruined city partially submerged in dirty water, corpses floating among the wreckage, the stench of death and decay clogging the air.

It wasn't the grand arrival I'd anticipated and I wrinkled my nose at the destruction while Alestro released a bawdy laugh, slashing the dead bodies with vines he conjured in his fists, like he was lashing a misbehaved mule.

"Virgo teaches us to respect the dead," I murmured, placing a hand on his arm to try and stop his vulgar display but he only shook me off.

"Virgo is also forever a virgin," he sneered. "Something the two of you look likely to have in common thanks to the Skyforgers and their ilk. I'd have thought you'd enjoy the sight of our enemies falling to ruin beneath us? Don't you want to change our fate, Septa?"

"I do," I agreed in a low tone, my cheeks heating from the insult. It wasn't *my* fault that my virtue remained intact but I knew not to prod that particular bear.

We approached the inner walls of the citadel and at last we found ourselves moving onto cleared streets, the cobbles swept and free of the dead or any debris at all.

I'd seen paintings of the palace which sat at the heart of Cinder Vale so as I leaned forward to peer out from beneath the canopy of our litter, a frown pinched my brow at what I found there.

It wasn't a towering building of black glass and stone. It wasn't even the ruins of such a place. Instead a grand castle squatted at the heart of the citadel, its walls white stone, carved with the emblems of our people. There were towers capped with blue, conical roofs, their tips pointing up to the sky as if making a claim there too. It was quite possibly the most beautiful building I had ever seen and it made no sense at all.

The litter came to a halt and Alestro leapt down from it, striding away to greet some of the warriors who lingered before the castle gates, asking them for tales of the battle.

I hesitated where I was, though I could see the others disembarking their litters too.

My hip had stiffened to the point of locking itself in place thanks to the weight of Alestro pinning that side of my body still for the journey down here and despite the hissed pleas I was shooting to Taurus in hopes that he might lend me enough stubbornness to push past the pain of it, I knew I wasn't going to be getting off of this thing easily.

"I've been awaiting your arrival, my lady," a deep voice growled and I couldn't hide the jolt of surprise which ran through me as my heart leapt in alarm at his closeness.

"Earl Tarlord," I breathed, bowing my head in deference while peeking through my lashes to get a good look at him.

He wore his warrior's garb, battle leathers in a brown so rich it appeared bronze, his dark hair falling forward around his face as he peered down at me from his staggering height, his eyes dark with unknown demons.

"No need for pomp and pretentious bullshit on the battlefield," he said, offering me his calloused hand and I noted the angry cut which curved across the edge of his palm between his thumb and forefinger before diving around to the back.

I hesitantly took his hand, careful not to touch his wound but he moved his palm against mine, those callouses forged on the hilt of his mighty war hammer grazing the softness of skin which had rarely seen a day outside the confines of our stronghold back in Avanis.

My palm moved over the cut on his hand and I made to draw back but he curled his fingers tightly to stop me.

"If the blessing of your touch doesn't heal it then nothing but time ever will," he murmured and my mouth dried out at the words.

I made to stand, locking my jaw against the pain I knew would come but suddenly he was bending down, his other hand moving to the small of my back as he tugged me upright, supporting my weight and taking the pressure from my leg. As if he knew exactly what was bothering me without so much as a glance at it.

He practically lifted me from the litter, turning us to face the castle and hooking my arm through his in a way that appeared formal but also took some portion of my weight, negating the pain of standing too heavily on my left leg.

"It's beautiful," I breathed, staring up at the castle where Avanis flags snapped in the wind on every tower.

"I thought the place required something new. Something which instilled the heart of our people right into the remains of their capital. So I destroyed what little remained of their palace and built one anew."

"You...built all of this yourself?" I asked, blinking up at the castle in astonishment. It had only been a few weeks since he had won the battle. He would have had to work tirelessly to build such a thing.

"You doubt my capability?" he asked and if I wasn't mistaken there was a hint of teasing to the words.

"I know you're incredibly powerful," I said quickly. "I didn't mean to imply–"

"I like to build in the wake of destruction," he said, cutting me off, clearly not insulted despite my fears. "War is a destroyer and yet our people have magic which can create so much. I leave my mark on every battlefield, creating something for those who will come after. This castle is a signal of our victory but also of a new beginning."

"Did you find the Sky Witch?" I asked eagerly, showing my desperation to have the curse upon Alestro broken and his shame at being unable to spill the secrets ended. But I wanted this done. I had worked so hard to secure a good place for me and my honoured husband. Every day that passed with the curse painting him into a fool, was another day I would have to work to wipe all memory of his failure from the minds of our people.

"Escaped during the battle, I'm afraid," Earl Tarlord said, his brow furrowing in frustration. "She was seen with her people as they fled on their flying island."

"Oh." I tried not to let the disappointment I felt at that revelation sting, but it was hard to do. With her still breathing, Alestro's shame would only linger on, staining me with his inability to provide our Earl with whatever secrets he held locked away in his mind.

"And what of the Void?" August's simpering voice made me flinch guiltily and I tore my eyes from our Earl to find the entire party had gathered around us, patiently awaiting his attention while he lavished it undeservingly upon me.

I tried to step away but he didn't release my arm, his thumb brushing softly against the skin of my inner elbow as if to reassure me.

I swallowed thickly at the gentle touch from a beast so brutal he had won the capital of Pyros for our people in a matter of hours. How had he looked at the end of that battle? How deeply had the blood of his enemies stained his skin?

"I've heard much about the Void," Earl Tarlord grunted and my gut twisted at those words. Of course it had been all anyone could speak of following the celebrations of our victory. Word had spread like a disease infecting every piece of our lands. The Void had surfaced at last and Cascada had claimed it as their prize. "We've called our people to action, sent word to outlying villages to move into the safety of the Earldoms' strongholds. I intend to rally half of our forces here and–"

"With the greatest of respect, Earl, it won't matter how impressive our numbers are if the Void nullifies our magic and the Raincarvers drown us all in the ensuing chaos," August said, his words like a poison which made every one of us recoil.

A growl sounded in Earl Tarlord's throat, something feline and wicked about the noise which sent a shiver through my skin. It was easy to picture him in his Manticore form in that moment, his hair becoming a lion's mane and wings sprouting from his back to further aid him in battle. But even that would be stripped of him if the Void appeared at our gates.

My Sphynx form would be stolen from me too. The thought of losing connection with that innate part of me made my heart speed with frantic panic. But I'd been thinking about this for the past few weeks, determined not to allow that fear to paralyse me and I'd had an idea.

"I say we just cut the heads from every Raincarver until we find the right one!" Alestro shouted before I might speak and the silence which followed his foolish bravado spoke far louder than any words.

"Do you think it would be so easy?" August sneered. "If so, perhaps you should run off on another little mission to do just that? The stars know that the information you gathered on your last expedition isn't going to do us any good any time soon anyway."

Heat rose in my cheeks at his jibe, the spattering of laughter which followed his words only further confirming my fears. Alestro was losing the respect of our peers. He was becoming the butt of their jokes. The fool who fucked the Sky Witch and came running back to us with nothing but a curse to show for his years of infiltration into the ranks of our enemy.

"I...had a thought," I said, uncertain what had possessed me to speak out. I'd meant to present this to the Earl in private, alone if possible, so that if it were a fool's musings I wouldn't be forced to face my own ridicule at the heart of his fickle court too. But everyone was looking at me now and I had little choice but to continue.

"We could divert the rivers and undermine the land," I said, forcing my words to come out clearly and loudly enough for all to hear. I'd spent weeks researching old siege strategies, studying the ways in which the cities had survived when they'd been surrounded. Most of what I'd found would be of no help to us but a few breadcrumbs from one piece of history mixed with the flavour of another had sparked an idea in my head. An idea which I'd run with, plotting in great detail, writing plans and filling countless scrolls and maps with my scrawled plots. Perhaps it was nothing, but maybe, just *maybe*, it was the scheme we needed to survive this.

"What land?" August asked, his tone scathing as always.

"All of it," I said hesitantly before forcing myself to go on with more confidence. "I took the liberty of planning out how it would work both here and back at Raglith where Stone Castle stands proud. Given time I could do the same for the other Earldoms and the coastlines too. Each and every village in fact if–"

August scoffed loudly and Alestro interrupted.

"My wife forever has her nose in a book, scribbling and muttering all night long while she makes these little plans of hers. It is a hobby which I assure you is as boorish as it sounds. But you know how Sphynxes can be about their books–"

"I know that Lady Septa is one of the most perceptive and insightful Fae I have ever met," Earl Tarlord growled, every syllable a warning which whipped the amusement from every face and promptly silenced my husband too. "And I also know, that were she *my* wife, her nights would be very much occupied with acts quite separate from reading. But perhaps your stamina is no match for hers."

Alestro's face burned hotly beneath the boils, his sharp gaze cutting to mine in accusation. But I had never spoken so much as a word of his inadequacies in the bedroom to any other, not even Getta who I confided in about almost all else.

"I…drew out some designs," I said, wanting to change the subject, the place where my skin still met the Earl's a raging vortex of sparking energy. I needed to pull away from him but he held me tightly for another moment before finally allowing me to go.

"Let us see them," he said finally, his green eyes pinning mine before he released me.

I turned towards the litter, realising that I hadn't in fact grabbed my bag when exiting the underbeast but thankfully it only took a few barked commands from our Earl for a guard to locate our luggage and bring my bag over.

I hastily cast a wooden table into place at the heart of our group, my heart pounding so frantically at the weight of their attention on me that I could do little more than create a solid structure with four legs. It was nothing on the perfection of the castle whose shadow we stood within but I refused to allow my insecurities to push in on me. I might have hoped to do this privately to avoid ridicule should my plans be judged poorly but I had no choice in the matter now.

I took several rolled scrolls from my bag and flattened them on the table, casting little stones into place to pin the corners down. Lastly, I placed a map of Cinder Vale right before the Earl, my sketches and scribbles annotating every inch surrounding the space.

"I'm not certain how accurate this map is but ignoring any inconsistencies for now, my plan is this. We dig. Here, here and here first." I placed a finger on every point of approach that surrounded the city. "Then if we still have time we fill in the gaps between them."

"Dig what exactly?" August drawled, tugging a sketch from the table and lifting it for his inspection.

Earl Tarlord took it from him and arched a brow as he took in the pit filled with sharpened spears, the jagged cracks which fell away deeply into the earth, countless traps and pitfalls.

"The Void can't cancel out magic which is already in place. We surround ourselves with land that has been undermined and cannot be crossed without plunging through its fragile surface into the pitfalls we have waiting for them. Let's see them march on us with their Void when the ground collapses beneath their feet and plunges them into a pit filled with spears. I don't think it will do them much good to Void anything then," I said proudly.

"They're Raincarvers," August pushed. "They'll simply form a bridge of ice or a river to carry their ships and–"

"That's what the chasms are for," I said quickly, pointing them out.

"Carved so deeply into the ground that any water which is cast there will sink away into them. And we would coax the heat of the earth into channels which encourage the lava to rise and steam to vent meaning any ice would be melted fast. We could build layer upon layer of these traps, so many of them ringing us that the Cascadians can't cast quickly enough to cross them. And above that we would place trebuchets and catapults, each triggered with tripwires to bombard them with raining death." I couldn't help but grin as I turned to look up at my Earl, my heart frantic as his green eyes simmered with what I hoped was intrigue.

"This could work," he said, a smile blooming to match my own, the first I'd ever seen him wear. "If they can't reach us, then they can't overrun us. We can defend against the Void and meanwhile plot a way to destroy it."

"The plan has merit," August agreed and from him that might as well have been a cry of applause.

"Truly?" I breathed, my eyes locking on my Earl who dropped the map he'd been holding and clasped my face between his hands, the thunder of his pulse rioting through his skin.

"You, Septa, cunning, clever, creature that you are, may just have saved our people," he said roughly, his eyes dropping to my mouth as I bit down on my lip. "Now let's go dig some holes."

VESPER

CHAPTER NINE

"Vesper."

I clenched my fists, trying to pretend I couldn't hear the call of my name, though it grew more insistent with every passing day.

I'd been plotting. Plotting and planning and scheming and… nothing. This place was like a vortex sucking me back in at every turn. All I wanted was to be set loose on my hunt for Cayde but there was no way that I could conceive to orchestrate that.

Prince Evard had been watching me closely. Princess Laurina too for that matter though I knew her focus was mostly due to distaste. She didn't appreciate having crossborn scum at the Generals' table, sat right before her at every meal, my pure existence a bane to her life.

Even Prince Roarson – the third brother and the one I generally regarded as little more than a philanderer with a penchant for bloodshed – paid me more attention now, though the king was as disinterested in everything as ever. Our sovereign looked even older, more gaunt with every day yet I still doubted his death would ever come for him despite the whispers about his ill health growing louder.

I wanted to heed Moya's warnings. Hell, I wanted to follow that fucking voice even if I wanted to snap Cayde's neck before doing so. But more than any of that, I wanted to climb the stairs in the east tower and meet the eyes of the man who lay beyond the door there.

I swallowed as I looked up at the tower walls for what must have been the hundredth time this week alone, my heart beating faster as I wondered if he might be looking back. I'd done what I'd had to but that didn't make it easier. He hated me now. There was no question of that, but still I found myself wanting to face his hatred over the simpering of the sycophants here who swooned all over me.

The same Fae who had sneered and muttered curses at my back for all those years now bowed and greeted me with bright smiles, trying to curry favour with the woman who suddenly had the power to choose which battles they fought in and decide how likely they were to meet their deaths in them.

It was sickening.

I stepped out into the training yard with my mind spinning and frantic energy making my muscles twitch. I needed a release and this was the best chance I had at getting one.

Mutters passed through the ranks of warriors who were already in the yard, those taking part in spars losing focus as my gifts drew their attention to me like moths to a flame.

"Will you watch me ride a pony?" a man shrieked from somewhere towards the back and a few others called out crude offers or claims of sexual prowess which I doubted they truly possessed. I ignored them all, shoving the one who dared approach me back with a sharp gust of wind and trying to ignore the pang of loss as I remembered the way Dalia and Moraine had always done that for me.

A match was already taking place in the main ring but there were a few benefits to my elevation to General.

"I'm up now," I called, taking a wooden staff from the rack of weapons which stood before the ring and testing its weight in my grip. "Any takers?"

My lips twitched as I felt the flickers of desire all around me, more than a few Fae wishing to go unnoticed in this moment, or hoping not to be selected, though of course they wouldn't admit to such. Cowardice was frowned upon in Stormfell. And bravery was rewarded.

As if my thoughts had summoned him into action, a brute of a man shoved through the crowd, calling out his intention to fight me. I eyed him with wicked appraisal, giving a slight nod before calling out for three more volunteers to join him. I didn't want to do easy today.

Several more Fae took up the challenge and I rolled my shoulders back as I stepped into the ring, ready to steal a moment of calm amid the crash of weapons and the pounding of flesh.

"No magic," I called, stating the rules. "If we're going to be up against the Void then we need to maintain our training without it. We need to be unstoppable with power or without."

Murmurs filled the training yard and I didn't need to eavesdrop to know what they were all saying. What use would fighting prowess be against warriors who could drown us with a flick of their fingers? They were right. But we had little choice other than to forge on. It wasn't like we were willing to concede defeat and surrender.

I didn't waste time announcing the start of the match, throwing myself at my closest opponent instead and sweeping his feet out from beneath him with my staff.

Carnage broke out instantly, bellows of effort and grunts of force, fists flew, weapons swung and I lost myself in the rush of the fight, relishing each blow I landed and embracing every strike of pain I received too.

It was a furious, frantic thing, my opponents keen to best me and win the accolade of having done so to wear like a mantle around their necks. But I was a wild creature, and I was too lost in my own fury for them to stand a chance against me.

I let the match drag on, minutes ticking by as I toyed with them, trading blows and grinning through the pain. The tang of blood coated my tongue and I could feel my cheek swelling from a punch I'd failed to dodge. But all too soon I had my prey disarmed or on their backs, tapping out and begging for mercy when it looked like I might not stop.

I forced myself to fall still, the staff tumbling from my grip with a solid thump as it hit the sand.

My chest rose and fell heavily, tangled hair falling into my eyes and I let them close as I tried to lose myself in the pain of my injuries, the rush of my win. But when I peeled my lids open again it was to find my head tilted back and my gaze pinned on the tower which held the man I'd betrayed for this pointless position.

Fae were clamouring around me, muttering pointless praise and offering me everything from tinctures to water to a turn beneath the sheets with them. I looked up at the man who had offered that. He was brutish and well built, a Minotaur if I wasn't mistaken. He wouldn't be gentle with me if I took him up on his offer and I certainly didn't want gentle.

But my eyes strayed beyond him once more, back to that lonely tower and the man I knew remained within it.

I spat a wad of blood from my mouth.

"Come on then," I said, jerking my chin at the Minotaur. "Let's see if you can handle me."

The bastard grinned at me as he took in my acceptance of his offer, and I fought back a growl in reply. But maybe this was what I needed. I was a creature built for sex and it had been a long fucking time since I'd had any of that. If this bull of a man could scratch the itch which was keeping me from sleep or at least stifle it for a few hours then I would make good use of him.

"I'm Jarod," he said reaching out to take my hand but I jerked it away.

"I don't care what your name is. In fact, I don't need to hear a single word from your lips. You can make better use of your mouth or I'll have no need of it at all."

He fell silent, his desire wrapping around me thickly, flashes of what he wanted to do to me pouring through my mind as my gifts devoured his power. He was inventive if nothing else, though his desire to tie me up while he fucked me would go unanswered. I was nothing if not dominant.

Jarod made to turn towards the city as we stepped out of the barracks, his fantasies giving me a rough idea of the layout of his home where he was hoping to take me, but I didn't want to waste time traipsing through the fucking city.

I flicked my fingers at him and shoved him down a small alley which led behind the stables where the cavalry was housed. I didn't need soft sheets and small comforts. I wanted rough and I wanted wild and he could take me against a wall well enough to deliver that.

Jarod made no complaint, grabbing me the moment we were concealed in the alleyway and pressing me up against the back wall of the stables, the rough wood coated with the scent of hay and manure. It was romance at its finest.

He pressed me back against the wall and leaned in to take my lips with his but I turned my head at the last moment, leaving him to press his mouth to my neck instead.

I tipped my head back, focusing on the trail his mouth left down my skin, the roughness of his lips and the bite of his teeth. He knew what he was doing at least but as my mind was overwhelmed with flashes of his fantasies of me I couldn't help but want to shove him off of me again.

I cursed, focussing on the desire that surrounded me and letting myself fall into it, feeling the way my body heated in reply, the power of what I was coming to life and causing a ragged groan to escape him.

"Take your clothes off," I snapped, shoving him back and I watched as he did what I said without complaint, unfastening his leathers and shucking his shirt first.

I eyed his strong physique with appreciation, taking in his powerful frame and forcing myself to think of nothing but the relief I might find if I could just take what I needed from him.

He looked at me, hunger in his eyes and I didn't need the flash of desire to tell me that he wanted my clothes gone too.

I resisted the urge to grunt in irritation and unfastened my leathers as well, still watching him while he kicked off his boots and unbuckled his belt.

He certainly wasn't shy, stripping himself completely bare while I tossed my jacket aside and tugged my shirt over my head, leaving my breasts contained only within the thin linen chemise I wore as an undergarment.

Jarod pointed at my trousers, clearly finding confidence in the baring of his admittedly impressive cock because he had the nerve to bark an order at me.

"Take those off," he said and I narrowed my eyes.

"That's not how this works," I told him scathingly. "You're going to get on your knees in front of me and take them off for me. Then you're going to see if you can make me come with your mouth before I decide whether or not to let you try it with your cock. And if you can't, I think the answer to that question is going to be pretty obvious."

His eyes flared with defiance for all of a moment but I simply tugged on his desire with my gifts and he dropped to his knees before me like a Reaper before the stars.

I leaned back against the wall as he unhooked my belt, once again focusing on the desire that surrounded me, the knot in my chest only tightening with every ragged breath that escaped my lips.

Jarod finally unfastened my belt, followed by my fly before tugging my trousers down with a sharp jerk which perhaps should have had me panting with the urgent desire to feel his tongue against my clit but instead had me wanting to snarl a curse at him.

I knocked my head back against the stable wall, trying to force my head into this but all it gave me was a view up out of the alley towards that same fucking tower which apparently had decided to haunt me.

Jarod gripped my undergarments and made to tug them down but I slapped him away with a force of air magic which had him on his feet and pinned to the wall to my right in the blink of an eye.

"I'm bored," I told him cruelly, yanking my trousers back up and fastening them without even bothering to look at him.

"You…what?" Desire pulsed from him steadily but with a sharp tug I stole all that remained of his magic from him and with it the only thing which had made this interaction worth my time too.

"Just jerk yourself off over the idea of how close you came to getting what you wanted from me. It's not the same but it's the best you're going to get."

He growled angrily, a moo of protest escaping him but I only smiled, his desire so potent that I knew he was going to do it if for nothing other than to claim the release his body was now so desperate for.

"Bitch," he muttered, fisting his cock and starting to pump it, his eyes still very much on me.

"You don't know the half of it," I replied cooly, stooping to grab my shirt and jacket from the ground and shrugging into them before striding away from him.

"Vesper."

"Yeah, I hear you," I snapped at the intangible voice. "But I can't do shit about it."

It called out to me again and I ground my jaw, pretending I couldn't hear it despite the fact that I could barely sleep for the racket it made while crying out to me.

It was so insistent. I hadn't been this loud before, not until…

I fell still, frowning to myself and wondering how I could have been so dumb. It had only gotten this loud, this insistent when I'd been right on top of the ley line the last time, the keystone within reach.

Was it possible that there was another one of those fractured points of power somewhere here? But if it was, then where?

I was so distracted that I didn't even notice my prince approaching until he was practically on top of me, his fingers snapping tight around my arm and his fury burning brightly in my face.

"Have you forgotten what you swore to me, Vesper?" he hissed, tugging me against him firmly and I had to fight the urge to resist as his magic banded around us and launched us into the sky.

I said nothing, swallowing back the anger which burned through me as I realised what I'd just done. I had forgotten the promise I'd made him, the way I'd sworn to belong to no one but him. I'd forgotten it because when I'd made him that promise the only thing I had desired had been to become his creature in every way. I'd been foolish enough to think he might have wanted me the way I'd wanted him for so very long but it came to me in a flood of realisation that now, I didn't want that at all. The thought of him owning me like that made me want to recoil. He was a man who had chosen marriage to another so very easily, who had used and coerced me in every way he could and yet still he seemed to think I would hold to an oath I'd only made in foolish naivety.

We landed heavily on the balcony of his chambers and he kept hold of my arm, hauling me inside before slamming the doors shut with a gust of wind and encasing us in a silencing shield.

"You will not disrespect me so blatantly," Dragor snarled, dragging me closer so that we were nose to nose and though my feelings for him were a tangled web of devotion, allegiance and honour, they were also tinged with a sour taste of betrayal I hadn't wanted to admit to myself. Because despite what lines he had drawn and what oaths he had coaxed from my lips, he *had* betrayed me. He'd corrupted and manipulated me and made me believe in something which never could have come to pass. And then he'd tried to force me to accept the scraps he tossed my way in place of the feast I'd been promised. But I was no dog to be beaten into submission. I was a wolf worthy of feasting, or at the very least, creating a banquet of my own.

"You have a wife. I assumed you had no interest in what I do with my body now," I spat, jerking free of him. "And you spoke of me seducing your brother too. So what difference does it make if I choose to claim my own pleasure from time to time? It's not like you truly want me anyway."

His eyes flashed with malice, the anger there awakening me to a truth which was so obvious that I realised I'd been staring at it from the very first moment I saw him.

"But that's not the point, is it?" I said slowly. "The point is the choice and who gets to make it."

"I am your prince, you swore an oath to me and that *was* a choice. You don't get to simply change the terms which bind you, Vesper Dragonsbane. You *are* my creature and you will act only in accordance to my commands!" he raged and though nothing but vitriol burned in my chest at his words it wasn't like I had any real reason to rebuff them. I hadn't even fucked the Minotaur and I had no desire to take a different lover either. I had no desire for anything at all aside from the vengeance which he refused to allow me.

"Fine," I bit out. "But if I'm a weapon then wield me. And set me loose on my enemy too."

"As easy as that?" he scoffed and I shrugged, defeat clinging to me. "And if I were to allow you to seek the man who wronged you would you be content then? Would you come back to me and be the sword at my side? Would you fulfil every desire I have of you? Would you do all I asked of you?"

"I've always done all you asked of me," I hissed, my voice breaking on the words. "And this is the only thing I ever asked for in return, yet you deny me it."

"Liar," Dragor spat. "You defy me at every turn, never more so than since you returned from that cursed Never Keep. Your head was turned by that place and the treason you committed there and you have never been the same since. You're tarnished by it and I told you before, I want you perfect, not stained by anything at all."

"Perfect?" I released a hopeless laugh. "I have never come even close to that."

Dragor surveyed me critically and I knew he agreed with me there at least.

I resisted the urge to say more, lowering my head instead and turning for the door.

"I'll remember the oath to you," I muttered. "So if there's nothing else, I'll just– "

Dragor lunged for me, grabbing my hand and jerking me back to face him again. I met his gaze defiantly, unable to cloak the roiling emotions which burned through my veins as he peered into my eyes as if hunting for something.

"What is it you want, Vesper?" he murmured, though the question seemed aimed more at himself than at me. "And why is it that when I look at you all I see is a desire for that Dragon you delivered to me?"

I flinched at that accusation, shaking my head in denial of it.

"He's nothing to me," I said though we could both taste the lie on the air as my words tainted it.

Dragor tilted his head as he considered me before continuing in a disparaging tone. "Don't tell me you fell for the lies of another Avanis bastard. What is it? Are their cocks bigger than the men in Stormfell can claim?"

"You tell me," I sneered, looking down at his crotch suggestively before tugging my hand from his grip.

Dragor chuckled, though a darkness simmered in his cold eyes.

"I have no concerns in that department. But I don't think that's it either. You do care about him though, don't you?"

"He was a means to an end," I replied mechanically, forcing my pounding heart to calm, ignoring the way my pulse echoed through my skull with every lie I spoke. "An end which you are denying me."

"Ah," Dragor said, nodding as if he'd suddenly gotten the answer he wanted. "Well you can calm yourself over the Dragon. I have him well in hand and I can promise you he harbours no longing for you in turn. He is in fact quite enamoured with the idea of your demise and would no doubt immensely enjoy it if I allowed him the chance to deliver it to you."

I said nothing. I'd already promised Bastian my death and I had no plans to renege on that bargain – the stars would curse me for it if I did. Though I supposed I was like Dragor in that sense, twisting the terms of our deal to suit my own ends. The realisation was less than comforting.

"This is how it will be. Perhaps if you have clarity on that you will stop with this defiance and find yourself comfortable in your place here once more."

"Perhaps," I replied, though nothing about the word offered agreement on that suggestion.

"Our most pressing concern now is the Void. Followed closely by the line of succession in our kingdom. My father is ailing and the time for him to choose his heir is fast approaching. All of my siblings have their own plans to turn his head and I need to know what they are. Evard wishes to use you as a key to gaining insight into me. You will encourage him in his efforts. Agree to wed him if he asks again and– "

I opened my mouth to protest but he held up a hand to silence me.

"*And* if it comes to it then you will bed him too – clearly your oath to be mine and no others' does not stand. So we may as well make use of the full range of your gifts."

The look on my face was clearly enough to convey my disgust at the idea of playing his seductress but he clucked his tongue dismissively and went on.

"Do not think this is something I ask of you alone. I have spies all over The Waning Lands who fuck our enemies and far more than that to keep their covers secure. Your flesh is the property of Stormfell just as every other part of you is, and despite your belief that you are a weapon best utilised on the battlefield I can see clearly enough that you are a blade which can cut both ways. And you *will*. You are my weapon so I will wield you where you are best suited to strike."

"I'm not a whore," I hissed.

"No one is offering to pay you for it," he spat in reply. "Now let me finish. Once I am crowned I will dissolve your marriage to my brother should you wish it – though you would be a fool to want to be anything other than an Aquila and you know it. But that is only one piece of this puzzle and by far the least important. The Void is our priority. We know that her power doesn't stall the magic stored in runes so we are working tirelessly to imbue all manner of weapons with as much energy as we can in preparation of their attack. But when we hit that battlefield your one and only task will be to capture her for our utilization. Do you understand me? The moment you bring her to me I *will* deem your loyalty assured and you *will* be allowed to hunt the man who called himself Cayde Avior and killed your precious sisters."

"Is that all?" I asked scathingly, the impossibility of what he expected from me allowing little else because I was so close to snapping that I wasn't certain how much longer I could stand there before I did.

"My wife desires a night with you in our chambers," he added as an afterthought like my question had actually been in want of an answer. "Though I do not feel inclined to take pleasure in your flesh while the stench of that brute still clings to you."

I recoiled, every piece of my devotion to this man peeling away like the shine falling from a statue, revealing the gold to be nothing but tin beneath.

"I'll have you before Evard does," he said, almost to himself, as if this were simply a matter of deciding what time to take his tea. "In fact, why don't you make him fall for you? Get him to spill his little heart out and tell you he loves you – he pretends at brutality but has always secretly desired love like a babe desperate for his mother's teat. Then I'll reward you with the fullness of my body and stain your skin with my touch before he marks you with his. I think I'd rather enjoy the knowledge that our act would crush him. It would go some part in payment to the bother he has caused me these last years."

In those words any last vestiges of delusional devotion I had felt to my prince shattered. Did he truly think my desire to hunt and butcher Cayde would equal my agreement to these terms? But the words of refusal which should have come at them didn't. Instead, a hollow acceptance fell over me. What did I care if I had to fuck his brother or his wife or any other bastard in between? If that was the price of vengeance then it was certainly simpler than any other I had attempted. Easier than capturing a Dragon. Easier than dreaming of some non-existent bond between us which had clearly never been more than a power play on his part.

I'd been foolish enough to imagine myself a life with this man, his secret obsession, but now all I felt towards him was disgust. Not that it mattered. He was still my prince and he was still the only one who could offer me the vengeance I so desperately needed.

"Speak," he commanded and I unfastened my tongue from the roof of my mouth.

"Yes, my Prince," I said finally. "I understand your orders."

A smile crept over his face like a snake slipping though long grass. "No more defiance?" he pushed.

"We capture the Void and you unleash me on Cayde at once?" I confirmed.

His eyes dropped to the vial of blood hanging at my throat and he nodded.

I nodded too then turned and strode from his chambers, the terms of my freedom clear at last.

HARLON

CHAPTER TEN

I reread the crumpled letter that had been left for me by Solomon Imai. It had been waiting for me upon my return to Never Keep all those weeks ago. I'd crushed it in my fist in rage, my failure a bitter taste in my mouth and my concern for Everest leaving me broken.

The stars have told me of your failure.
I have left for The Enclave to consult with them
on these dire circumstance.
Remain at Never Keep until my return.

That was it. All I'd been given for my efforts. And now I was abandoned here, unsure when or *if* the Cardinal Reaper was going to come back. I'd fallen into a mindless routine, following the Grand Maester's orders and working to assist in the instruction of the new wave of warriors that had arrived here.

But with every day that passed, my failure weighed heavier on me. Thoughts of Everest's choice plagued me. She'd turned from me, the trust between us had fractured and I had no idea how to restore it. It made me doubt my faith in Solomon, but those doubts could never be voiced. Had I really betrayed Everest in his name? I'd been trying to protect her. Now she was in the hands of her father and it was only a matter of time before news of the Void reached us.

I should have been excited at the prospect of my land's potential victory, but I was riddled with doubts. She'd seemed so shattered when she'd walked into her father's arms, like she had no other choice in it. He would fiercely protect her now that he could use her, but she didn't belong beside a man who had done nothing but bully and berate her all her life. So yes, perhaps we would win the war, but I was starting to realise Everest meant more to me than that.

It was a blasphemous thought; the war had always been a priority, but I hadn't been handed a sword to fight in it in the end. No, I was here. Confused by my fate and what the stars had planned for me. Because all I really felt was lost.

A flurry of movement in the Reapers' Quarters made me look up from the letter and I stuffed it back in my pocket – the place it had lived ever since I'd found it.

"He's back," Reaper Lily said, seeming worried and Reaper Jaspin frowned, leaning close to her to speak in a whisper but I could still catch his words. My heart thundered. There was only one Fae they could be referring to. The man I had been waiting for all these weeks. He had retuned at long last.

"Then we must do what we can to please him."

"All Reapers will assemble in the Astral Sanctuary immediately,"

Solomon's voice boomed out through the Reapers' Quarters, carried to us by magic, the sound setting my nerves on edge.

Relief found me though. He might have answers now, a direction for me to follow. Perhaps he would send me after Everest again, which in truth was all I really wanted. I'd even considered slipping away in the night, taking a boat and heading for Cascada alone. But my gut had kept me here, reassuring me that Solomon would have a plan upon his return. He'd been conversing with the stars all this time. He had to know the right action to take or he would not have come.

For the first time in weeks, I moved with energy in my step, sweeping along with the other Reapers. I hadn't made much effort to befriend them. In my past life, friends had come easily to me, but it was impossible to know who to trust among them. Which of my fellow acolytes had been recruited to the mass of Reapers who'd been working to summon that terrible monster into this world and which of them remained innocent to their devious work? So I kept to myself – finding the solitude grating and missing Everest all the more fiercely. Somehow, the longer I spent here, the more it felt like the path of a Reaper didn't belong to me. But today I might just find purpose again.

We hurried into the Heliacal Courtyard where snowflakes where swirling down from the grey sky, landing lightly upon the gold-cloaked shoulders of my comrades. The shine had quickly worn off of my status. My attempts to speak casually with the training neophytes were met with murmurs of fear, muttered prayers and confused glances. I wasn't one of them anymore, but I didn't feel like a Reaper either. So where did I belong?

The Astral Sanctuary was dark except for the glimmer of everflames that ringed the stone room, casting eery, flickering shadows on the statues of the zodiac deities.

Solomon was waiting there, standing tall at the far end of the chamber, his back to us and his head bowed as if in prayer.

We gathered behind him, me taking a position at the front of the group, anxious to meet his gaze and find reassurance waiting for me there. I'd been longing for this moment; I'd had nightly dreams about it and waking deliberations of it too. He'd confided in me, made me his most trusted confidant and I couldn't wait to discuss Everest with him and how best to protect her.

When the door closed with a firm thud, he turned, casting a silencing shield around the space and settling his penetrating gaze upon us all.

I lifted my chin, hoping his eyes would turn my way, but they didn't.

A knot tied in my stomach.

Something was wrong.

"I have spent many days consulting with the stars," he announced. "And they have answered a number of riddles for me. For weeks here at Never Keep, I must admit I spent much time working to uncover a terrible secret that had been kept from me."

Murmurs of concern broke out around me.

My pulse quickened, hope filling me at the realisation that he was finally about to punish those who had summoned that monster. Between the power of the loyal Reapers and the Cardinal, they could likely destroy it this very hour too.

"It troubled me deeply what I found here, the knowledge of an ancient creature summoned to the precipice of our world."

The murmurs grew, fear ripening the air and I sensed bloodshed was coming for those who had defected.

Solomon raised a single finger to silence his flock.

"But the stars have assured me I was a fool all along. I should have trusted you, my faithful Reapers, to act in the name of the almighty sky. It was my own ill-guided doubts that turned my gaze from the path of truth."

A frown burrowed into my brow, those words riling up a storm in my heart. I wanted to shout in defiance of them, but forced my tongue to remain still and take stock of what he was saying.

He went on and it was impossible not to notice the excited glimmer in the eyes of the Reapers around me. Those I'd tailed for weeks, eavesdropping on them whenever I could, sneaking after them at all hours of the night. The Fae who should have been dropping to their knees and begging for forgiveness for their heinous crimes but were being praised instead.

"You have been doing the stars' work and I have come to you now to apologise for my own folly. I did not see the gift you had brought us before. But I see it now. My eyes are wide open, dear Reapers. And the whispers of our beloved stars have told me what we must do next."

"Praise be!" Reaper Lily cried, lowering to her knees with a choked sob.

Jaspin fell to his knees too and one by one they followed like dominoes, the traitors among us who had allowed neophytes and acolytes alike to be butchered by that vile monster. I looked to Solomon, one of the few still remaining on his feet as the rest of the Reapers bowed, whether they were guilty or not, but no matter how hard I glared at the Cardinal Reaper, he didn't look back.

"The stars have named the creature Caelum and have directed me to be its master – an honour I will bear the weight of. I will ensure I act in the best interests of The Waning Lands."

"No," I blurted, stepping forward and causing all eyes to dart my way. Including Solomon's.

"No?" he inquired, raising a single eyebrow. "And who are you to defy the word of the stars?"

He looked at me as if he barely knew me, and his gaze was a knife to my throat, telling me to back down. My pulse rose in my throat, trying to quiet my words and I fast remembered who I was talking to.

"I only mean that... are you sure, Cardinal Reaper?" I backtracked, seeing the wrath in his eyes. Perhaps he just wanted me to play along, then the real plan would be revealed later.

A hiss of whispers broke out, accusing eyes carving lines into my flesh. Questioning our leader was as good as questioning the stars themselves.

"Of course I am sure," he said in a hard tone that allowed for no dispute. "I am their divine ear. Their pious listener. They have told me of their desires, do you dare go against their wishes?"

"Of course not." I bowed my head, then forced my knees to bend, dropping to the cold flagstones to join the rest of the Reapers. It felt like an act of platitude instead of subservience.

None of this was right.

Surely Solomon had some greater plan here? This was a ploy to draw out those who had defied him. He would tell me of it as soon as this was done.

"Caelum has been gifted to us to restore balance in The Waning Lands. It is a powerful weapon capable of great things, greater even than the Void itself."

Ice crawled through my veins, my muscles bunching tight at what I feared he was about to declare.

"The stars have told me plainly what must be done," he said firmly. "The Void must be brought to me, then I will ask the stars what action I should take with it."

"*Her*," I ground out through my teeth.

"What was that?" Solomon's voice tremored through my bones.

I looked up, jaw tight and heart thrashing. "Her, not *it*."

"The girl is a vessel, nothing more. And she will be *my* vessel soon enough."

I was on my feet before I knew it, lunging at Solomon only to find my legs bound by vines of his making and I went crashing to my knees. He stepped toward me and leaned down, speaking in my ear, a breath of a whisper but it was the sharpest threat I had ever heard. "Fall in line, Hadlin. Or you will bear the weight of your sins."

I sneered at the flagstone beneath me, head bowed and irritation flaring through my skin at how quickly he had forgotten my name. It was an insult to all he'd asked of me.

"I tried to bring her here," I growled. "I did everything you requested."

"Some people will always be triers, but I value *doers* among my ranks." He stood up straight, his vines snaking up my arms, around my waist and forcing my back to bend even further. He addressed the room, stepping past me and leaving me there to contemplate his dismissal.

"I hear Caelum is unsatiated. He craves the blood of war and the taste of carnage. We must offer it to him in the form of our sinners. All of you, gather the wrongdoers of the Keep, any neophytes who have crimes to their names." A flurry of motion sounded as the Reapers hurried to exit the room until I felt sure only Solomon and I remained.

"What's your true plan?" I called as his footsteps tracked away from me toward the exit.

"This *is* my true plan, Hadlin," he growled. "Be thankful that I feel merciful this day. One more word against me or the stars' wishes and I shall let Caelum feast upon your worthless bones."

With that, he left me there, my muscles bunching against his binds and a bellow of frustration escaping me. I'd done everything he'd asked and this was how he repaid me?

Everest's distrust of him had been well placed after all. He might have still been acting in the name of the stars, but what if it called for her death? What if he handed her to the monster under their instruction? If she was ever put in danger, so help me, I would dissent. For there was no world in which I would allow that fate to pass.

EVEREST

CHAPTER ELEVEN

The journey through Pyros had turned into endless festivities. Every town or city we reached along the river was empty, but with every new celebration that broke out among our army, the more bored I became.

This wasn't true victory. We were planting flags and declaring sovereignty over a nation that wasn't being defended. It pissed me off in all honesty. We were acting like pigs in a mud pen, rollicking in our own shit while never realising that we were next on the menu.

The warriors of Pyros were no meek creatures. They were going to fight back, but Father wouldn't listen to my ideas of leaving a full battalion at each location. He left his shining flags with just a handful of Cascadians in each town and on we sailed as if no Pyros sword was ever going to be swung against us.

His ego was going to be our downfall if he didn't start preparing for attack. We were underestimating the most powerful warriors of the land of fire and I'd seen firsthand what they were capable of.

There was a change in the wind at least. After a long journey north, we were closing in on the northern boundary that divided Pyros from Stormfell, Father's self-assuredness leading us on to the land of air. We had only truly seized a strip of land running through Pyros but Father wouldn't listen to reason when I'd tried to encourage him to spend more time in the land of fire to claim it fully. But he dismissed me, acting as if it was his already. It was arrogance in its maddest form but even the word of the Void couldn't sway him this time.

There was one small positive to be gleaned from this insane plan. The people of Pyros may have vanished, but I was confident that the Skyforgers would meet us head on. At long last I might partake in my first true battle and prove my prowess. I'd been born for this moment after all, the gift of the Void in my veins only confirmation that I had always been fated for glory on the battlefield.

"Oh bother, good golly, this is a bother."

I looked up at the voice I knew so well with a thrum of excitement, gazing over the edge of the White Mare and knocking away the Fae who had been braiding my hair with flowers.

Down among the cavalry who had been following us along the river, my dear friend Galomp was working to untie his boots where they hung from a cherry tree. I'd know him anywhere, from his pale skin to his equally pale hair and his impressive height. The cavalry was marching past him, war horses swerving around his large form as he tried to climb the tree and unsnag them. A few warriors sniggered at him as they passed by, sharing looks that made my lip hook up into a snarl.

I hurled myself over the side of the ship to a chorus of gasps, wielding the river to catch me and carry me to the water's edge. I flung myself onto the bank and horses reared up to avoid me, their riders crying out in shock as I went racing through them.

I made it to the tree Galomp was struggling to climb, grabbing hold of a branch and hauling myself up to the top where the boots were hanging, frozen in ice. With a growl in my throat, I melted the ice with my magic, and they fell to the ground with a soft thump. Galomp didn't look at them though, he was staring directly at me, eyes wide and jaw agape.

"Hello," I said brightly, so damn glad to see a friendly face. Someone who wouldn't fawn all over me for the sole reason of my newfound power.

I leapt from branch to branch, and he climbed down too until we were standing in front of each other with a tide of war horses sweeping past us on both sides.

"Oh boy," he gasped, then he fell to his knees, bowing low to me. "Praise the stars for our Kysharna."

"*No*," I groaned, my heart sinking at his reaction. "Kaské, please don't." I tugged on his arm, trying to pull him to his feet, but he wouldn't budge.

"Quick – salute the crack of dawn," a woman with icy blonde hair crowed, tipping a salute and nodding to Galomp's ass. Several warriors around her followed suit, then they all broke into heinous giggles.

I stepped around Galomp as he hurriedly tugged the back of his trousers up to hide his ass crack.

"Hey," I barked at the blonde woman, and her giggles fell dead in her mouth as her eyes found me. Perhaps she hadn't expected to find me among their ranks, her gaze missing me before. But she sure realised who I was now.

"Kysharna," she whispered in horror.

"I'm not your saviour, tiska." I blasted her with water, sending her flying off of her horse, over the heads of her friends and right into the river. Her shriek was akin to a dying cockroach and drew attention from all around. Laughter broke out as her head breached the surface and I set my gaze on her friends.

"If anyone harasses him again – *anyone* – you'll answer to me," I growled. "Spread the word. Because I'm not afraid to have your rank stripped."

I turned my back on their paling faces and found that Galomp had finally gotten to his feet.

"Oh boy," he exhaled. "I am not worthy of the great Kysharna's protection."

"Don't call me that, I'm just Everest to you," I insisted, brushing some twigs out of his blonde hair.

"Miss Everest."

"Just. Everest."

"Oh boy."

"And you just got promoted, Galomp. You're now my…" I scrambled for a title. "My personal sentinel. And as my sentinel, you'll stay with me up in the White Mare." I tugged on his arm but he didn't move an inch, even when I dug my heels in and leaned right back.

"I cannot," he said with three head shakes.

"I order you to," I said, and his throat bobbed.

"Okay then, I can. But what of Lalakin?" He pointed to the sandy mare who was tethered to another tree nearby. She was a beautiful thing, her golden colour glimmering in the light. That was no cheap war horse.

"She comes too." I shrugged, heading back for the ship, and Galomp followed me, leading his horse to the shore where I forged a bridge of water all the way up to the White Mare.

The Fae who had been braiding my hair watched with wide-eyed dismay as I led Galomp and Lalakin on board. I directed them to feed the horse the finest apples we had and to house her somewhere comfortable for the journey. To punctuate my words, Lalakin shat all over the deck and let out a heinous fart. They didn't question my word despite the horse's turd, and Galomp followed me like a shadow as I led him to my quarters. It was plenty big enough for both of us, and there was a hammock strung up which I was more than happy to sleep in so he could have more space in the bed.

I released a sigh of relief as I perched on the large writing desk. "I feel like I can breathe again. Can we play a game? Or do something completely normal? Even if we just comment on the weather, anything but more praise and flattery."

Galomp regarded me warily, then his shoulders relaxed. "Yes, my friend. I would most enjoy that."

I grabbed a deck of cards from the drawer and tossed a few cushions on the floor so that we could sit together. He reclined on them, taking in my quarters with interest before returning his attention to me.

"So, you are the Void."

"I am. But I don't want that to change anything between us. I want you to see me exactly as you used to see me."

He tilted his head to one side. "You look very much the same, Miss Everest. Apart from the flowers in your hair. Oh, is that– " His eyebrows raised as Calcifiend crawled out from my curls. "It is your blue lizard!"

He leaned in to pet Calcifiend's head, and the Sayer Dragon chirped happily, crawling onto Galomp's hand and giving him a lick.

"Oh boy, I think he likes me."

I smiled the realest smile I'd smiled in weeks. "I think so too, Galomp. So, tell me everything you've been doing since we parted."

"I was with my uncle for a while, Miss uh…uh… Not miss. No miss." He tapped his forehead. "Everest."

My smile widened a little more. "Did your uncle receive my donkey?"

"He did indeed. He would like to thank you, M-Everest. He shall be here soon, in fact. He is following along on his strongest donkey to commend us after our victory in Stormfell. In fact, Commander Rake himself has asked me to go meet with him and lead him to us. I will be sad to miss the battle."

"He's part of the Magistrine, right?" I blurted, hope rising as I realised I might just have a chance to tell him of the monster.

"Oh boy, yes he is."

"I'd love to speak to him," I said.

"You will get your chance. I am sad I cannot stay with you. Especially as you have named me your sentinel. Oh bother, I do not like to let you down."

"You're not, Galomp. If you fetch your uncle, you'll be doing me one hell of a favour anyway."

"That is good indeed. He is most excited to meet you."

Calcifiend clicked his tongue at me, and I met the little creature's gaze, my heart stumbling in surprise. It was like looking into Kaiser's eyes, as if I was seeing into death and he was staring back at me. I took the Sayer Dragon into my palm, lifting him high to peer deeper into his eyes. My heart thumped at the base of my throat and Calcifiend gazed back without blinking. I could almost feel Kaiser, like he was here in this room breathing down my neck, making demands of me, summoning heat to my flesh.

It burned, this hollow ache in my chest. This hole where my enemy's hate had once lived. Could I declare that the hate was gone now? Was his death equal to peace?

No…not even close.

Galomp cleared his throat. "Oh boy, are you going to kiss that lizard?"

I looked up, breaking the spell that had held me like a butterfly in a jar. "What?"

"You looked rather taken with him."

"No, what? No, Galomp!" I grabbed a pillow and tossed it at his head, and he boomed a laugh, the sound like fire catching in an icy storm. My laughter joined his and I fell into the joy of his company, recalling how I'd once denied his friendship. I wouldn't do so again.

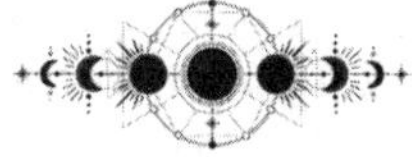

It had taken three more days to reach Stormfell but finally, I stood at the prow of the White Mare, Voiding the boundary between Pyros and the land of air, the magic dissolving in an archway that would allow us through. I guided it out to the shore where the cavalry were waiting, the tension in the air palpable.

Father placed a hand on my shoulder, his fingers squeezing firmly. "That's my girl. We'll make our mark on the land of sky this very day. We head for Pomair where we'll gutter out the Skyforgers' magic and extend Cascada's empire even further.

"We haven't even secured Pyros yet, shouldn't we– " I started, but he cut over me as if he hadn't heard me speak.

"They'll know we're coming; that's for certain. They'll have had spies watching us for some time now, but they have no defence against you, my child. This will be an easy triumph."

I nodded, giving up trying to sway his mind from this path. We were here now, and I wanted to flex my Void and prove I could really win this war for Cascada.

I'd never seen the Skyforgers bow to anyone though; they weren't going to take this lying down. I'd heard that a lot of their people often chose suicide over capture, falling on their own swords rather than allowing themselves to become prisoners of war. I couldn't imagine them bending the knee willingly. But then again, my Void had cut through the armies of our enemies before. They would be powerless this day and we would not.

The ship turned to the east as the river met with the sea, veering toward the towering city of Pomair on the jagged peninsular of land that stuck out of Stormfell like a crooked finger daring Fae to come closer.

They city's sandstone walls were bright under the high sun and glinted with the fortune of the Skyforger's land. It was a symbol of the grandeur they were used to, the sharp spires and effigies of the sun and wind combined in the decorative facades of the buildings' walls.

A fortress sat high up on the hill that overlooked the sea, an observatory doming over the top of it that marked the place where they studied the stars. But it was more than that. Father had told me of Pomair and the city's observatory which acted as a watch tower; I could feel the eyes of the Skyforgers from that very structure now.

The city was beautiful, there was no denying that. This first glimpse of the land of air made my lips part in awe at the power woven into every structure. They had clearly built this place to be noticed from the sea, a warning to all who dared traverse closer. But we would not be deterred.

They weren't hiding from us like the people of Pyros, they were here awaiting their fate, be it death or fortune.

Our ships carved through the calm ocean, the warriors around me controlling the water and sending us toward our destiny upon a rolling wave that carried half of Father's fleet. The cavalry were crossing a rocky land bridge to our right, charging on to attack the city from the east while we headed directly in from the south.

"Now," Father urged and I knew what he wanted.

I let the Void tear from me, sending it out across that city and suppressing any magic it found, stealing it from the grasp of the Skyforgers and leaving them exposed. It was power in its purest form, the Void's energy flowing from me in a dark and ominous wave.

A cacophony broke out from our cavalry's ranks and I spotted the pits that had been dug and concealed on the shoreline, waiting for our horses to cross them and sending them tumbling down onto spears awaiting them below.

Our warriors changed tactic, casting ice across the ground to stop any further pits from breaking their ranks and a path was formed, our war horses falling seamlessly in line with one another to follow it.

"Shield!" Father bellowed and I twisted back to look at the sky as giant burning balls of pitch were launched at us from catapults hidden beyond the city walls.

I stared at the ice shield that was being forged above us by my comrades who were clustered behind me, avoiding the null power of the Void. Despite their efforts a few of the fireballs broke through the gaps before we could close them. My heart juddered as one of them slammed into the water in front of us while another struck the ship to our right and a bellow of anguished cries ripped the air apart.

I cursed, halting my Void power to aid in fortifying the ice shield as Father stepped closer to me.

"That's it," he growled. "Cast the Void again once we're on shore. Don't let those dirty Skyforgers get a moment to strike."

"I won't," I assured him.

The wave we were riding guided us to shore and the moment the host of Cascadian ships landed, bridges of ice formed directly from their decks and our warriors poured out onto the white sand.

More balls of burning pitch rained down on them and as Father led the way to an ice bridge, blood-curdling screams carried up from the beach. I sprinted along one of the ice bridges, spotting the metal bear traps buried in the sand which were closing on the legs of some of our people below. I kept my Void subdued as more ice bridges were formed, climbing higher to avoid the beach that was now stained with blood. My heart rioted as the ice bridge lifted beneath my feet and I made it to the street, leaping down onto the cobblestones with Father at my back.

Warriors raced ahead of me and I unleashed the Void once more, cutting off their magic as a line of arrows fell from the sky. Five of them fell dead and I cried out in horror, "Stay back – get behind me!" I pulled the Void away from them, allowing the magic to return to any who still lived.

Father grunted, holding my arm firmly and a tight formation of warriors closed in around me.

"Stay close – as we practised!" he bellowed, then took off, charging away through the throng of warriors who surrounded me.

"Wait!" I screamed trying to break through them. "I can fight!"

I was shoved backwards, forced into the middle of the rows of warriors who were forming a barrier around me and shielding from above.

"Just focus on Voiding our enemies," one of them called to me and I glared at him.

I tried to get through once more, but they pushed me back and the look in their eyes told me there was no chance they were going to let me escape. The Void still raced from me, guttering the magic of the Cascadian warriors around me and I worked desperately to wrangle it, pulling it away from them as all hell broke loose.

I couldn't keep it away from every Raincarver here. It was impossible to be so precise.

"We need to get to higher ground!" I bellowed and thankfully, they listened to me, keeping closer and heading for a hillside to the east of the city where the cavalry were fighting with our enemies. But as we raced away from the streets and out onto open land, I spotted the hulking form of Ironwrath nestled between two mountains beyond the fray. Skyforgers were pouring from it on windriders, all of them using the contraptions to fly instead of wings or air magic.

A swarm of them rushed out over our heads and I angled my Void in their direction, growling when my power didn't affect the runes in their windriders. A flash of pink hair made my breath catch and among the mass of Skyforgers above me, I spotted her. The Sky Witch was here.

Cries of death carried from the battlefield and I forced my gaze onto our path, my brow furrowing at the knowledge that I may just clash with Vesper today. We were standing on opposite sides of a battle after all and only one of us would see victory.

As arrows spilled from the Skyforgers on their windriders, I knew I had to move fast to ensure this fight remained in our favour. But with the Void tearing blindly out from me and affecting my own people as much as it was the enemy, I didn't know if I could do so in time.

VESPER

CHAPTER TWELVE

I barrelled through the clouds on my windrider, adrenaline surging through my veins as I drew back the string on my bow and took aim at the Raincarvers below.

The legion under my command were following the orders I'd given them down to the letter and I couldn't deny the grim satisfaction I found in flexing my newfound authority. Not that it came close to making up for the price I was expected to pay for it.

At my back, a flock of Skyforgers swept through the air on windriders. I'd claimed every Sinfair in Prince Dragor's army for my legion and the other commanders had given them up more than willingly. But I knew something they didn't about the Sinfair and unlike those Generals who had always seen us as little more than cannon fodder, I knew the determination and resilience of their kind unlike any other. No one on this battlefield had more to prove than a Sinfair and none would fight harder to do so.

I whistled sharply, the note carrying on the wind and commanding my windrider force to split in two as I spotted a group of Raincarvers preparing to launch a giant wave into the sky at us.

We sped through the air at speed, the wave hitting nothing but the thin clouds which divided us and with another sharp whistle every one of us had picked a target and fired our bows down on them.

Raincarvers screamed as we pierced their army like a pincushion, fifty soldiers falling at the attack while the rest fought to throw up shields of ice but we were already circling away from them.

Across the battlefield I could see Dragor's tactics for dealing with the Void coming into play, the cannons and catapults firing tirelessly, the mechanisms not reliant on magic and so immune to the debilitating power of the Void. But the Raincarvers had adapted and were shielding against the blows as often as they were able to strike true.

Only my legion seemed unperturbed by the way our magic had been stifled and I smiled grimly because there was only one reason for that. I glanced over my shoulder at the pale faces of countless teens among my ranks, some of them here on their first battle but all of them were used to one thing the other warriors here weren't – they had no magic to fight with in the first place. Even those who had graduated Never Keep had spent years fighting before their magic was Awakened and were well practiced in making the most of every other option available to us.

I took in the battlefield as we circled, picking a new flank of the enemy army to strike at and directing my warriors toward it. The Raincarvers were boastful and fervent in their attacks – clearly believing themselves to be the victors of this battle already and I could see that their new weapon was affording them the advantage, but it wasn't over yet.

A legion of Raincarvers surged forward, spears of ice clutched in their fists as they ran at General Imona's ground forces. I cursed, whistling to my own legion to get them to turn, but I could already see that we were going to be too late. Our forces had been blocked by the Void and though they raised their weapons and ran bravely into battle, the Raincarvers were rousing their water magic against them. They would be drowned in a matter of minutes before ever getting close enough to strike their enemies with their blades.

I slit the tip of my finger open on my next arrow then took aim at the woman barking commands to the Raincarvers from the back of a warhorse and sent an arrow spearing through her throat.

She fell into her ranks with a bloody gurgle and I grunted as the blood magic I'd cast snapped taut between us, forcing her body to rise from the ground and swing her sword at her own people.

There were cries of confusion but her battalion surged to the east, still running for my people, my act not nearly enough to stop what was about to happen. But as I braced for the sight of a hundred Stormfell warriors being drowned before me, the spears and waves of water which had been brewing in the hands of our enemies fell to nothing in their grasp.

The Raincarvers cried out in shock, their magic escaping them in an instant and I knew that only one thing could be responsible for that.

As the two magicless forces collided beneath me and my legion took aim where I'd directed, I whipped around, my eyes sharp on the Raincarver force to the south.

Air magic flooded my veins as I hunted the endless ranks of warriors and I gasped in surprise, calling a storm to my fingertips, but it was snatched away from me just as quickly.

The Void.

I shot to the right, hurtling through the air until suddenly my magic returned once more, right when I was positioned above the thickest of the Cascadian ranks.

I sped on, urging my legion along behind me, directing them at targets as we went until I reached the edge of the fighting and still my power remained with me.

I slapped a hand to the rune on the side of my windrider, topping up the power in it even though I knew it held enough energy to sustain us up here for hours. But on a battlefield I was never short on magic. The desires of those desperate to survive and claim glory filled my reserves beyond measure.

"Andre, Becca!" I barked and the two warriors sped closer to hear my commands. "Take word to the other generals – the Void can only strike in straight lines – the ranks to the east still have access to their magic but if she blocks them she blocks her people too. If we can figure out where they have her positioned then we can move into the spaces between her power and even out this fight once more."

They nodded their understanding and sped away.

"We strike where we're needed," I told the rest before leading them back across the warring armies to the ranks which were being blocked by the Void and were most vulnerable because of it.

"Alissa," I called to the warrior who I'd chosen for my second. "Take charge while I'm gone, keep your focus on their commanders and– "

My words were broken apart by an ear-splitting roar. Every warrior on the battlefield seemed to pause their fighting to whip around and look to the mountain to the north as a sight forgotten to myth and legend emerged from its shadow.

My lips fell apart as the steel grey Dragon raced across the sky, fire blossoming from his jaws and a pair of powerful wings beating in perfect synchronicity at his back.

I stared at Bastian in awe as he tore through the sky, healed, *flying*.

A breath of agonised relief escaped me as I watched him speeding into battle, my mind so caught on the impossibility of him flying, of his wing having been fixed, that it took a blast of water colliding with me to remind me that we were still in the midst of war.

I cursed as I was knocked from the sky, tumbling over and over as I fell, my clothes saturated, my windrider almost spinning from my grip.

With a determined growl, I tightened my hold on it and swung my leg back into place, launching myself skyward mere inches above the heads of my enemies.

Air magic rushed back into my possession just as they noticed me there and I blasted them with a hurricane which sent them all smashing into one another and flying away.

I shot back into the sky, my eyes finding Bastian once more and my surprise soured tenfold as I spotted the man riding valiantly on his back.

Prince Dragor was clad all in white as always, his pale hair hidden beneath a silver helm, his sword raised in command as he pointed to the western ranks of the Cascadian army where their ships filled the river which had brought them here.

Bastian followed his command at once, dropping low and raining down Dragon fire on the ships, blasting them to pieces and setting the world alight in his wake.

I recoiled from the sight of him being ridden like a glorified warhorse into battle, this king of beasts reduced to little more than a stallion beneath the heel of a master I'd had stepping on my own neck for far too long.

Alissa had already led my warriors away to do my bidding and for several too-long minutes all I did was speed between the projectiles launched my way and stare at the Dragon who had come to fight for people who weren't his own. What had Dragor done to make him agree to this?

It took me several moments of hurtling through the sky to realise I was flying for him, heading towards the beast I'd been too much of a coward to face until now.

A herd of Cascadian Pegasuses sped into the sky from below me, thirty or more of them surrounding me in an instant, horns lowered as they prepared their charge.

"Shit." I twisted my grip on my windrider, yanking its nose skyward and shooting for the stars as fast as I could go. The Pegasus herd whinnied furiously, taking chase and though my windrider was fast, I knew it wouldn't outpace them endlessly. I needed to outmanoeuvre them but we were in an empty patch of sky, not a single obstacle for me to use to my advantage.

I threw my hand out, blasting air magic at them and knocking them back. Before I could get too excited about my move, the magic was wrenched from me, the place in my chest where power had been brimming to the point of overflowing now vacant.

For a moment I thought I was fucked but then I heard the wild, desperate screams coming from below and I looked down. It took me a second to figure out why around thirty naked Fae were tumbling toward the ground with terrified cries of alarm before I realised I was looking at the Pegasus herd, their ability to shift also stolen by the Void and death rushing for them at speed.

I winced at the sickening crack of their bodies hitting the ground, flattening the warriors beneath them and taking more into death alongside them.

My head snapped up as I realised I now knew which direction the Void power had come from and for the briefest of moments my gaze met the wild, horrified eyes belonging to my kitty cat.

I grinned and she looked inclined to vomit in reply. I wasn't certain if she'd just saved my ass on purpose or not but I did know that I'd been tasked with capturing her at all costs.

The knot of Cascadian warriors surrounding her was thicker than anywhere else in the field and of course it was – they were guarding their prize with all they had. But that wasn't going to stop me.

I scanned the ground quickly, picking out several Fae from among the ranks of my enemy and swooping straight for them in a sudden, violent dive.

I drew my bow, smearing a drop of blood from my split finger across the tips of six of my arrows before taking aim and loosing them one after another.

A volley of arrows were fired in return but I sped away from them, leaning low on my windrider and zigzagging to avoid their aim.

I felt the strike of my arrows in their targets like the strum of fingers down my spine and fell into the call of the ether.

It shrieked my name as I gave myself to its dark power and I muttered a promise to listen to it later before drawing it to my command in thanks for the six souls I was sacrificing in its honour.

The dormant power roiled at my gift and with a jerk of my fist the Fae I'd targeted all turned their weapons on their allies.

Chaos broke out in the ring of guards surrounding Everest as they found themselves defending against their own and in the melee she broke free, sprinting towards the battlefield like she'd been waiting for the opportunity to do so.

Everest didn't see me speeding through the clouds above her or circling around behind her where the crash of my air magic returned to me like an old dog racing into the doting arms of its master.

I dropped like a lead weight, speeding up behind her with a lasso of air magic whipping ahead of me just as she swung for her first real opponent.

My air magic yanked Everest off of her feet a breath before she could decapitate the Skyforger and she screamed bloody murder as she found herself hoisted into the air beneath me.

"Let me go or so help me I'll rip every bit of power from your limbs!" she yelled as we shot for the sky, her hair billowing across her face so that she could see her captor and I laughed darkly.

"Go ahead, kitty cat. I'd like to see how the power of the Void will save you from a fall from the heavens themselves!"

"Vesper?" she growled indignantly but my chance to reply was stolen by the tremendous roar of a Dragon and a blast of fire which nearly roasted us both alive.

We weren't the only ones making use of the clouds.

I cursed, yanking on the magic holding Everest and drawing her to me. She landed heavily on the windrider behind me and the machine lurched downwards violently.

"Hold onto me," I barked.

"Fuck you," she snapped but she wound her arms around my waist all the same, gripping me tightly enough to prove that she didn't want to risk falling into that battlefield. She may have been able to catch herself with water magic before she went splat but from up here in the clouds there was no way of knowing if she might land among Cascadians or warriors from Stormfell.

"You have the Dragon," she hissed angrily as Bastian lit the clouds red again and I veered away from him, not wanting to end up burned alive.

"You met him on the battlefield at Cinder Vale," I said in agreement. "I captured him the same night I left Never Keep."

"You lied to me," she accused.

"Says the Void."

Silence fell for a moment and then she released a growl of frustration. "Fine. We both withheld the truth. But this is bullshit, Vesper. I saw that man wielding earth magic on the battlefield – how did you convince him to choose to ally with air?"

"He didn't choose it," I said, looking back at her, my gut twisting with guilt. "I took that option from him. And I know he wouldn't have made the decision lightly. Though I can guess what Dragor gave him in return for his allegiance."

I'd known it the moment I saw him crest that mountain with his wings intact. Bastian had nothing left to lose but he'd had a whole lot left to gain. I couldn't even blame him for accepting a deal which returned his wings to their magnificent glory and saw him able to take to the skies once more. It was the same choice I would have made if I was given it.

"My people will kill him. The first Dragon seen in hundreds of years and he'll end up the last, just like that." She snapped her fingers and I might have punched her for the disparaging comment had I not been able to see the sadness in her brown eyes at the declaration. It wasn't that she wished that fate upon Bastian. She feared it.

"I wouldn't count on it."

"I can't Void him," she said, almost to herself. "Is that a Dragon thing?"

"More like a crystal thing," I grunted, realising too late that I probably shouldn't have divulged that much to her. But the lines between us had always been too easy to blur.

"Crystal?" she questioned and I cursed my own stupidity.

"It's the reason he was stuck in his Dragon form in that cavern. It keeps him trapped," I said, realising that those crystals might just be a very real way to resist the power of the Void. An army in their Order forms was formidable indeed.

"The ether is still calling my name," I blurted, uncertain if I was trying to distract her or just pleased to have someone I could tell about it. "I think it wants me to repair more keystones, return the natural flow of the ley lines."

Everest looked at me as we sped through the clouds, the sound of battle growing distant between us.

"Oh."

"That's so helpful, thank you," I drawled.

"I'm hoping to get in contact with someone from the Magistrine to help with that monster at the Keep," she said almost defensively.

"Hoping to? Sounds like you've been busy working on that then."

"I am the Void, you know? I have a lot going on," she replied defensively.

"I guess we all do," I said with a grunt of frustration because it wasn't like I'd done much of anything to deal with that monster either. "I'm a General now – and I have a new name too though I don't much like it. Oh and a prince wants me to marry him."

"Prince Dragor?" Everest recoiled and I snorted a laugh, the screams of the fighting enemies now so distant it could have been the crashing of the sea against the shore, though the bellow of the Dragon was less easy to ignore.

"No. Evard."

"Isn't he the one who collects the heads of his enemies and keeps them in a great chamber somewhere deep beneath the palace?" she asked with distaste.

"Apparently so. Though I've never seen them myself."

"Well, he sounds…lovely."

"How's being the Void going for you?" I shot back at her.

"Great," she said enthusiastically, though there was a flicker of something in her eyes that told a different story. "Pyros basically rolled over and gave us their lands. So now we just have to get Stormfell and Avanis into line and the war will end and– "

"Oh, kitty cat," I sighed, angling us towards the ground. "This war won't ever end."

We landed on a rocky outcrop so far from the battlefield that I knew she wouldn't be able to Void anyone from here. Or at least I hoped she wouldn't.

Everest dismounted and half-heartedly drew a dagger.

"Like that, is it?" I asked, drawing one of my own in turn.

"It has to be," she replied bitterly though the point was aimed at the dirt.

"Does it?"

The question hung between us because the answer should have been obvious. We were enemies born and bred, designed for nothing more than to kill one another. Worse, she was the one thing which could decide the fate of this war. I should have taken her directly to Prince Dragor not to this rocky crag in an abandoned corner of Stormfell. But there we stood.

Everest frowned. "I don't want to hurt you."

"Cute that you think you could," I teased and her frown deepened.

"I could Void you."

"Mmm, and I could taint your blood with a curse that would rot you from the inside out and make you claw the flesh from your own bones in desperation to rid yourself of the pain of it before you died. Want to find out which is more effective?" I took a sprig of yarrow from my pocket and crushed it against the tip of my still bleeding finger, ether rushing to answer my call and making my pupils dilate.

"Don't do that," she demanded and I shrugged.

"I thought this was a stand-off?"

"It's a fucking shit show, that's what it is!" Everest burst out. "I'm supposed to be down there winning my first battle and you're supposed to be…well, I don't know, but not here with me twenty miles from the battlefield talking shit to the wind."

I sighed, turning my head so that I could gaze out toward the battlefield too, though there wasn't much to be seen from such a distance besides the cloud of dust that had been thrown up from the clash of war. The warriors who fought on the ground were reduced to a stain of darkness against the land and nothing more. A blight upon the greenery. And wasn't that the truth of it?

"Sorry I didn't kill the Fury for you," I said. "But I'll do it if I ever lay eyes on him again."

"No need. I did it myself. I set myself free."

"Did you now? And how did you manage that despite the bond?" I asked curiously.

"Well…I'm the Void, so…"

I broke a laugh and she smiled too though there was a hint of sadness in her eyes. Weren't we just a fucking pair.

"Vesper…"

My name urged me into action, whispered in voices only I could hear once more.

"I have orders to capture you and deliver you into the hands of Prince Dragor," I said, returning my focus to my kitty cat, my heartrate settling a little as I met her brown eyes with mine.

"I'll die before I let you capture me," she hissed, all feline.

I arched a brow, sweeping my hand out to remind her of where we currently stood and how we'd gotten here.

"And what would you call this if not captivity?" I drawled.

"I see no chains," she scoffed. "No cage. No prince for that matter either."

The corner of my lips twitched into what was the first smile to have tempted me in weeks.

"I missed you," I told her.

Everest's brows rose in surprise. A flicker of movement drew my attention to that little blue lizard she kept as a pet as it crawled up onto her shoulder to peer at me too. "I missed you too," she admitted, her cheeks heating at the words as the smile captured my lips in fullness. "No one is quite so brazen," she added quickly. "Or sharp of tongue. You are amusing company, even if you're my sworn enemy. And I can't imagine you simper to anyone either."

"Simper? Don't tell me you've been subjected to the heinous company of ass-lickers since your elevation in the ranks of your army. I can't bear to think of us as similar in that regard – though I suppose there is true reason to fawn over you as the great and powerful Void. Whereas I find myself celebrated for accomplishments I'd sooner not lay claim to."

"Well, you'll be a princess soon. So I suppose you'd better get used to it."

"No," I disagreed, the truth of my words coming so easily to my tongue. "I won't. It occurs to me here on this rock, in the middle of nowhere, while a battle I'm supposed to be fighting in rages on without me, that I won't become a princess or any other kind of pawn. Not now and never again."

The sincerity of that declaration struck something deep within my bones as if a call had gone out and roused me from slumber. What was I even doing here? I should have taken Everest straight to Prince Dragor but instead I'd spirited her away from him with all the haste I could muster.

"Then what will you be?" Everest asked, a note of caution to her voice.

"That is the real question."

She arched a brow at me and I gave her a wicked grin.

"Want to chase monsters into the dark with me and follow the call of my name into the forgotten places of this world?" I offered.

Everest balked like I'd offered her up a steaming turd instead of a chance at freedom and she shook her head as she backed up a step, the point of her dagger finally finding its way to aim at me with purpose.

"I'm the Void," she said forcefully as if I'd somehow questioned that.

I considered her for a moment, the way her eyes flared with defiance and the deepest desires of her heart reached out to coil around my senses. She wanted to be the one who brought this war to an end. She wanted to be the Void in all the ways I had no faith she could be. She wished to use that power to force peace upon The Waning Lands. But how could there ever be true peace with one land ruling over the others? Perhaps her power could subdue Pyros, Avanis and even Stormfell – though I doubted it could do so truthfully because she couldn't be in all lands at once, in all cities and all towns, ready to stifle any uprising or rebellion. But even if that did come to pass, her power didn't grant immortality. My land and the others would only have to wait for death to come for her and they'd rise up once more. And they'd all be sending their assassins her way too. If there was going to be an end to the war then peace would have to be chosen by will, not force. But I could see that she wouldn't be convinced of that by me.

"I'm done," I said finally, sheathing my dagger and releasing my hold on the ether, its power rushing from me like an exhale of icy wind. It abandoned me with a soft cry of my name and I knew in my heart that my mind was made up. "Get the fuck out of here, Everest. Run back to your army and turn their attention to Pyros or Avanis but leave me the hell out of it."

"That's it?" she demanded as I backed up, tapping the rune on the side of my windrider to bring it to life once more.

"That's it," I agreed. "Turns out, I really am a traitor after all – so I figure I might as well do the thing properly."

"What is that supposed to mean?" she shouted as I launched myself into the air, abandoning her to a rock in the middle of nowhere.

"It means that you should probably run if our paths ever cross again, because I can't be certain of what I'm going to do next. But I know in every dark corner of my fractured heart that I'm not going to be shackled any longer."

Everest called after me as I sped away from her but I didn't turn back. I was seeing things clearly at last and it was time I showed my prince exactly who owned me now.

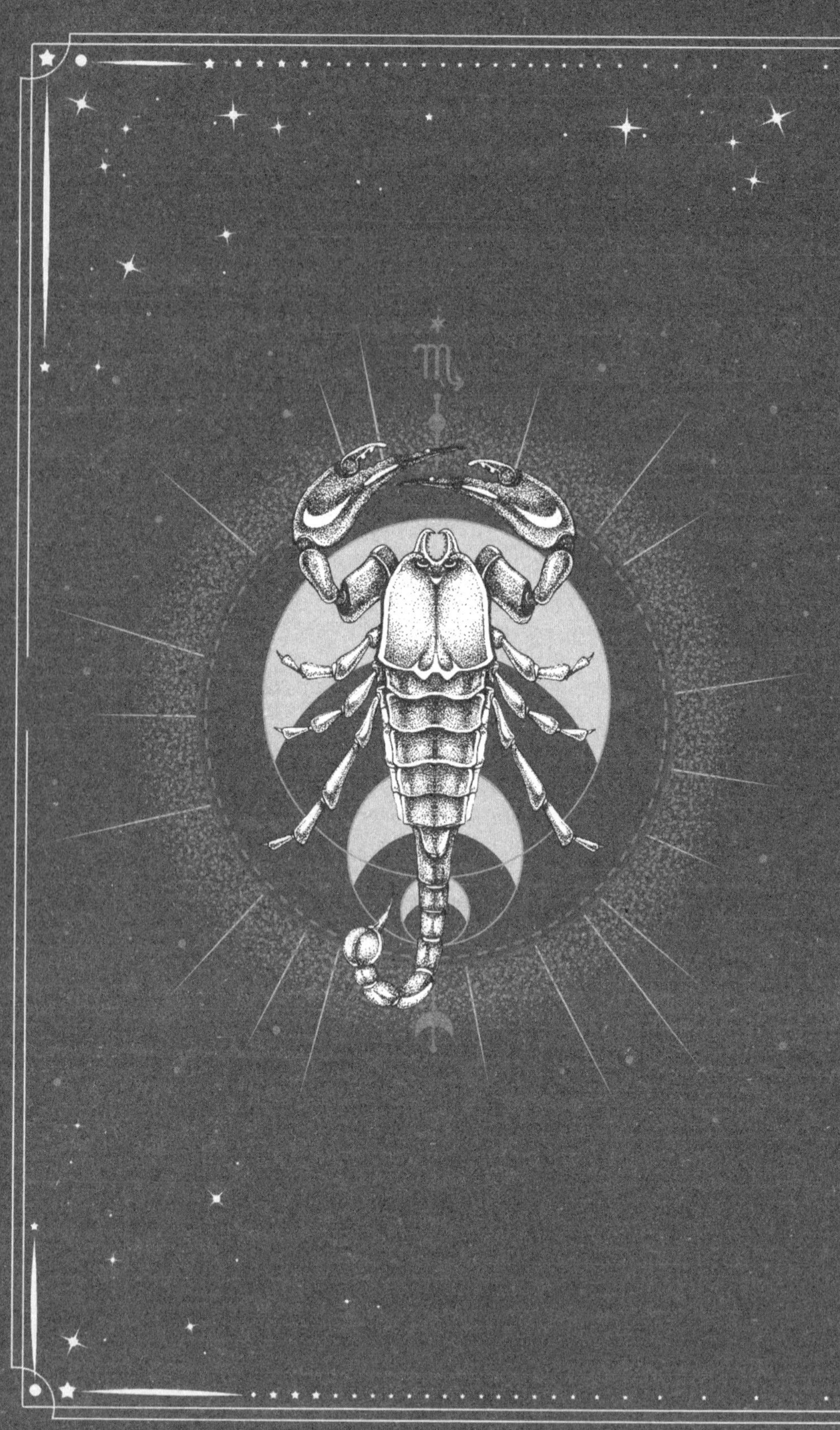

RANSOM

CHAPTER THIRTEEN

"We won't let it happen again, we'll triple the reinforcements around you," Father said fiercely, pulling Everest into a hug she didn't seem all that eager to accept. But she melted after a couple of seconds.

When she had been snatched away by the Sky Witch, I'd thought it was the end for us. That the rotten bastards of air would kill her or keep her for themselves. Without the Void protecting us and with not nearly enough preparation in place for the battle, Father had finally called a retreat.

He'd cast a hundred foot wave that had held back the tide of our enemies and allowed us time to escape. That wave had crashed against the walls of Pomair, toppling buildings and spreading carnage where their air shields failed, but it wouldn't have been enough to gain the upper hand again.

Despite our fears over losing the Void, Everest had turned up marching in from a mountainside, running to meet our retreat at the Pyros boundary and saving our asses once more when she cut a temporary hole in it to let us through.

She'd spewed a heroic story about fighting her way free of the Sky Witch but that infernal air-wielder had gotten away too.

Now in the wake of our failure, there was only one thing anyone could focus on. The Dragon.

The memory of that iron grey beast was still seared into my mind, jarring me into a new era of war. I could still see the faces of the screaming Cascadians who had burned up in its almighty flames. I'd felt the heat of that fire against my skin. I'd thought it would claim me too, but somehow I'd managed to flee.

Where had that beast of legend come from? The Dragons were lost. So many rumours had been spun about their disappearance and now the fucking Skyforgers had seized one. How could it be?

Even with a Dragon shifter bolstering the ranks of our enemies, we should have been capable of winning the fight. Father was growing sloppy, believing us unbeatable with the Void on our side, but there hadn't been proper tactics laid to prepare for true battle. And with Everest randomly Voiding sections of our own army as well as the enemy's, it had been in fucking shambles even before she'd been torn from the battlefield. Now we were holed up in a town in the north of Pyros, most of our army laying camp beyond this old tavern where Father's inner circle had taken up residence. And the mood was decidedly shit.

"I don't want to be guarded. Let me fight," Everest grumbled, pulling out of Father's arms. "If I lead from the front it will be easier for me to target who I use the Void on. I can keep it away from our army but only if– "

"Nonsense," Father cut in. "You would be exposed at the front, a sitting duck to be shot and plucked. There's no sense in it. You must spend time on practising to wield the Void so that you can direct it more proficiently. Now come, eat with me." He slid an arm around her shoulders, leading her to the large fire that had been started in the hearth. Agatha had cooked a stew and promptly filled two bowls for the two of them. They sat, speaking in low tones and my jaw tightened.

I stalked over to them and when Agatha didn't offer me a bowl, I snatched one for myself and dropped down onto the arm of the chair Father was reclined in.

"Back up." He waved a hand at me. "Go sit over there or something." He pointed at a dank corner where a repetitive drip from a leak in the roof had created a greenish puddle and I balked in horror.

"Oh, so I'm not invited to your private conversation?" I snipped.

Everest raised her eyes to me, seeming deep in thought, a taut line crossing her brow.

"No you're not," Father said and my heart twisted at his rejection.

"Fine, I'll go over there and sit on my own then."

"You do that," Father muttered, turning away from me and casting a silencing shield around himself and Everest before continuing to speak with my half-sister.

Agatha let out a low guffaw and I shot her a glare, tossing my bowl of stew onto a side table with a clatter and prowling away again. I wouldn't sit there and be dripped on like some toad forgotten in a hole.

Fucking rich that was. I'd been discarded like an old turnip that wasn't good enough for eating.

I moved behind the bar at the back of the tavern, helping myself to a bottle of rum and pulling the cork out with my teeth, spitting it aggressively in the direction of Jacobin who was perched on a bar stool.

He sneered at me, resting his elbows on the surface and leaning closer. "No good having a tantrum, eh Ransom? Just because Daddy's got a new favourite, you don't need to throw your toys out of the bassinet."

"Shut your mouth or I'll ram my fist in it," I warned.

He chuckled. "Nah, you wouldn't cause a fight among Rake's closest confidants. I reckon he might just sling you out with the rest of the inferior warriors if you did that. Without his favour shielding you, they'll chew you up and spit you out, boy."

I slammed my fist down on the bar in front of him, my knuckles whiting as I fought the urge to punch him. He flinched a little at the strike, telling me he knew I could take him if I wanted to.

"I possess plenty of Father's favour."

"Strike me then. Test it and see, Ransom Rake." He smiled, revealing that he'd lost a couple of teeth in the battle with the Skyforgers, his gums reddened in their absence.

My fingers flexed, the urge to give in to his goading consuming me for a second, but I cursed as I snatched my hand away instead.

His smile grew, his eyes a taunt that said he saw the cracks in me. Because the fact was, what he'd uttered was likely true and I couldn't bear to swallow the bitter pill of it. Father's warriors had once respected me, but they were growing less and less courteous by the day.

I huffed out a breath then took a long swig of rum, the heat of the alcohol burning through some of the rioting rage in my chest.

A creak sounded above me and my gaze slid to the ceiling in suspicion just as Agatha started playing a piano in the corner. Jacobin turned to watch her, clapping along while a few more of Father's cronies started up an out-of-tune song, all of them drunk on ale already.

No one seemed to have noticed the creaking sound besides me and while their attention lay on their celebrations, I slipped out from behind the bar and through a door that led to the stairwell.

I started the climb, my hand closing on the hilt of my sword at my hip as I crept higher, my pulse warring beneath my flesh. I should have alerted Father and the others but something held my tongue as I climbed. Perhaps I was in the mood to prove myself. Or maybe sheer stubbornness at their dismissal made me less inclined to speak up. I certainly didn't want to be ridiculed for jumping at bumps in the night.

At the top of the stairs I pushed the door wide and stepped into a large bedroom with low beams on the ceiling. A carved wardrobe stood opposite the wooden bed and my eyes were drawn to it, narrowing on the engraving of a ram on the door. I remained still, holding my breath and listening for several beats until I heard a shuffle of feet from within the wardrobe followed by a hissed whisper.

"Ow, Casey, you're on my toes."

"*Quiet.*"

"I *am* being quiet. It's you that– "

"Shhhh."

Three voices, all female.

My gut dropped as they fell silent again, contemplating my options. Walk away. Do nothing. Pretend I never heard them. Or unveil them, drag them downstairs and hand them to my father.

Or maybe…

My throat thickened as I made my decision, striding across the room and pulling the wardrobe open. The first made to scream and I slapped a hand to her mouth. The second came at me, aiming a punch to my head, but I grabbed the hilt of my sword in warning and she backed up.

"Quiet," I growled in a soft voice, releasing my sword and taking my palm from the girl's mouth. They were a little younger than me, eighteen or nineteen perhaps. The fact that they hadn't cast magic was telling enough. They weren't Awakened.

All of them were blonde, sisters clearly from their similar features. They wore the garb of the Flamebringers, but it was obvious what they were anyway.

"They'll find you if you stay here," I whispered, feeling like a traitor to my land. But I had to deal with this problem fast. Father would likely use this room tonight and there was no chance he wouldn't discover them hiding here.

"'They'? Aren't you 'they'?" one of them hissed, her eyes frantic with fear.

"Yes…but I…well I don't kill innocents." I raised my chin. "Others will though. So get to the window. Climb out and head north from here. Don't use the main streets and avoid anywhere around the town hall. The whole of the Cascadian army are here."

Their faces paled. "Mother told us not to leave," the shorter of the three squeaked. "She said she would go for supplies, but it's been three days– "

"She's not coming back, Meredith," the one with the blue eyes said darkly and Meredith's eyes glittered.

"She will, Gail," Meredith squeaked back but Gail shook her head solemnly. "Won't she Casey?" She looked to her other sister who appeared to be the middle child, her hair cropped short while the others wore it long.

"I don't know," Casey rasped.

"Where is everyone else?" I asked, my curiosity sharp. They were young, maybe naïve enough to tell me. "It seems like the whole of Pyros has vanished."

"I don't know. But Mother wouldn't leave the tavern, she said rogues would take it," Gail muttered. "It seems she was right."

I nodded stiffly. "Come." I offered my hand to the smallest one, Meredith, and she hesitantly placed her palm in mine, letting me guide her out of the wardrobe.

"You shouldn't touch him," Gail growled.

"Shh," I hissed, the sound of the music suddenly falling quiet downstairs. "You need to hurry." I led Meredith to the window and her two sisters tiptoed after us. I slid it open just as the sound of footsteps padded up the stairs, making the hairs rise on the back of my neck.

"Go," I said forcefully under my breath, helping Meredith climb out onto the roof first.

I grabbed Gail's arm to push her out too, but the door burst open and Casey let out a cry of fright.

Jacobin stood there, his eyes widening at the sight unveiled before him and a sick smile twisted his lips.

"Ransom's caught some hideaways!" he bellowed and more footsteps came pounding up the stairs. It was all happening too fast. I was frozen.

My fingers tightened on Gail's arm and Casey grabbed a lamp, swinging it right at my head and sending me stumbling aside. Meredith tried to drag Gail out of the window with her but Jacobin leapt at them while I recovered from the daze, seizing Gail by the elbow and knocking Casey to the floor.

Agatha appeared next, catching Meredith's ankle and hauling her back inside, rousing a chorus of screams from her and her sisters.

"Wait," I rasped, but they were already dragging them away, carrying them downstairs kicking and screaming.

One second past. Then two. A heavy thump in the base of my brain urging me to do something. But what?

I threw caution to the wind and chased after them, panic rearing in my chest as I lost control over the situation, taking the steps two at a time.

Father had risen to his feet and Everest was up too, staring at the girls who were being presented to the room. I met my sister's eye, a sense of disquiet passing between us that made her frown. But I simply didn't know what to do. Maybe nothing. Just bury my head in the sand. The alternative was treason.

"Ransom found them in the attic room," Jacobin said keenly and a few more of Father's men slinked closer, eyeing up the girls like prey.

Agatha had a tight hold on Meredith and the young Flamebringer thrashed in her grip.

"My mother will have your guts for stepping into her tavern," Gail spat at my father and his brows arched.

"Will she now? And where is this mother of yours?"

"Gone. Like the rest of them," Casey answered bitterly.

"Ain't that a pity," Jacobin purred, caressing Gail's neck and she cringed away from him.

My shoulders tensed and I took a step forward, unsure what I intended to do. My instincts were rioting. The pounding in my head was growing to a wild crescendo.

"They're no threat to us," Everest spoke, commanding all eyes in the room. "We'll let them go."

Father shot her a look, considering her for two eternal seconds. "Yes, that's what we'll do." He nodded, looking to Agatha and Jacobin and a heavy breath fell from my lungs in a wave. "You two, take them to the woods. Up near that waterfall we passed. Release them there."

"Of course, Commander," Jacobin simpered, bowing his head

a little, his fingers curling possessively around Gail's arm. Tension stiffened my shoulders. This was not over yet.

"In fact, I'll come with you to ensure the job is done properly." Father adjusted his belt, striding toward them and directing them to the door as his hand closed on Casey's. They dragged the girls from the tavern and blood pounded heavily in my ears. I stared at the door as it swung shut, jaw tight, mind roaring.

Father's men seemed a little disappointed as they returned to their seats, picking up their tankards of ale and falling back into easy conversation. But Everest and I remained on our feet, our gazes meeting once more.

"I think I'll go too," I muttered, making a move for the door and Everest shadowed me at once.

"You shouldn't go out there, Void," grunted a burly warrior as Everest passed him. "You should stay here where we can keep an eye on you."

"Oh fuck off, Pidley," Everest snapped, overtaking me and leading the way through the door so I had to jog to catch her.

The army had made camp surrounding the road, stretching out to the east and west and some of them glanced our way, calling out praises to their Kysharna. There was no sign of Father and the others already and my gut tightened, a sense of foreboding falling over me. I didn't trust Father to release those girls. At the very least, he would torture them first for information. And that was bad enough, but if he left them alone with Agatha and Jacobin for any length of time, who knew what they would do to them? I'd seen their violence firsthand. I knew the depravity they liked the taste of. Flamebringers or not, I couldn't see innocents brutalised.

Everest darted down an alleyway as soon as possible to leave the army behind and I fell into step beside her. For a second I swore her dark curls moved around her neck, revealing something blue shifting within them. But it must have been the way the moonlight was falling upon her, either that or my mind was cracking.

I pulled at my hair, feeling a few strands come away in my grip and swallowing the hard lump in my throat. I'd been losing more and more ever since we'd entered Pyros. And in truth, maybe before that too. Since the battle at Cinder Vale, I'd gained a small bald patch on the back of my head that was only covered because of the thickness of the hair around it.

"Are you going to admit what the hell you're planning right now?" Everest hissed at me, quickening her pace as we rounded out of the alley and the woodland came into view ahead, rising up from the town toward a high waterfall.

"I'm helping Father," I lied.

She cut me a look. "Helping the greatest warrior in Cascada with three girls who look young enough to be unAwakened?"

"Yeah," I grunted.

"You always were a dumbass, Ransom," she muttered. "I know exactly why you're here."

We darted across the final street and made it into the cover of the trees, the sound of the waterfall carrying to us from up ahead. I flicked a silencing shield around us to hide our approach and Everest glanced at me again.

"You don't know shit about what I want," I muttered.

She weaved through the narrow trees and I hurried to keep pace with her. For someone several inches shorter than me, she sure did know how to move. I'd always had trouble keeping up with her when it came to the hunt.

"I'm not fool enough to believe they're just going to let those girls go," she admitted tightly.

"You think Father will kill them," I stated.

She fell quiet. "I don't know. Yes, probably. Maybe not. Whatever he decides, I have to find out."

"And then what?"

"Why are *you* here, Ransom?" she threw back, evading answering. "Hoping to pick up a few tips on interrogation? Perhaps try them out for yourself on innocents?"

"I'm here for the same reason you are," I said.

"Which is what?" she demanded.

"You don't want to see innocents get hurt. Neither do I."

She gave me an assessing look. "And how do I know you're not just here to try and get back into Father's favour? That's all you ever cared about before."

"You can believe what you want to believe. I don't give a fuck." I tried to take the lead but she sped up, refusing to let me pass.

"You do give a fuck. Far too many fucks actually. I see how envious you are of my position beside Father. I see how much you miss being his number one."

"And I see how much you relish it in return. It's pathetic really. He snubbed you your whole life and now you're just his lap dog, taking a few pats while you can get them and thinking they make you special."

She pressed her lips together, saying nothing in answer to that but I was pretty sure I'd hit a nerve.

Everest suddenly turned and pressed her back to a tree. The waterfall was roaring close by, but it didn't quite drown out the sound of voices ahead.

I slunk into the shadows, casting concealment spells around me while noticing Everest was struggling with hers, her left hand useless to command the extra movement she needed for the intricate spell. I tossed a few up around her and she offered me a scowl in thanks.

"Don't do me any favours," she hissed. "I was handling it."

"Sure you were," I drawled. "The loner doesn't need anyone, does she?"

"Suck a dick."

"Gladly."

She rolled her eyes at me then shifted around the tree a little, falling quiet as she surveyed the group.

The three girls were on their knees between Father, Agatha and Jacobin and I noted Gail's dress was torn at the front, nearly revealing one of her breasts. Rage rolled up my spine, my Merrow Order prickling to come out. This was wrong. Every bone in my body said so.

"I'll ask you one more time kindly before I do so unkindly," Father said dangerously. "Where are the people of Pyros hiding?"

"We don't know," Gail spat.

"We don't know anything!" Meredith shrieked and Agatha back-handed her.

Everest's shoulders tensed in time with mine.

"Agatha, release your Order," Father commanded and she shifted, her hair turning to snakes as she let her Medusa form come out to play. The serpents snapped and hissed as she kneeled down and Gail gasped as one of them bit her, injecting her with the venom of her kind. It would act quick, paralysing her for a number of hours but at least it wouldn't kill her.

Gail's limbs drooped heavily and her sisters cried out to her as she crumpled to the ground. Agatha cast chains of ice to hold Casey and Meredith back, and a snarl curled my lips.

Jacobin kneeled down, gripping Gail's throat. "Pretty, pretty," he murmured. "Will your sisters sing like canaries when they watch us carve you up?"

"Fuck this," Everest growled, reaching into her hair and pulling out a small blue lizard thing with wings.

"What the hell is that?" I hissed.

"This is Calcifiend," she announced, which was hardly an explanation. Then she whispered to the damn animal like it could understand her. I couldn't catch what she said to it but the little beastie clicked its tongue then took off on its wings and sped back the way we'd come.

I opened my mouth to demand answers but Everest sprinted off into the trees to our right without another word.

I stared after her with a sneer, unsure what maddened path she was on. As her sudden absence settled over me, uncertainty crawled through my skin. What was I supposed to do now that I was alone?

Gail's screams coloured the air as Jacobin cast an ice blade in his grip and sliced it along her arm.

If I walked out there and made a stand against my own father, I would be declared a traitor of my people. His son or not, I doubted he would take kindly to that. I wouldn't raise a sword against him either way. So what the fuck was I supposed to do?

A roar of alarm carried to us from the town and my head wheeled back in that direction. The scent of smoke trailed on the air and between the thick boughs, I could just make out the glint of fire rising from one of the rooftops.

My pulse quickened.

Pyros had come. We were under attack.

"Deal with them," Father clipped, striding for the trees.

"The Flamebringers have shown their faces at last." He raced into the trees and I held my breath when he passed me, watching him disappear into the night.

I turned back to the group as Agatha and Jacobin shared excited looks and Jacobin's hand slid down Gail's dress. My fingers closed on the hilt of my sword, a burn in my veins telling me to do something, to fuck the consequences. As I stepped forward in an act of certain treachery, a wild cat sprang from the trees, a white leopard landing on Agatha and knocking her to the ground. She lunged for her throat, my sister in her Order form a vicious thing to behold as she tore and slashed and bit, not stopping even when Agatha screamed. Her snake hair tried to sink its fangs into Everest but my sister ripped them clean out of her head with her teeth and tossed the writhing things on the ground, leaving Agatha wailing in agony.

Jacobin ran to help her, but I raced forward to intercept him, sword raised and heart in my throat. I hesitated at the last second and punched him in the chest instead. It knocked him flat on his back and Everest ripped Agatha's throat out in a vicious attack then she leapt onto Jacobin, slashing his face with her claws and silencing his baying yell with a bite that snapped his spine, ending his life in a reign of purest pain.

Everest lifted her head, blood staining her white fur and a savagery in her eyes that made me want to kneel before it. Agatha and Jacobin's bodies were laid to waste at her paws, their faces still twisted in anguished terror.

Casey and Meredith gathered around their paralysed sister, hugging her tight in relief.

"Thank you," Casey croaked, staring at Everest then at me. I shook my head because I hadn't really done anything at all. Yet in my heart, I had. I'd made a stand against my father. I'd had a hand in his warriors' deaths.

Everest took a step toward me then stiffened, looking down in alarm. She'd stepped on one of the mutilated snakes, its fangs digging deep into her paw.

"Shit," I gasped as Everest staggered two steps then collapsed at my feet.

"Run," I barked at the girls and between them, they managed to carry their sister away into the woods. "Don't stop. And don't come back!"

I lifted Everest into my arms, cursing into the night air and looking around in confused desperation. This venom was going to take some time to wear off. I had to hide her somewhere she could recover and come up with an iron clad alibi for this shit show of a bloodbath.

I'd been bitten by a Medusa before and it had been hours before I'd regained full movement in my body. If we were gone that long, it would be more than a little suspicious.

"Alright, I've got a plan. You're gonna have to trust me, runt."

She gurgled a mewl that said she abso-fucking-lutely did not trust me but she didn't have a choice. I ran for the trees where she'd laid her trap, finding her clothes stashed there.

"Can you shift?" I asked.

She blinked once then turned into her Fae form and I dropped her haphazardly onto the ground, not wanting to touch my naked sister. With a blast of water, I cleaned the blood off of her then rolled her around in the grass a bit to dry her off while she grumbled and grunted.

"Okay, step one complete," I announced.

I jammed her clothes onto her as quickly as I could then lifted her up again, tossing her over my shoulder like a sack of shit and running back to the town.

"Pyros is here," I voiced my worries out loud. "We can wait out the fight and- hang on…" The sounds carrying from the town didn't sound like a fight at all.

As I got closer, I found the flames were being doused by jets of water rising up from the far side of the buildings ahead, a new fire catching again as soon as another was put out. A small blue lizard flew out of a window where the latest fire had started, smoke trailing after it and it all clicked together.

I glanced at Everest. "You told your lizard thing to start the fire."

She grunted which I took as an affirmation.

"Clever little runt," I said in a jibe, but hell it actually had been a decent plan. It had drawn Father away from the girls and given us an opportunity to free them. But it was a crime we were now partners in. A secret that could never be uttered.

I crept closer to the town then took the alleys back to the tavern, hoping upon hope we'd beat Father there. A quick glance through a back window assured me that the rest of father's men had exited to join the commotion and that gave us a chance.

I shoved the window open and tossed Everest through so she landed with a thump on the floorboards. I climbed in after her and accidently kicked her in the ass as I went.

She growled as I picked her up and ran for the basin behind the bar, using water magic to flush out the venom in the bite on her hand. She sagged against me like a ragdoll as I held her up with one arm, her toes scraping across the floor and her head lolling against my shoulder.

I propped her against the bar while I grabbed the bottle of rum I'd been working on earlier, downing a long swig before holding it to her lips.

"Drink." She swallowed when I poured it between her lips, then

I splashed a healthy measure on her clothes to give her the scent of a real drunk bitch.

The front door opened and my heart jolted as Father walked in, looking as pissed off as a cat in a cloud of dog farts. His gaze cut to me and Everest sank slowly off the bar to the floor at my feet with a long groan.

"I knew I could outdrink the runt," I laughed, hoping it didn't sound too strained as Father cut us a look.

"Ransom," he barked, glancing at Everest at my feet. "You fool. You've inebriated our fucking weapon."

"Is she needed?" I tried to sound concerned. "What was all that shouting about?"

"Looks like there's a few stragglers in this town fucking with us. But not to worry, we'll flush them out by dawn." He pushed a hand into his hair then glanced back at the door. "I'd better check on Agatha and Jacobin."

I smiled casually. "Sure. I'll put the Void to bed."

Father nodded stiffly then exited the tavern again, leaving me with a breath sighing from my lips. "He's gonna be pissed when he gets back," I muttered. "Let's hope he assumes that those Flamebringers shifted and killed two of his best."

I scooped Everest up, heading for the room I'd discovered upstairs, wondering why it felt right to have sent two monsters into death this evening with the aid of my sister. She might have been a runt, but she was a fearsome runt I supposed. And so help me, we were bonded by this secret now. Because if Father ever found out what we'd done, we truly were fucked.

BASTIAN

CHAPTER FOURTEEN

My footsteps thumped against the flagstones as I walked a pace behind the man who had chained and bound me so prettily. I supposed to anyone else this might have smelled a lot like freedom, but to me it stank of horse shit. Nevertheless, I'd made my bed and this was all there was to it.

Dragor strode along before me, the smugness which radiated from him making me want to gag. I'd never been the type for pomp and pretention, though it was clear this man who called himself a prince revelled in such things. I was a prize pig about to be put on display and the mere thought of it was rankling against my last nerve.

He was claiming the battle at Pomair as a victory, though I wasn't so certain that was the truth of it. The Void's disappearance had certainly levelled things out but when the armies turned their backs on one another and fled the field it had seemed more like a mutual understanding of subjugation. But the way Dragor told it, he had sent the Cascadians running in fear.

I supposed they had abandoned Stormfell, so in that sense he was right. But I very much doubted that would be the last we'd see of them.

"If you prove you can behave yourself among polite company then I will allow you to have more freedom within the castle," Dragor said, tossing me scraps which I had no real choice but to snatch from his hands.

"And these?" I asked, raising my wrists to indicate the metal cuffs which adorned them. They'd been fashioned to look decorative but they were blocking my magic as solidly as any cuffs might.

"Perhaps, in time I will allow you to remove those among company too. But you might…slip and it wouldn't do for you to reveal your Avanis heritage to the court, or anyone else for that matter. I will remove them once you return to your rooms for the night as agreed."

I sneered at his back, the deal between us feeling claustrophobic already. I rolled my shoulders, trying to dispel the memory of him riding me in my Dragon form but it was something I was going to have to get used to. I reminded myself that it had been worth it if it meant my wing was healed by that Reaper he'd brought to me. But even flying through the sky after so many years hadn't been as liberating as it should have been with a parasite taking a ride.

The music reached out to capture us in its net as we approached the ballroom, the sound of hundreds of Fae revelling within making my hackles rise. I'd never been a particularly sociable creature even before my years of isolation and I had no inclination to become one now.

I kept my gaze over the heads of the crowd as we stepped into the opulent room, the foreign music washing over me too loudly, the embroidered dresses and suits appearing all too alien. There was a refinement to these people which mine had certainly never claimed in my time. I wasn't certain if that had changed now but I doubted it somehow. We were a wild people, bound to the earth and beholden to it too. Our festivities had felt more primal than this show of wealth and power, our people losing themselves to the calls of the flesh and the wildness of nature.

Dragor led me through the crowd who clamoured to get a look at me, the same word echoing among them like they were stalagmites passing a note of music through a cavern.

Dragon, Dragon, Dragon.

The fascination over what I was wasn't new to me. Even when I'd been born there hadn't been others of my kind, the Dragons of old had been long gone and my existence had been hailed as a symbol from the stars themselves, hidden from most.

Dragor paraded me around the opulent hall, the watchful eyes of the three huge zodiac statues seeming to follow me wherever I walked. The Gemini twins were curious in their observations, Aquarius almost pausing in his eternal water pouring, Libra's scales creaking on the cusp of judgement.

I missed the great effigies of my own element, the tremendous bull of Taurus, the bountiful beauty of Virgo, and the great sea goat Capricorn who I owed my own birth allegiance to. I missed the flowers which coated the walls of every home I'd ever known in Avanis, the way the buildings were so full of life and magic that they seemed to breathe.

Here everything was cold, pale stone. Any decoration came in the form of tapestries and statues created to be impressive or recount tales of war. Perhaps other parts of Stormfell were different but nothing in this place spoke of it being a home. It was the commanding capital of a nation of warriors and little else. I might have pitied its people if

I wasn't drowning in contempt for them already.

Dragor led me straight to the long table at the head of the room which had been laid out for the royals alone, a single chair set just to the side of it which he pointed out for me.

"It is a great honour to be seated so close to the Aquilas," he warned me in a low voice. "See to it that you don't prove yourself unworthy of the boon."

I said nothing, snatching a glass of wine as a servant approached us with a tray filled with them. I drank it in one, the taste tart and not to my liking. "Do you have ale in this place?" I asked and the servant looked to Dragor who sighed but nodded his allowance of my request.

I kept my silence as I stood beside him and started work on the ale once it arrived, staring stoically though the throng of dancing bodies, the feasting not yet begun, though my stomach growled with hunger.

Dragor spoke with Fae he deemed important enough, introducing me to them, though I said nothing and barely even acknowledged them at all.

I didn't care about the self-important Lords and Ladies, I certainly wasn't interested in the women who enquired as to my eligibility, and I couldn't care less about impressing his counsellors.

Dragor's irritation with me only showed in the slight flaring of his nostrils. He could say nothing. I had agreed only to behave myself. There had been no requirement of small talk or even politeness. Perhaps he was wishing he'd been more specific but I was of the impression that he should just be glad I wasn't reducing this entire castle to cinders.

And then there was her.

My spine straightened, a growl rolling up the back of my throat and my muscles tensing.

Of course she was here. I should have expected nothing less but as

I stared at her across a sea of dancing courtiers, all I could feel was fury.

Dragor stilled beside me, shooing away the Fae he'd been talking with and placing a hand on my forearm.

I snatched my arm away and he was only lucky I didn't break his jaw for good measure.

"Keep your hands off of me," I warned him and he straightened at the threat in my words, though clearly he thought better of biting back at me here and instead turned his focus to where mine remained.

Vesper hadn't moved. She still stood on the far side of the dancefloor, a dress of deep navy coated in gold brocade clinging to her figure in a way that made me ache, the flared skirt skimming her knees, the bodice tight and strapless. It shouldn't have been legal for a woman to look so enticing while being so deceiving.

I snarled at her and she raised her chin.

Any other Fae would have known to run from me, my skin heating with my inner fire as the rage I felt towards her threatened to consume me whole. But of course she didn't run. I didn't think she even knew how to.

Vesper strode straight through the dancing bodies, magic flicking from her fingertips and forcing a path into place for her as she approached me, not a hint of regret or fear in her grey eyes. All bravado and bullshit, the same witch she'd been when we first met.

Dragor hissed an instruction at me not to hurt her but I only growled again.

Vesper didn't slow even though every other Fae within my vicinity backed away, their instincts warning them of the danger which was building. She had to be able to feel my violent desires aimed at her but still she didn't balk.

Her steps were confident and measured, her eyes locked on mine and a slow smile spread across her seductive lips as if this were nothing but a game we were playing.

She curtsied for her prince, dipping low, but never once looking away from me.

When she straightened, Dragor waved her aside and she moved to stand before me instead, his gaze following her with malicious intensity.

"Hello, Dragon. Come, dance with me," she purred, her gifts creeping from her and skimming through the air towards me. She knew I could resist her, she knew her ploy wouldn't work, yet still she tried.

The Fae surrounding us started calling out to her, offering themselves up in my place with frantic desperation, though she cast a wall of air around her to force them back.

"Oh for the love of Gemini!" a man groaned beside me before dropping to his knees and shoving his hand down the front of his britches to tug at his cock.

Two women on the other side of her gave up on trying to win the Succubus's attention for themselves and pounced on one another instead, kissing passionately and tugging at the bodices of their dresses as though they intended to fuck right here on the dancefloor regardless of the audience.

Dragor hissed a warning at the two of us not to turn his ballroom into a brawl but he may as well have faded into dust for all the attention either of us paid him.

Vesper cocked her head, every part of her a dare in that perfectly fitted dress. I swallowed down the lump in my throat as I scowled at her, all the words I wished to hurl her way jamming there and festering. Because I wouldn't be offering her my wrath. Not here. Not on her terms. I could see through this play of hers to the spark of need in her grey eyes, the corruption in her soul so clearly visible to me that I could only wonder at how no other Fae seemed to see it at all.

"I'll dance for you!" a guard yelled, breaking into a vibrant set of movements with flamboyant arm flourishes and a lot of hip thrusts.

She ignored him. She ignored the woman who had just ripped her dress open to reveal her tits and the man who was pouring a glass of wine down his chest and massaging his nipples through the wet material. She ignored the groans and cries for release, the stench of arousal on the air. Every inch of her focus was locked on me. And me alone.

The royals were staring down the table at the commotion, Dragor looking thunderous as he pushed to his feet, his ire pinned on her, and despite my every intention, I shoved to my feet too, ending this before he did.

"Fine," I snapped, taking her hand and yanking her against me forcefully so that our bodies were flush and her other palm landed obediently on my shoulder, though she had to stand on her tiptoes to reach even in the stiletto heels.

I slid my free hand around her spine, drawing her closer still, stalling the breath which tumbled from her lips as I leaned down to speak against her lying mouth.

"Is this what you wanted?" I asked in a low tone only for her.

"No," she admitted, that word hanging between us, my glare boring into her storm-grey eyes, a thousand furious words falling still and fading away because what was the point in any of them? She was no more deserving of my rage than she was of my attention but still she chose to steal both regardless.

We weren't on the dancefloor but as the music struck up, I took the lead and moved her to the rhythm of it.

She stumbled at first, the steps I took clearly unfamiliar to this enemy of mine, both through a difference in our cultures and every change in trend and style which had taken place in the years I'd spent trapped beneath the ground. But she only tripped once and my hold kept her in my arms. Then she used her gifts to sense what I wanted, her magic making it all too easy for her to follow my lead as I pushed her into a dance to which no other Fae here knew the steps.

I said nothing, pushing faster, our feet moving to the music, her body firm against mine yet soft in all the right ways too. She was so fragile in stature for one so stoic of heart. But despite appearances I knew she wouldn't break easily.

I backed her up onto the dancefloor then spun her so suddenly that any other woman would have fallen flat on her face. Perhaps that had been my intent – to embarrass her, to wound her ego as she'd wounded my heart, for the stars knew nothing beat in her cold chest for me to aim at.

But she didn't fall, she spun out and back, her leg kicking up the way the dance required and I caught it, her knee hooking over my elbow as I dipped her back and a woman gasped at the scandal of the movement.

I jerked her upright, keeping hold of her leg and our bodies became one as I dragged her across the dancefloor, her hands finding my cheeks, eyes boring into mine.

I pushed her harder, faster, our breaths growing frantic and movements more animal, more carnal. She appeared to care as little as I did, only focused on the movements I demanded from her and keeping up with the pace I set.

When the music fell still we were left pressed together, our bodies slick with perspiration, our breaths colliding, chests heaving, hearts pounding. And all I could see were those grey eyes peering into mine as if she had the right to see straight through me the way she so clearly did.

Silence rang out for several seconds and a lone fae clapping forced my eyes from hers, my focus finding Dragor who was applauding our debauched display from his seat, though his expression was anything but pleased. The sycophantic congregation soon joined him, their dropped jaws closing, scandal turning to delight as if we'd simply been set to entertain them and hadn't cleared the dancefloor with our power play.

"I need to speak with you," Vesper said, her words hidden in the applause, fingers knotting in my shirt as she felt me withdrawing.

"We have nothing to say to one another," I growled, straightening, but she held on.

"I have plenty," she disagreed, her eyes flicking to the balcony doors so briefly no one else would have caught it.

A prickle of curiosity stirred in me despite myself and she gave me a cunning smile as she sensed it before straightening and releasing me. She curtsied like a well-practiced courtier and didn't bother waiting for me to bow before turning and striding away.

She was quickly swallowed by the crowd, her gifts drawing Fae closer to beg the favour of her company or the honour of her next dance and irritation prickled through me at their display.

I jerked around, ignoring the offers of a dance from several women who had flocked to watch us before pushing through them and the rest of the crowd towards the balcony doors.

The air outside was cool but the bite of winter had abandoned it along with the snow and the darkened landscape which I could see beyond the city limits was teaming with new life.

I ran a finger beneath the collar I wore, the green gemstone which had stopped me from shifting when embedded in my skin now clasped in a band of iron grey metal which was carved with runes and imbued with magic I had no idea how to break. With the collar I could shift, my Dragon form available to me at all times, the metal able to adapt to my change in size. But it wouldn't come off.

It was better than the cavern. I had to remind myself of that daily and likely always would.

Footsteps approached but I could tell by the pace and weight behind them that they weren't hers.

I turned to look at an unfamiliar man as he stopped beside me, offering a bow I was certain I hadn't earned.

"Prince Dragor wishes to let you know that you are free to return to your rooms. He appreciates how exhausted you are and thinks a rest may be in order."

"Does he now?" I asked darkly, straightening my spine so that I loomed over the messenger and he squeaked in alarm before shifting suddenly into a Tiberian Rat, his clothes puddling on the ground at my feet. He took off with another squeak of fright and I snorted my amusement before turning my eyes back to the view.

A gentle breeze tumbled over me from my right and I frowned as it swirled around me, noticing a scrap of white among it and snatching it from the air on instinct.

A small, folded scrap of paper sat crumpled in my hand, a few words visible on its edges. I unfolded it, my forearms pressed to the stone balustrade and my body hiding the note from view.

You're as subtle as a sack of crabs.
Take the long route through the east wing on
your journey back to bed.

I crumpled the paper in my fist, turning to look for her, but of course she was nowhere in sight.

The feast was being laid out in the ballroom, long tables filling with Stormfell's most important citizens, the royal family lording it over all of them. The other Fae on the balcony were hurrying back inside and I caught a glimpse of pink hair at the table closest to the royals.

Well, if she was feasting then I had some time to myself.

I kicked my boots off, followed by my socks and the shirt I unfastened with ease. Shucking the elaborate ensemble in favour of my own brutal flesh was liberating in its own way. The trousers followed, leaving my body clad in nothing but ink and the collar I couldn't remove.

A few scandalised and excitable cries came from within the ballroom as some of the Fae there spotted me but I ignored them, snatching my clothes from the floor and balling them together before leaping from the balcony and shifting in midair.

My gut plummeted as I fell, the shift not going exactly to plan, the years since I'd done such a thing having blurred my memories on how best to execute it and my clothes tumbled out of my grasp.

My tail slammed into the palace wall with a deafening boom, my belly pointing toward the sky in place of my spine and I cursed internally as the ground rushed up to meet me.

I threw my body into a cumbersome roll, my wings snapping out, one of them decapitating a decorative tree in the process before I manage to launch myself skyward again.

A flutter of movement caught my eye and I spotted some of my clothes dangling from a lower balcony. I twisted to snatch them in my claws, breaking the balustrade as I did so and sending a flurry of rubble down into the courtyard below.

But then I was off, powering towards the silvery glow of the moon through the clouds, a roar escaping me as the bliss of flight enraptured my soul.

This was what I'd dreamed of in the dark, the rush of wind and thrill of speed, every moment of it exhilarating in a way that was entirely my own. No one could steal this from me, not truly, not even when my wing had been broken and butchered. This was still an experience that was mine alone because there was only one of my kind.

I wasn't certain how long I spent in the clouds, circling the mountains and releasing as much of the pent-up energy in my body as I could before finally returning to land on the balcony outside the ballroom.

The fires had burned low, the revellers long since retired to bed and only a single man awaited me, the same Rat who had delivered Prince Dragor's message earlier and now promptly scurried away to no doubt report my return to him too.

Not that I could have truly left. A deal is a deal after all. Especially one sworn on the back of the stars.

I looked down at the clothes which I'd dropped from my claws and found only my trousers had made the journey back to the ground. In hindsight I likely could have just left everything here but I'd been planning on landing in the city and finding a tavern – the problem there had come with the lack of open spaces available for me to land in and the small rooftops which I'd doubted would hold my shifted weight. So now I had returned to the palace and would have to traverse it in nothing but my trousers. I supposed it beat having a shirt and wandering the halls with my cock out.

I strode through the ballroom, my stomach growling over the banquet I'd missed, then I passed the guards who were still manned at the door, the flickering sconces offering the only light to the wide corridors. I wasn't hugely familiar with the castle yet but I knew which way was east so it didn't take me long to find my way to that wing and as my chambers lay at the top of the highest tower there, it wouldn't be difficult to locate those either.

A door on my left clicked open and I tensed for an attack but instead slender fingers grasped my wrist and Vesper tugged me inside.

"You took your time," she griped, releasing me as she closed the door and flicking a silencing shield up over us.

A fire was burning low in the hearth illuminating a sparsely furnished chamber in a dim orange glow. Vesper's chambers held as little of her personality as they possibly could, the place which should have been her haven seeming more like a cell than my own rooms. There was a rack of weapons to the rear of the space, an armoire and a chest which I assumed held her clothes, a small table with a single chair and a bed. No trinkets, no paintings, nothing hanging on the walls aside from the drapes which were closed over her window and they couldn't have been more bland if they'd tried.

Which left me with little else to look at besides the traitorous wretch who had led me to this place. She'd changed out of the lavish dress, her petite figure clad in a linen shirt which looked to have been made for a man, though it hung almost down to her knees. Her feet were bare, pale pink hair mussed from sleep and the rumpled sheets confirmed the suggestion.

"For someone who claims to have been awaiting me, you clearly took the time to rest."

"I set magical alarms keyed to your signature to wake me when you passed. Don't flatter yourself into believing I'd allow myself to lose sleep over you," she said but there was something in those words which didn't ring true.

I folded my arms and leaned back against the door, tempted to simply turn and leave. I had nothing to say to her. Nothing kind anyway.

"Out with it," she demanded.

I arched a brow.

"I can feel what you want, Bastian, so I know you're biting your tongue against all the curses you wish to hurl at me. So go ahead, say them. I can take it. I know what I am."

"You're a fucking liar," I spat, shoving away from the door and prowling towards her.

"I'm all the bad things," she agreed without flinching. "And I never claimed I wasn't."

"No," I scoffed. "You just do this, don't you? You take all the labels like 'witch' and 'liar' and 'heartless cunt' and you wear them like badges of honour."

"That last one is new," she said, stepping forward to meet me, refusing to back down from my glare.

"I can see what you're doing," I growled, my blood heating with the ire I felt towards her.

"What's that?"

"You make yourself the target, offering yourself up like a punching bag so that you can take all the insults, all the judgement, all the hatred, and forge armour out of it. You wear it like a second skin and you think there isn't a Fae alive who can see through it, especially in the face of all that grief you carry around with you. But you can't hide from me, spectre. You let that armour crack when we were out in the wilds and I caught a glimpse of who you really are beneath it."

"And who's that?" she asked scathingly. "Because I've spent my entire life trying to figure that out."

"You're just a lost little girl who no one ever loved yet can't stop herself from craving it, even though you do everything in your power to make yourself unworthy of it."

My words hit her like a slap, her grey eyes brightening and her fist curling at her side.

"Come on then, spectre – hit me. Hurt me, punish me, shove me away and prove your point all over again. You want everyone to hate you? Well done, you succeeded. You want me to yell at you? Then here you go. But I *know* you. I've *seen* you. And you can run from that all you like but it doesn't stop it from being the truth."

"There isn't anything to see in me," she hissed, her body tight with tension and I could tell she was fighting the urge to strike at me with all she had. My feral little creature. "I am precisely what I claim to be and I want nothing more than what I have always told you to be the truth. I am still breathing because I have a life to end before I give up on my own. I'm going to hunt the man who called himself Cayde Avior and take great pleasure in his agonising death. That's it. That's all there is–"

"That's all?" I scoffed. "So you don't hear your name whispered in the dark now then?"

"No," she ground out but it was a lie and we both knew it.

"And I suppose you felt nothing at all when you saw me flying into battle with that bastard on my back?" I pushed.

She shook her head defiantly but I saw the way she swallowed back her truth.

"Liar," I growled again, stepping forward so that she had no choice but to step back, my chest knocking against her, my bulk crowding her in. She wanted to run but fuck that. She hadn't given me the courtesy of doing that, so I wouldn't be offering it to her either.

"Why should I care what you do?" she hissed, her eyes a raging vortex of emotion which she couldn't hide from me.

I took another step and she was forced back once more, then another and another until she was flattened against the wall and still she didn't strike me, still she didn't push me away because she knew as well as I did that I could see straight through her bullshit.

"You care that I flew. You care that he shackled me to his will and you fucking care about *me* too which is precisely why you did what you did. Because you're scared. You're terrified of this and so you wanted to sabotage it but that doesn't stop me from seeing you. I can hate you, but it doesn't make me blind."

"There's nothing to see," she protested angrily, her hands finally coming up between us, her palms flattening to my chest as she shoved me back.

I conceded a step, barking a bitter laugh as I turned for the door and stalked away from her.

"Fuck this," I muttered, reaching for the handle.

"Fuck you," she breathed in reply and I whirled, fury lighting inside of me because she was still lying. She'd summoned me here, she'd wanted me to come and then she'd run scared again, baited me, begged me to tell her all the worst of herself and was about to get her wish. I'd leave here and she could break on her own terms, wallow in her own self-assured sense of wickedness and get precisely what she'd wanted. But I wasn't going to let her use me to validate her own self-loathing. She could stare right at the truth of herself before doing that.

I crossed the room in six powerful strides, taking hold of her and turning her back to me before shoving her against the wall.

"What are you doing?" she hissed, trying to fight me off, but I caught her wrists between my fingers and pinned her hands to the wall above her head. Her breaths grew ragged, a curse slipping from her lips and I fisted my free hand in her pink hair, forcing her to turn her head and meet my gaze.

"Shift," I growled at her, and she stilled, her eyes widening before going blank.

"I don't know what you–"

"My cousin was a Succubus. I know well what your kind are and what you're capable of. I know every secret of your Order and most of all, I know that you can shift. But you never do. Why is that, spectre? What is it you're so desperate to hide?"

She tried to fight me then, really tried, but it was too late for that. She'd let me capture her and I had her pinned exactly where I wanted her.

"Shift!" I bellowed in command, and a tear slipped from her eye as she shook her head, sagging in my hold, fighting the urge with all she had.

I let my fingers move through the silken strands of her hair, leaning in to speak against the shell of her ear.

"You won't ever stop lying to the world and yourself if you keep hiding the worst of what you are in the shadows. So why don't you stop hiding and show me something real for once? You asked me here because you want something, not because you felt moved to let me curse you out and name you every heinous thing you work so hard to embody. So stop being a coward and *shift*."

She panted in my hold, her muscles bunching against the command, head shaking in refusal but another tear slipped down her cheek.

I pressed even closer to her, the heat of my Dragon fire enveloping us both as I let my fingers fall from her hair and skim down her spine through the linen shirt she wore. She shuddered at the touch, and

I fisted my fingers in the fabric before tearing it open, revealing the bare skin of her back and the words which she'd inked there.

I ran my calloused fingers back up her spine, splaying them wide to caress the edges of her shoulder blades, the command on the tip of my tongue once more, but she gave in before I had to say it again.

A broken sob escaped her full lips as she shifted, the beauty of her features growing impossibly sharper, more alluring to the point of fantasy. She looked like an ethereal being, not meant for this world but destined for something far greater. It was a beauty which was painful to behold, striking a chord in the echoing recesses of my chest, but that wasn't the biggest change which her body underwent.

I pulled my eyes from hers to look at her spine, at the two broken stumps where her wings should have been, the ends of them long since healed over, the black, leathery skin encircling the place where the fullness of her wings should have spread wide from her back.

I'd suspected this but it still stole the breath from my lungs, words thickening in my throat and stalling there.

In the silence, I released my grip on her wrists but she didn't move away from the wall, her eyes moving to the floor as tears slipped down her cheeks.

My hand was still pressed to her spine and I slowly moved it across her skin, caressing the ridge of her destroyed wing and stroking the silken smoothness of the flesh there.

She shivered at my touch and I caressed the other stump too, feeling the heartbreak of this loss in my core. I'd gone hundreds of years without the use of my wings, one of them broken and mangled. But I'd had hope to cling to in the dark. They hadn't been taken from me entirely. The brutality which had resulted in this…

"Did your prince do this to you?" I snarled, fury rising up in me at the thought of her enduring this agony at the hands of another but to my surprise she shook her head.

"When I first joined the Sinfair at fourteen, I was assigned to the barracks with the other recruits. They hated me for my birth. They were all highborn and simply working off some shame their families had earned. So when I started to outshine them all they took it as a personal affront. I ignored their threats and took the beatings when they came – I could outmatch any of them anyway. At least, I could when they were alone…"

My fingers shook with fury as her voice cracked at the words, the truth of what she'd suffered for nothing more than being crossborn making my hatred of this endless war expand tenfold.

"One night they all came for me at once. The entire squadron – nineteen of them. They said…they said I didn't deserve to fly because I wasn't really air-born and they…"

She shifted again as a heavy sob escaped her, the ruined legacy of her wings fading from sight, her features settling into their usual beauty. She didn't turn to face me but I drew her around, cupping her face in my hand and making her look at me.

"I'll burn them all," I promised her and the edge of a smile tugged at her tear-stained lips before she shook her head.

"I ended them myself," she admitted and of course she had. "They left me lying in the street, bleeding and beaten, probably hoping I'd die as they stole my wings away as trophies. It started to rain and I watched my blood mix with the muck of the street as it created little rivers between the cobblestones. I felt the ether then for the first time. I didn't know what it was, or how to call on it really but it took my blood in payment, it accepted my sacrifice and it gave me the strength to get back on my feet. There was a broken bottle lying in the alleyway where they'd done it to me so I picked it up and I went seeking revenge."

"I hope they died screaming," I growled and again, that beautiful, broken smile confirmed it.

"Earned myself my first lashing for the privilege," she told me. "Five for each life I took. Ninety-five in total. It almost killed me. And if truth be told I would have welcomed death then."

Dragon fire burned hot against the back of my tongue, my fury on her behalf rising so high that my fingers shook with it. But before I could lose control of the beast inside me, she took my hand in hers and gripped me tightly.

"What of your wings?" I asked her. "The Reapers could reattach them if you kept them – I can find one and make them do it. I'll–"

"They burned them," she admitted bitterly. "I dragged a single bone from the fire but it was broken and blackened with soot after their abuse of it. I begged to be healed but the Reapers themselves told me there was nothing they could do without having the wings to hand and even then it wouldn't have been likely. Then they placed me with a new legion as I was the only remnant of mine and that was where I met Dalia and Moraine. They hated me of course and I hated them in turn. But then one day…I don't know, I guess we just forgot to hate one another and found something else."

"Family," I told her firmly. "You found your family."

More tears pooled in her eyes as she nodded and I cursed the stars themselves for the cruelty of the fate they'd dealt her.

I lifted her into my arms, the sweet scent of her skin enveloping me, the blazing rage in my chest dimming despite all the promises I'd made myself. She leaned her head against my chest as I cradled her there and I carried her to her bed, placing her beneath the sheets.

Her fingers curled around my wrist for half a heartbeat as I made to withdraw and something twisted in my chest at the sharp sting of her truth. She was alone. And that was a feeling I knew all too well.

She tugged her hand away sharply as if realising what she'd just admitted to with the gesture and my resolve shattered at the thought of her replacing those walls around herself. I said nothing as I gave in to the ache in my chest and followed her into the bed.

Vesper sucked in a sharp breath but said nothing as I wrapped her in my arms, my own rage at her fading to a lingering bitterness in the face of all she'd endured.

She curled in on herself, her cheek on my chest. I ran my fingers back and forth over her shoulder blades, precisely where her wings resided, as if my touch could soothe the lingering pain there.

Silence wrapped us in that moment, the seconds dragging into minutes, our pulses finding a rhythm with one another, two broken souls seeking refuge in a shared embrace.

"The ether still calls to me," she admitted as the darkness curled in around us, the fire dying away. "That's why I wanted you to come here. I thought… Tell me what vow binds you to Dragor."

I sighed, knowing I'd been a fool to accept the deal of the air kingdom's prince. But if anyone could understand the deep longing I'd harboured to return to the sky on my wings then it was her. She knew why I'd agreed to his terms.

"I swore to obey the commands of Stormfell in aid of its survival until such time as the war is done or death releases me from my oath."

"Of Stormfell?" she asked, lifting her head to look up at me in the darkness and I nodded. "Not *his* commands specifically?"

"I believe he wished for my compliance to be a gift to his father – proof that he was the most worthy of the crown. Not that I imagine he intends to let any other Fae command me regardless."

"I could command you," she said slowly. "I'm a General of Stormfell. I could command you to run–"

"How would that aid Stormfell?" I asked, shaking my head, though I hadn't considered that she might be able to command me as she suggested and I wasn't at all certain that was a good thing.

"Then I'll command you to help me follow the voices in my head. The disruption to the ether is a threat to us all – Stormfell included. Whatever is summoning me is close at hand – I can feel it."

"What of your own oaths?" I asked.

"I cannot hunt the man I need to kill until my prince releases me to do so. But he never forbade me from seeking out the faults in the ether and I have free access to the lands of our people. So I wouldn't be breaking the terms of my agreement by following the voices that call to me."

My lips tugged into the hint of a smile as I considered her suggestion. It was a small rebellion but I was hungering for a mutiny of any design.

"Alright," I agreed, drawing her close and letting my eyes fall closed.

She shifted in my hold and I wondered if she was going to protest my presence in her bed. But she only adjusted her head on my chest so that her ear was pressed to the steady pounding of my heartbeat and the two of us let the darkness claim this truce.

HARLON

CHAPTER FIFTEEN

Since Solomon had lost all interest in me, I'd gained one advantage. It was all the easier to sneak around Never Keep and watch the inner circle of the Reapers who were assisting the Cardinal Reaper with the monster. Or Caelum as he now referred to it.

The blood sacrifices in Never Keep had increased daily, any neophyte in training who broke even the simplest of rules disappeared in the night to be fed to the beastly thing which lurked beneath our feet.

The shift in the Reapers that Solomon was using for his dark plans was too obvious to ignore. They consulted with the stars every hour they didn't disappear down into the bowels of the keep.

I was able to follow them though, slipping through the dark passages and watching through a crack in the wall as they worked on creating a huge underground chamber where a dark abyss stood at its centre. The wielders of earth magic carved out the new space and there they worshipped that hole, bowing to it, casting bones and blood into its depths.

That was where Caelum lurked. But last night I'd discovered something terrible.

I'd watched Solomon hold a wicked ceremony in that chamber, spying on them as they tortured and mutilated three neophytes then threw them into that horrid abyss. The Cardinal Reaper had said something truly alarming then.

"Upon the night of the blood moon that is set to rise in the coming months, the magic of the moon herself will be able to summon Caelum from its world into ours. The creature will cross into The Waning Lands as predicted by the stars and it shall be a god among us!"

The Reapers had cheered and praised the stars for the gift of Caelum while I'd shuddered, backed away and run. Run and run all the way to my bedchamber where I'd paced in turmoil.

I'd come to an idea that was risky, perhaps futile. But I didn't know what else to do. And today was my only chance to enact it.

With the morning light on my back, I walked down to the black sand beach where Wandershire was sailing across the rough sea. The sky was clear today, a rare sight on the isle where it so often snowed. In my pocket was a letter that felt as though it was burning a hole right through me. It was weighted with a thousand hopes and an equal amount of fears.

As the floating town came ashore and the great metal legs drew it part way out of the water, I hurried toward it among the handful of Neophytes who had already arrived to seek wares from the traders.

The golden steps rolled down onto the sand to offer us access, and I was the first on board, striding through the narrow streets and heading straight for the tower at its centre. I rang a bell at the door there, heat burning its way up the back of my neck as if I was being watched. But I was just paranoid. No one was looking at me. And even if they were, I had every right to be here. It wasn't uncommon for the Reapers to seek wares from Wandershire.

The door flew open and I came face to face with the man I'd been looking for.

"Mr Angelico, I'd like a word in private," I asked.

His eyebrows rose, his green gaze tracking over my face. "It's not often I get Reapers at me door. Come in then, I wouldn't want to leave your star-gifted ass out in the cold to freeze."

I stepped inside and he snapped the door shut behind us before leading me upstairs. My heart thrashed as I followed him, unsure how many questions he might ask of my request and how well I would be able to lie in answer.

"I recognise your face, lad," Mavus revealed as he led me into his bureau. "You're a friend of a friend, I believe."

"You helped Everest escape from the Fury once," I said with a nod. "Did she mention me?"

"Mention ya? She gushed about ya, lad. You're Harlon Brook, ain't ya?"

"Yes, were you a good friend to her?"

"I tried to be, lad. I fiercely respect that girl," he said.

"Good. Then I have a task for you." I took the heavy pouch of gold out of my pocket and dropped it on his desk, noting the sea of maps there. Plenty had been marked with Xs, and I wondered what the meaning of them was.

Mavus licked his lips, reaching for the pouch and weighing it in his palm. "That's a hefty lot of gold there. You must want somethin' mighty bad."

"Not bad. Important. I want you to find Everest for me and give her this." I took the letter from my pocket, the seal on it forged by the fiercest magic I'd learned in my acolyte training. None should be able to open it but her.

He arched a brow, plucking the letter from my grip and twisting it between his fingertips. "A message for a lover perhaps?" he questioned.

I nodded. "She means everything to me," I growled.

"I can see that," he breathed, gazing into my eyes. "And she means a great deal to me too, you know?"

I frowned, wondering how close Everest had gotten to this Fae. He had looked out for her once but I didn't know what price she'd paid for the privilege. But maybe he really did care about her.

"Tell no one of this," I warned. "It must stay between us."

"You got a deal, lad. I don't share me client's dealings. You have my word on that."

I nodded, meaning to leave but I glanced back, my heart urging me to ask one more question. "Do you know where she is?"

I couldn't go to her myself, not after betraying her trust. I hated myself for how I'd acted. How I'd tried to force her to come with me against her will. I prayed to Scorpio that she would forgive me and that she'd lay her trust in the words in that letter.

"A little birdie tells me she's in Pyros with her daddy," Mavus said and I grimaced at the reminder.

"Pyros is a big place, how will you track her down?"

"I have eyes everywhere." Mavus grinned. "Don't you worry about it, lad. I'll find your girl and give her your love letter."

I nodded, letting him believe that was what it was.

"It must reach her as soon as possible," I pressed.

"I'll set sail for Pyros this very day, you have me word on that." He painted a cross over his heart then grabbed his pipe off the table and stuffed some fogweed in it. The sweet scent filled the air as he lit it and toked on the end.

"Thank you. I'll double that pay if you can reach her in under two weeks," I promised.

"You know how to charm a fella, you do," he purred with a cat's smile. "I'll make every effort to squeeze more coins from you, Reaper."

I smiled tightly then headed for the door, my gut sinking as I left the fate of the world in the hands of Mavus Angelico. But I had to stay here and keep a close watch on the Reapers and their monster, so what other choice did I really have?

Kaiser

CHAPTER SIXTEEN

The wedding was held in the grandest hall in Ravensview, the stone chamber vast in height and length with wooden beams criss-crossing above that were decorated with black and white drapes. The traditions of our people were blended with that of our newfound allies. The Vampires.

Mirelle was dressed in a black gown which was encrusted with diamonds on the bodice, glittering like the night sky. Her dress mirrored the ebony suit of her new husband. Lazarus Astrophel looked imposing in his finery, the underlying savagery of his kind always hinted at in the depths of his hazel eyes. We stood in rows, us on the left side of the hall while the Vampires clamoured and cheered from the right. Their arrival had driven fear into the hearts of many Fae of our land, and I could still taste that fear now. But at the encouragement of the ruling gang leaders, everyone had fallen in with this plan. Perhaps seeing the logic of it and the strength it would glean our nation.

Magpies watched from wooden beams crossing the hall above us, their eyes focused on their queen while Mirelle and Lazarus led the ceremony, speaking out the words that guided them into marriage beneath the stars' watch. They laid their hands on each other's wrists as they declared their union. And so it was done, my mother married to the new leader of the most formidable Vampire Coven of his kind.

The Vampires roared with raucous enthusiasm as Lazarus took Mirelle's hand and lifted it high to announce their union was done. Our people were quieter. Hands clapping more stiffly while uncomfortable glances were exchanged, the underlying fear among the Fae of Pyros bolstering my magic reserves.

I felt North's eyes on me from my left and looked his way, finding a crease upon his brow. While I tried to decipher it and unpick my own feelings on the marriage, North leaned closer and whispered his truth.

"I don't like this, Kai."

"It's a tactical move," I muttered under my breath. "We're unbeatable with them on our side."

North nodded, but the crease on his brow only deepened. "But they're bloodsuckers."

"That we are!" Lazarus crowed at him, his gaze locking onto North, his heightened Vampire senses clearly catching the words from his lips. "Bloodsuckers he calls us."

The Flamebringers quietened, shoulders tensing, the atmosphere growing suddenly heavy. The Vampires hushed at Lazarus's words too, throwing sharp glances our way. This marriage may have been intended to unite us, but it was clear it was not going to be as simple as that. Too many years of hatred stood between our people and theirs. But Mirelle was a Fae of strategy. And this choice would likely be her greatest play in the war yet.

For all the logic behind it, my skin prickled with the sense of an oncoming fight. If this tension was not shattered, it might come to blows.

"Your prejudice is showing, young North," Lazarus growled, flashing his fangs at my brother.

"No Vampire shall harm a single Flamebringer," Mirelle said in a simple yet sharp tone.

Lazarus inclined his head, his lips twisting in a smirk. "Indeed," he agreed, his fingers tightening on her hand. "We only harm our common enemies. Which brings me nicely onto your wedding gift, Mirelle." His eyes sparked with something sinister, a look I knew well from my enemies.

I held no sword at my hip today, but my fingers flexed for the kiss of a hilt. My lust for violence had not been eradicated by my newfound emotions. In fact, there was something even more tempting in it now. An outlet I hadn't known I'd needed before.

The iron doors at the back of the hall flew open and in strode two Vampires in coat tails, dragging a filthy-looking man between them. He screamed and thrashed as they hauled him down the black-carpeted aisle and tossed him at the feet of Lazarus and Mirelle.

The two Vampires bowed low then moved to join the masses of their kind.

Lazarus took hold of the man by the hair, dragging him up to kneel before them and taking a ruby-encrusted dagger from his hip. He offered the blade to Mirelle, bowing his head slightly to her in an offering. "An enemy spy of Avanis. We caught him on our way here sniffing around a little too close for comfort to your hiding place."

Mirelle had sent a group of her sons and daughters to send word to Lazarus of the engagement and a date for the wedding – since North was still teaching me how to control and understand my emotions, she'd decided not to send us too.

When Lazarus had left Cinder Vale upon our last meeting, he'd left word of a meeting place in the south of Pyros where Mirelle could contact him should she change her mind on the proposal. It hadn't taken long for Lazarus's response to arrive and his people to follow ours to Ravensview. It was a great risk to lead them here, but there was no way out of our current predicament without taking such a chance.

Our spies had watched the Cascadians march through our towns and claim victory over our land despite the fact that we hadn't been there to protect it. Mirelle had ordered that no battalion was sent to defend our lands.

She was playing the long game, and despite the disgruntlement of her people, they continued to follow her. She'd earned their trust in many ways during her rule, from providing safe havens from war to civilians, to bounties of food for her people.

So her position as the most powerful gang leader in Pyros held firm even in the face of her seemingly reckless decisions.

The Avanis spy had fallen quiet, looking from Lazarus to Mirelle in dawning understanding. "You… you cannot be wed," he rasped.

Mirelle took the blade, sliding her hand into the man's hair too and interlocking her fingers with Lazarus's in a show of oneness.

"The queen of fire has coupled with the king of sin," she purred then she slashed the spy's throat in one clean swipe. The man buckled forward, but their fingers remained knotted in his hair, keeping him upright. Lazarus took the blade and stuck it in the man's chest with a brutal stab that sent a crack reverberating through the hall. Then with his free hand, he clasped Mirelle's throat and she let him draw her forward into a kiss that proved to every Flamebringer and Vampire in attendance that they were one. His mouth on hers was possessive as hers was in return. They were two powerful forces that were now poised like cobras to strike venom into the earth of enemy lands. Together they were unstoppable. And the burn in Lazarus's eyes and the dark smile that tilted Mirelle's lips as they parted left no room for argument. They would forge victory together.

Some of the fear festering among our people faded from my hold and I nodded to North, assuring him that this was working. But the tension didn't drop from my brother's shoulders as our mother and Lazarus released the dead man and he slumped to the floor, leaving a pool of blood spilling out at their feet. They paid no more attention to him as they stepped over his corpse and strode from the hall hand in hand, drawing each other close in a show of true alliance.

"There's no going back now," I said to North whose face was growing pale. "It's the most powerful move she could have made."

"So we're just meant to accept them now?" He jerked his chin at the Vampires across the room, their celebrations growing in crescendo as everyone began to file out of the hall.

We followed on with our brothers and sisters gathering around us, the energy humming from the Flamebringers much darker than that of the rejoicing Vampires.

"Yes, I believe we are," I answered, unsure how I felt on the matter. It was an ingenious move. I'd even suggested it to Mirelle once. But that idea had come from the tongue of a man who had not known his own truth. I wasn't sure I knew my truth even now. But I did know the logic behind this marriage, and logic was something I had long relied on.

"Fuck," North cursed. "Look at them. All of them. Wait, look at *that* one. Why does he have to be hot? It makes it harder to hate him."

His gaze narrowed on a Vampire man who seemed entirely relaxed in the company of a nation that had long disliked his kind. He was swigging from a wine bottle and offering it to friends without care.

"I thought you didn't court men anymore," I commented, and North jammed his elbow into my ribs.

"I don't wish to court him," he spat. "He's a damn parasite."

"But if he wasn't?" I mused.

"As you say, I don't court men anymore," he muttered. "Not since–" He cut himself off. "Well, you know."

I did know. And at the thought of it now, my heart did something unusual. Somewhere between a tug and twist. I recalled how broken North had been by the warrior he'd fallen for two years prior. A man a few years his senior who had regularly journeyed back and forth from war and who'd declared his undying love for North.

It turned out, he had declared such a thing to several others, but before North could confront him about it, he'd died in battle. It had left my brother in a strange state that I hadn't understood back then. I wasn't sure I understood it now either. But I'd always understood one emotion even then. Fear. One of North's greatest terrors was finding himself back at the mercy of a disloyal man he couldn't escape his love for. So, he'd sworn off men. Perhaps because they reminded him too much of the past or perhaps because he believed he might find more loyalty in women. It wasn't logical, I supposed it was based on emotion. I hadn't thought to ask him about it in all honesty and now I realised what a shitty brother that made me.

"I am…sorry you went through that," I said, repeating what he'd taught me about expressing myself in such a way. It didn't quite sound like myself though. As if the line was rehearsed rather than natural. What I actually wanted to say didn't make a lot of sense but North had urged me to trust my instincts, so I blurted it out anyway. "I will cut ribbons from the flesh of any Fae who tries to place a mark on your heart in such a way again."

North's eyebrows raised then he grinned widely. "There's the psychotic truth in your words I've been waiting for. You've been on your best behaviour lately but it's growing rather dull. I don't think you're a sweetheart kind of guy, freyin."

"Then what would you call me?" I asked, wondering if there might be some clue in the label he gave me. Something that might fit me better.

"Just keep following those feelings and you'll find out. Be unapologetic. Be real. That's all you have to be, Kai."

My mind immediately darted to Everest Arcadia. Be real? Fuck, if I was real with him over her, North would not be so encouraging.

I shut my eyes, connecting my mind to Calcifiend's and finding her in her bedchamber on the White Mare ship dressed in nothing but a dark green slip that hugged her body as close as a second skin. She was speaking to Calcifiend, letting her thoughts out and exposing her inner truths to me unknowingly. My cock stirred to attention at the way her mouth moved around the words, how her nipples pressed to the silken material and her bare legs shifted against the sheet beneath her.

She was a temptation I couldn't help but indulge in. All I had to do was close my eyes and there she was. When she'd spoken to Calcifiend about me, I'd listened with rapt attention.

"Sometimes I feel strange about it. Not regret exactly but... I don't know. He was so broken. There are things about him I didn't understand, but I wish I could now. My mind can't put it to rest if I'm honest. Sometimes I dream of him. Sometimes he feels so close I can almost smell the cinders on his skin. Sometimes I wish I could smell

that scent again for real. But that's just for you to know."

Those words had haunted me since I'd heard them uttered from her lips. She thought of me and not entirely with the ripe hatred she'd always felt. There was some deeper meaning behind her words. Something close to regret. Perhaps I'd understand it better if I only knew my own emotions well enough.

It ripped me apart inside to be in the dark like this, always confused, on the cusp of grasping understanding only to miss the mark. North's teachings weren't simple. It seemed I could feel more than one emotion at once, even ones that contradicted the first.

How was I meant to figure myself out when nothing was clear cut? Especially when it came to Everest. She was the root of the most complex confusion I was afflicted with. My riddle to solve. But I never seemed to get closer to comprehension when it came to her. When I looked at her, sometimes all I wanted to do was slide my fingers around her throat and make her pay for her father's crimes. Other times, like now, I wanted to rip that thin slip from her body and rake my tongue over her tempting flesh.

She spoke to Calcifiend and my ears pricked up as her full lips moved around the words.

"What would happen if I really did join forces with the Sky Witch? Would we actually get very far in a 'free life' hunting monsters? We'd be caught eventually. Tortured slowly, executed even more slowly. What's the point in risking everything just to be chopped up into itty bitty pieces beside my enemy?"

Calcifiend clicked his tongue in answer and I mulled over Everest's musings. I'd witnessed her interaction with the Sky Witch during the battle at Pomair. I'd watched through Calcifiend's eyes and seen the truth. I knew the secrets they shared. And I was starting to form a plan that was a risky kind of madness. It might just be the second most brazen act Mirelle could make. And it might return me to silka la vin's company. A thing I craved in a way that was dangerous to my own people. But the desire for the Void was sharp enough. The Flamebringers wanted her back in our possession. I wanted her back in *my* possession. So were our two desires really that unaligned?

I thought of the dagger she'd stuck in me. I kept it in my chambers, often eyeing my name where it was etched on the hilt, thinking of the rage she must have poured into the forging of that blade. It really was a fine thing. I'd never seen a dagger as well-made as that and I felt a strange kind of attachment to it. Perhaps because of how close it had come to causing my death.

North's elbow jabbed me, bringing me back to where we were. We'd entered the banquet hall, the oval room decorated with black and white drapes and a feast laid out fit for royalty. Musicians played their stringed instruments and the Vampires thronged on one side of the room while our people kept to the other once more.

"Holy shit, my star-damned eyes!" North exclaimed, clapping a hand over his face and it only took me half a second to realise what he'd seen.

Mirelle and Lazarus were on a raised stone stage at the centre of the hall, fucking each other with wild abandon. Mirelle's dress had been ripped to shreds, still clinging to her body in pieces, but her breasts were exposed as Lazarus sucked one of her nipples while she straddled him and he thrust his cock into her from below.

A strange and uncomfortable knot formed in my gut and my features twisted at the sight before me. I felt…sad? No that wasn't quite it. Despondent? No…not that.

Mirelle gasped with pleasure, her fingers drawing blood on

Lazarus's neck before he flipped her over with a burst of Vampire speed, pinning her beneath him with a palm on the back of her neck and sinking his cock into her once more. The sounds that left them were pure animal, like beasts mating without care of whose eyes fell on them. But I knew they did care. They wanted everyone to see that this marriage was no farce. This would leave no room for rumour or muttered words about who had tricked who into this wedding. As plain as day, they wanted one another. Or at least that was what they wanted everyone to believe. The truth in it, I didn't know. But I did know Mirelle had no qualms about doing what needed to be done to ensure Pyros fell into line.

Still, I couldn't quite name my emotion around witnessing this. There was an itch in my skin which I didn't like. Perhaps this was dejection?

Mirelle yanked Lazarus's hand from the back of her neck and arched her spine, raising onto her knees and pushing back her hips to meet every thrust he offered her.

She touched a hand to her throat and words poured from her lips that were amplified around the room with magic. "We are in union. Vampires and Flamebringers alike. Dance, talk, join hands. We are one!"

Mirelle cried out as Lazarus forced her into an orgasm that everyone in the room witnessed. Their queen coming apart at the seams for a man who went against everything Pyros had once stood for. But perhaps that was the point in this; to demand a change from our people.

Lazarus followed her into his own release, cursing through his teeth and groaning with pleasure. He smiled a wicked smile, leaned down to whisper something in her ear, then scooped her up and shot from the hall in a blur of speed that left everyone turning to look for them.

The door banged shut with finality and I tugged North's hand away from his face.

"It's over," I grunted.

"Thank Aries for that," North growled.

"North… what emotion am I feeling? It's like ants in my skin."

"That's disgust, freyin," he said, dry retching a little. "You should have looked away."

"Oh," I said in realisation, wishing I had.

"I need a drink." He made a beeline for the banquet table where a sparkling wine fountain was waiting, but I only had eyes for the Vampires and Flamebringers. Because they were moving toward one another, hesitantly at first, but as hands were offered for dances, drinks were passed out and laughter lit the air, I realised Mirelle had played this game perfectly.

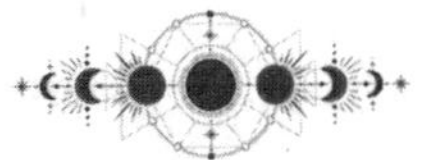

The party grew increasingly wild and when North headed for the dancefloor to grind against a Vampire woman, I decided it was time to call it a night. He'd been refusing to talk to them all evening, calling them bloodsucking leeches and sneering whenever they came close. But after he'd polished off a bottle of sparkling wine, his tune had started to change. *'They can dance well though, can't they?'*, *'I suppose it will make us stronger against our enemies'*, *'Do you think it feels good when they bite you?'*, *'That one's giving me the eye'*, *'I think I like it'*.

I'd refrained from drinking a single drop. I hadn't indulged in any alcohol since my newfound emotions had awakened. North was concerned that I might lose a grip on myself if I did and as I frequently found myself slipping into rages and breaking things without ale or wine in my system, I'd decided to follow his advice.

With North enjoying himself on the dancefloor, even letting the Vampire woman lick his neck and – shit, now she was biting him. Yes, he was definitely drunk. Maybe I should have extracted him from the situation, but when he let out a keen Wolf howl, I remembered he only did that when he was enjoying himself or running into battle. And as he wasn't doing the latter…

As I made it to the exit, Mirelle darted from her seat at the circular table where the other gang leaders were sat talking with Lazarus and his coven mates. She had returned about an hour ago in a dark red dress the colour of blood with bite marks on her arms, and the statement wasn't lost on me. Lazarus was marked in return, her fingernails having painted his skin in scratches. The Vampire nodded to me and I nodded in return.

"Kaiser Brimtheon," he spoke my name with knowledge behind it. He knew of me. So he likely knew of my importance to Mirelle too. "Come drink with us."

"I don't drink," I declined but Mirelle took my hand, guiding me to the table and giving me a look that told me I was not to leave. A magpie flew down to land on my mother's shoulder, crooning when she petted it.

It looked like my plans for an early night whilst spying on Everest Arcadia were not going to come to fruition. The feeling I experienced over that left a sinking sensation in my chest.

"We were just speaking of our shared dislike of the Reapers," Mirelle said openly and my intrigue piqued. I'd not heard her speak so frankly of that truth before.

The gang members nodded, telling of their own feelings on the matter. I'd thought all this time I was one of the few Mirelle had confided in on her suspicions of the Reapers' manipulation. But it appeared I was very wrong about that and she'd kept them well informed of our findings.

"Do they know of the monster too?" I tested the water, daring Mirelle to shut me down. To see what trust she really laid in the people at this table. Vampires included.

"We do. We have named it the eschaton star as it is a devourer of life – though we do not believe it is truly a kind of star," Lazarus answered and his coven nodded.

"You have been busy," I muttered to Mirelle and she smiled that ruler's smile of hers. She never showed her true hand, it seemed. Not even to me.

"The Reapers will not be easily overthrown," Lazarus said.

"Surely it's not even possible?" Gavrin Simmer piped up. "They're the most powerful Fae in all The Waning Lands. They hold multiple elements to their name."

Lazarus opened his hands before him, casting fire in one and a twist of air in the other. "As do some of us," he said darkly, a sinful look on his face.

Two of the five Vampires in his Coven opened their palms and showed they held two Elements as well.

Gasps and mutters broke out among the gang leaders and even I raised an eyebrow.

"Even so…" Lydia Ashworth breathed, looking to Mirelle. "Do you really believe we have a chance at taking down the Reapers? The war I believe we can win. But them…"

"They are just Fae," Mirelle said sharply. "And they are no warriors. They have no scars from battle. They do not know the inner workings of war. We have the advantage. And the Vampires will provide more to us than just their power. They have allies of their own."

I looked to my mother with curiosity, that little spark of energy in my chest having become one of the more familiar emotions to me. "What allies?" I asked.

"That is for us to announce," Lazarus cut in, giving Mirelle a firm look. "As promised."

She nodded to him. "A promise I will keep."

"Are we sure the Reapers are as corrupted as you say?" Gavrin asked cautiously.

"I've spent many years spying on them," Mirelle said firmly. "They have lied to us all. They are no more in the stars' favour than you or I. It was all a ploy for power. The fear of the stars is what they use to control us, don't you see?"

Gavrin nodded quickly. "Forgive me, I will trust you on this, Mirelle. You have always led us true. But I still believe overthrowing them will be a great challenge."

"We require the Void," Mirelle said and my eyes flicked to her, examining her expression though she gave little away.

"How will we get hold of her again?" Lydia asked.

"I will handle that," I answered firmly. "And I believe I have some other knowledge that may assist us." All eyes swung to me. "The Void has a tenuous alliance with the Sky Witch."

A clamour of surprised chatter broke out and Mirelle laid a hand on my arm, drawing my eyes to her.

"This is news indeed."

"I've been gathering intel," I said. "Calcifiend is watching the Void."

"Then you know her location," Mirelle gasped.

"Yes, and I know how we should handle this," I said and a most naturally wicked smile curled my lips. "I have a plan."

"Tell us everything," Mirelle urged and the words slipped from my lips, connecting one dot to the next, until a great and unshakeable plot was formed.

VESPER

CHAPTER SEVENTEEN

I drew in a deep breath of the crisp Stormfell air, the tension which had been lining my limbs for the past weeks lessening at last. It felt good to be making this decision for myself, even if I still wasn't at liberty to make the one I truly wanted.

But Cayde's time would come. I'd put out missives to several of Stormfell's spies in Avanis in hopes of at least discerning his true name in anticipation of my hunt, and hopefully they'd get me a location too. Being promoted to General did have its perks. One of which being the look of utter indignant outrage on General Imona's face whenever I had the displeasure of seeing it. That woman hated me to the bones of what I was and now she was forced to treat me with the respect of an equal. I took great pleasure in making certain she did so as often as I could.

The mountain paths were mostly trodden by the hooves of deer or perhaps foxes, bears, wolves, but not many Fae, and I found that suited me just fine. I'd always been more like the wild creatures of this land than its dignified population anyway.

The wind brought the whisper of my name to my ears as I walked, each syllable slipping over me, tugging on my fingertips, urging me on.

I was headed north, the song of the ether guiding me in an almost perfectly straight line towards the top of world – or at least to the tip of The Waning Lands where the magical barrier containing our continent stood.

When I was young I used to think about what might lay beyond the gleaming dome which trapped us all here. What savage continents might exist beyond ours? But as I'd grown I'd come to realise that there was more than enough savagery trapped within The Waning Lands to keep me occupied, and my questions about the mysterious world beyond it had faded.

I'd been travelling alone for two days and the temperature was plummeting the further north I headed, lingering well below freezing all through the day, the mountains shrouded more heavily with snow than their counterparts which surrounded the capital.

I wondered if the landscape up here ever felt a reprieve from the bite of snow.

I'd taken my leave without seeking permission face to face, instead leaving a note for my prince informing him that I had matters of ether to attend to and would return once they were done. No doubt he assumed I was in the cavern of lost souls with Moya and the other Sages, tending to my skills in blood magic. It was one of the few things which stood true against the Void after all, so my focusing on it made sense. But my real destination was a little further afield.

I glanced up at the sky, trying not to question or doubt, but that night in my chambers felt like a dream hazed in shadow, a reality which couldn't have truly come to pass. The morning had brought the harsh light of day down upon us and I still wasn't certain what it had revealed. But I'd given my orders and we'd made this plan between whispered secrets in the dark before the sun rose and I had no other option than to trust in our plotting now.

If he didn't come then I couldn't blame him. But Moya was right – I'd been treading this path alone for too long.

I trudged on, my boots leading me into deeper snow as the path led me into a valley between two mountains, the pair of them straining up towards the grey sky as if racing to reach its embrace first.

The cold was painful now, its teeth digging into my flesh and gnawing at my bones. I was going to have to put up an air shield soon to block the worst of the wind but out here in the wilderness I had no one to draw magic from. No way to replenish my power once it was gone. And I had a feeling I would need every drop I had once I reached my destination.

A shadow fell over me and I jerked my head skyward, squinting up at the endless blue above me, the sunlight blinding me as it reappeared and the dark blight which had passed over the sky vanished behind the western peak.

My fingers curled around the hilt of my sword and my pulse quickened to a pace I'd come to realise it only reached for one Fae.

Snow catapulted from the tip of the mountain as a Dragon so large it engulfed my view of the sky burst into view over its peak, his claws clipping it and knocking enough snow loose to cause an avalanche which came tumbling towards me in a rush.

My lips twitched into a smile as I watched the wall of snow racing down on me, magic burning my fingertips as I held it back and counted the seconds, allowing death to reach out for me, letting it think it might just get a chance to claim me at last.

I shot from the ground with barely a moment to spare, snow hitting my boots hard enough that one was almost ripped from my foot and my ascent became a spiral in which I pirouetted towards the sky.

Bastian nearly collided with me, his steely eyes wild with panic as if he had thought me dead for a sliver of time.

I used my magic to direct myself away from him, launching myself through the valley between the mountains in a rush which propelled me clear of the avalanche before I dropped to the ground once more.

The mountains clustered even closer to the path where I'd landed and Bastian was forced to circle above me, unable to land in his enormous form.

I tilted my head back to watch him, the frigid air twisting around me as he beat his powerful wings.

A heavy bag fell from his claws with a solid thump, missing me by inches and I arched a brow at him, wholly unimpressed by the move.

He shifted next, plummeting from a height of around twenty feet in his Fae form, his naked body dropping towards the snow before a vine shot up from somewhere deep in the rocky ground and snatched him into its grasp.

A thrill raced through me at the sight of him wielding his magic, the act so forbidden and so pure all at once. I'd never seen earth magic wielded like he did it, with practice and care, its intent to aid instead of hurt. My only real experience of the power of Avanis had been in battle and I found far more appreciation for Bastian's magic than I did for wooden spears and jagged stones shot at me with ill intent.

He prowled towards me, his body thick with muscle, the ink and scars which marked his flesh a map I wanted to learn the secrets of.

"If you like, I can just leave my clothes off," he said, stopping before me so that I had to raise my chin to meet his gaze. "That way you can stare for as long as you like."

My smile darkened, a tendril of lust coiling from him as he looked into my eyes. "Go ahead. I've always wondered what happens to a man's cock if it gets frostbitten."

Bastian barked a laugh, stooping to retrieve his pack from beside me and pulling it open to take his clothes from it. "That would be a crying shame," he said. "Especially when you've been having such sordid thoughts with it in mind."

I scoffed lightly, my eyes now on his back as he turned it to me while he dressed. The tattoo spreading across his dark skin stared back at me, a sky full of stars falling down on a depiction of The Tower from a tarot deck. I'd seen it before and asked him about it too, not that he had given me a real answer. But out here in the wild parts of the world I found myself wanting to know more.

"Tell me why you inked The Tower into your flesh," I demanded, my tone brokering no refusal and more than enough to make most Fae quiver into submission.

But Bastian wasn't most Fae.

He stood, yanking his trousers up as he turned to me, though he left the stays at his waste undone and they sank low on his hips, threatening to fall again.

"Tell me what The Tower means to *you*," he suggested, his voice a growl of warning which told me this was a wound he wasn't fond of poking.

I considered him then shrugged a shoulder as I gave him his reply.

"The Tower is…danger, crisis, destruction."

"Do you happen to a have a deck with you?" he asked, not giving my answer any attention.

"Funnily enough, I do." I took my own pack from my shoulders and opened it, rummaging in the bottom of it until I located the intricately-decorated tin which housed the deck I carried with me and pulled it free.

"Shuffle it," he instructed and I arched a brow at him before doing as he'd asked then holding the deck out for him to pick from.

Bastian drew The Tower, flipping it over for me to see before handing it back. "Again."

I shuffled the deck once more and this time he took the top card, revealing The Tower before returning it to me and getting me to re-shuffle it so he could draw it three more times. The card he pulled never changed.

"How are you doing that?" I asked, the corner of my lips twitching as I suspected some trick but he only released a low growl in reply.

"If you think I'm somehow fooling you then go ahead and draw for me." He stepped back and I had to resist the urge to move forward and reclaim the closeness between our bodies.

I eyed him suspiciously then shuffled again, doing so twice to make certain the deck was thoroughly mixed before drawing a card from the heart of the pack.

The silver border that edged the card flashed in the sunlight as I revealed The Tower once more.

"Since the moment I was born, every time I try to read a deck, every time someone else tries to read one for me, The Tower reveals itself first."

"That's…odd," I said slowly.

"It's fate," he corrected grimly.

"Fate? You think yourself marked by The Tower?"

"It's inked into my skin, isn't it?" He took the card from my fingers and scowled down at it.

"You put that there yourself," I replied flatly.

"I did. When I finally gave in to the inevitability of its hold upon me. The Tower marked me as a bringer of ruin and it did its work through me more thoroughly than you can even imagine. In every way you might think up. I have destroyed every good thing, every bad thing, every *real* thing which has ever come close to me in one way or another. It made me a monster in war and marked me with its curse in life."

"Some things need destroying," I said, reaching for the card, my hand falling over his as he refused to relinquish it.

"Perhaps," he admitted, his voice soft and rough, the wind threatening to snatch it away from me. "But I grew weary of destroying everything a long time ago. And there are some things I do not wish to taint with the weight of my corruption."

His silver eyes met with mine and took them captive, his gaze piercing my soul in a way no other's ever had.

"The Tower doesn't just mean destruction," I said slowly. "It can mean liberation too."

My fingers moved over his and he turned his hand to capture mine, the tarot card flattened between our palms as he drew me closer.

"Would you have me liberate you then, spectre? Is that why you keep drawing me back to you?"

"Maybe," I agreed, stepping closer to him so that the heat of his skin enveloped me, his powerful body looming over my own, the scent of him on every inhale, my wants for him on each exhale. "Or perhaps I know that I am worthy of nothing short of destruction and I'm in need of your help to ruin me."

"Be careful what you wish for."

My gaze fell from his eyes to his mouth and I found myself stalling there, aching for something I shouldn't have wanted. Magic thrummed in my veins, the place where our hands were connected buzzing with it and without thinking it through, I lowered my walls and let my power reach out for his.

Bastian's reply was instant, as if his magic had been holding back by a thread which snapped at the demand from mine.

A gasp parted my lips as his power rushed into me, the heavy weight of his earth magic coiling through my limbs and making every piece of my body hum with awareness. This was more intimate than a kiss, more treacherous than any other move I'd ever made against my prince, more dangerous than I should ever have allowed myself to endure. But it was the first time I had felt truly alive since my sisters had been ripped from my arms too.

"Vesper..."

Bastian turned away from me sharply, his hand tugging free of mine, the tarot card which had been trapped between us fluttering down to the snow behind him.

"Who was that?" he growled, his shoulders rolling back as he tensed in anticipation of an attack.

"You heard it?" I asked, the ether crying my name louder in reply.

Bastian shot me a confused look, his hand curled into a fist.

"Can you *still* hear it?" I pressed because the ether was still calling out to me but he wasn't reacting to it anymore.

"No. What was that?"

"It's the reason we're here," I said, reaching out to take his hand again, my magic racing up to meet with his but his gaze hardened as he pinned it on me and this time he didn't allow his power to merge with mine. "There's another corrupted keystone nearby. Or at least that's what I assume the ether is guiding me towards. I figured I'm the least likely suspect to be sent on a quest to save the world from darker forces of nature, but maybe that's why they chose me for the task. No one would ever suspect me."

"Or perhaps it's because you're one of the most competent Fae I've ever met. And the ether knew well that you were capable of achieving anything you might set your mind to."

"Careful, that sounded like a compliment," I teased.

"I already told you, spectre, you're the one who needs to be careful around *me*."

Bastian returned to dressing himself and I said nothing more, my eyes trailing over his tattoos, his scars, the stories I had no right to ask about yet wanted to hear him tell.

"Can you locate any caverns beneath the ground here?" I asked when he had pulled a warm coat on and finished lacing his boots.

"I can try." Bastian knelt down, scooping mounds of snow aside as he hunted for the frozen earth beneath. Once he found it, he laid his palm flat against it and closed his eyes as he sent his magic roaming into the dirt and rocks below.

The silence stretched as he hunted but I held my tongue, my eyes searching the sky and trailing the flight of a solitary bird which was passing over the mountains.

"There are no caverns beneath our feet," Bastian said finally, standing once more. "But there is something near the top of that peak." He pointed towards the western mountain and the ether screamed all the lounder inside my head, urging me closer, confirming his assessment.

"How easily can you replenish your magic?" I asked him, eyeing the climb with distaste.

It would take us hours to make it up there on foot but if I could fly us up there then we would be done all the sooner. The slope was too steep and inaccessible for Bastian to easily be able to land us in his Dragon form but air magic could be manipulated more precisely than landing a beast as big as a barn.

"More easily if you let me spend some time with that pretty necklace you so like to wear," he replied.

"We'll see about that." I stepped up to him and took his hands in mine before wrapping us in a net of air magic and hurling us into the sky.

Bastian cursed at the sudden propulsion, his grip moving to my waist even though I had hold of him well enough without him needing to pull me tighter.

It was tempting to drop him and see if he screamed but as he dragged me against his chest I found myself content to stay in the cage of his arms.

Bastian called out directions but I didn't need them. The ether was screaming now, my name a wretched lullaby which it was intent on singing until I forced its silence.

I followed the call, speeding towards the side of the mountain, a rocky ledge coming into view between the snow and a small crack beckoning us to slip through it.

We landed softly and the ether fell deadly silent. This was the place.

Bastian made to release me but I gripped his jacket and dragged him closer as I reached for him with my gifts and tugged at his desires.

I was expecting him to bombard me with another sordid fantasy but the vision which came to life within my mind wasn't of us tangled in wicked knots beneath silken sheets. It was of open skies and the wind beneath his wings, the stars shining brightly as he dove into the dark with no destination in mind and nothing to stop him from just flying on and on forever.

The soft brush of his fingers through my hair snapped me out of the daydream and I blinked up at him as he silently wiped a tear from my cheek, his gaze mirroring my old hurt back at me.

"Your prince may not have been the one to take the butcher's knife to your wings but it was his kingdom's rules which gave the motivation to those who did it to you. He and all of his rotten brethren deserve death for that single crime alone."

I swallowed down the words I wanted to give him in answer to that. I may have resigned myself to my treason but that didn't make it easy to speak it aloud. I was still a part of that kingdom, still a cog in its corrupt machine, and still trying to imagine any other way that life might pan out for me without it.

"Let's go," I said simply, stepping back from him with my magic overflowing and my old wounds stinging.

I moved to the jagged entrance to a cave which had likely seen very few Fae in all the millennia it had stood there, then led the way into the dark with a beast at my back and the ether urging us onward.

Our footsteps echoed in the darkness as we crept into the tight space, the light snatched away as soon as we turned the first corner, though at least the walls opened up a little.

"It would be real nice to have fire magic around about now," I muttered, squinting into the nothingness ahead and Bastian turned a dark look on me.

"That has to be a joke? You do know that Smoker flames have nothing on Dragon Fire? Mine burns hotter, faster, further, longer. It can melt most known substances from metal to comets, forge weapons of great power, shatter the shields of–"

"Prove it then," I taunted and he stilled, eyeing me dangerously and I couldn't deny the thrill I got while locked in this predator's gaze.

"You're baiting me? You really are a foolish little mouse."

"Squeak, squeak," I agreed, the edges of my lips tugging upward as a growl rumbled through his chest.

A blast of Dragon Fire tore from his fist so suddenly I flinched, the heat washing over my frozen limbs for an all too brief moment before it hurtled away into the darkness ahead, leaving the imprint of what it had illuminated onto the backs of my eyes.

We were in a cavern which opened up before us with a wide, yawning hole at its heart.

I stepped up to the edge of the hole and Bastian reached his hand out, letting more flames fall from his fist to spiral down into the darkness and out of sight.

Deep beneath us, something noticed.

This was nothing short of madness but once again I found myself striding straight towards the unhinged option.

I took hold of Bastian's arm as the flames died out and together we stepped into the abyss.

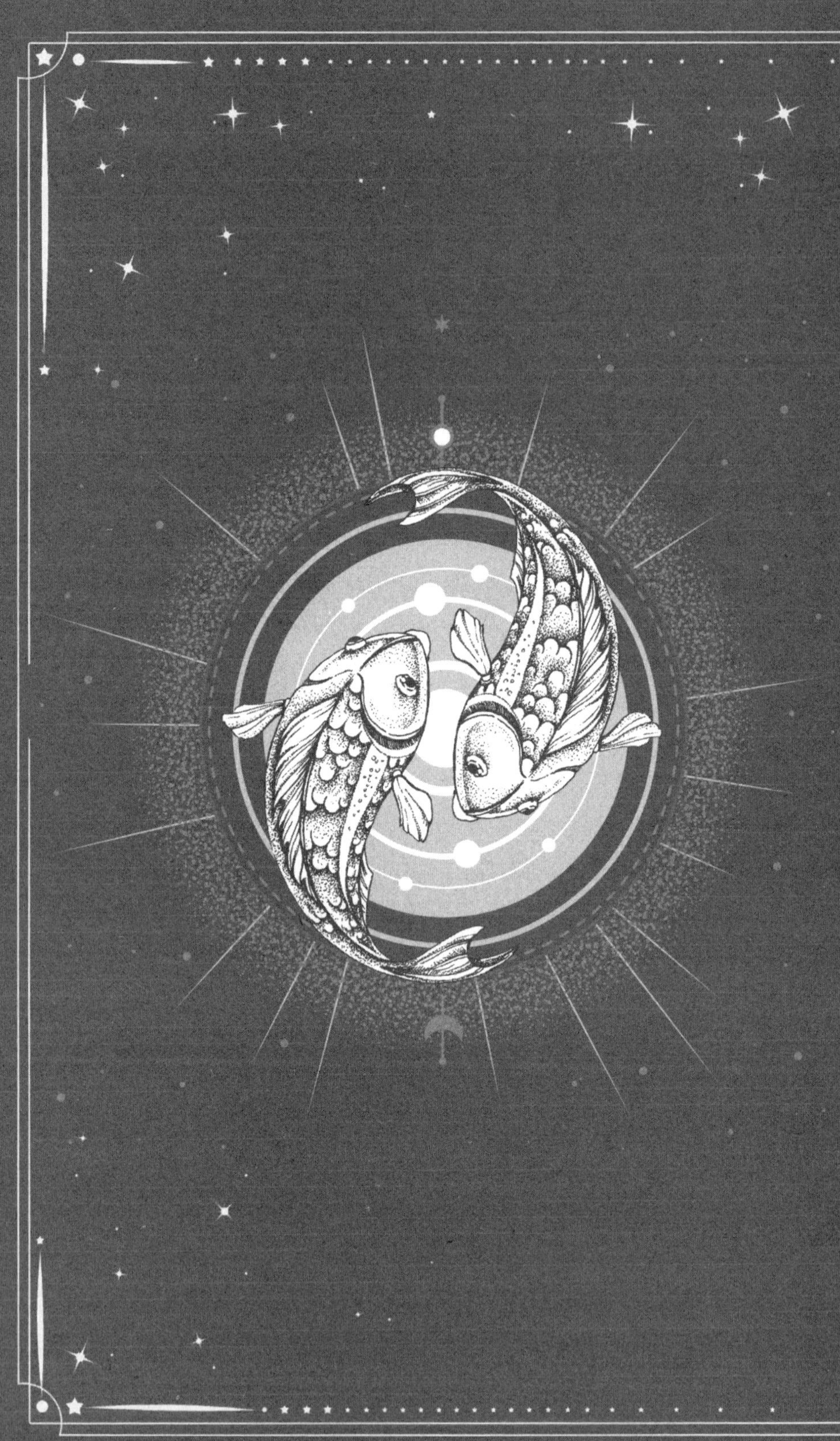

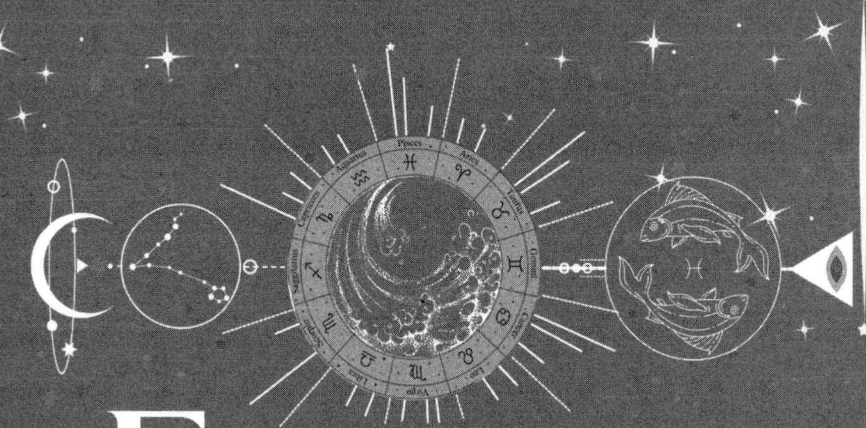

EVEREST

CHAPTER EIGHTEEN

The Astral Sanctuary came into view over the hilltops, gilded bronze by the morning light. We'd anchored the ships and Father had handpicked a group of thirty warriors to travel on foot and horse to Leergaith in Pyros.

Excitement grew among the Cascadians around me as we closed in on the Reapers' sanctum where Galomp's uncle was waiting to commend us for our victories. He was going to be disappointed when he heard of our failure in Stormfell.

My heart thudded out of rhythm as I closed in on the Astral Sanctuary. Were the Reapers here just like those at Never Keep? Did they know of the monster that lurked beneath the fortress?

I couldn't trust a single one of them anymore. Not even Harlon. My dearest friend. He'd turned his back on me and chosen them in my place. The sting of his rejection burned all the deeper at the sight of one of the Reapers' holy places. The twelve-sided building jutted up toward the azure sky, lurching toward the hidden stars among the vast blue. It was beautiful, but was it just a facade that hid a terrible lie?

My father had commanded I travel within a litter, carried high like a boast to the Reapers. I'd refused, stolen Galomp's horse from the White Mare's holding cells and ridden off ahead of the group toward our destination. It hadn't been long before I was flanked by Father's warriors again. Ransom was among them, now riding close on my right, but rarely uttering a word to me.

We hadn't said much to each other at all since he'd witnessed me killing Jacobin and Agatha. I wasn't sure what I'd say even if he tried to whisper to me of it. Ransom was no ally. But we were bound by that secret now. And I couldn't help but wonder where his conscience had grown from. Thankfully, when Father had discovered their bodies, he'd fallen for our ploy and believed the Flamebringer girls had shifted into their Order forms and killed them.

Ransom, for all his flaws, was not the cold-blooded killer I'd expected him to become. He'd wanted to see those girls safe just as I had. And knowing that my half-brother was not all bad when I'd seen him as a villain for my entire life, was a strangely hard pill to swallow.

I nudged the sides of Galomp's mare, Lalakin, to urge her into a trot and the group followed, picking up the pace around me as we drew closer to the Reapers' place of worship. There was one thing that urged me onward, one single thing that caused an escalating hope inside me.

Here, Galomp awaited me alongside his uncle. A man of the Magistrine, whose power was absolute. He could bring news of the monster that was threatening our continent to the rulers of our nation at long last. And once a plan was decided, I could travel with them to Never Keep, Void all those who stood in our path and help the

Cascadian leaders to cast that wicked beast to ash.

So, between the days of endless travel and the sour mood that had been left by our retreat at Pomair, I finally had something to hold onto again.

When we reached the paved white path that led through a row of elm trees to the Astral Sanctuary, we guided our horses to the surrounding woods, dismounted and tethered our animals in place. Father tied his black stallion Karkinos beside Lalakin, walking close to me and resting a firm hand on my shoulder.

"Stay close," he commanded, nodding to his warriors in a silent order and they all flanked us.

Up close, I could see the intricate designs in the sanctuary's walls, the effigies of the twelve zodiac signs staring down at us in judgement. Even Pisces didn't seem so welcoming, the two fish, glaring at me with a harshness I'd never felt from them.

A shiver tracked down my spine as we stepped through an archway into a rectangular courtyard of ragstone. Gold-cloaked Reapers milled around it, many turning our way in curiosity while our people bowed in deference.

"Praise the stars," one called to us.

I could have sworn I felt all of their eyes on me beneath those gold hoods, burning deep. They knew exactly who I was and something in my bones told me that was no good thing.

"And praise to those who tread their destined path," we all answered in return, though the words tasted like a slick of oil in my mouth.

"We have come to meet with the great Donavon Wader of the Magistrine," Father said to them, spewing charm as he bowed again. "And to ask the stars for guidance while we are here of course."

"You must pray to them first," a Reaper woman said, pointing to the open door of the Sanctuary. "Then and only then, may you ask for more."

"Of course." Father bowed his head a third time then pushed me onward through the courtyard, climbing the three steps into the sanctuary. The chamber was a grand space with zodiac statues flanking each of the twelve walls. Cushions were laid out before them for Fae to kneel and candles lit the space in an ethereal glow. Incense thickened the air, the scent of it reminding me sharply of Never Keep and the horrors I'd witness there. At the centre of the sanctuary, a group of Reapers were singing in a low hum, a prayer to the stars that reverberated through the walls and made my heart shudder.

I finally had room to breathe when Father parted from me and headed off to praise the current ruling sign of the sky while the rest of his warriors followed to say their own prayers.

Ransom followed suit but I drifted away toward the far end of the chamber where an open door led out of the sanctuary, revealing a courtyard beyond and a stone building that must have been part of the Reapers' quarters. There were no Reapers watching and with everyone kneeling, falling into murmured pleas to the stars, I slipped away without notice. I passed through the courtyard and found the door to the building cracked open. Inside, I crept through a hallway where paintings of watchful eyes peppered with stars stared at me from all sides.

My hackles rose, my instincts making magic tingle at the fingertips of my right hand. But as I pushed through a door at the far end of the corridor, a breath of relief fell from my lungs.

"Galomp," I called as he turned to me between two mighty book shelves, the expansive library around us stretching up three floors.

He stood with an older man who I had only ever heard descriptions of. Donavon Wader was nearly half Galomp's height with a carefully clipped grey beard and bright blue eyes. His left arm was missing from his battle days and there were a few faint scars across his nose, but instead of the hardness I was used to seeing in battle-worn warriors, there was a warmth in his eyes that was entirely inviting.

"I'm Everest," I announced, walking toward them.

"This is the girl?" Donavon asked his nephew excitedly.

"Oh boy, indeed it is, uncle." Galomp took hold of Donavan's wrist and led him toward me.

I bowed my head, unsure how to address a member of the Magistrine but Donavon waved a hand at me to dismiss the formalities.

"None of that," he said, breaking away from Galomp and drawing me into a hug. He was short enough to bend me over to do so and I stumbled in surprise. "You sent me a fine donkey, Miss Everest. I am more than grateful."

"Just Everest," I corrected as he released me. "And you're welcome."

"You're not 'just' anything." He appraised me, his eyes bright and shining. "You're the Void."

"I am." I raised my chin, proud of that very fact but I was glad when Donavon didn't start fawning like the rest of Cascada.

"Well, my nephew here says you've been hoping to talk to me. I would be more than happy to lend my ear to the saviour of our people."

"I'm no saviour. Not yet anyway," I said quickly. "But I might be, if you take what I'm about to say seriously." I stepped closer to him, glancing over my shoulder and casting a silencing shield around us.

Donavon frowned in surprise. "You speak of something not even the Reapers can hear of?"

"Yes," I hissed and I glanced at Galomp who nodded encouragingly. Not that he knew for certain what I was about to say. "It's about the Reapers you see…"

"Go on." Donavon's frown deepened.

"They're not what they seem," I whispered despite my silencing shield. "They're harbouring something at Never Keep. A monster. A vicious creature intent on destroying Fae kind. They've roused it from some unearthly place and now it wants to devour the land."

"A monster you say?" Donavon gasped and I hurried on, hopeful of his reaction.

"Yes, and that's not all. This beast is wielded by the Reapers. I saw it do terrible things. Killing students on the orders of the Reapers. They're responsible for it. And I believe..."

"Yes?" he pushed.

"That the Reapers are not what they seem. I believe those at Never Keep and perhaps many more, perhaps all of them in fact, are using their power to control us all." The blasphemy spilled from my tongue like acid and Donavon's face paled.

He stepped away from me, looking to Galomp in confusion, then back to me with something closer to fear. "How can you speak such words?" he rasped, clutching the collar at his throat. "It is a strike against the stars themselves."

"But the monster–" I started, stepping toward him but he cut over me in a cry.

"Whatever the Reapers are doing, it is the work of the stars!" He retreated again, bumping into Galomp who was frowning from me to his uncle.

"I know it's hard to hear, but you have to listen," I implored. "I saw it with my own eyes. Galomp saw it too." I turned to my friend and Donavon looked up at him, shaking his head in refusal of his nephew's involvement in this.

"What do you have to say about this?" Donavan hissed. "Surely you don't share the same sentiment as this girl?"

"I do not think Miss Everest is a liar."

"Foolish boy," Donavon sighed then looked back at me in anger. "Do not play tricks on my nephew. He is a good boy. Do not slip poison in his ear."

"I didn't," I growled, anger raising the hairs on the back of my neck. "I know what I saw. And if we do nothing, that monster will destroy us all."

Donavon shook his head several times, backing up again. "You may be the Void, and by the stars, I respect your position in this war. But I pray for you and your soul that you may beg for forgiveness from the heavens for your lies."

"I am not lying!" I argued. "If you would only listen, I can tell you what I saw in detail. There is no denying it."

"Enough!" Donavan's hand trembled as he pointed at me. "That is enough of this. Do not bother me again with this drivel. I will not speak a word of this to anyone, and be thankful of that Miss Everest. But you best hold your tongue."

I hissed like a cat as he hurried past me and lurched for the door to escape me, disappearing down the corridor and leaving me there with Galomp.

"I will talk to him," Galomp said. "Do not worry, Miss Everest."

"Don't put yourself at risk," I said, but Galomp lumbered out too and it seemed there was no stopping him. "Kaské," I cursed.

I stood between the mahogany bookshelves with a heavy breath falling from my lungs, my shoulders dropping and a stone falling into the pit of my stomach.

I'd been waiting on this moment for so long, I'd never considered he would turn me away. The devastation of that reality caught me in its hold and I couldn't break free.

The words of that terrible monster reverberated through my mind as I recalled leaping into the abyss where it lurked.

"Soon, I will step between the boundaries of this place and that. Then your world will know me in the splintering of the earth, in the spitting of every fire, in the strike of the howling wind and in the flooding of the four lands."

I shuddered at the way that dreaded voice had sliced through my skin and spoken through my bones. I'd been so wrapped up in being the Void, I'd convinced myself the Magistrine would handle the monster headed our way. But now that possibility had shattered before my eyes and I was faced with the fact that the terrible being was coming and no one was stepping forward to stop it.

"Poor, poor lonely gal," a familiar voice crooned out from between the bookshelves and I tensed in horror. "I didn't have to hear those words falling from ya lips to know that conversation didn't go so well."

"Mavus?" I snarled, disbanding the silencing shield around me and stalking towards his voice.

"Lemme guess what ya said to him…" he purred from behind a bookshelf to my right but when I sprinted around it, there was no one there. "You want someone to help ya with ya little problems. You thought the Magistrine was the answer. That they'd listen to the revered Void and answer your every request." His voice came from the left this time and I raced in that direction, hunting the gaps between the bookshelves in fury.

"Come out!" I commanded. "Come and face me for what you did."

"What I did?" he asked sweetly, his voice now sounding from far across the library. "I only did what I always do, lass. I made a living out of dealing with secrets. It's my finest trade, truth be told. There was no choice in it for me."

"No choice?" I spat. "You sold me out. I could have been killed!"

"Killed?" he laughed, the wildness of it carrying from my left again. I ran that way, a growl in my throat as I hunted for the bastard of a trader. "You're the great and wondrous Void, Everest Arcadia. People would trade more than a pretty penny to keep you alive. Nah, I didn't try to kill ya. I freed ya. I cast ya into fame and glory, just as you always told me you wanted. Now, how can you go punishing me for that?"

"Show yourself!" I yelled, sick of chasing shadows.

"I saw ya speaking rather passionately with that Magistrine fella. I bet you were tryin' to convince him that those Reapers ain't the pious, good Fae they preach to be, weren't ya?"

My answer was nothing more than a growl. How could he possibly know that? Was I really so readable?

"Ah, so I was right," he said with a smile in his tone, his voice now coming from behind me instead of in front. I spun on my heel, certain he was using magic to throw his voice around this library, but my flesh was too fuelled with adrenaline to give up.

I turned to the shelf beside me and blasted it with a shot of ice that punctured it and the subsequent five shelves next to it, sending books scattering into the aisles.

Mavus darted into view three shelves away, leaning down to look at me through the hole, his green eyes sparkling. "This rage is poorly aimed, lass."

I sent another blast of ice tearing through the holes and Mavus darted away. I didn't run to him this time, changing tack and raising myself up on a pillar of water to hunt him from above.

"You and me both know the truth of this place," his voice called from further into the library and I willed the water to carry me that way. "Who else shares that sentiment with ya? Who else are you gonna turn to?"

I launched myself forward, eyes locking on him at last, his blonde curls hanging about his shoulders, his handsome face wearing a smirk. I used the water beneath my feet to propel me down and I slammed into him, knocking him to the floor and casting an ice blade in my grip which I pressed firmly to his throat. Rage rippled through my skin for what he'd done, but something held me back as I stared into his eyes.

"You're hesitating," he rasped, his hand landing on my side with the promise of a counterattack.

"I wouldn't bother trying anything," I hissed. "The Void won't allow it."

He frowned in intrigue as he noticed the power ebbing from me, its roiling magnitude spilling into his flesh and rendering his magic useless. His throat bobbed, a flash of something in his eyes telling me that he had not expected to end up at my mercy.

But I still didn't slit his throat. I'd held so much anger since he'd sold my name to the ears of my enemies. But now he was here beneath me, giving me that relaxed look of his that said he feared nothing, and I was conflicted.

"You're all alone again, doll. No friends. Not one. But I never stopped being ya ally in all this. I only gave up your secret to elevate ya to greatness. And it worked, didn't it? I even tipped off your papa about your situation with the Flamebringers and got the whole of Cascada sent out to rescue ya."

"You can't have known what would happen once you shared that information," I growled, but I had to admit he was making a strange kind of sense. Especially for a man like him who never acted predictably. It was easy to picture Mavus coming up with such a far-fetched plan and truly believing it would work, but that didn't make it right even if it was the truth.

"Okay, okay, maybe I went about it a little cock-handedly..."

"A *little* cock-handedly?" I snarled. "You went rogue. And I get the feeling that's you through and through. Always ready to sell your so-called allies for a few coins."

His gaze darkened and his mouth pulled down in a savage sneer. "Nah, that ain't the cut of me, lass. You're wrong there. I make moves that ripple through these here Waning Lands. I may not belong to one of the four territories, and a nomad I surely am, wandering here and there, but it all plays its part in this great war. I matter in it, see? I am crucial to it in ways not you nor anyone has yet to notice. But that's exactly where I like to be. In plain sight, yet never truly seen."

"I should kill you."

"That you should. But I got a feelin' fate ain't done with you and I yet. You owe me, when you think about it. For this golden life of yours."

I pursed my lips. "Yeah, well this golden life isn't so golden after all."

"No?"

I shoved off of him, falling onto my ass at his side and pressing the tip of the ice blade to my finger in irritation. Maybe I was just a sucker for his bullshit, or maybe my anger had never truly belonged to Mavus, but either way, I didn't find I wanted his death now that it was offered to me.

"No. What are you doing here anyway?" I clipped, refusing to drop my ire despite the fact that it was obvious I'd decided not to kill him.

"Well ya might just be glad ya didn't kill me before you found out." He reached into his crimson coat pocket and took a letter from it, offering it to me.

I accepted it curiously, finding the seal already broken as I unfolded it and stared at the words on the page.

Dear Ever,

Firstly, I'm sorry. With all my heart and with everything I am, I owe you the greatest of apologies. I should never have tried to force your hand in coming with me on that battlefield. You were right about everything. Your fears were well founded and I see that now, so I desperately wish to right my wrongs.

I don't know who else to turn to and I hope this burden isn't too great to bear, but I've discovered a secret that will lead to the certain destruction of The Waning Lands if action isn't taken.

The monster we both witnessed at Never Keep is being brought into this world upon the blood moon in a ceremony led by the Reapers. I've been stealing the tomes they've been studying to prepare, reading as much as I can through hours of the night before returning them. It seems the blood moon's magic will allow the beast to pass from its world into ours. There are even prophesies that speak of it. One named the Luna Portas described the great summoning power of such a moon allowing 'reverent gateways to open' and 'otherworldly summons' to occur.

It must be stopped, Ever. I've learned so much of its terrible desires and the chaos it will reap from our land.

I believe you are the answer. I have read the Elysium Prophecy over time and again, the one that lays beneath the Keep, hidden from the eyes of the four nations. It must be the truth, buried deep by the Reapers for their own gain. I believe it is speaking of this moment.

'Seek the Void, for it shall guide the
chosen ones to their glorious path,
a weapon of purity, and the gift of null.
In a web of lies and cruelty, fate will favour
the peacemakers of destiny.'

The Reapers are surely responsible for the 'web of lies and cruelty' so with the gift of the Void, you can unite the 'peacemakers of destiny.'

I've learned all I can of the Void's powers from the books kept in the Reapers' library. You would not believe the knowledge in these tomes that they keep from the rest of the world. Magic we cannot even fathom. The Void power is spoken of in many prophesies and even great philosophers gained whispers from the stars about it. The power you hold is greater than you know. It's believed by some to be power imbued with starlight itself and it can counter the greatest of magic.

I trust in you Ever. I witnessed what you did on that battlefield in Cinder Vale. You cut off the magic of the four armies, thousands upon thousands of Fae rendered powerless by your hand. So I propose, you and only you, could have a chance at Voiding the magic of the blood moon.

Please, Ever, you must do this, if not for me, for you, for Cascada. Find anyone who will assist you. Anyone you trust who might fit the description of a 'peacemaker of destiny', bring them to Never Keep on the night of the blood moon. I will meet you at the ten towers upon the hour the moon rises and lead you to the chamber where the ceremony will commence.

Forgive me for placing this responsibility on you. But I know if anyone in The Waning Lands can do this, it's you. My Ever.

Domerna sil oceania,

Harlon

P.S. Be careful. Solomon has sent a group of Reapers to capture you. I don't know what he'll do if he gets his hands on you. Be sure he never does.

My hand trembled, my eyes devouring those words once, then twice to be sure of them.

"I took the liberty of reading that," Mavus announced smoothly and I snapped my head up to look at him. "Fine, fine magic Harlon had put on that letter too, but I'm a master of breaking magical seals. It's what keeps me so well-informed in this land."

"So you know," I exhaled, the weight of Harlon's words pressing down on me. I couldn't even muster the energy to be angry at Mavus for prying in the face of this deadline. The blood moon… When was that? I knew it was soon, but was it weeks, days?

"I know everything there is to know. I learned of the monster before this here letter, but now I know it is comin' to me great land to destroy us all and I can't be havin' that."

I stared at him, finding a sudden ounce of hope to latch onto. "You'll help?"

"Aye, lass. I'll help ya. I've been itching to have a stab at the Reapers for some time now and it looks like my name is being called by the blessed stars at last." He clutched the bundle of amulets at his throat and kissed them all, smiling darkly.

I nodded quickly, shifting closer to him, knowing I couldn't fail Harlon. Because of course I forgave him. The thought of him alone among the Reapers at Never Keep made my gut tug and I shot a prayer to Pisces to watch over him.

"Alright, that makes two of us then," I said, a rush of adrenaline racing through my blood. "But who else can we–"

The door opened across the room, the squeak of hinges telling of someone's arrival. I didn't know what the Reapers might think of finding their library in disrepair so I shoved to my feet and planned to make a quick escape.

"We'd better get out of here," I whispered to Mavus as I slinked to the end of the aisle, chancing a look at the door. There was no one there so I crept toward it at a fast pace, about to dart out of it when a hand caught me from behind.

I was spun into the arms of a red-haired Reaper woman and within half a heartbeat, I knew I was in trouble. Vines blasted into me, launching me back against the wall and pinning me there as more vines grew from the wall itself, coiling around me in a wild knot.

"You fool -knock her out!" a male Reaper crowed from behind the redhead. "The Cardinal Reaper wants her alive."

Harlon's warning echoed in my head and I cursed myself for not being more prepared. A snarl left my lips as the Void tore from me in a potent wave, the vines dissolving as the redhead ran at me with a syringe in her grip. The vines dissolved around me as I stole their magic away and I darted aside as the redhead tried to stab me in the neck with the needle.

My heart rioted as I spun around and raised my hand, casting a huge wave which sent them both flying back into one of the aisles.

I froze them in place just as Mavus came running toward me, looking to the Reapers I'd attacked.

"You gotta kill 'em, lass," he said wickedly. "They've seen us both here. And they could spin a web of lies about this attack. For your sake and mine, they gotta die. I'll do it for ya if ya can't bottle it."

I turned the ice encasing the Reapers to sharp blades that dug deep into their flesh and killed them fast, a sneer twisting my features.

"I can bottle it," I said coldly, meeting Mavus's gaze.

"Indeed, it seems ya can." He tilted his head as he regarded me, like he was seeing the power I possessed and taking stock of it. "Well lass, how's this for an idea – I'll travel with ya onto your next destination and we can have a little chit-chat about how we're gonna handle that monster. The blood moon is just a few weeks away and there's no time to spare." He offered me his hand, a deal waiting to be struck. And though I knew Mavus's deals were wrought with trouble, I was in need of allies who were willing to place their life on the line for the sake of the world. Mavus didn't exactly strike me as a 'peacemaker of destiny' but he would have to do.

I slid my palm into his and he smiled like the cat who'd gotten the cream. And there I went, following some instinctual madness, taking chances on my enemies again.

BASTIAN

CHAPTER NINETEEN

The dark consumed us but it had nothing on the oppression caused by the weighted power in the heart of the mountain.

Vesper led the way onward through the endless tunnels. We had to have been trailing through them for hours already and I could tell the caverns made her uncomfortable.

But for me, being beneath the ground was as natural as breathing. My home had been carved into rock and soil, my childhood memories rife with explorations of tunnels not unlike these. Though of course my years of captivity beneath the ground had tainted the comforting feeling I'd once found in places such as this. Not that I thought this particular cavern could have been considered homely under any circumstance. It was dank, and the stench of dark magic fouled the air even if I couldn't communicate with it the way my dark-hearted companion did.

The Faelights we'd cast to allow us to see showed little beyond the slate-grey walls around us, so my focus fell all too often on the way my sweet spectre moved.

She was a born seductress but it wasn't simply the sway of her hips or the curves of her body which held my attention. It was the way she prowled towards danger without so much as flinching.

"Were you born without fear or was it beaten out of you?" I asked her, though the answer was likely to deepen my hatred for the people she claimed as her own.

"Fear is a pointless emotion unless being actively used to avoid death," she murmured, not looking back at me, her pale pink hair brushing the base of her spine as she tilted her head to look up at the tunnel's roof.

It was more words than I'd gotten out of her in the last hour and I knew it was because the cries of the ether were close to deafening her, even if she hadn't spoken of them. They were calling out to her so powerfully that I could have sworn I heard them myself now, even without my magic connecting to hers.

"You're certain this is the right thing to do?" I asked, not for the first time and she ignored me, not for the first time either.

"You should stay here."

Vesper didn't so much as glance at me as she strode around a corner and out of sight, leaving me to slam into the air shield she'd erected to stop me from following.

Bitch.

"I thought we were in this together?" I yelled, my voice echoing through the caves and hiding the sound of her footsteps as they disappeared ahead of me. By the time the echoes had faded, so too had any further sign of her.

I cursed her, slamming my fist against the unrelenting air shield, wondering why the fuck she'd just abandoned me here after bringing me so far.

There was only one answer which came to me and I snarled at the thought. Was she trying to protect me? After everything that had led us to this place, was she truly choosing this moment to attempt self-sacrifice in place of following her own selfish desires?

I snarled, striking the shield once more before turning my focus to the wall at my right and placing my palm against it. Magic poured from my fingertips and the stone sighed as it melted beneath my touch, becoming sand which spilled down to the ground, creating a path for me to follow.

Except, when I took a step closer to it, I struck solid air again, Vesper's shield tightening like a snare as if she'd known what I would do and had already instructed her magic to thwart me.

The mountain groaned, rocks shifting and re-settling, the change I'd made to this ancient infrastructure causing unknown stress to the make-up of this entire place. It had been foolish to do such a thing but I'd long since accepted that this woman made a fool of me regularly.

I considered my options. I was powerful, but even my own ego had limits and I could admit that I would burn out very quickly if I tried to wield my earth magic over an entire mountain. And the both of us would be crushed down here long before I could get us free of it.

I dropped to one knee, placing a palm to the ground, reaching out with my magic to–

Vesper screamed somewhere in the tunnels ahead and I shoved myself upright, her name tearing from my lips.

I threw my weight at the air shield then threw my magic at it when it failed to shatter.

Vines slammed into the invisible wall, pounding on it with the full force of all I was, cracks forming across its surface as I yelled her name again.

The sound of her voice echoed away from me through the tunnels and her scream was cut short abruptly.

The air shield shattered but not because of me. Her hold on the magic had been fractured.

"Vesper!" I roared, breaking into a sprint, diving around the turn she'd taken and only stalling for a moment as I found two more paths awaiting me. I didn't know which she'd taken but my magic was roaring beneath my skin and I only had to brush my fingers against the closest wall to feel the echoes of her passage and know she'd taken the righthand path.

I ran down it, my boots a continuous thunderclap which resounded off of every wall.

I took turn after turn, my Faelight barely keeping pace with me, my shadow lengthening to the point where I could hardly see the path within it, but I didn't slow.

I stumbled out into a cavern with the keystone at its heart, the stone pillar carved with the faces of Gemini on one of its three sides, the scales of Libra on the next and Aquarius presumably on its rear.

But I only had eyes for the woman bleeding on the floor, crushed herbs scattered beside her. Vesper's pink hair pooled around her, stained with blood from a wound at her temple which was bleeding too much, her skin paling unnaturally.

I ran to her, dropping to my knees and hauling her into my arms.

"Can you hear me?" I demanded though she lolled unresponsively in my grasp.

I tore a strip of cloth from my shirt and pressed it firmly to the bleeding wound on her temple then sealed it firmly in place with my magic, making a clay which dried against her skin.

"Vesper," I snarled, gripping her jaw as her head rolled aside. "Open your eyes."

My heart was racing to a frenzied pace, panic rushing for me as I gripped her more tightly, all the things which lay unsaid between us simmering in the air. All the reasons I had to despise her, the truth of my infatuation with her, all of it caught in my throat and threatened to choke the life out of me.

I grasped the collar of her fighting leathers and jerked them open, pressing my fingers to her throat, feeling for a pulse which came all too faintly when I finally located it.

"I'll get you back to Stormfell," I told her, drawing my hand away but it caught on a chain around her throat, the vial of blood which hung from it falling against my fingertips.

Power slammed into me at the contact, a rich and violent power which spoke to some deep part of my soul but was nothing like the magic of my element.

Without thinking, I took a dagger from my belt, my hand seeming to know what to do, that power guiding my actions while I fought to understand them.

I cut into the pad of my own thumb, blood welling and dripping onto the little vial then spilling onto her throat.

I watched transfixed as it raced across her tanned skin, rolling up to her jaw before dropping from her neck and into the tangles of her hair where it met with the blood that had risen from her wound.

I jerked upright, my spine straightening, my head snapping back, my hold on Vesper almost failing as a rush of power swept into me.

I gasped as it flooded my mind, the roiling intensity of it so potent I could hardly remember who or what I was.

But the weight of her body laying too still in my arms brought some semblance of what was happening back to me and a simple word clawed its way free of my throat.

"Please."

Power roared around me, *through* me, consuming everything, my vision blurring, muscles tensing. It was ecstasy unlike any other, it was sinful and punishing and achingly beautiful and it had taken possession of my soul.

I felt myself falling into the endless well of it, the draw so intoxicating that I didn't once consider trying to refuse its call.

The crash of a fist striking my jaw sent me tumbling back into myself. Not all the way, but enough for me to look into a pair of storm grey eyes which were wild with furious terror.

"Let go!" she shouted, her bloodied fist ready to strike me again.

My lips parted but no reply came. The power calling me back to it, the oblivion it promised tempting me away. I so wanted to lose myself to it, wanted to let it have me and be done with the world and all the suffering it had offered me.

Vesper hit me again but I hardly felt it. I wasn't there anymore. I was drifting away on a current which led to nirvana.

The rush of dark magic dragged me deeper, claws which should have been painful sinking into my soul inch by inch but leaving bliss in place of agony. I would never return from this. I never *wanted* to return from this.

Onward the magic raced, with me its willing prey, dark pressing in all around me, a silence so thick it held weight over me.

A deep growl summoned my attention and from the lost confines of myself I spied something shifting in the dark, something foul and ancient, something hungry and desperate and utterly insatiable.

A pair of bright and piercing eyes flashed open, spearing me in their gaze, promising my annihilation. I was trapped before a beast of myth and magic so terrible the sight of it anchored me in horror, unable to run or fight or so much as yell a plea for my worthless life to go on.

"I see you," the voice of chaos snarled, its words ricocheting through every piece of me. It spoke no language I knew but somehow I understood it, the voice resounding through the fibres of my being.

Cold lips snapped me out of the dark a heartbeat before I could be consumed by it.

The world rushed in on me as Vesper kissed me harder, her hands clasping my face, nails biting into my jaw, teeth taking hold of my bottom lip.

And then there was only her, and I was grasping her waist and hauling her closer, my tongue parting her lips, a growl echoing from my throat into hers. She was my one light in an endlessly dark sky, my spear of hope which I clung to even now after her betrayal. She was all I had and as I devoured her mouth with my own I found she was all I wanted.

Vesper gasped as I pushed up onto my knees, kissing her harder, tasting desperate tears which had tracked over her full lips.

I kissed her like she was the only tether which held me in place on this lonely planet and I knew that was the truth of it. She had become my only reason to continue on. All I'd ever known and loved was lost to me but this broken, grieving soul was a mirror of my own. I was the reflection of her pain inside and out. We were wrong for each other in every way but the fit of her lips against my own couldn't have been more perfect. Her kiss lit me up and cast the shadows away from my soul, her light burning through me and awakening the darkest desires of my heart.

I had been fighting it until that kiss. I didn't want to need her the way I did; I didn't want to hunger for her like a starving creature in her absence, but that kiss was all I needed to prove to me that I was already lost to the spell of her and there would be no breaking it.

I was hers.

In all the darkened corners of my being I had become so close to nothing at all, but she was summoning me forth and making a claim on all I was. I wasn't even certain she had meant to make it. But clarity found me in the taste of her lips against mine and I gave up all efforts at resisting. She had pulled me out of the dark. And I was her monster in servitude for that.

"You came back to me," Vesper gasped against my mouth, her fingers knotted in my hair as she opened her grey eyes and took me captive within them.

"I would have let the dark have me," I confessed, running my hand down the side of her face. "There was something monstrous waiting for me within it. But you hauled me free."

Her eyes bounced between mine, her brow pinching in a frown.

"Ether isn't sentient," she said slowly. "What do you mean?"

My chest rose and fell as if I'd been fighting in battle for hours, my hold on her tight as if I feared she might escape me, though she made no attempt to retreat from my grasp.

"The magic drew me under as if tugging me through water. I felt like I might drown but couldn't summon a single reason why I wouldn't wish to do so."

"Ether isn't something you should toy with. You were a fool to dive into it for my sake."

A growl vibrated through my chest at the way she dismissed her life so easily but she wouldn't allow me to divert the conversation from its topic.

"Tell me all of it," she demanded.

"Just as I thought I would be lost to the pull of that torrent of magic, something spied me in the darkness. It told me it saw me. Its rage dug into the depths of my bones as it peered at me."

"And then?" she hissed, her face pale and fingers biting into my flesh.

"Then you pulled me free."

Vesper cursed, pushing out of my arms and standing. "I don't think our work here is secret any longer," she said.

"And what does that mean?" I asked, standing too, missing the heat of her body against mine.

"Nothing good," she muttered, her attention moving to the keystone. "But I managed to fix the flow of power in this place before it overwhelmed me."

"I found you on the verge of death," I growled, my focus moving to her temple but where I had bound her wound with earth magic I found only dirt and blood staining her hair. The wound was gone. The ether had healed her once more.

"Looks like my luck hasn't run dry yet," she said. "But yours almost did."

"I was saving *you,"* I replied fiercely, her accusation rankling at me.

"I've never needed saving before." Her walls were up once more, her anger over that kiss clear in her eyes. "Besides, I was the one who rescued *you* in the end."

"You did," I agreed, grazing my thumb over my bottom lip where the sting of her teeth still lingered in the best possible way. "Your methods were unorthodox."

"Lust has long been a weapon at my disposal."

I closed the distance between us, gripping her jaw tightly and forcing her gaze to meet with mine.

"That kiss was no petty lust, Vesper," I uttered, daring her to deny it. "You will not dismiss it as such."

She swallowed, her throat brushing against the side of my palm, her eyes falling to my mouth.

"No," she breathed, her fingers curling around my wrist as though hoping to keep me exactly where I was. "It wasn't lust."

Her admission surprised me but before I could press her for more of the truth, she withdrew, pushing my hand from her skin and turning her back on me.

"We'll be missed if we're gone much longer," she said, stalking away into the dark. "We should return to Stormfell before they link our absences."

I frowned after her as she strode away but she offered me nothing further and I was left with no other choice but to succumb to her demand.

The secret which had passed between us remained in that cavern but I didn't simply leave it there. I took the brief taste of her heart with me as I licked it from my lips and I made certain to savour it as I followed her into the dark, knowing now that I would follow her endlessly. No matter what twisted paths she might take.

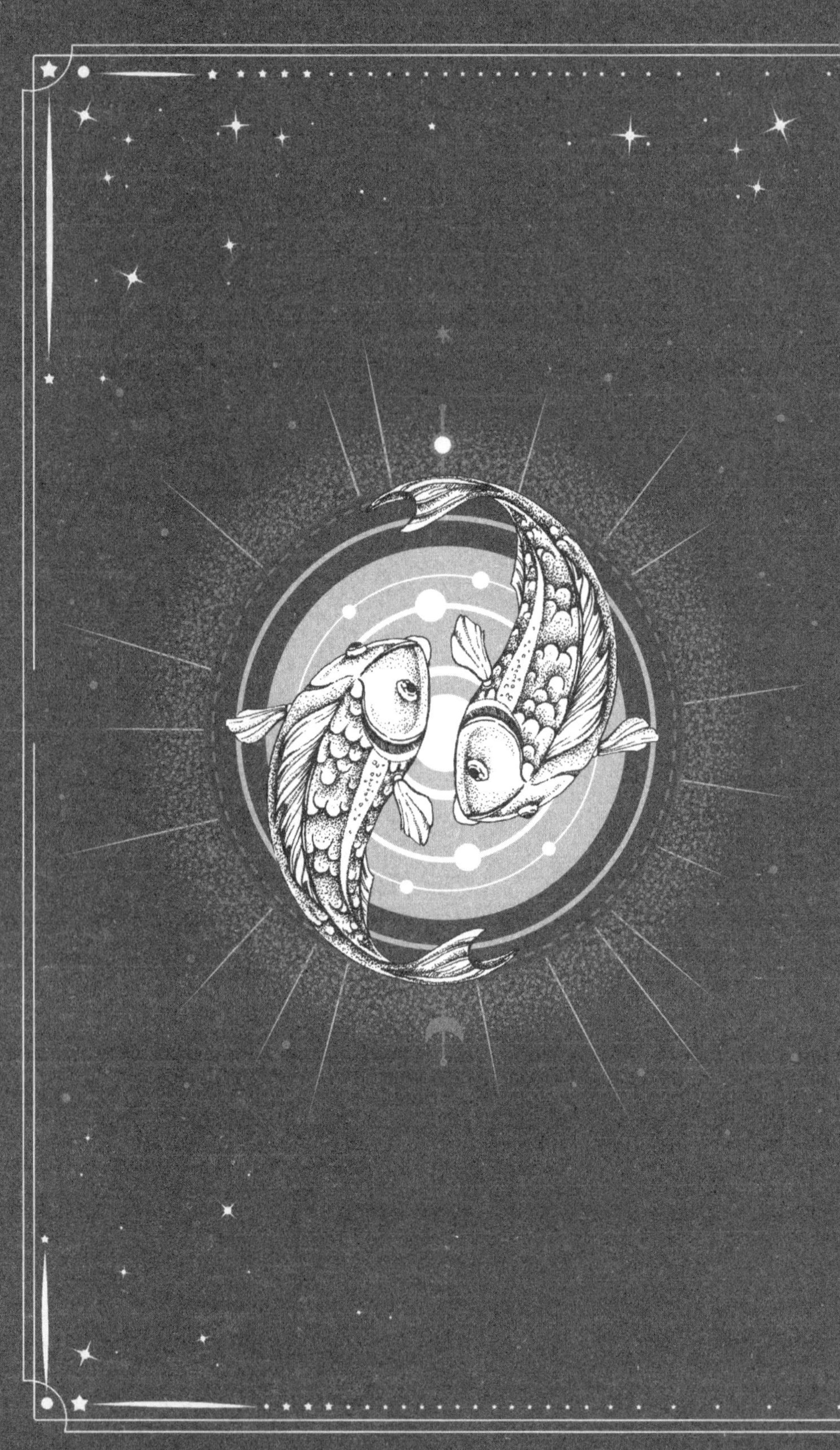

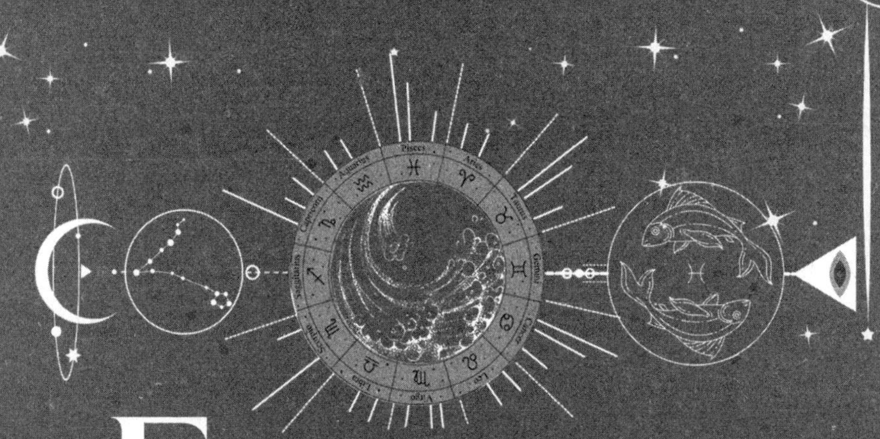

EVEREST

CHAPTER TWENTY

Mavus followed our fleet onboard Wandershire, slipping onto the White Mare now and then during our journey toward Cinder Vale. We laid our plans in secret under the guise of me doing trades with him and Mavus kept the Cascadian warriors content as his workers were able to offer fresh food, fine meads and supplies. No one questioned his presence, Wandershire well-known for following armies around to earn some coin.

Father had finally decided to conquer Pyros fully and seeing as there was still an Avanis stronghold at its heart occupying Cinder Vale, that was where we were headed. If we couldn't find the citizens of Pyros then we could at least find ourselves a battle with the Stonebreakers. And as Mavus and I couldn't do anything about the monster until the blood moon, I was happy to seize a victory in the meantime.

We were closing in on Cinder Vale now, navigating the canals that drew us all the closer to our enemies and a true battle. After our failure at Pomair, I'd been practising daily to control my Void better. If I focused, I found I could steer the power here and there, curving it around my people and sending it onward where our enemies would be waiting. It certainly wasn't perfect but my accuracy was improving the more time I spent on it.

Mavus liked to watch my drills, helping to line up Cascadian warriors, splitting them into groups of allies and enemies in various orders to help me hone my skills. Father was too busy laying his plans for the coming attack to pay us much attention and he hadn't questioned the amount of time I spent with Mavus, perhaps assuming we were friends or perhaps not really caring.

I'd decided to keep Galomp in the dark about the plans I was weaving with the trader, not wanting to include him in a traitorous plot against the Reapers. I couldn't live with myself if I led him to his death. So I'd encouraged him to ride with the cavalry once more since his uncle had decided to return to Cascada with news of our 'victories' in Pyros.

I hadn't sent Galomp away without a token though, a silver brooch I'd forged now proudly worn on his breast that named him as my personal Sentinel. That would stop anyone daring to breathe a nasty word in his direction. And it had quieted his apologies about his uncle's reaction to my request. He'd parted from me with the words 'I believe you, Miss Everest. Even if the rest of the world does not,' and I'd wondered if I'd made a mistake in keeping my distance from him. But Galomp was too pure for this mission; it was too deadly a task to rest on his shoulders.

After my latest practise session with the Void, I retired to my quarters with Mavus swaggering in after me, a glass of water grasped in his hand which he glugged freely from.

He slung himself in an armchair, kicking his feet up on a footstool and Calcifiend landed on his arm, promptly receiving tickles under his chin. I cast a silencing shield before bringing up the subject that both of us were itching to discuss.

"It's all well and good plotting to destroy this monster, but two of us isn't enough to pull this off and you know it."

"That I do, lass. We need a team of spirited Fae. The kind who would walk into their death knowingly for the chance to expose the truth."

I'd been thinking about the Sky Witch ever since I'd received Harlon's letter, sure she would take on this task. But I didn't know how to tell Mavus I was open to working alongside a Skyforger. "There is someone…"

"Who's that?" His eyebrows lifted, a keen curiosity burning in his green eyes.

Trusting this man was not something I did easily. I was willing to place my neck on the line for attempting to stop the monster coming to this world but Mavus had proven he would sell my name for the right price. What was to say he wouldn't do so again? But he did seem to be in on this plan whole-heartedly, though I didn't yet understand why.

I ignored his question and asked my own instead. "Mavus… why are you really doing this? You don't strike me as the kind of Fae to place his life on the line for the greater good."

"Are *you* doing this for the greater good?" he threw back and I frowned, considering that. My reasons were selfish as much as they were for others. I wouldn't see Cascada fall because of that monster beneath Never Keep. But I was doing this for Harlon too.

"Harlon isn't safe among the Reapers. Now that he knows about their lies, I think he might leave with us after we deal with this monster."

"And then you'll kiss and run off into the sunset together," Mavus said through a teasing smile, but it wasn't cruel.

I blew out a breath of amusement, thinking on that. Once upon a time, I'd have jumped at the chance to run away with Harlon. But now…

"So you want to go rescue your boyfriend," he taunted. "And you want to know what's in it for me? Well let me tell you. It ain't what you'll be hoping to hear, I'm afraid. I have no boyfriends to rescue meself. No. What drives me is different than most folk. See, I'm a real pursuer of chaos, lass. I like to shake the tree and see what falls out." His eyes flashed menacingly. "And that Reaper tree has been producing the finest fruit around here for far too long. I'd like to see what happens when those fruit start to fall. Mayhem is what I thrive on. It's what makes me burn inside, do you get that?"

The air shivered with the intensity of his words, the truth of them ripe and undeniable.

"So what's to keep you loyal to me during all this? What's to say you won't sacrifice me to save your own skin if we get in too deep? You may like chaos, Mavus, but I know you value your life above mine. So say I go through with this with you by my side, how can you assure me you won't turn on me?"

He considered my words, stroking Calcifiend as he did so before finally giving his answer. "Perhaps I can't do that, lass. Does that mean you won't go through with this anyway? If you have those doubts crawling through your mind, will it stop you on this path now you've begun down it? Truth is, you need me to pull this off."

"You need me too," I pointed out. "Without the Void, you won't get past the front gates of Never Keep."

He grinned wickedly. "That's where the trust lies then, ain't it? You and I need each other. So shall we stop nattering about death and deception and lay our plans good and true? I fancy saving the world, that's all you need to know."

I nodded slowly. "Fine. I can likely bring one other Fae to this plan. She's powerful. Together, we've done the impossible, we can do so again. But I'm not going to name her until she's agreed."

"Can you trust her?" he asked.

"I can."

"Good," he purred. "Get her agreement and then she and I can meet, how's that for a plan?"

"That's going to be a challenge," I murmured. "But if I can find her, I think she'll join us."

"I could always find her for you?" he offered in a purr.

I said nothing in reply.

"If we don't trust each other, this will never work, lass," he urged.

"It's up to her if she wants to offer her sword to our plan. She can introduce herself to you if she chooses this fate."

"Then find her. And do it sharpish," he said in a growl, pushing out of his chair. "And if there's any others you can think of who might fit the bill, you'd best bring them too. We'll need traitors a-plenty to achieve this."

"I'm not a traitor," I growled. "I'm trying to protect my people."

"Traitor to the Reapers. That's my meaning, doll." He chuckled low in the back of his throat. "You're a little touchy about that word though. What other traitorous acts have you been committing lately?"

I pursed my lips, ignoring that question and asking him one instead. "Who will *you* bring to this mission?"

He released a dismissive breath. "I wouldn't trust the Fae of Wandershire with this. They'd sell our names for coin quicker than a mouse can squeak for cheese."

"They learned from the best," I jibed and Calcifiend flew to land on my shoulder, nuzzling my cheek.

"Ha, that they did, lass. That they did." He saluted me and sauntered to the door, glancing back as his hand rested on the handle. "We'll strike upon the blood moon regardless even if it's just you and I and Harlon against that beastie. You'd better be ready to shake the tree, Everest Arcadia. Because once the fruit starts falling, there's no going back."

The bellow of Father's voice cut through the air, amplified by magic and making the ship tremble with the force of it. "The time is nigh! All warriors assemble on the decks and dive into the canal!"

We'd been waiting for this moment since Father had sent word of his plan to all legions and now it was here, adrenaline burst through my veins. This was our chance at our first true victory, and I had to prove myself out there. Cascada was counting on me.

I grabbed my armour from where I'd hung it on the wall, the dark green metal shimmering with all the new lacquers I'd applied to it. I'd attempted a mix of my most tested concoctions, hoping that one wouldn't cancel out another, and I supposed I might find out now. This metal wasn't just fireproof, it was stronger than iron, it could provide warmth in freezing temperatures and was even light enough that I could swim in it.

I pulled on the armoured plates, positioning them over my clothes and tightening my boots before strapping my newly-made sword to my hip and racing for the door. My weapon was forged of the best steel I could buy from Wandershire, the metal tinted green to match my armour and the hilt carved into the shape of Typhon. It wasn't perfect and it didn't feel as right in my palm as my dagger had, but I could always improve it. I just wished I'd thought to take my mother's sword back from Kaiser when I'd killed him.

Mavus opened the door wide, noting my armour with an intrigued eye, perhaps weighing up the price it might fetch. "I like to observe the battles sometimes, can I join ya?"

"Do what you like, you're a free man aren't you?" I answered with a smirk then we raced onto the deck together.

The White Mare had weighed anchor within a thick forest that rose up the canal banks on either side of us and Wandershire was nestled among the trees. At our rear, the Cascadian fleet had stopped too and warriors were leaping from gangplanks into the blue water. They slipped away like arrows darting beneath the surface, using magic to propel themselves downriver towards our target.

"I'll see ya shortly, lass. I'd better not let the big boss man see me hounding you about," Mavus muttered then raced for the other side of the ship and created a wooden bridge that led him back to shore.

Father was directing Fae into the canal close by and I marched his way, my wild curls blowing back over my shoulders in the breeze. I felt Calcifiend hiding among them, quickly disappearing into their masses as I made it to Father.

"You'll travel with Ransom. I'll be close behind," Father said. "You remember the plan?"

"Of course," I said fiercely.

"I've got a cunning plan this time and a secret or two up my sleeves." He grabbed the back of my neck and placed a kiss to my forehead. "Get going, child. Let's claim Cinder Vale and herald our victory to the sky." He released me, leaving my skin buzzing with the warmth of his affection before he shoved me toward Ransom who was standing next to the closest gangplank. His serrated Merrow scales glimmered against his skin, the dark blue colour of them catching rays of sunlight and highlighting the sharp spines that lined his arms and shoulders. My hatred for him had made me disregard the beauty of his Order. He was a fierce creature in all senses, but he was a rare and magnificent thing too.

Ransom grabbed my shoulder, yanking me toward the gangplank. "After you." He smirked like a heathen and I remembered exactly why I despised him as he threw me straight over the side of the ship. I gasped as I hit the water, kicking up to breach the surface.

Ransom slammed into the water beside me, splashing me with a huge wave before surfacing with a gasp. "It's fucking freezing."

"Scared of a little cold, Ransom?" I taunted.

"Shut it, runt," he tossed back, but somehow we both smiled.

Mavus launched himself into the water from the river bank, swimming over. "Fancy carrying a little limpet to Cinder Vale, lass?"

"Come on then," I encouraged Mavus, drawing him closer and he wound his arms around my neck, latching onto me with his ankles. I wielded the water beneath us to keep us afloat. He was damn huge. And it didn't help that he was gripping my head for support.

"Aren't you that trader guy?" Ransom said in realisation.

"Mavus Angelico, pleased to meet ya fella. You're Everest's brother, am I right? The one who got a lugfish stuck on his cock?"

Ransom shot me a glare that could have burned through steel. I smiled sweetly.

Mavus leaned closer to Ransom to whisper in his ear, causing me to lean sideways in the water. "Did ya like it a little bit? You can tell me the truth, fella. I can see in your eye you liked the way that fishy felt."

"Shut your damn mouth!" Ransom swung a punch, but I chose that moment as the right one to dive, wielding the water to drag Mavus and I under the surface with Calcifiend clinging tightly to my hair.

Mavus let out a laugh that became a stream of bubbles trailing behind us but as I guided the water over us to allow an air pocket to form, his laughter became clear once more. We sped down the canal at a tremendous speed, the feeling of the water against my skin like a balm as it recharged my magic.

We were heading straight for Cinder Vale, a secret army gliding under the water's surface. When the canal took a sharp right, I knew we were approaching the city, that the warriors ahead of us would already be arriving, enacting our plan.

The crash of a thunderous waterfall made the water vibrate around me and I rose to the surface quickly, chancing a look at the way forward.

The Cascadian warriors were pouring over the dam which must have been mended with earth magic since the battle, the canal spilling down into the city where the Avanis stronghold had formed. I caught sight of the new palace made in the place of Mirelle's structure of glass, this one a regal stone design, a monument to Avanis's victory. But it would not remain theirs any longer.

I pulled us underwater again, not even needing to guide us to the powerful waterfall that was tearing down over the edge of Cinder Vale and spilling our warriors into its belly. We were yanked over the edge and Mavus's arms locked tighter around me as we free-fell, my stomach lifting, adrenaline soaring through my blood. It was five seconds of pure excitement, then we were flowing through a river again, only this time Cascada was guiding it. The warriors split it into several forks and I remained on the central one that speared its way through the destroyed houses like an arrowhead, tearing toward the citadel which had been rebuilt.

The first wave hit the walls and it sounded like a crack of thunder echoing through the water.

I launched myself skyward, propelling myself out of the water with Mavus still clinging to me fiercely and I cast a ladder of ice ahead of us on the wall. We hit it with force, but I clung on and Mavus slipped from my back, snatching hold of the rung beneath my feet as water frothed up beneath us.

Pyros may have gone underground but Avanis spies must have been watching us travel this land. So the Avanis forces had retreated into these walls and awaited our attack but they hadn't known when we would strike.

I climbed fast, racing for the top of the wall while warriors did the same on all sides, hundreds of our people sprinting for the top. I spotted Ransom climbing one to my right, his muscles tense with exertion.

The Void hummed inside me, ready to be unleashed. This day would be ours. No more mistakes.

We made it to the top of the wall and I looked down at the swarm of Avanis warriors that were waiting beyond.

Explosions tore out around us as our enemies shot cannonballs at us from below, but as their magic tried to join the fray, I guttered it out. I balanced on the top of the wall with all eyes finding me, recognising what I was as my enemies' power faltered and they raised weapons instead.

Hundreds of Cascadians dove down to attack, using water to guide them to the ground. But there, pitfalls and hidden traps opened up before the enemy lines, sending our people to bloody deaths.

Ransom stepped close on my right and a line of Father's best warriors filed up beside him. On my left, more of them gathered close as they fought to defend me, blasting away any cannonballs or arrows that came my way.

I couldn't draw my focus from Voiding the warring Avanis soldiers below, but something told me Mavus was no longer close by. My suspicions were confirmed when I spotted him running over a wooden bridge which he cast beneath his feet from the top of the wall to one of the buildings ahead. He shot a look back over his shoulder, meeting my eye and winking before slipping away through a roof hatch no doubt in hunt of loot. Even in the midst of battle he only had a mind for coin.

I focused back on my enemies and noticed the way Avanis were moving as they retreated, side stepping, avoiding secret traps laid beneath their feet. They knew where each of them were hidden, luring our warriors towards them as our people advanced.

"Freeze the ground!" I cried, and my command was taken up by the warriors around me as they realised what was happening too, all calling out to our comrades to aid our warriors.

And as Cascada moved in and the Void echoed out through our enemies, I knew this time we would not be stopped.

SEPTA

CHAPTER TWENTY ONE

The walls surrounding us shook and quaked as water crashed against them from outside.

I backed up, though where I thought to run to was beyond me. Most of the Fae who were unable to fight had fled Cinder Vale the moment we'd realised the Void was coming for our newly-claimed stronghold.

Most. But not me.

I had ignored my Earl's urgings to flee, instead taking up position in the heart of the castle he'd built here, unable to bear the thought of running while knowing he fought against such devastating odds.

Alestro had been thrown into one of the mechanical beasts which tore tunnels into the ground and returned to the safety of Avanis so that the secrets still locked within his mind were protected. But for reasons unknown to me, my Earl had allowed me to make my own choice in the matter of staying here. It had been clear he'd wished to see me safely away from the fight but I'd refused and he'd accepted my decision.

So now I stood with no company besides August who muttered curses into the shadows and kept himself firmly on the far side of the chamber to me. He stayed clear of the window but I did not. I couldn't. I had to *see.*

My heart pounded in my chest, its frantic pace matching with the destructive force of our warriors as they fought with sword and axe, refusing to back down even as their power over the earth was stolen from them time and again.

Earl Tarlord was among them, holding fast in the front line, cutting down Raincarvers by the dozen, their blood coating him from head to toe.

I didn't dare blink for fear I might miss the swing which ended his life, terror burning a path through me as I awaited the fate which seemed so inevitable but hadn't come calling for him yet.

My eyes roamed all parts of the battlefield within the citadel and as I scoured the towering wall which ringed the castle I stood within, a gasp stalled in my chest. There she was. The Void.

Wind tore her long and curling hair away from her face, her features impossible to distinguish at this distance but the light glinted off of her green armour as she stood with her arms raised, that terrible power pouring from her. Cascadian warriors were positioned all around her, defending her from every attack that shot her way.

I watched in hope as a legion of our Pegasuses and Manticores swept through the air towards her, keeping high to stay out of the line of her attack. Their bellows and whinnies of pain cut the air in two as her protectors targeted them with spears of ice and blasts of water, knocking them from the sky one by one. Their numbers fell from a hundred to fifty, to twenty, twelve, eight, three–

The last of them were almost upon the Void, a Manticore's serpentine tail whipping out to strike at her and hope blossoming in my chest like a spring bloom. They were almost there, they'd made it, they were going to end this and finish her and–

The Void raised her head, her hands following the motion as her attention locked on the pair of Pegasuses and the Manticore who were moments from taking her life. Power ripped into them and their Order forms were torn away, the warriors shifting against their will, their animalistic bellows turning to the screams of Fae as they tumbled naked and helpless from the sky.

I flinched as their bodies were dashed against the wall, their blood leaving a trio of stains beneath the feet of the beast they'd come so close to ending.

The Cascadians cheered, the Void joining the celebration before returning her focus to the battlefield where my people had been gifted a few short moments of being able to wield their magic once more.

Earl Tarlord had made the most of his power in those fleeting seconds, and my lips parted in awe as I took in the bloody trail ahead of him where at least thirty Raincarvers had been impaled upon spears of wood which had shot up from beneath their feet. More still were scrambling to escape a giant chasm he'd opened behind them and as the Void stole his magic away again, he ran into battle, swinging his axe and cutting into the floundering forces before him, taking full advantage of their distraction.

It was a sight to behold. But it wasn't going to be enough.

I moved closer to the window despite knowing the risk in it. Magic tingled against my palms in case I needed to defend myself but there was little else I could do from here besides watch and I was enraptured by the horror before me. I'd heard tales of war my entire life but never once had I been close enough to witness it like this.

"Step back, you fool," August hissed.

"I can't," I told him plainly because it felt like my heart was out there on that battlefield, carving a bloody path through our enemies while risking all to do so.

An explosion tore the world apart and I screamed as I spotted the giant wave surging across the battlefield directly for us. My cries cut off abruptly as water crashed into the window and shattered it, sweeping me into its grasp before I could so much as attempt to run.

I was swept off of my feet, broken glass from the window slicing my arms and legs, tearing my gown and herding me towards the wide staircase at my back.

I kicked and fought, vines bursting from my hands as magic tore from me but I was tossed like a leaf in a whirlpool, unable to see beyond a rush of bubbles which burst from my throat in place of a terrified scream.

The vines I fought to catch myself with failed to grab anything and I was hurled down the staircase in a vortex of motion, all directions blurring together, all sense of my place in the world lost.

The last of the air in my lungs choked its way free of me, my chest burning as I fought the urge to suck down water.

I crashed into something solid and coughed, water searing into my lungs, my death rushing for me too fast. But then the water washed over me and away, dropping me to the stone floor and leaving me in a sodden, hacking lump at the base of the giant staircase which led to the room I'd just been standing in eight floors above.

I choked and gasped as I forced the water from my throat, my fingers clawing for something to grasp so that I might pull myself upright once more and somehow closing on a warm, dry hand.

I blinked up through matted, saturated strands of blonde hair and found a man I thought I recognised, his skin kissed by the sun, his smile warm, though turning cunning.

"Who–" I began but my question was cut off by a bark of wild laughter that escaped him.

"Well, well," he murmured, his face melting, shifting, features rearranging, body expanding. "Thank you very much for this gift."

I screamed as I stared up into the face of Earl Tarlord, the impossibility of the transformation striking terror into my soul even as my mind battled to understand what was happening.

Incubus. He was an Incubus and he'd taken the form of my most desperate, passionate, secret desire. He had stolen the face of my Earl right from the hidden, aching chambers of my heart.

The blade came for my throat so fast I had no hope of escaping it, my scream the only thing faster than its approach and my horror the last thing I was likely to ever know.

But before the stranger could carve my throat apart with that wicked blade, a figure fell down the stairs with a startling cry and collided with him, the knife knocked aside and gifting me an unexpected chance at escape.

I scrambled upright, pain lancing down my leg as I moved too fast, the wall cold at my back.

"My apologies, Earl," August gasped as he fought to get off of the Incubus who had stolen the form of our leader and horror lanced through me at how easily he'd been fooled by this charlatan.

"That isn't our Earl," I barked, magic blossoming in my fingertips.

August frowned at me, his lips parting on words which were cut from the air with a wicked slash of the blade the Incubus still held.

I screamed as blood poured from August's throat, my eyes locking with the familiar green of my Earl's, my death sparking in them. But I couldn't die. I was the only one who knew this Raincarver had forged this wicked plot, the only one who could warn my Earl of the danger posed by our enemy.

A wooden blade formed in my fist and the Incubus barked a laugh as he glanced at it. That was all the distraction I needed. Because I was no warrior, but I had long understood that my strength lay in cunning where others favoured brawn.

The wall at my back melted as my hand pressed to it, the stone parting under my touch, allowing me to fall backwards through it.

The Incubus bellowed a curse in my Earl's powerful voice, his dagger speeding through the air for me. But I'd already stumbled into the room beyond, and the stone wall reformed between us at once. Dully, I heard the thump of the blade striking the now solid wall but I was already sprinting away.

Pain daggered up my leg and into my hip, the punishing pace I set far too much for my brittle bones to endure but I didn't slow for so much as a beat.

My magic wasn't powerful but it was more than enough to turn every door I passed through to stone, blocking the way at my back, feeding me more time to escape.

Nothing but battle and bloodshed lay beyond the walls of the city but I had no choice other than to run for it.

The wooden dagger I'd forged to distract my enemy was still held tightly in my fist and as I stumbled around another corner, I paused to cut the sodden layers of my skirt off at the knee, the weight of my dress too much to bear.

Scraps of green fabric fell to the ground and I raced on, ignoring the agony in my limbs, the thunderous sounds of war beyond the walls, everything fading to insignificance because I *had* to warn Earl Tarlord of my folly. I had to tell him about the Incubus the Raincarvers had sent to infiltrate our people.

If they managed to execute such a heinous plan then I knew all of our people would be doomed. The false Earl would betray every one of them before anyone suspected anything, leading them into a trap I couldn't fathom the depths of.

Heavy footsteps pounded stone at my back and fear spilled through me like oil dripping over rock. How had he managed to catch up to me?

I couldn't move as fast as my pursuer. I couldn't fight him off if he caught me. I could only run and keep running and ignore the pain which was begging me to stop.

I turned another corner then threw myself at the closest wall, magic parting the stone for me as if it were a curtain, my heart leaping as the footsteps thundered closer at my back.

Stone reformed behind me and an anguished sob caught in my throat. The main doors were close now, the courtyard beyond them heavily guarded for a final stand we all knew was coming.

I could make it. I *would* make it.

Every step onto my right leg sent a flash of blinding pain through my body, my pace slowing despite myself, my desperation the only thing keeping me upright at all.

Those pounding footsteps were behind me again as he threw open a door and sought me out again, and I cried out as I threw myself forward even faster.

Agony exploded through my hip and I fell just as a blast of ice speared through the air, crashing into the wall ahead of where I'd just been. Luck appeared to be favouring me and I shot a prayer to Virgo in thanks for her protection.

I turned wild, terrified eyes back at the man wearing my Earl's face, throwing my hands up as he took aim for me again.

Magic exploded from me, a wall of dirt burying me instantly, wrapping me in its embrace and hurling me towards the doors which led out of the castle.

I rolled and tumbled within the ball of dirt, my cast sloppy and unruly but somehow doing what I needed it to as the pounding of magic struck the outside of it but failed to reach me.

I sped for the doors, water spilling through invisible cracks in my magic as the bastard chasing me worked to flood it and drown me inside.

I coughed and spluttered, mud caking me, water building up and taking the place of my air.

The impact of the doors bursting open sent more pain spearing through my body and the ball of mud exploded around me, sending me tumbling free of it and out into the courtyard beyond.

I coughed and wheezed as I raced into the heart of a legion of Stonebreakers who were retreating from the battlefield at the command of a wild and brutal man coated from head to toe in the blood of his enemies.

"Tarlord!" I yelled, my voice raw and jagged.

I pointed back to the castle doors and Tarlord's gaze swept from me, bedraggled and mud-stained to the man who had been hunting me.

The Incubus's face changed in the blink of an eye, the form of Earl Tarlord replaced with that of a man I'd never seen before. It happened so quickly I wasn't certain anyone else had seen the form he'd stolen from my desires.

The real Earl yelled a command at his men and magic was fired into the castle, spears, vines and blades all rushing for the Incubus but he threw a wall of ice into their path.

The ice shattered under the weight of so many attacks but beyond it there was no one left to capture or kill.

"We retreat to Avanis," Earl Tarlord barked, his voice that of the commander who so many warriors rode willingly into battle behind.

The legion moved quickly, racing across the courtyard towards the last of the great machines which remained above ground for our retreat.

I shook my head, calling out for them to pursue the Incubus, though my words fell on deaf ears as none so much as glanced my way.

Earl Tarlord turned back for me though, striding across the cobbles and taking my hand in his, hauling me to my feet.

"That Incubus stole your image from my mind," I gasped, tears burning the backs of my eyes as I peered up at the man who had only ever shown me respect and kindness. And now I'd repaid him with this betrayal, offering up such a dangerous weapon into the hands of our enemies.

"You gave an Incubus my form?" Tarlord asked, his voice low and rough, his gaze fixed on mine as if we weren't caught up in a desperate retreat on the losing side of a battle.

"I did," I sobbed, clinging to his hand where he still held me, desperation surging in my soul. "I'm so sorry, I'm so–"

"An Incubus takes the form of the most desperate desire of your heart, Septa," he said, dismissing my apology and forcing me to face the truth of that claim.

I blinked at him, my cheeks flaming at the realisation of what I'd just admitted to him. To myself. I was married. He was my Earl.

I had no right to look at him the way I did, to think about him the way I often found myself doing. I knew it wasn't right. I'd tried to fight it. I'd worked to pretend it wasn't real. But now my truth had burst free of my lips without permission.

"I'm sorry," I repeated quickly, my gaze dropping to the floor as I tried to back away but the pain in my leg had me stumbling instead and he caught my arm to steady me.

"You're sorry?" he asked slowly.

The pounding of hundreds of boots surrounded us as the Avanis warriors made their retreat. The Raincarvers were at the gate. The Void was coming. We should have been running for our lives but instead his bloodstained fingers caught my chin and forced my eyes back up to his.

"Septa…"

His words fell away and I knew he was trying to think of something to say, some way to let me down kindly.

"I know it's foolish," I said quickly. "I know you'd never…I mean I'm so...and you're… Besides I'm married and–"

Only that last protest seemed to register with him and his gaze darkened before he turned away.

"We need to leave this place. The Void will not be vanquished this day," he said abruptly. "But we have learned much in this encounter and I'll require your assistance in planning for our next run-in with her."

My embarrassment was doused a little with the pride those words summoned. He valued my input, my opinion. That was far more than I had ever hoped to gain.

I nodded my agreement and we turned for the underbeast. Even the short distance between us and them seemed impossible as my hip barked in agony but Tarlord appeared to know that without me saying a word.

He lifted me into his arms and strode straight through the lines of his warriors, cradling me to his chest.

I said nothing. My heart was beating too fast to allow words to pass my lips anyway. But what a pair we must have made, the bloodstained warrior and the mud-stained scholar both leaving the battlefield as one.

I didn't even see the projectile which was launched at the castle walls before it struck.

We were thrown away from it and I was sent tumbling out of my Earl's arms as rock and dust exploded all around us. I hit my head hard, breath whooshing from my lungs, every piece of me singing with pain.

I coughed and spluttered as yells of panic broke out around us and the Raincarvers poured in through the great hole they'd blasted in the castle wall.

I spotted our Earl lying in a pool of blood, his eyes closed, body limp.

"Tarlord!" I screamed, trying to get up but something had fallen across my legs and was pinning me in place.

Three of our warriors ran into view and I sagged in relief as they spotted our Earl, inspecting him quickly and yelling among themselves.

"He's still breathing!"

"Make a stretcher!"

"Hurry!"

I watched with my heart in my throat as they spun earth magic at a furious speed, a stretcher forming between them, vines hauling our

Earl's unconscious form onto it before they grabbed him and broke into a run for the final underbeast remaining above ground for our evacuation.

My relief was so palpable I only remembered to cry out for their help at the last moment. One of them turned, spotting me, hesitating.

But the Raincarvers raced into the courtyard between us and with a sorrowful look, he turned and sprinted with the others as they fought to get onto the underbeast with our Earl in tow.

A sob caught in my throat as I watched them diving through the open door, Tarlord safely making it inside. Spears of ice crashed into the metal hull as the door slammed shut behind them.

The underbeast blared to life, sinking into the dirt so fast that the tear which slid from my eye didn't even make it to my jaw before they were gone. Without me.

And I was left to face the unlikely mercy of our enemies.

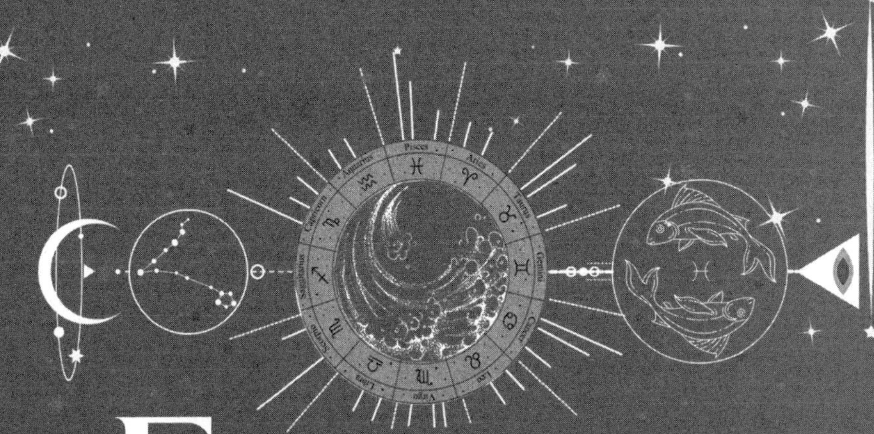

EVEREST

CHAPTER TWENTY TWO

It was over. Cinder Vale was ours and as I hurried through the ruins of the citadel with Ransom at my side and a ring of warriors closing in around me, I could hear cries of surrender up ahead. Father had led his ranks that way. As we stepped through the tall gate that had been half ripped off its hinges into a courtyard of stone at the base of the new castle, I saw them.

Lines of Avanis warriors all on their knees. I stole the magic from them swiftly but it was clear they were done regardless. Their faces were pale, their eyes downcast, defeat written into their faces that spoke of pain. But this was a mark of what was to come now. More of our enemies would surrender in future and it would happen easier and easier once they knew our army was undefeatable.

Father strode in front of the rows of around fifty warriors who had laid down their weapons, barking out a victory speech that echoed all around the courtyard and carried to the ears of our army.

I shared a hopeful look with Ransom, my heart finally finding a steadier beat. This might be the beginning of the end of the war, our first true victory.

I noted some civilians among the surrendered warriors, those who had perhaps been brave enough to attempt to build a new home in foreign lands. A woman and her partner held hands, heads bowed, but eyes lifted in a show of hatred towards Commander Rake pacing in front of them. I couldn't even take in the words he was spewing about our greatness, our invincibility. He prattled on while I crept toward the front row and felt Calcifiend rearranging himself for a better view on my shoulder, peeking out at the Stonebreakers before us.

Father finally finished his speech and I walked to his side with my chin raised. "Our mercy will help build the peace we're hoping for one day," I said.

His eyes narrowed on me, a harshness to them that I hadn't witnessed since he'd noted my power.

"Mercy?" he spoke the word like it was something dirty. Something that didn't belong on his tongue. "These people are less than rats." He spat in their direction and a jolt went through my heart that made me back up. The venom in him was brimming to the surface, the spines along his arms bristling menacingly. He was stained with blood from the kills he'd made this day and it suited him all too well.

"They will fall in line now that they know they cannot defeat us," I said fiercely. "You must see them as people under our rule now. People whose needs must be catered for."

"Silence," Rake snarled, warning coating the word. "No daughter of mine will cater to the needs of vermin. We will win this war with an iron fist. We will strike fear into the hearts of all those villages, towns and cities we are yet to claim. They will bow to us because they know we will not be merciful when the day of retribution comes." He threw out his palm and a curved blade of ice burst from it, spearing along the line of the surrendered people of Avanis and slitting their throats open before it sped back along the other rows. Screams could barely escape their mouths before it was done. All of them slumping forward, clutching at the gaping wounds, blood pouring in a terrible, unstoppable wave.

"No!" I yelled in horror, falling to my knees before a woman who was trying to stop the bleeding, clasping at the wound in an effort to save her. But there was no undoing this. Death was coming like a plague and I was helpless to keep it at bay.

Father caught me by the back of the neck, dragging me upright and shoving me into the arms of Ransom.

"Take her away," Father snarled and Ransom dragged me backwards through the crowd of Cascadians, my brother meeting my gaze with equal revulsion mirrored in his eyes at our father's act.

I fought him for all the good it would do, his strength outmatching mine as always and as a cheer went up from the warriors around me, I gave up fighting. Instead, I shrank from the monsters around me, taking in their jeering faces, the victorious smiles upon their lips. How they applauded such bloody, cruel deaths of unarmed Fae.

Bile crawled up my throat, rage ripening in my gut and burning a passage through my veins.

"How could he?" I rasped, feeling so alone in it all, forgetting my brother had hold of me.

"He has no heart," Ransom answered in a barely audible whisper. "It rotted away long ago. I admired him for that once. How ruthless he could be."

"And now?" I looked up at him, throat tight, muscles knotted.

"Now I'm not sure of anything anymore."

"Neither am I," I agreed, leaning into him instead of away. Preferring his company to all others around us who beat their fists in the air and called for more bloodshed. And it was me who had secured their victory. I was the reason those people had been butchered.

More Avanis captives were dragged before my father by a group of his favoured warriors and my gaze lingered on one woman among them with flowing red hair. She was covered from head to toe in mud, her dress torn and bloodied. She looked broken, desperate and my heart shattered at the sight of her.

"Take these prisoners to the White Mare," Father commanded in his booming tone. "We'll have them uttering the secrets of their Earl's plots by nightfall."

Ransom pulled me along faster, his arm latched tight around me while reality left me spiralling. I wasn't fighting him now. I wanted to get away from this place of bloodshed. As far away as I could. And yet I had no idea where I would go. Where I belonged apart from here. Somehow, after years of despising Ransom, I found he was the only person left on this battlefield I could stomach.

Though perhaps there had been one more. But Mavus hadn't reappeared. If he'd survived this fight, he'd most likely headed for Wandershire and we'd soon meet again to lay plans for the night of the blood moon. It seemed that was the only thing in the world which I had left to hold onto.

VESPER

CHAPTER TWENTY THREE

The stone walls of Wrathbane Palace felt less oppressive as I walked between them, though nothing much had changed. But I found I no longer felt the keenness of my lonely existence while stalking along the stark corridors.

I had an ally in my rebellion.

We'd returned to the palace weeks ago, Bastian flying back to his rooms a day before I returned to the city on foot. And my prince hadn't suspected a thing.

Of course he still watched my movements, tracked my interactions, be they with the kitchen staff or while training my Sinfair legion, but he hadn't made any further demands of me. Nor had he released me to hunt Cayde down. And I was growing more than tired of his excuses.

Still, the war was raging, the Void causing havoc across The Waning Lands. I'd even heard the Cascadians had stolen Cinder Vale from the Stonebreakers. There was good reason for my prince to keep me here if the only considerations were strategy for battle. But I was no longer interested in passing the time between bouts of warfare only to recuperate and head back into the fray once more. What was the point of it all? No one ever won.

I knew it was treasonous to have such thoughts, but the more I tried to stop myself thinking them, the deeper they dug their way into my mind.

I'd been summoned once again to a feast in the ballroom and though I wished with all my soul not to attend, I knew I had to keep playing my part if I ever hoped to be let off of my leash and freed to kill the man whose death I yearned for.

So I strode through the corridors in a midnight blue dress which was even more beautiful than all the others I'd been gifted. Its silver brocade spun a web of stars over the skirt which was cut short above my knees in the front but pooled into a wide train at the back. A gift from Prince Evard who seemed disinclined to take my hints at rejection seriously.

Dragor had forbidden me from denying his brother's proposal in full but I was fast approaching the end of my patience with the pretence that I was considering it. And if Evard thought that pretty gowns were the key to my heart then he really didn't know me at all.

Guards stood either side of the doors as usual but as I approached them a hand grasped my elbow and tugged me aside into a small smoking chamber.

I had a dagger to the throat of my prince before I had the chance to recognise him and Dragor arched an eyebrow at me in warning.

I bared my teeth, reminding him how foolish it was to try and sneak up on me, then I reluctantly stowed the dagger back into the sheath at my hip beneath the folds of my skirt.

"What is it?" I asked as his gaze dropped over me.

Dragor sighed, irritation in his expression. He released me, his attention moving to the door for a moment before he spoke.

"You are not to overreact," he told me firmly, my spine straightening at the warning.

"To what?"

"My father ails in his final days," Dragor murmured. "We all know it. The readings have confirmed it. But of course no one is allowed to breathe a word about it. Which means–"

"Your siblings are all making their last power plays," I said in understanding, my mind racing over what they might do now, what plans they'd all bring together, who would die, what secrets might emerge.

"They are," Dragor growled angrily. "And I won't be made a fool of. So I'm warning you to play the hand you are about to be dealt. Accept it. Don't make a scene. Do nothing at all."

"Or what?" I hissed, resentment bubbling up inside me as I took a step away from him. "You insist upon me proving my loyalty to you over and over again but you do not reward me for doing so."

"Reward?" Dragor sneered. "And what reward would a lowly creature such as you imagine you deserve?"

"Only one," I replied, my fingers coiling around the vial of blood which still hung from my neck, the power contained there pulsing. It felt as though I held a beating heart in my fist. My sisters were listening. They could feel my rage.

Dragor clucked his tongue and I made to stride from the room before my anger got the better of me but he threw his arm out to block the door before I could leave.

"Fine," he barked, his pale eyes flashing dangerously. "I don't have time for this. Play your part, make no protest, *smile,* and await the culmination of my best laid plans. It will serve you well in time. And if you can manage that then I shall release you from your oath to me so that you can hunt the bastard who you so ache to destroy."

I fell utterly still. So much time had passed since I'd found myself stained in the blood of my sisters and ruined by the loss of them that my all-encompassing need for vengeance had been forced from a boil to a simmer. But it was still there, waiting, for *this*.

"Swear it," I breathed, releasing my grip on the vial of their blood so that I could offer him my hand.

Dragor scowled, his fury over me forcing this from him clear. But I'd lost any trust I'd once placed in him to keep his word, unless the act of doing so was bound in magic.

With a jerk of motion he seized my hand, his lips parting to make the oath. But I spoke before he could, not wanting his slippery words to create a loophole for him to wriggle free through.

"I swear to make no scene nor raise any protest to what will unfold within the ballroom tonight – so long as my life or the life of those I care deeply for is not threatened."

Dragor arched a brow at my provision but said nothing to deny it, making me relax at least a little. He wasn't planning on executing me then and I would be free to protect Bastian too. The stars knew he was the only Fae in this place I gave a shit about anyway.

"And if I uphold this bargain then you will deem my loyalty to you assured and our past agreement fulfilled. You will then release me to hunt down the man who pretended to be Cayde Avior so that I might seize the vengeance I am owed."

"I swear to those terms," Dragor agreed and a clap of magic rang out between our palms, binding us both to the stars.

I stared at him in surprise, uncertain of what fate I'd just agreed to but so overwhelmed with relief that I didn't even care. No matter what happened within the ballroom tonight, I would be on the hunt for Cayde at the next opportunity.

I'd have my vengeance.

I'd fulfil my promise to my sisters.

Dragor released me and strode from the smoking chamber and I was left to reel in the sudden freedom I'd been granted. My pulse raced and my head swam. I was free at last. I could enact the punishments I'd been fantasising about for all these months upon the monster who so rightfully deserved them.

Just as soon as I faced whatever awaited me in the ballroom.

Tension tangled in my gut as I made to follow my prince but I stamped it down because nothing I might have to endure would change my mind on the decision I'd just made. Vengeance was owed to me and I was long overdue on its collection.

The first thing I noticed as I strode into the ballroom was the fact that it was far fuller than usual. It seemed every courtier in the land had made sure to be in attendance and I supposed the rumours of the king's ailing health had called them all forth from their homes no matter the cost.

No one would want to miss the king's decision on his heir. His choice would shape the entire kingdom after all.

Faces turned my way and trailed me into the room, a few whispers passing from ear to ear. I felt for their desires but none seemed fixed on me beyond the usual explosions of lust and desire.

I'd been in residence at the castle for long enough for most of the courtiers to be able to control themselves around me now but I still had to endure a few cat-calls and shrieks of devotion.

As always, I ignored them, my feet carrying me past the dancefloor towards the tables which were laid out with a glorious feast.

I wasn't sure if I was surprised to see King Aquila in his normal place at the heart of the royal table. Certainly he didn't strike me as the type to ail away in his bedchamber, but if the whispers of his demise were true then it must have been some feat to force himself into attendance.

My attention swept over the pair of Reapers who lingered beyond his chair and I wondered if they'd deigned to heal him so that he could attend. Would that count as interference in the war? If they healed one of the leaders of the fighting lands could they conceivably be perceived to be showing favour to us?

Then again, the Reapers had healed *me* at Dragor's request so they clearly weren't beyond doling out their secret magics for the right price, be it coin or bargain.

There was a prickling of tension in the air as I moved to take my seat at the banquet. The king hadn't officially started the feasting yet so I wouldn't be able to eat anything but I'd rather sit alone than endure the idle chattering of the court.

My eyes roamed over the sycophants who were edging closer to the royal table, my gifts gleaning insights into what they were hoping to gain from an audience with the princes or princess of our kingdom. Land, marriage, promotion in rank, the only one of interest to me was the man who hoped to be granted permission to wed his pet goat, claiming his own Satyr Order form meant it wasn't bestiality but was in fact a natural match for him.

I wrinkled my nose, hoping the goat managed to escape his clutches before the nuptials were performed.

I accepted a glass of wine from a waiter, ignoring him as he babbled incoherently about the colour of my eyes and instead looking across the table of royals.

King Aquila seemed to be lost in thought, his focus elsewhere and brow furrowed.

Dragor was tense. I doubted anyone else would have noticed it but his spine was straighter than usual, his fist balled tightly where it rested on the table.

Princess Laurena looked…smug. Discomfort tugged at me as I focused on her, her desire for power so consuming that it almost had me hungering for the death of her father too.

Of all the Aquilas, I wished for her selection the least. She clearly hated me but I wasn't petty enough to allow that to affect my thoughts on the matter. My issue with her was how she despised everyone like me. Every Sinfair would suffer beneath her rule – she might even have them all killed. Her hatred for the other elements was so visceral that she couldn't see beyond it, refusing to accept us as anything other than foreigners unworthy of the element of air.

I took my attention from her, hoping she had no good reason to be looking so smug and glanced instead at her brother Roarson, the second youngest Aquila and the most likely to lose his temper if provoked. He seemed unusually reserved tonight though, sitting back in his chair, refusing to speak with any courtiers who tried to approach. In fact, if I had to guess, I would say he was waiting for something…

I followed his gaze towards the statue of Gemini which towered over the room at my back. There were a large group of Fae standing near it but his focus seemed to be on the statue itself. Was he praying to the stars? Asking Gemini for intelligence? By all accounts, he could do with a greater dose of it.

I returned my focus to the royal table and was surprised to find Prince Evard looking straight back at me. His roguishly handsome features pulled into a wicked grin as he stood and knocked a knife against his wine glass to call the attention of the room towards him.

The silence that fell in reply was chilling. Not a cough, not a sneeze, not a shuffle of movement followed, as if every one of the gathered crowd had been waiting for this very moment. And now they all held their breaths so as not to miss a single piece of it.

"Father," Evard called out clearly, his focus shifting to the king whose eyes slowly turned to meet those of his son in answer. "It would be my great joy and privilege to announce my union this night – if you would be so kind as to grant your approval of the match? In times of war it feels…self-indulgent to waste time on extravagant celebrations so I instead seek your permission to confirm the marriage here and now without wasting time on any such frivolity."

A shadow shifted in the dimly-lit space beyond the royal table, a man bigger than any other here drawing my gaze to him like a spark of fire catching on sawdust. There was no stopping nor denying it. And the blaze broke out beneath my flesh as my eyes met Bastian's.

So it was him who I was looking at as Prince Evard spoke my name into the silence. Him who I watched as the king barked a laugh of surprise and delight at the chaos this marriage could bring. Him whose body rippled with energy, violence dancing in every piece of his flesh as the king gave his approval and confirmed my marriage without me so much as speaking a word. And him who turned and disappeared onto the balcony as I was forced to hold my tongue against any protest I might have made.

And so I moved from Crossborn to Sky Witch, to Dragonsbane and finally Aquila. A leap I never could have dreamed of making when

I was fighting for scraps in the waif house. And one I couldn't afford to deny now that I knew with all my heart that I wanted no piece of it.

Because this was the price of my vengeance. And even if a crack juddered through my heart as I watched the shadow of a Dragon tear away from me beyond the windows, there was nothing in this world more dear to me than the fulfilment of my vow.

KAISER

CHAPTER TWENTY FOUR

I waited in the shadow of a mighty larch perched upon the riverbank. The great ships of Cascada were anchored ahead of me and the White Mare stood out starkly under the silver moon. Not long ago, Wandershire had stood off in the trees to my right, but it had crawled away around an hour ago, the chugging and whirring of its magically-driven engines disappearing into the night.

My gaze had not waivered once from the White Mare.

Upon that vessel was the woman I'd come hunting for. Guided by Calcifiend who had showed me her location. I couldn't name the emotions that seared my heart now I was finally this close to her. I could only liken this feeling to that of violence. The heightened roar of sensations when I fought a bloody fight. She was invoking this wretched ache in me and I was sure only she could quiet it too.

At a tug in my mind, Calcifiend came to me, flying from the cabin I knew she was housed in. But she wasn't alone. She had entered there with Ransom Rake hours ago – her tormentor. A man she had feared not so long ago. But I'd felt nothing of that fear when I'd followed them along the riverbank. I'd heard their chatter through the mind of Calcifiend and how they shared in their discontent over their father's doings.

I'd watched that vile man kill the surrendered warriors of Avanis through the eyes of my Sayer Dragon and it had brought on a wave of rage that I still felt thrumming through me now. Every time I recalled my family, all I could see were their vicious deaths at the hands of that Fae. All I could feel was a burn that blistered the inside of my chest and made me want to kill so viscerally that I became nothing but a beast.

North had taught me to contain it as best he could, but it was difficult to focus on my task and not hunt down Abraham Rake and cut his worthless head from his shoulders in a bloody display of retribution.

No.

I took a breath as North had taught me.

I had to wait.

Calcifiend flew to me, his blue scales catching the moonlight so he glinted like a firefly. He swept into the shadows and landed on my hand, offering a wet lick in greeting.

"Hello, fiend," I growled, brushing my thumb over his head and he clicked his tongue.

Warmth coiled through me at being reunited with my creature.

"How do you think she will react to seeing my face risen from the dead this night?" I murmured and Calcifiend let out a small trill. "Hm," I grunted. "I do not think she'll take kindly to me."

I drew the dagger from a sheath at my hip, the one she had driven into my chest in a promise of murder.

"Silka la vin," I muttered, my tongue wrapping around the words as if I owned them. I had once. She had been mine. My fearsire. Bound to do as I bid. But there would be no coercing her now.

This plot would be no easy feat to complete. Mirelle was the only one I'd told, not even North knew the madness of my plan. That was why I'd come alone. North wouldn't be pleased when he found out I'd left him behind. We'd faced dangers together before but perhaps none so risky as this. Even Mirelle had refused it at first, but I'd assured her that with or without her permission I would be doing this.

So here I was, lurking in the shadows, awaiting my moment. My little killer was right there, closer than she had been since she'd driven a blade into my chest. How her eyes had blazed, how her hatred had echoed through her beautiful features, but there had been something else there. Something I couldn't name. And still I wasn't able to identify it.

Something close to pain but not so sharp.

North would know, if only I'd told him. But that would have meant unveiling this dark secret I was holding, the far more selfish reason I was here upon this hillside, hiding within the trees. I would have come whether Everest was the Void or not. I would have found her one way or another. If I'd had to stalk the world barefoot, starved and unarmed, I would have done so to find her. Because something had twisted between us when she'd broken the magical link of Nightfire.

She was no longer mine, but I was hers. Me; this shell of a man who couldn't name desire from envy or hate from love. No matter how many times North explained them to me, whenever I thought of Everest, I felt it all. A tumult of emotion that swung from a heated assault of fury to a need that was laced in all things sweet and all things savage. The only thing I knew was that I wanted her in some form.

And my intention was wrought with darkness. This was not desire – certainly not in the way North described it. It was something wilder that seemed tethered to the stars themselves, my fate soaked in this want. It was inescapable.

So tonight would lay me bare and the cards would fall as fate decided.

I wasn't sure I cared about her reaction, only that we were reunited at last. Then Aries and Pisces alike would spin us a new destiny, because we were surely bound by something deeper than I could understand.

For a Fae of another land to drive me to the brink of mania, there had to be magic at hand. Perhaps I would be granted answers once her eyes fell upon me again. Even if those answers were draped in bad omens.

If I knew anything about the workings of the stars, it was that they were not logical rulers of the sky. They had greater plans and I was just a pawn among them. It felt as though they had guided me here, and following their call might just give me the answers I needed to unlock the confusion of my mind.

So here I'd wait until Everest was alone and then I'd find out if the stars would grant her my death a second time.

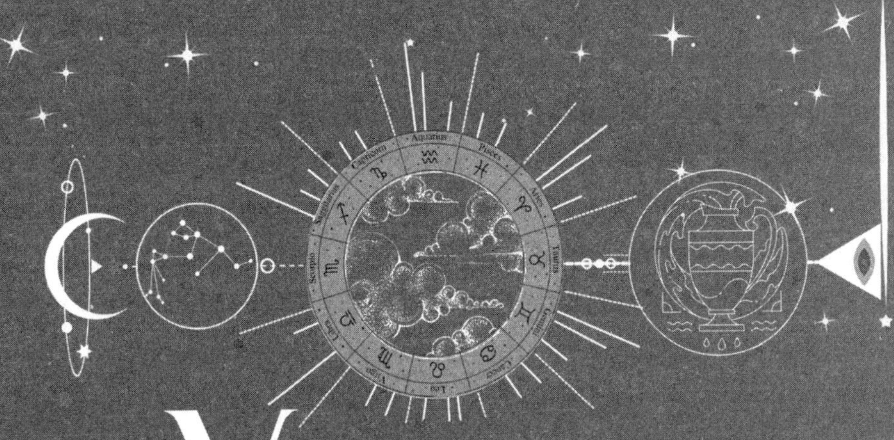

VESPER

CHAPTER TWENTY FIVE

The evening of my wedding had passed in a whirl of simpering nobles and conniving courtiers. I could not leave the festivities, nor did I really join in them. My…husband had forced a single dance from me then murmured a promise in my ear that this elevation would see me become queen.

I found I cared nothing for the promise of the title even as he held it out before me like some titbit to tempt a monster.

I knew what would come next. He thought I'd help him seize that crown. He thought I'd take part in the bloodshed his claim would require so that I might secure myself that position.

And that was precisely why Dragor had unleashed me. He wished for me to hunt Cayde now because he'd been unable to stop my marriage to his brother and had found no way to turn it to his benefit. So he wanted me gone until he decided if he might still have use for me, or if he would kill me himself. I knew him well enough to understand that those were the only options he was considering for me now. And as I moved around the dance floor or endured the gushing courtiers, I felt his eyes on me, that decision spinning over and over within his mind like the roll of a dice.

Though of course I knew Dragor wouldn't mind finding a reason to rescind that star vow either. So I had played my part and done exactly as promised. I raised no objections; I caused no scenes.

But my thoughts weren't in this room of grandeur and political intrigue. They were racing through the sky with a Dragon who had walked out on me.

I didn't know what Bastian was thinking. We'd made no oaths to one another, nor ever spoken of the tether which seemed to keep drawing us back together.

My thoughts lingered on the press of his mouth to mine but he had made no attempt to kiss me after we'd left that place of hellish design. Nor had we spoken about it since.

So we had no promises binding us. But still I felt the tangled knot of guilt inside my stomach growing with each second he chose to remain away from my company.

"I've had your things moved to my chambers," Prince Evard spoke into my ear and I whirled, resisting the urge to pull a dagger on him and instead cutting him with the sharpness of my smile.

"And I suppose that's where we're headed now?" I replied, contempt on each syllable though none but him was close enough to hear it.

Evard smirked at me. "Yes. Though don't fear – I still have no intention of bedding you, wife of mine."

"I had never thought you wise before this moment," I said because I would not be fucking Prince Evard this night or any other. Our supposed marriage could stand unconsummated or be dissolved for all I cared.

"Let me guess – if I tried to put my cock in you, you'd have returned the penetration with one of your own? But your tool of impalement would be a little more metallic and pointy?" he chuckled at his own joke and I arched a brow at him.

"I would never threaten a royal," I said innocently, though we both knew he'd been correct in his assessment.

"And I would never be foolish enough to underestimate you, Vesper Aquila."

I fought against the curling of my lip at the name and thankfully he didn't seem to notice it. It was one thing for me to refuse to bed him, quite another for me to admit that I found the idea of being an Aquila repugnant.

"Come," he said loudly, offering me his arm and drawing the focus of several courtiers. "My chambers are quite large – you'll find there are multiple beds for you to choose from for our wedding night. And several hard surfaces too, if you prefer."

I snorted in amusement, taking his offered arm and letting him guide me towards the exit.

"Oh, you wouldn't be able to handle what I prefer," I purred.

I could feel Dragor's eyes burning into my spine as we strode from the ballroom but I didn't give him the satisfaction of looking back.

I supposed if one good thing had come from Evard's surprise wedding it had been that my prince hadn't been given enough time to follow through on his threat to make me join him and his wife in their bedchamber before it. I wasn't sure what lengths I'd have gone to in my refusal of that command but it might have gotten bloody and made a true traitor of me.

Guards swarmed at our backs as I allowed Evard to lead me deeper into the palace, away from Dragor's wing and towards the north side of the sprawling building where his chambers were located.

I said nothing about the crowd of Fae Evard kept close for protection but I didn't much like having so many eyes on me.

When we reached his rooms we had to wait while his guards went in and inspected them, which I did…until I didn't.

Evard tried to catch my arm as I stalked through the opulently decorated doors which had been cast in iron and set with rubies depicting the outline of a Sphynx – Evard's Order form, but I evaded him and strode on in.

The guards were busy searching the closest rooms and I glanced at them as they checked behind doors and in the shadows beneath beds, using their magic and Order gifts to aid them.

"Do you always have so much protection in place?" I called back to Evard who hesitated by the door then muttered a curse and followed me inside.

"It is a precaution. In times like these there are many who would profit from the death of an Aquila. You'd do well to bear that in mind."

I scoffed. "You think I haven't spent my life wary of assassination? You do know who you're talking to, don't you?"

He eyed me for a long moment then shrugged. "We aren't all as capable of defending ourselves as you, my dear."

"You were trained for war and have fought in many battles, haven't you? You lead an army, even if it is the smallest of the four–"

"Small does not always indicate weakness," he interrupted me. "As you should know well."

He earned a true smile from me for that then I shrugged and turned away from him, heading further into the sprawling wing of the palace which was reserved for his use…and mine now, I supposed.

"Anyway, I am more of a tactician as you know well and I long ago stopped risking my life on the front lines. My army are hand-picked for their attributes and carry out tasks which the forces of my siblings would be incapable of. I know my worth, as does my father, and I am far better suited to plotting from the rear than charging into battle at the front the way Laurena, Roarson and Dragor do."

I nodded in acquiescence. I knew enough about him to appreciate the truth of his claims. He was cunning and clever in warfare and stood out among the siblings for those qualities.

The guards moved with us as Evard kept pace with me, a clunky, mouth-breathing, heap of shadows at our backs. It really wouldn't do.

"This isn't going to work for me," I pointed at the crowd of ten guards who were less than six paces behind us and I stopped so abruptly that they stumbled and tripped into each other as they hurried to halt too.

"You get used to it," Evard placated.

"No. I'm worth every one of these assholes put together and more in a fight. You don't need them this close when I'm with you."

Evard ran his eyes over me then nodded once. "That is true. Assuming *you* aren't the threat."

"Oh," I purred, my gifts coiling from me as I sought out every underlying desire to flee from me in the room and tugged on them. It was harder than focusing on the most forefront desires of my targets but I'd been practicing with the subtleties and found this game quite easy now. Besides, all Fae who knew me feared me – at least a little. The guards gripped their weapons and straightened their spines. Evard alone stood without reaction but his pupils dilated as the desire to defend himself from me struck him. "If I were, you'd already be choking on your own blood, *husband*. And don't think a handful of guards, or even an army of them would be enough to save you from that fate if I chose it for you."

I let the disquiet in the room build for a count of three then dispelled it just as suddenly as I'd called on it, giving the man who had dared to force my hand into marriage a predator's grin.

Evard assessed me for a long moment then snapped his fingers at the guards and pointed them toward the exit.

He didn't have to say a word and they all hurried to obey, scurrying from the room like rats abandoning a sinking ship.

"Can you tell if there is anyone else in my chambers?" Evard asked me.

I made no effort to disguise my boredom at the question and sighed before I answered. "The only desires I can feel coming from this side of that door are your desperate ambitions to seize the throne when your father passes into the afterlife and my desperate ambition to leave this place and go on the hunt for my enemy. And now that I've played the part of the willing wife as my prince requested, I'll be off to achieve that goal."

I turned to walk away from him but Evard caught my wrist.

A dangerous move if ever there was one.

I gave him a single chance to release me, my warning nothing more than an arched brow.

Evard smiled, his eyes bright with calculation. "I know you seek to kill the man who secreted himself among our people and murdered your sisters-in-arms when revealing his true nature."

I stilled, surprise halting my escape. No one in Stormfell knew of the things that had happened back at Never Keep besides Bastian, who I was sure wouldn't have spoken a word of this. No one but me and Dragor, unless my prince had lied about that too.

My hand fell to the dagger concealed beneath my skirt and Evard shook his head.

"No need for that. I'm not looking to hurt you. I told you this match would be advantageous for us both. I'm a powerful man and I needed a powerful wife. There are none who come close to you in that regard. But I don't want you to think this arrangement between us is one-sided. I know you seek vengeance. I know my brother will have unleashed you the moment he realised he couldn't stop our nuptials. He will want you to disappear on me now, to run off in pursuit of revenge and leave me looking like a man whose hand in marriage was unwanted. But I can offer you something far better than the simple freedom to hunt your prey."

"And what's that?" I asked, my voice dangerous with warning. I could gut him before he could so much as scream and be gone before his guards even came looking for him. I was free from my star bond to Dragor now. I could go after Cayde and let death have me the moment he was vanquished. So what if I was named a traitor if it was the cost of me fulfilling my oath? Though even as I thought that my gut twisted uncomfortably, my oncoming demise not as comforting as it had once been.

"I will give you the whereabouts of the man you hunt. I've already been working on it and am certain I'll be able to give you all the information you could ever want about him within weeks."

"Why should I believe you?" I sneered. "It serves your agenda to keep me here while the future of the kingdom is being weighed and decided."

"It does," he agreed. "But I am a man of my word if nothing else. Come, I'll show you."

Evard turned from me and strode deeper into his chambers. Reluctantly, I followed, my eyes moving over the lavishly decorated hallway with gold-leaf coating the doorframes and exquisite tapestries and portraits lining every wall. The focus of the art wasn't vain or filled with warfare the way Dragor's chambers were. Evard had chosen landscapes and animals from all across The Waning Lands to adorn his walls. I was surrounded by colour and beauty.

My new husband didn't so much as glance back as he led me into his study, either brave or foolish enough not to mind opening himself up to attack so easily. Or perhaps he knew that I could kill him without much effort whether he faced me or not.

Evard's study was located in the base of a tower, its curved walls creating a cosiness I hadn't expected in this cold castle.

A fire had already been built in the grate before us and the warmth of it washed over me as I stepped into the prince's personal space. Red and gold rugs covered the wooden floor before his desk, and there was a collection of comfortable chairs clustered closer to the fire. Papers and books were spread over the desktop with blots of ink staining the wood and scribbled notes in every empty margin.

I tipped my head back to look up into the open space above us. The tower extended over five more floors above our heads, the heart of it open while the walls were crowded with the biggest collection of books I'd ever seen. It was his own personal library, little wooden walkways and curving staircases leading between the shelves, the roof itself painted like a dark sky with the constellations of Gemini, Libra and Aquarius all depicted upon it.

There were no windows in here at all. it was a sanctuary hidden from everything beyond it, nothing here aside from us and the written words of thousands of others.

"Do you like to read?" Evard asked, noticing where my attention lingered.

"I don't often get the time," I admitted.

"And when you do I'd wager it's all military strategy and training techniques?" He smirked at me and my lack of answer was confirmation enough. "Well, if ever you wish to broaden your tastes in the written word, I would be a more than willing guide to help you find a tome which will satisfy your desires. For now, I'd wager *this* is the most interesting thing to you in here."

He took a ledger from his desk, knocking several sheaves of parchment aside as he did so, and offered it to me.

I moved closer to him to take it, the leather cover warm as I took hold of it.

My other hand moved to grasp the vial of blood at my throat before I even fully noted the weight the book seemed to hold. Ether crackled around me expectantly.

The ledger had nothing at all marking its cover, nothing to tell me what I might find inside it, but there was a potency to the air which told me this was important.

Evard moved away from me, dropping into a comfortable wing-backed chair beside the fire and waving a hand in invitation for me to join him in another.

I hesitated but something about the thin ledger I held in my grip made me think I'd want to be sitting down when I opened it.

Without a word, I moved to take the seat opposite him, the chair's cushions curving around me impossibly comfortably.

I released my hold on the vial of my sisters' blood and carefully opened the first page of the ledger.

I sucked in a sharp breath as I stared into the face of the man who haunted my nightmares depicted in a portrait so life-like he almost seemed to look back at me from the lines of fine paint.

Cayde was smiling knowingly in the image, his dark hair pushed back from his eyes.

The sight was like a punch to the gut.

At the base of the image was a note on his name, rank, training, the reasons for him becoming Sinfair. All of it false, of course. All of it simply a recounting of the lies he'd woven around himself while secreting his way into our kingdom.

"He did a very good job of falsifying his persona," Evard said, though I couldn't raise my eyes from the image of the man who I hated so viscerally it hurt. It was all I could do not to shred the paper into a thousand pieces and cast it into the fire for good measure. "Even when I knew to look for the falsehoods it was difficult to discover them."

Evard waved a hand to encourage me to turn the page and with my fingers trembling from the rage I was forcibly restraining, I did as he wanted.

The next page held another portrait, this one of a large family gathered before an imposing manor house. There were two teenage boys in the painting, the younger of the two darker in features, an arrow drawn in red ink pointing him out amongst the group.

"Those were the family he chose to pretend to be a part of for his false identity," Evard said, relaying the information which had been recorded alongside the portrait. "The ones he and his companions killed so that he could take the place of the youngest, Cayde. It was a very well done thing. Every member of the family murdered, every person in the town closest to their stronghold too – and of course all of the staff who worked for them and ever had worked for them. They hunted them all – there had been a cook employed at their manor four years prior and they'd even tracked her down where she'd relocated and managed to murder her too. It looked like an accidental fall down a flight of stairs but of course now that we know what we know, it is obvious what truly happened. In fact, I was unable to find a single living Fae who had known the real Cayde Avior as a teenager. There were a few who knew him a little as a child but they couldn't confirm or deny whether this man was one and the same. It was very well done indeed."

"Did you show me this just so we could sit here congratulating the bastard on his duplicity?" I hissed and Evard paused, seeming to realise how close to the edge I was before he went on more tactfully.

"No. Of course not. I only meant…you couldn't have known, Vesper. No one could have known."

My throat thickened at the tenderness with which he delivered my name. He sounded as though he really was sympathetic to my pain, as though it meant something to him too. Dragor had only ever seen my grief over my sisters as an annoyance. Perhaps I'd sworn myself to the wrong prince all those years ago.

Not that I trusted this one any more than I trusted the others.

I said nothing but I turned the page again and this time I found something far more tantalising awaiting me on the thick parchment. A name.

"Alestro Sharbone," I breathed and it was a curse upon my tongue.

"That took quite some doing," Evard said and I could tell he meant it. This information had not been easy to come by. "But, there he is. That is his true name. Everything you might wish to know about the man he was before leaving Avanis. His lineage, his training to some extent, there is an image of him in his Drake form though I suppose you witnessed that yourself–"

"I did," I muttered, sparing a glance for the squat, bull-sized lizard which I'd once thought must look something like a Dragon. How wrong I'd been. A Drake was short-legged and its snout was squashed, it looked more like a winged toad than a Dragon and in size the comparison was laughable.

"The next page details what we know about his betrothed – likely his wife by now – Septa Thorngrove. Not a lot to say about her really. She isn't a warrior, just a breeding tool with a highborn name."

An icy chill rolled through me as I looked at the portrait of the pampered looking noblewoman. She had long, red hair and cool eyes. Not a scar to be seen on the skin left exposed by the cream dress she wore. Did a creature such as her even know that war waged on beyond her walls? Did anything of worth so much as wander through her vapid mind?

"He was betrothed to her before he came here?" I clarified and Evard nodded, watching me closely.

My skin slithered at the memory of his hands on my body, his mouth against mine, his cock inside me. Had his fiancé known he would be bedding the enemy in his mission? Did she care?

And more to the point, why did *I* care? I'd known he'd used and tricked me. I'd known that nothing he'd said or done with me had held any truth to it. But knowing that all the time he'd spent taking pleasure in my flesh he'd been betrothed to another somehow heightened my disgust for him even further.

"Did you love him?" Evard asked curiously.

I scoffed, my gaze snapping from the image of Septa Thorngrove to the eyes of the man who had made me his wife.

"Love?" I spat. "I have only ever felt that emotion for two people in this world and he is the one who tore them from me. I was tricked by him, yes. And he spun pretty words which made me feel wanted and stole a little of the loneliness from my soul for a time. But it was never anything close to love."

"I'm glad for you then. At least you don't have that burden upon you."

I had no words in reply to that so I flipped the next page of the ledger while Evard went on.

"Unfortunately I have little else. His allegiance is to Earl Tarlord so we can assume he returned to him but my eyes within the Earl's court were unfortunately severed before any word of Alestro's return might have made it to my ears. Everyone is fearful while the Void roams The Waning Lands and I have not been able to confirm his location for you…yet."

"Earl Tarlord rules from the Stone Castle," I said, snapping the ledger closed, my mind briefly turning to the memory of the bloodstained warlord I'd seen on the battlefield at Cinder Vale. Earl Tarlord's reputation was a terrible thing and seeing him in the flesh had only confirmed the fact that he'd earned it. But the Earl wasn't my target so I dismissed any concerns I had about facing him. "So that seems like as good a place to start my hunt as any."

"He doesn't actually. Or at least he isn't in residence there at the moment. I know that much. He took Cinder Vale and remains there–"

"All the better. Pyros is closer–"

"And then the Void took it from him in turn. I am yet to discover if he perished in the battle or escaped it. If it's the former then Alestro might be among the dead too or–"

"I cursed that bastard as he ran from me and the power of that magic still remains strong in my blood. I can feel it. He hasn't met with death yet."

Evard nodded, accepting my word on the matter.

"Good."

"Is it?" I asked.

"Yes. You need to take his head yourself. Any other fate would be too easy for him."

I eyed the prince with suspicion, uncertain why he would show such understanding to my cause.

"What do you want for this?" I asked, my gifts coiling around him as I hunted for his desires, his motivations.

He was a complicated man and his wants were muddled. Ruling them all, I felt his ambition for the throne of course, but as I pushed that aside and hunted for the other wants of his haunted soul, I found some more interesting desires. He was hungry for knowledge in a way that was admirable, keen to see the war ended and peace falling too – which truthfully surprised me as I'd found most other men in positions of power like his to be fond of warfare and bloodshed.

When I dug deeper, hunting for the desires he held in regards to me, I was surprised to find he really did wish to see me seize my vengeance. He also wanted me at his side when he claimed the throne – a little of that desire was for petty victory over Dragor but part of it was because he enjoyed the idea of raising a Sinfair into the position of Queen and making a statement to the entire kingdom which spoke of equality within Stormfell. I looked for lust, tugging with my gifts to try and unearth it, wanting to know if he'd been lying to me when he denied wanting sex, even if the desire was buried deeply. Evard could clearly feel the pull of my gifts though and he sighed.

"I told you plainly I do not wish to consummate this marriage. I assure you that the knowledge of our abstinence will not become widespread but I suppose it would serve you to understand a little of why I have no desire to bed you, or any other Fae for that matter. As well as to make it all the clearer to you as to why this union will be more than beneficial to you."

"I assumed you just had no interest in the act," I admitted, letting my gifts fall away. "I've never sensed any lust on you."

"And you won't. I don't feel any. Not since…well, let us simply say that I loved someone once too. It was a secret guarded so absolutely that I believed no one at all knew of it. Until of course I was gifted her head in a box by a man I should have realised was my enemy long before that day."

"Truly?" I breathed because surely such a story, such a scandal, would have found its way around the court like wildfire. How had I never heard a whisper of such a thing before?

"Yes. And none know of it, so I shall know if you speak it beyond this moment."

"I won't," I told him, though why I was offering him my word on anything I didn't know. "Did you get your vengeance?"

"In some ways yes, in others…not yet. But I will. So you see, I do understand your need for revenge. Can you trust that I will help you claim it?"

I stared at him, peering into his eyes as if I might pick apart his soul in the process. My gifts tangled around him, hunting for any sign of duplicity but all he seemed to want from me was allegiance.

"Yes," I said finally.

"Then work with me. Our union puts me in the same position as Dragor so far as inheritance is concerned to my father. We both have wives able to provide Heirs and neither of us have gotten them pregnant."

"How do you know his wife isn't pregnant?"

Evard gave me a cunning grin. "Because I may or may not be responsible for slipping a contraceptive potion into her tea once or twice a week. Believe me, *I'm* more likely to get pregnant than she is while consuming that concoction."

I breathed a laugh, knowing it was wicked to do so but Dragor had only taken that bitch for his wife because she was supposed to be good for breeding. How long would he continue to stomach her while she failed him in her only task?

"You are a far more powerful match than he has made with Alexandrius. He was a fool not to see that before. Our father doesn't give a shit about noble bloodlines but he *has* noticed *you*. Your legion of Sinfair are already proving themselves notorious in battle. Join them with my forces and our tactics will see us surpassing all of my siblings where warfare is concerned and truly, that is all my father cares for. He wants to win this fucking thing and I do too. I'm bored of endlessly fighting. I want it done and I believe that with you by my side we might see that happen. I don't want to die before I see peace like so many of my ancestors have."

"So I'd be your wife in name only? You won't expect me to make you an Heir eventually?"

"I told you, I am not capable of such and have no desire to ever be. But you can take lovers as you like. Perhaps we will find one among them who could do the job of producing an Heir for us too. I think perhaps that is the only kind of love I might ever be able to feel again. That of a parent... But if you don't wish to birth your own children then we can claim an orphan or five."

"You don't care if I take lovers?" I asked suspiciously because why would a prince of Stormfell have no objections to his wife's adultery?

"You're a Succubus. I'm sure we can spin it so that it appears to be the most natural thing in all the world, whether I'm royal or not. We can even give them titles. The royal harem. Whatever you wish. Anything will be within our power – just so long as we make it to the throne."

"You're mad," I said, shaking my head in disbelief. "You think the kingdom would love a crossborn queen who keeps a harem?"

"I think the people of our kingdom will love whatever they are told to love. Take a good look at my father and you'll see the truth of that. He is not so very lovable but he wins battles for them, so they praise him as their beloved monarch. And if we won them the war…"

"You really think he would choose you as his Heir?"

"With you at my side, I think we have a real shot at it, yes. So what's it to be?"

I thought his offer over. It really was madness, but for some reason it was tempting too. If I looked at this as just another promotion, then all I was really accepting from him was more power. He wasn't asking for any kind of commitment from my flesh, he didn't want any attempt at romance. And on top of that, he might just be the key to me finding and killing Cayde. After that, all deals would be off regardless.

"I'll take your word that you will deliver me all the information I need for my hunt the moment you receive it. You won't delay or weaponize it, hold it over me, or use it to gain further favours from me. Nor will you try to stop me when I have all the information I need to go after him." I offered the prince my hand for a star bond, and he eyed it with interest.

"Fine. But in return, I'll take your word that you won't betray, sabotage or assassinate me."

I gave him the smile I reserved for my victims, and he gave me a cunning grin in reply. We weren't so very different, this prince and me. Just monsters wearing different skins, both wickedly corrupt beneath them.

"Deal."

"Deal." His hand clasped mine and magic crashed between our palms, binding us to those promises.

And just like that, I became a princess of Stormfell.

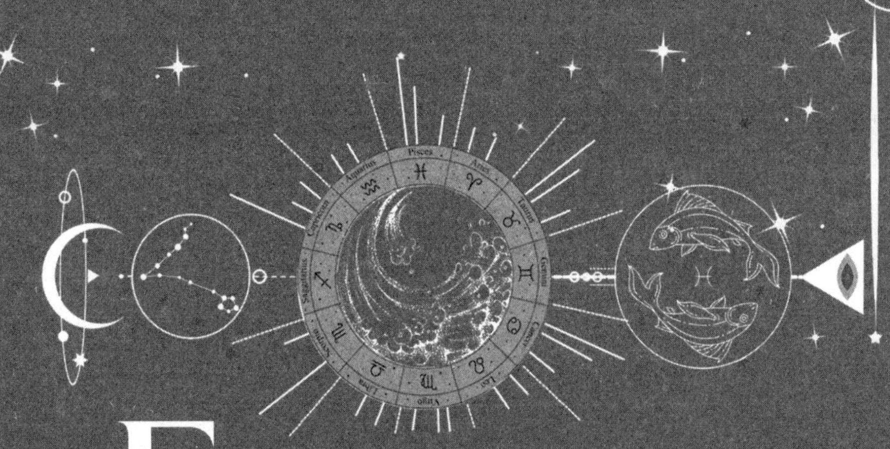

EVEREST

CHAPTER TWENTY SIX

I woke to the firm grasp of fingers to my throat and the scent of oak and cinders filling my senses. My eyes flew open, the Void tearing from me in a torrent and slamming into my attacker. Two red eyes glared down at me, becoming all the darker until they were an abyss of purest ebony. Those eyes had haunted me in my nightmares but this felt too real. Too impossibly tangible to deny.

But I had to deny it. Because this wasn't really happening. It had to be another dream wrapping me in its unforgiving hold, never letting me forget him.

Then he spoke, and there was no hiding from reality. It shattered something within me, the devastation of my failure to kill this Fae a crushing blow to my soul. But then the broken pieces found a way back together, remaking me anew.

I tried to deny the rush of relief that took me hostage, but it wouldn't let go. He was alive. Kaiser Brimtheon. My tormentor in the flesh. Somehow, he was here despite the blade I'd driven under his ribs and into his heart. Had I really missed?

My brain was catching up too slowly to the reality that I was in grave danger. He'd come to kill me, to seize his revenge. But in the face of it, I could only do one thing and that was to utter the desperate question searing my tongue.

"How did I fail?" I exhaled and for reasons I couldn't fathom, reasons I wouldn't dare let myself look at, I felt a tear slip from my eye and trail down into my hair.

He caressed my throat, his thumb brushing my pulse point as his grip eased. "You didn't," he growled and the sound of his voice made some part of me ache. I hated him as fiercely as any other day I'd stared him in the eye, but it hurt to hate him too.

"I was killed well and true," he said with grit. "But I was reborn. Thanks to you."

I pushed up from the bed and he retreated, his hand falling from my throat as he sat beside me and we came face to face. Too close. As if we were a breath away from a kiss. But I should only ever wish to lay my mouth on his if it was laced with poison.

"What does that mean?" I demanded, heat rising in my skin like molten fire.

I should have cast an ice blade in my grip. I should have finished what I hadn't before. But instead I sat there, unable to drag my eyes from his. The man who had haunted my dreams and written himself into the essence of my skin, impossibly here on the White Mare in my cabin. He was the monster I'd thought I'd slain and I had craved him ever since. Like a starved beast, I fed on tainted meat, knowing it would only destroy me to do so. But I was unable to stop.

"It means the power of the Void freed me from the dark and barren cage I have long been a captive to. There was a spell on me that held my emotions in a trap. I could not feel a thing. Not until I met you. Your Void unleashed me from time to time until, at last, it broke the bars in totality. Now I am a new man. A man that knows nothing of who he is or what he wants. Nothing except the knowledge that I had to find you again so that I might understand why, when I look at you, I feel so many things. Some that eat at me until my insides are raw, others that twist until I cannot breathe, and a few that make me feel as though I am bleeding on the inside. But then there are those that soothe, a balm to the wounds you cause me. Those are the ones that confuse me most. The ones I cannot identify as hate or ire. Perhaps you can name them for me?"

I stared at him with no words coming to my lips, processing all he had told me. If his story was true then this Fae was not the heartless heathen I'd known before. He was a stranger, but in ways, perhaps he wasn't. I'd seen him in the depths of his rage; I'd felt the power of his wrath. Yes, I knew some of the real Kaiser. And that should make me far more afraid than I felt. Because with him looking at me the way he was, as if I held his bloody, beating heart in my palm, I only felt lost.

"I cannot," I said, my voice a dry rasp as my thoughts tumbled into each other. "Have you come to kill me?"

Kaiser rose from the bed, turning from me and stepping deeper into the shadows of my cabin. He slinked through the darkness like a wraith and it suited him well. I could only see part of his face as he glanced my way, his brows drawn low, his dark hair falling forward towards his eyes. I could almost taste his inner turmoil, how he was trying to hold himself in check and I didn't know what he might do in the next moment. Ice slid over my right palm but I didn't cast a blade. Not yet.

"You think I would not have slit your throat while you slept if that was what I was here for?" he barked, the loudness of his voice making my heart jolt sharply. No sounds came from out on the deck, no footsteps running to my aid. He must have cast a silencing shield.

Calcifiend caught my eye as he flew from a shelf and landed on Kaiser's shoulder, his glowing tail lighting up the anger lining my enemy's face.

I shoved out of bed, everything falling together too fast, abruptly knocking my senses back into me.

"You've been spying on me," I accused in a gasp.

All this time. All this fucking time I'd had Calcifiend with me, assuming Kaiser could no longer watch me through his eyes. But he had been. He had never lost his connection to the Sayer Dragon.

"Yes," Kaiser snarled, turning to me again, seeming caught in a violent rage. "And you have tormented me every time I saw you through his eyes." He grabbed a chair beside the desk and hurled it against the wall, smashing it to pieces.

I cast a blade of ice in my hand, raising it at him as I bared my teeth in warning. "You've lost your mind."

"Yes, it is well and truly lost," he spat then he laughed and it was a cold, merciless thing. "Will you kill me again, silka la vin? You'll be needing this, surely?"

He produced my dagger from his belt, offering it to me with a mocking sneer. "It has my name engraved upon its hilt. It was always intended for my death. So here." He tossed it onto the bed beside me, and I snatched it, wielding it in my left hand while I gripped the ice blade in my right.

"Why did you come here?" I demanded, still holding back on attacking him for reasons I couldn't name. My pulse was rioting uncontrollably, the tension mounting towards something calamitous.

"I told you. I came for you."

My shoulders tensed, my Order form bristling with the urge to come out. "You're not taking me anywhere. I killed you once, Fury, I'll do it again."

"See? That's the problem, isn't it?" He shook his head at me, pacing from one side of the room to the other, not seeming to care about offering me his back even though I could have driven a blade into it. "We're enemies. It's written by the hand of fate itself. Don't you think I haven't realised that?" He turned to me, tapping his temple. "But something in here is arguing with that." He thumped his fist to his chest. "Or maybe it's in here." He yanked his shirt up, showing the jagged, risen scar that marred his ribs from where I'd stabbed him. It was struck through by the diagonal scar I'd given him years ago, running from his shoulder down to his hip.

My throat thickened, something about seeing the scars I'd placed on him feeling oddly bitter. But there was validation in it too. I'd done that. I had cut down the monstrous Fury.

Yet here he still stood.

"You're making a canvas out of me, silka la vin," he said, his voice gravelly and wrought with hatred. "But why is it that I've grown fond of these marks? Why is it that your eyes upon them makes me want to pin you to that bed and sink my teeth into you?"

Heat blazed up my spine and no words came to my lips as I pictured that very thing. Him towering over me, pushing me down and tearing my clothes from my body. His teeth leaving marks on me in penance for the marks I'd left on him.

I cleared my throat and hurled abuse at him to shut down the errant thoughts. "Because you're fucked in the head," I hissed.

"You're confused. Maybe your emotions are darting all over the place uncontrollably. It doesn't mean anything."

"It means everything!" he bellowed, lurching toward me, and I raised my dagger to point at his heart, exactly where I'd aimed to kill him before. He didn't slow, letting the tip of my blade press to his chest while his eyes never left mine, and Calcifiend took off from his shoulder to land on mine instead, clicking his little tongue like he was trying to calm us down. But I couldn't pay him any mind. He was a traitor just as he always had been.

"I am torn between hatred and something far more wretched which wants me to commit every sin to claim you as my own," he said in a hiss that was as wicked as a serpent's. "I feel none of this towards any other Fae but you. There is no confusion in that. But I do not yet know if I wish to kill you more than I wish to kiss you."

An inhale jammed in my throat, that admission ringing out a truth in my own soul. Because it was the same taboo confliction I'd denied to myself. But he was my enemy and he was clearly lost to madness. I couldn't trust a word he said. And even if I dared admit this forbidden want in me, I would never, ever give in to it.

"You killed my mother," I said with vitriol, grounding myself in that knowledge and the hatred it invoked in me.

"I did," he agreed and I couldn't read what he felt about that from the dark pits of his eyes. "And your father killed my family."

"I played no part in that," I growled. "Your hatred doesn't equal mine. I despise you, Kaiser Brimtheon. I will never feel anything other than abhorrence towards you. The fact that you still breathe is a burden to my soul. I won't rest until I put you in your grave for good."

"Then do it," he purred, his voice softening to a wicked taunt. "See if you can."

I dissolved my ice blade and turned it to a violent blast of water, sending him flying backwards, smashing through the door and out onto the deck beyond. I ran after him, launching myself onto him with a cry of anguished rage as I straddled him and raised my dagger high above his heart.

He smiled at me. Fuck. His smile was a twisted riddle I couldn't unravel. My cry fell still in my throat. My blade came down too slow. His hands coiled around my wrists and he yanked me close, my body pressed to his, my face lowering so our mouths were just a breath apart and my hair fell down in a spill of curls around us.

"No," I exhaled, but it was so weak. Like I might as well have said yes.

Every nerve ending in my body was alight and blazing as his fingers knotted tighter around my wrists and my dagger rested uselessly between us.

My lips grazed his and all I wanted was to betray my own flesh and taste the twisted wants of my enemy.

No, I wasn't going to do this. I wasn't going to let him take that sinful bite of me. But maybe I was.

A thump of footsteps came at me in a blur and strong hands hauled me off of Kaiser. I looked up to find my father there, his eyes widening at the sight of the Fury laying on the deck.

"You're The Matriarch's boy," Father spat in recognition.

Kaiser lunged from the floor with a roar of utter hatred pouring from him, the sound cracking apart something in my chest as he tried to get his hands around my father's throat.

Father snared him in chains of ice and more restraints were added by the warriors running to his aid, forcing Kaiser back to the deck on his knees. Father sneered down at him, pushing me behind him.

"Is he Voided?" He spoke to me and the quiet stretched as I stared down at Kaiser, warring with the confliction of my soul.

"Everest?" Father prompted.

"Yes," I breathed and Kaiser's eyes whipped to mine, narrowing like I'd betrayed him before a bellow of anger left him.

"I'll kill you, Rake," he snarled at my father, his muscles straining against his tethers and a look of merciless violence in his dark eyes.

Father released a dismissive breath through his nose. "Take him to the brig and lock him up with the other prisoners."

Kaiser was dragged away and I stared after him in confused anguish, feeling Calcifiend slip into my hair as he let out a low grunt of sadness. The Fury was shoved roughly down the stairs below deck and jeers filled the air.

I could barely hear the words my father spoke to me next.

"Good job, my child." He laid a hand on my shoulder. "We'll have him squealing the location of The Matriarch by dawn through a mouthful of blood."

With that, he strode away to follow his captive below deck and all I could feel in my heart was fear, so deeply tangled with my blood that I had no doubt Kaiser was feeling every ounce of it too.

BASTIAN

CHAPTER TWENTY SEVEN

Prince Dragor had tightened his grip on me since the announcement of Vesper's marriage to his brother. And truthfully, I'd done nothing to resist his demands. He wanted me close and only permitted me to leave his side when he was resting for the night or taking meetings he didn't want me listening in on.

Tension was mounting in Wrathbane Palace. Every single Fae within its walls was on edge.

The king had chosen his heir. And though he still might change his mind before death stole him into its clutches, the word had gone out that he had made his choice. Of course he hadn't announced it though. He'd written his decision onto a scroll which he kept in a sealed box that was with him at all times. The box would only open after his death and in the presence of all four of his children.

The suspense had everyone full of anxiety. Everyone but me. I was simply hoping the oncoming revelation would provide something stimulating enough to tear me from my spiralling hollowness.

This place wasn't meant for me. It was too cold. Too barren. I missed the sight of the rolling hills, blue skies spreading endlessly above them. I missed the scents of the forests and the richness of the greenery that filled my homeland.

I didn't allow myself to dwell too long on what else I missed. The company of my family and friends, the familiarity of my own name on the lips of someone who cared for me.

They were all lost to me long ago.

And my legacy was to become the puppet of my enemy.

Dragor was in a foul mood, his wrath spilling out at any Fae unfortunate enough to cross his path. He'd called on Vesper twice since the news of her marriage to his brother had been announced and he'd been refused twice too.

His plans for her were falling apart and his rage at her grew just as my torment over her built too.

"Go," Dragor snarled at me. "Have a few hours to yourself. But I expect you to be present for the morning meal."

I needed to expel some magic and he knew it. Dragor might have permitted me the full use of my power now but it was hard to wield it when we were constantly surrounded by courtiers and guards who were not allowed to know that I wasn't air-born.

I turned and stalked away from him as he headed into his chambers, no words leaving my lips, my hands aching with the desire to release my power from them. ideally in a way that resulted in his death. Though we both knew my vow to him ensured I did no such thing.

I rolled my shoulders back, resisting the call of the skies. As much as I would have liked to take flight in the darkness I knew I needed to make use of my magic first. But my power was still lower than I'd have liked. Dragor was careful not to let me have access to treasure, ensuring I wasn't able to replenish my magic at any real rate. The collar I wore at all times was valuable of course, but whatever foul power clung to the green gemstones imbedded in it seemed to nullify my ability to recharge from it.

I climbed the stairs of the eastern tower, taking them two at a time and ignoring any Fae I came across. They were mindful to keep out of my way, their apprehensive eyes clinging to me as I passed them. I had no desire to speak with any of them regardless.

There had only been one person in this cursed place whose company I sought out and now I had no desire for hers either.

But fate liked to kick me whenever I thought to make a decision for myself. So, as I opened the door to my chambers, I found her there waiting for me, sitting on my bed, her pale pink hair loose around her shoulders, a cream and gold gown fitting her perfectly and suiting her not at all.

"Get out," I snarled, gripping the door as I held it wide, fire licking up the back of my throat, my Dragon roused in anger.

"And if I refuse?" she asked, not moving an inch. She should have been born to Avanis because she was as cold and immovable as stone.

"I can force you." I didn't move towards her. Holding my place at the door was the best form of restraint she was going to get from me.

Vesper looked me over, her eyes roaming across my body in a slow assessment which ended with the hint of a smirk on her pretty lips.

"Perhaps," she agreed. But still, she didn't move.

I growled at her, baring my teeth like the beast I was, my restraint close to snapping.

"We should talk." She flicked her fingers and a sharp gust of wind snatched the door from my grip, slamming it shut. A silencing shield followed, engulfing us both.

Rage burned in my gut but I held it in check, my hand moving to the lock and turning it with a sharp click.

Her smirk grew.

"Stop that," I sneered.

"Stop what?"

"That fucking death grin. The witch's mask you so enjoy donning. I've seen beneath it and I don't care for its return."

Her smile faded, her lips pursing in place of it.

"You're angry," she stated as if that were some revelation.

"And you're a fucking hypocrite. Did you only come here so we could toss obvious facts at one another?"

Her brow furrowed, her lips parting, and for a moment I thought she might be going to offer me something real. But then her gaze shuttered and she stood, smoothing down the skirt of her dress.

"This was a mistake. I'm leaving."

She strode towards me, chin high, cold, grey eyes meeting mine and challenging me to stop her.

But I didn't want to stop her. I wanted her to walk out of that door and keep fucking walking. I wanted to forget everything about her from her traitorous lips to her devious soul.

I stepped aside as she reached the door, moving my gaze to the wall while she turned the lock and pulled it open. The solid stone of the wall looked back at me. Empty. Vacant. So void of colour and life, like everything else in this place. Everything but her.

She would keep walking. I knew her well enough to understand that much. If I let her go now, she wouldn't return. Her pride was too fragile to allow it. The fact that she'd come here at all was more than

I would have expected in the first place. My dismissal would be a bruise to her ego which she wouldn't risk a second time.

This was it for us. I could listen to the sound of her steps retreating and close this door between us for good. Or I could take one last chance on the only bit of hope I'd managed to find in this fucking hell of a land and time.

Vines snapped from my fingers before I'd fully made my choice, the length of them banding around her waist and hauling her back into the room, all the way into my arms.

A soft gasp escaped her as I shoved her against the door to close it again, one hand pinning it shut above her head, the other turning the lock once more.

"Tell me," I growled, bearing down on her, my height so much greater than hers that she was forced to tip her chin right up to meet my gaze. Strands of pink hair kissed her cheeks where I'd dishevelled them, and bolts of lightning sparked in her pupils where she wore her anger at me without any attempt to conceal it.

"Tell you what?" she breathed and I exhaled another growl, warning her how close I was to losing myself to the beast within me.

"I've seen your demons, spectre. I know what this place has taken from you." I took my hand from the lock and moved it between her and the door, running my fingertips up her spine where the dress left it bare and tracing the place where her wings should have been able to burst free of her flesh. "So don't bullshit me. Tell me why you sold your soul to this place all over again and accepted that monster's hand in marriage?"

"We're all monsters here, Bastian. Did you forget that just because I have a pretty face? I'm the same as the rest of them and you know it."

"You're worse," I spat and she stiffened before pushing up onto her tiptoes to close the distance between us further.

"Oh, I know. I've carved up every piece of myself on the path to claim that title. And now here I am, wearing a crown to prove I earned it."

"You didn't earn shit. You just let them pull your strings and then you thank them for the scraps they feed you in payment for being a good little witch whenever they need to trot you out and make use of you. Do you think you escaped Dragor by trading him in for his brother?"

"I'm not a fool."

"Are you sure? Because you look like a damn fool from where I'm standing. Dragor will kill you for this."

"Dragor will simply try to use me the way he's always done. He'll want me feeding him secrets about his brother and staying in place for whatever other plans he has. Besides, from where *I'm* standing you're the one who looks the fool. Who do you think told me to go along with the marriage?"

Her hand slapped against my chest as she tried to force me back a step but I only bore down on her further, my chest pressing against her as I boxed her in against the door.

"Dragor wanted this too?" I demanded, my mind racing with the knots she'd tied herself in.

"Of course he did. I'm beholden to him, aren't I? Just like *you* are – in case you forgot. Though I made use of his demand on me and managed to sever my ties to him."

"How?" I snarled.

"He wanted me wedded, and I wanted off my leash. So now I'm free. I can hunt down the man who killed my sisters and–"

"Then why are you wasting your time hanging around here? Don't tell me you came to say goodbye?" I scoffed at her, shoving off of the door and stalking away, unable to bear how fucking stupid she'd been. Why would she entangle herself further with these people? Hadn't she admitted that they used her for her entire life? That she'd done nothing but suffer under their rule? Why bind herself to one of them in marriage?

"I'm not leaving yet. Evard is using his connections to find Cayde for me–"

"Of course he is," I said on a bitter laugh, turning to face her from across the room. "But, let me guess – he doesn't have all of the information just yet? He's *really* close to figuring out where the man you wish to kill is hiding *but* it will take a little longer. And in the meantime if you can just hang around here and play wife, suck his cock and thank him for the pretty crown he lets you wear while doing it, then that's all fine isn't it? It's all worth the price so long as it gets you what you want. Eventually. Whenever he can manage it. Just… not yet."

Vesper scowled at me, her own fury rising with every taunt, every accusation, every truth. But she wouldn't back down, so of course she exploded instead.

"What's the problem, Bastian?!" she yelled. "Did you think that maybe somewhere, deep down among the messed up shit we both grew up in there was a connection we'd forged which might end up in marriage one day? Be real. You're a Stonebreaker and I'm–"

"Forgetting that I own your death, *princess*," I growled, the title holding so much scorn it dripped from my tongue like acid.

"And you can have it. Sooner than either of us thought, I'll be claiming Alestro Sharbone's head and you can have mine in turn.

What was it you told me? You were looking forward to snapping my pretty neck one day? Well me too, Bastian. I wake up every morning hungering for the day when my constant suffering in this infinite grief will end. So don't go thinking I'll try to escape our bargain, because I'll run willingly into your murderous hands just as soon as I can."

She took something from the pocket of her gown and hurled it at me before turning and unlocking the door once more, slamming it behind her so hard that the walls rattled with the shock of it.

I turned, meaning to throw my window wide and leap from it in Dragon form, but my boot struck the package she'd thrown at me and I looked down at the deck of hand-painted tarot cards in surprise.

The edges were gilded in real gold leaf, their backs painted with small leaves and flowers. This deck was old, rare…incredibly valuable. I could feel the power of it recharging my magic with only the toe of my boot touching it. I dropped to one knee and flipped the deck over, the cards parting as I did so to reveal a single card.

The Tower stared back at me with wicked malice. Destruction, chaos. My life embodied.

I could still hear her footsteps on the stairs as she tore away from me, each one like the stab of a dagger to my chest.

I was doing it again. Destroying everything in my path.

I ran for the door and ripped it wide, vines pouring from my fists and tearing after her. I caught her in my tethers and she fought back, air magic howling up the stairs and knocking me off balance. But I dug my heels in and pulled, dragging her back to me, refusing to let her run. Because she was all I had in this world. And I couldn't simply let her go.

I caught her as my vines hurled her back into the room. Her elbow slammed into my chin with such force that I released her again just as fast and she landed on her feet, whirling on me furiously.

"You can't just–"

"I can." I took her face between my hands and kissed her ruinous mouth before she could bend her tongue around more poisonous words. She didn't mean them anyway. Or maybe she did and I just didn't fucking care. Because nothing in this place meant a thing to me aside from her, and I was done pretending that wasn't the case.

Her lips parted for my tongue and I kissed her so hard I stole the breath from her lungs, my hands pushing into the pale pink strands of her hair as I pulled her closer and refused to let go.

Vesper's hands curled into the front of my shirt and she tugged me closer still, her body pressing to mine, her nipples hard through the thin fabric of her dress.

Our kiss was devastating, annihilating, the death of all that was and might have been. The birth of something lethal, which was bound to end in the total demise of us both. But she was the only thing in this world which I desired and I refused to deny myself her any longer.

I tugged at the neck of her dress and dropped to my knees, my mouth roaming down her throat as I went, then over her collarbone and finally to the curve of her breast. I pulled harder and the fabric relented, freeing the fullness of her breast to me so that I could seize her nipple with my mouth.

She moaned my name into the emptiness of my bed chamber and I relished in the way it echoed from the walls.

I didn't care what claim any other man had made on her or whose wife she was supposed to be. She was mine. I would make it so this night and every other. And I'd fight for the right to keep that as the truth so long as I had breath in my lungs.

Vesper tugged on my shirt hard enough to tear it, her hands cold against my shoulders as she explored my body with rough passion.

I kept pulling at her dress, my mouth moving down with the fabric and when it finally pooled at her feet, I leaned back to gaze up her exquisitely bared body as she stood before me in only her undergarments, stockings and heeled shoes.

"Why are you looking at me like that?" she asked, her hands in my hair, her expression full of lust.

"Because I'm going to devour every inch of you and I'm simply deciding where to start."

"In that case, I can help you make your decision." She raised her foot, placing her shoe against my chest and smiling down at me like the predator she was. "Take that off."

I gripped her ankle tightly but instead of falling into line and doing as she'd demanded, I ran my other hand up the back of her leg, my callouses catching against the smoothness of her stockings. I forced myself to go slowly, worshipping the feel of her skin against mine, watching her as the anticipation of where this climb might end filled her grey eyes.

I reached the top of her stocking and curled my fingers into the fabric, rolling it down and shifting closer to her at the same time, forcing her knee to bend until I could turn my head and brush my teeth across the soft skin I'd exposed.

Vesper cursed, leaning back, her grip on my hair pulling tight. I pushed her ankle, forcing it up and over my shoulder while running my mouth up the inside of her thigh until I met with the fabric of her undergarments.

I kissed her through them, the material drenched with the taste of her desire and her cry of pleasure echoing from the vaulted ceiling.

"I could get used to that sound," I said into the wetness of her cunt and she bucked against me, trying to back up as the vibrations of my deep voice sent a message straight to her core.

I took hold of her other leg, gripping her tightly as I lifted her off of her tiptoes where she'd been precariously balancing to claim this pleasure from me. But I didn't want her to be worrying about falling. I wanted her to ride my face while I fucked her with my tongue and made her scream my name until she was hoarse.

Vesper's thighs tightened around my jaw, her ankles locking at my back as I took hold of her ass with both hands and buried my face against her wetness.

I tugged on her undergarments with my teeth, taunting her with what was to come, teasing her with a lap of my tongue along their seam which just managed to graze the edge of her entrance.

"Please," she gasped and I wondered if any man had ever made her beg before. Somehow I doubted it. And that only made me hunger for her to do it all the more.

With a growl, I allowed the smallest spark of Dragon fire to roll up the back of my tongue until it set light to her undergarments and burned them from her flesh.

I closed my mouth over the flame to douse it before it could do more than heat her skin and her yell of alarm had me grinning into her cunt as I buried my face against it and sank my tongue inside her.

She cried out louder then, her spine arching backwards, her grip on my hair threatening to pull it out but I didn't care. I was lost to her, wild from the taste which coated my lips. I slid my tongue out of her and slid it up onto her sweet clit, capturing it between my teeth.

Vesper came hard and fast at the single bite, her thighs clamping shut around my ears and drowning out all sounds but those of her pleasure and the thundering roar of her pulse.

I fell onto my back beneath her, dragging her weight down onto my face as I continued my feast, and she started to ride me just as I'd dreamed she would if ever I got her in this position.

The silken fabric of her stockings caught and frayed against the rough bite of my stubble, and I relished the destruction, wanting to see her pretty gown spoiled too. She was too wild a thing for lace and silk. This sweet monster of mine was designed for leather and bloodshed, dirt and grit. And I so wanted to see her pretty facade ruined at my hand.

I lapped at her clit, pulling her down onto me hard, her hips rolling to chase the pleasure I was offering, her muscles tight with the oncoming release. I growled into the heat of her, the pad of my tongue stroking her clit in a long and thorough demand.

Vesper came for me again with a ragged cry and I skimmed my hand beneath the curve of her ass to sink my fingers into her wet heat and feel the way her pleasure pulsed through her body.

"I want to feel that while you're wrapped around my cock," I said before sucking her clit into my mouth again.

She moaned my name loudly and I peered up the length of her body as she toyed with her nipples to seize even more pleasure for herself.

"Aren't you still afraid I'll ruin you?" she panted, throwing me a knowing grin as she rocked her clit against my tongue, utterly in her element, a creature of sin and sex.

I growled deep and low, pressing my lips against her so that she was forced to cry out for me again, and that smug grin was wiped from her features.

"I'm starting to think I'm ruined either way, spectre. No other woman could ever torment me the way you do."

"You're right," she agreed, though the words were laced with a bitterness I hadn't wanted to hear from her. Her muscles had tensed, her whole demeanour shifting. "There's not many in this world like me."

I stilled in my devoted worship of her clit and lifted her, pushing her back so that she straddled my chest instead of my face.

"I didn't say there weren't *many* women like you," I said roughly, pushing up onto my elbows so that I could peer into her shuttered eyes, the truth of what she was thinking still there for me to see, though she was clearly trying to hide it. "I said there was *no other.*"

"Succubuses are rare–" she said as if it were some practiced line, but I wasn't going to allow for her bullshit when it came to this between us.

"I couldn't give a shit if there were a million more of your kind in this land or any other. None would be *you*, Vesper."

I leaned forward to kiss her as she opened her lips on a reply which was almost certainly another dismissal of my claim on her.

She kissed me willingly but I could still feel those walls in place so I deepened it, my mouth slowly exploring hers. And as she gave in and let her tongue roam over my own, the taste of her euphoria passing between us, I let the walls around my magic fall away.

Vesper sucked in a sharp breath as she felt the press of my power against hers. There was a purity to the offer, a level of trust which I hadn't given anyone in a very, very long time. Only her.

She hesitated but finally her barriers fell down too, her magic colliding with mine in a way that was alarmingly intense and breathtakingly intimate all at once.

She broke our kiss, her forehead falling against mine and her hands coming up to cradle my jaw.

"I trusted a Stonebreaker once before," she said, a tear slipping down her cheek as the weight of her grief pressed in on her. "I don't think I can do it again."

"Then don't," I expelled a heavy breath and pushed aside the desperate ache in my body to continue what we'd started because no matter how much I wanted to, I knew she wasn't ready for me yet. "I won't be a mistake you make, Vesper. I won't be a distraction or a scratch to that itch beneath your skin. I don't want you because of what you are but I don't expect you to blindly believe me on that either. So I'll be here for you and I'll tread whatever path you need to walk too. Because you're it for me. The only thing I have in this forsaken world. And I'm willing to become your shadow so long as you can swear to stop keeping me in the dark."

Vesper frowned as I withdrew my magic, shattering the connection between us before I shifted her carefully off of me then stood, offering her my hand.

She accepted, allowing me to draw her to her feet and I crossed the room to grab a tunic from my armoire to offer her.

"You don't want to finish what we started?" she asked, still frowning as I strode away from her and pulled back the covers on my bed.

"No," I grunted, removing my boots but leaving my trousers on and tightly fastened as I laid down. "Not until you're ready."

"I'm no virgin, Bastian. I know how to fuck for pleasure's sake–"

"And I'm no plaything for you to use at will. So I'm not going to claim you until you're ready for me to, spectre. You can have my mouth and hands as often as you want them. But I won't give you all of me until you're able to give me all of you in turn."

"You're serious?" she asked and I could feel her power surging around the room, tasting my desires. "I know how badly you want to–"

"Want and will are not the same thing. I desire far more from you than a simple release of tension for my cock and I won't change my mind on the matter. Now get into bed. It's fucking freezing in this place."

Slowly, she gave in, her eyes staying pinned to me as she pulled the tunic over her head and finally removed the torn stockings from her legs.

My cock throbbed with unsated desire as she sank onto the sheets beside me but I only drew the covers over us and pulled her into my arms.

"Someone might find me here," she said, though she didn't make any move to leave.

"None dare to approach my chambers while I'm here," I said dismissively. "Though I suppose your husband may notice you missing from your marital bed."

Silence stretched for several long minutes but just when I thought she'd fallen asleep, she spoke again, her lips brushing over my chest where my heart thumped heavily beneath her.

"It isn't like that. Evard doesn't share a bed with me. He doesn't expect that or even want me that way. And even if he did, I wouldn't have…I'm not a whore," she finished bitterly as if I had ever accused her of such.

I couldn't help the smile which tugged at the corners of my lips at her confession though.

"I know you aren't," I said in a low voice, my fingers twisting through her hair. "And that does simplify things for us."

"Why?"

"It makes it far less likely that I'll have to murder him."

Vesper laughed unexpectedly, her hand slapping down on my chest. "It's treason to even joke about that."

"Treason? I'm not air-born, love. Everything about me is treason. And I'm fairly certain that's the only reason you're even in my bed right now. The danger turns you on."

"Everything turns me on," she taunted, that self-deprecating humour coming all too easily to her tongue.

I caught her chin in my grip and turned her gaze up to meet mine. "Don't do that," I warned her. "Tell me if I make your body ache with desire, tell me if your cunt is wet just looking at me, tell me if arguing with me is fucking foreplay to you – but don't sell me bullshit and don't put yourself down just because others have tried to turn those weapons on you in the past. You shouldn't laugh with someone calling you a whore any more than I'll allow them to keep their tongue should they be fool enough to say it within earshot of me."

Another jibe tugged at her tongue but she swallowed it back, knocking my hand aside before dropping her head down onto my chest once more and speaking in a soft voice instead. "Okay."

"Tell me about them," I urged when it seemed she might succumb to sleep instead of continuing our conversation.

Vesper hesitated as if she was going to ask who I was referring to but she clearly read my desires to hear her answer instead. Her whole body tensed and I said nothing as I waited, wondering if she would be willing to share the most precious pieces of herself with me or not.

Finally, she spoke.

"Dalia was a heathen. There's no other way to describe her. She was born in hellfire and devoted to chaos and she was afraid of *nothing*. And Moraine probably seemed to be the more level-headed of the three of us, the one who thought things through – and she was that. But she was also the wildest when the moment required it, the fiercest, the bravest."

A tear fell heavily against my chest but I only continued to hold her in my arms as she spoke of them, the little vial of their blood laying against my skin where it still hung from her neck.

Vesper told me stories of warfare and espionage in their company, her tears slowly ceasing as she allowed herself to remember them clearly at last and I smiled while I listened to her. Even though my heart ached at the loss which had shattered her already damaged soul. But this was the real woman beneath the mask, the true heart of all she was. And no matter how much pain had gone into building her into the creature she now was, I didn't want to turn my gaze from any of it. So I held her in my arms and drank in every word she spoke.

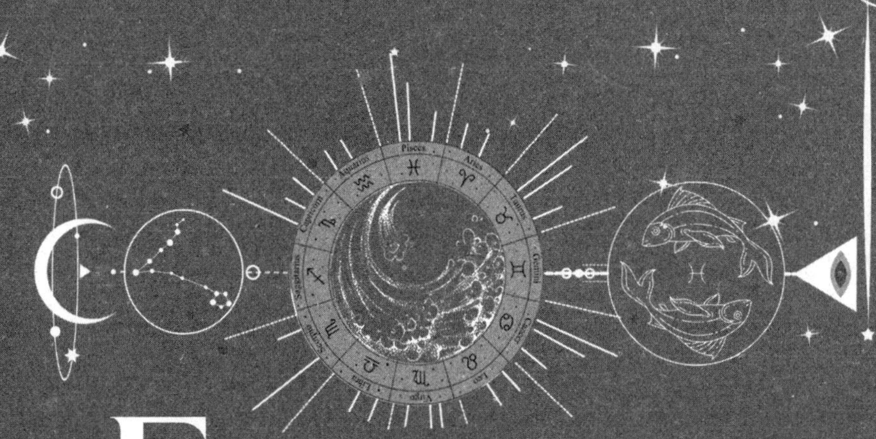

Everest

CHAPTER TWENTY EIGHT

After Father had taken Kaiser below deck, I'd been corralled by four of his fiercest warriors, manhandled back into my quarters for 'my own safety' and locked away like a princess in a tower. The growl that had left me when they'd locked the door in my face had been nothing short of feral.

They remained out there guarding me while I paced my room, confused, angry, lost. I didn't know what to do with the knowledge that Kaiser was both alive and now below deck, being mercilessly tortured by my father.

I should have wanted that. I should have been yearning to go down there and cut into him myself. But instead, I found myself torn to ribbons inside. Some part of me was screaming for his freedom and I didn't know why. Perhaps it was some lasting mark from the Fearsire bond, but in truth, I knew that was a lie I was trying to convince myself of. It was deeper than that. Something beyond magic. Something that had haunted me ever since I'd driven my dagger into his chest. The same dagger I held in my grip now, turning it over and over as I examined his name.

The thought of Kaiser's body being marked, beaten, bruised sent a shudder down my spine. I squeezed my eyes shut to fight the thoughts away, but they wouldn't leave. Why did they torment me so?

I realised the sound of voices beyond my door had ceased and I hurried to it, pressing my ear to the wood. I cast my Void out into the space beyond, seeking the source of the warriors' magic but I found none.

They were gone.

My gaze fell on my dark green armour on the wall, my matching sword hanging beside it. Calcifiend let out a mournful trill and flew to me from the bed, landing on my arm and tugging at my sleeve with his teeth.

"I don't know what I'll do if I put that on," I breathed to him, an itch growing in my skin.

Calcifiend let out a despairing noise that tugged at my heart and I met his gaze, shaking my head.

"Going down there is madness," I told him but I walked toward my armour, as if drawn to the green shimmer of the plates. "But not going down there isn't an option."

Calcifiend let out an excited click of his tongue as if he'd understood what I'd said.

I grabbed the armour, pulling it all on and sheathing my sword on one hip while tethering my dagger to the other. As I whirled to leave, I caught sight of myself in the mirror and my throat tightened as I saw my mother in my face. Was she watching me now from some place beyond death? Was she screaming my name and demanding

I remember the sins of my enemy?

I shut my eyes, seeing it all. Kaiser's emotionless eyes.

The basilisk venom.

The fire.

The heat, the smoke, the scent of singed skin.

I opened my eyes to look down at the scar on my palm. A stain of war. Tit for tat and tit for tat. Where did it end?

"I can't turn from this," I hissed at the mirror, at my mother. "If he is to suffer then I will at least be there to see it."

Those words fell from my lips like an offering to my flesh and blood. But they didn't feel like the real reason I was going below deck.

I lifted Calcifiend to my hair, letting him crawl in among it despite my confliction over him spying on me. But it felt like I was on a precipice and I had to jump now or forever miss my chance. So I couldn't spare time to think about the betrayal. I just had to act.

Hurrying across the room, I pressed my hand to the lock and froze it, shattering it to pieces. With my pulse thumping heavily in the back of my head, I strode out and slipped across the empty deck.

Fires lit the hillside where our people had made camp, thousands of Cascadians still enjoying the night as they continued to relish in their victory at Cinder Vale. I turned my gaze from them and made a passage down the stairs that led toward the brig, my mind honed onto one thing.

Him.

When I made it two levels down, I heard screams. A woman crying out for Capricorn to come down from the stars to save her. A man begging for death. The cries for help answered by callous laughter.

I made it down the next level and came eye to eye with the heavy wooden door that led into the brig, not wanting to see beyond it but refusing to turn from the terrors awaiting me there.

I pushed through the door, coming face to face with the brutal reality of torture beyond. Men and women were strapped to racks, strung up like pieces of meat while others called out to them from cells that lined the cabin. From their clothes, I could tell they were from Avanis. A faction of the upper class Fae that had surrendered to us at Cinder Vale. These were prisoners of war. And my father and his warriors showed no mercy as they cut lumps out of their flesh and made them bleed and bleed.

Father's man Goshart was flaying a woman with a whip, beating her and asking nothing. No questions. No reason for the torture except the clear pleasure he was taking from it.

I hunted for father and found him with Ransom, dragging his son close by the back of the neck. He pushed his son toward a man strung up on a wooden rack, arms tied above him with magical-blocking cuffs and his legs tethered in place too.

Kaiser's shirt was half ripped off him; bloody marks lined his arms and chest, clearly placed there by the knife in my father's hand.

My breaths came more raggedly.

Ransom shook his head, retreating from Kaiser as Father offered him his knife, and all the while I went unnoticed as I strode closer, my mind a sea of red.

"Like this, son," Father said, twisting towards Kaiser and casting a whip of water that knotted around his neck and cut off his air supply. Father regarded Kaiser's chest as if deciding where to cut next and I winced as he sliced a shallow slash across the scar my dagger had given him.

"Where is your whore of a mother hiding?" Father demanded,

releasing the tether around Kaiser's neck so he could speak.

"Fuck you," he spat and Father slammed a fist into his stomach, making Kaiser growl.

Father lunged to the side, opening a cell and grabbing a woman out by her hair and slicing her throat right in front of Kaiser so blood splattered him. "You want to die, you Flamebringer bastard? This is what will happen to you if you don't give me the location of The Matriarch!"

Ransom stared down at the dying woman on the floor with a pale face and shaking hands. Horror resounded through my bones at the ruthless death my father had delivered.

The warriors around us cheered as Father tossed the doomed woman to the floor, the sound drilling into my skull. They were so caught up in the blood lust of the torture that they hadn't seemed to notice my arrival.

I prowled closer to my father, seeing him for what he was like a veil was lifting from my mind. How had I ever craved this man's respect? Why had I wanted his approval? He was nothing but a vessel for death. A beast who lived for the kill.

He didn't care who fell to his sword. He had long ago lost the will to care for anything more than victory.

"I'll let you live if you give her up," Father offered Kaiser. "And if you tell me now, then maybe I'll make her death swift. If not, I'll cut ribbons out of her flesh and flay her good and slow. I'll make her scream for days and days. I'll enjoy her pain alongside all my warriors. I'll let them play with her all they like."

A cry of assent went up from Father's grunts, their twisted desires colouring the air as they shouted out the sickening things they wished to do with her.

Monsters.

Kaiser roared out in fury, his eyes blood red and promising death for Rake's words. But something was keeping his Order in check and I noted the range of strange potions laid out on a table at the centre of the room. Order supressing powder was among them.

"Come on Ransom. It's time you learned to have a little fun." Father grabbed his arm and yanked him closer to Kaiser again. "We'll work together you and I. And by dawn we'll have his secrets spilled. There's much to enjoy in this game. If you don't want him, pick another to play with." He gestured to the cells where more prisoners gazed out in terror.

"No," Ransom said, his voice barely above a whisper, but I caught it.

"What was that?" Father growled as Ransom backed away, shaking his head.

I was close now, close enough to smell the blood on Kaiser. To see the Avanis woman fall still at my father's feet. But amidst the carnage, only one Fae saw me. Kaiser's eyes burned into mine, his head lifting and a strange frown crossing his face as if he wasn't sure if I was a figment of his imagination. His muscles bulged like he wanted to break free, his jaw flexing and his eyes wild with the darkest of emotions.

Father's fist slammed into Ransom's cheek, sending him stumbling backwards. "What's wrong with you?" he sneered at my brother. "This is your birthright. You wouldn't be in this world if it wasn't for me."

"Neither would I," I said loud enough to be heard and Father and Ransom turned to look at me.

"You shouldn't be down here," Father snapped, glaring at me. "Get back to your quarters."

"I thought it mattered that you were my father," I hissed, ignoring his dismissal. "I thought I needed your approval. I have always wanted you to look at me like I'm something more than a runt. And now you have, but I finally see what you are and I find I don't want your approval after all. I don't want your wicked blood running in my veins. I'll spend the rest of my life rejecting the parts of me that resemble you. Because if being a Rake equals *this*." I gestured to the cruelty around me. "Then I'll have no part in it."

"You *are* a part of it," Father sneered. "You're the reason we defeated Avanis. You're why all these people are here. You can't wash your hands of that. You're a Rake through and through; it's time you embraced it."

I shuddered, glowering at him for branding me that way. "I would never have assisted you if I knew it would end in this needless bloodshed," I snarled.

"Needless?" Rake barked a hollow laugh. "These rats deserve to feel the wrath of Cascada upon their bones. Their pain will echo down through their bloodlines and strike fear into the hearts of all who come against us. We torture them to bathe in the victory of our great people. Our *better* people. It's an offering to Pisces, Scorpio and Cancer themselves. I'll paint myself in the blood of my enemies, man, woman and child until all of them are crushed and gone. This world will be won soon enough. And when it is, they will all perish. No babe shall be born outside of our superior water element and we'll cast any mistaken ones into the ocean!"

The Fae in the room cheered loudly, a roar of assent at such a vile statement.

My mother's voice echoed inside me, but I heard something different in it this time.

Never rest, Everest.

She'd wanted me to pursue all the rioting wants of my heart. She'd encouraged me through every step I'd taken to become a warrior but she'd also taught me mercy, love and compassion. This man, no, this *monster*, had taught me nothing except that brutality was the mark of a great Fae. But he was so wrong about that and I'd been an eskindo lidenti – *fucking idiot* – to ever believe it.

I'd sought the approval of a man I'd placed on a pedestal, this so-called exceptional warrior who was revered across our land. But if this was who they revered then they either didn't know the truth of him or they were as despicable as he was. And I was done being his puppet. Done standing at his side and done being his latest trophy. I was tired of the limelight and tired of being celebrated. And most of all, I was tired of ignoring the call of my innermost desires.

Ransom was watching me with riveted attention but no one else in the room seemed to notice the shift in me.

Father turned his back on me, prowling into another cell and dragging a woman out by her red hair. She had magical blocking cuffs on her wrists and was caked in mud. Her screams were met with more cheers and something twisted inside my skull as she let out a terrified cry.

"Wait, stop," the woman begged and I noticed she struggled to walk, like she was injured already.

A snarl peeled my lips back as my father tossed her onto a wooden bench and pinned her there by the throat.

"I like it when they fight," Father purred as the woman clawed at his arm uselessly, his dark eyes gleaming with menacing cravings. He took pleasure from her fear and the stars only knew what he'd do to her if I walked away. He didn't even ask a single question of her before he carved a blade down her cheek and she screamed as blood poured.

My mind quieted as my decision locked into place.

It was like I'd taken a dose of battle stims, my fears gone, my mind set. I was done denying who I truly was and there was a freedom in that which I'd never tasted before.

"Watch and learn, children of mine. This is what it is to be a Rake. We punish all who are not of our land, for they are nothing but maggots for us to crush beneath our heels." Father tossed the woman to the floor and caught her wrist, slamming her arm down on the bench and raising a knife from his hip to cut her hand off. She tried to fight free, shoving him, struggling with all her might as panic took over. But her movements were pained, jolted like she was in agony and I was done watching her suffer.

I struck like a viper. Fast, efficient, unstoppable. My dagger cut through flesh and bone as I lunged, the name Kaiser Brimtheon kissing the skin of my palm upon my dagger's hilt as if thanking me for this act against his family's killer.

My father's right arm fell onto the bench with a wet thump, fingers unlatching from the woman's arm. His scream was a roar that filled every space in that terrible room and the hairs on the back of my neck stood to attention.

Shock staggered through the brig for all of two seconds then bellows of 'traitor!' came from all sides. Magic crackled in the air as Father's warriors turned on me and I stifled it with nothing but a thought, the Void making quick work of muting their power.

"No more," I spat at Abraham Rake as he stumbled away from me, clutching at the gaping wound on his shoulder.

"Get her!" he roared, his voice riddled with agony.

Warriors came at me from all sides and I turned to my right, blasting three vicious balls of jagged ice at the Fae running my way.

They were thrown backwards from the force, chests ripped open and screams tainting the night as they hit the far wall and shattered the wooden hull. They flew out into the canal beyond but I had no more focus to give them as two more lunged from behind me.

I twisted around with the litheness of my Leopard form, capturing a woman in a dome of water and snaring the man in sharpened ice chains. Goshart had been my second victim, the man who was one of Father's favoured warriors. The woman began to drown but Goshart didn't have as long left in this world as the chains sliced through his body and cut him apart in a display of bloodshed that made Father roar again.

He made for the door in a flash of movement and I sent an ice blade flying into his back so he slammed to his knees with another cry of anguish. Ransom stared on from across the room, shock written into his face, but he made no move to stop me.

Four more warriors came at me in a blur and I leapt onto a table to avoid the swipe of their knives. I wielded the element of water, the beauty of it singing in my veins as it poured from me in a crushing weight of ice, spilling down on top of the four Fae, snapping bones as they crumpled to the floor beneath it.

I took on the final wave of warriors, using whips of water to hurl torture devices at them, slicing through flesh, causing a riot of screams. There was so much blood and death and I relished in it all, making them pay while their victims watched on in shocked delight. I made it hurt right up until the end, then I sent them into violent deaths and silence fell like nightfall.

Then there was only Father. His whimpers puncturing the quiet. Voices rose too, calling out to me from among the tortured Stonebreakers, encouraging me on.

I didn't walk toward him though, instead I turned for Kaiser, untethering him from the rack so he fell heavily to his feet beside me. I offered him my dagger but he shook his head.

"Together, silka la vin," he growled, his voice a dark river that bled into the most secret places inside me. He caught my chin between his finger and thumb and turned my face toward my father as he whispered in my ear. "Yon kiden shriveed haset raya, nord o sil oceania."

The use of my language sent a shiver rolling down my spine. *You have earned his death, warrior of the ocean.*

I was so caught up in the rush of the bloodlust, I didn't think twice about offering my back to Kaiser and stalking toward my father. I could feel him close behind me like a brutish wraith and it felt so terribly right to seek out death as one.

Father dragged himself away from us, cursing and shouting out for help. Not even Ransom offered it, my brother silent as he watched on.

There were yells going up on the hillside beyond the White Mare but I couldn't turn from Abraham Rake. The man who had crushed me beneath his heel too many times to count. The one who had declared me useless, a runt, a worthless daughter. But here I stood above him with all the power in the world in my grip and he could finally see how wrong he'd been to brand me those things.

"Who's worthless now, Father?" I hissed venomously before I stuck my dagger into his chest.

Kaiser grabbed an axe from a rack of torture implements, heaved it above his head and yelled, "For my mother, for my father, for my brother – they await you in death and I send you into their arms now where only torment awaits!" He swung the axe down, Father's shriek of terror cut off for good as he cut his head from his body.

The cheers of the captives rang out, emphasizing my betrayal against my own people.

I met Kaiser's gaze, the spell between us breaking now this act of solidarity was done and wariness took its place once more.

The word traitor cut through the air, bellows of my name sweeping from the hillside as the Cascadian warriors camping there stared in through the hole I'd blasted in the side of the ship.

Ransom walked toward me with wide eyes and I took a step back from him, half expecting an attack, unsure where we stood with each other now.

"You've done it now," he said shakily, looking to father's dead body then to the hoard of angry warriors baying my name.

"I have to run. I'll push you into the river to cover for you." I reached for him but he shook his head, grasping my hand instead. "I want out of this fucking life. Wherever you go, I'm going too."

"Ransom no–" I gasped but Kaiser cut in.

"There's no fucking time for this. Void them, Everest."

I looked to the hill as magic came blasting our way and I guttered it out, letting my Void sweep over my own people in an act of certain treason.

I looked to the Avanis captors, making a firm decision and using whips of water magic to rip the doors off their cages and tethers to free them all. Then I blasted a hole beneath our feet, grabbed the arms of the two people who had long been branded as my enemies and dragged them down into the embracing water below, tugging the Avanis captives with us.

The White Mare began to sink while we were swept away within the canal, guided by my magic as my mind scattered into a million pieces. I was a traitor to my land. I had nowhere to go. Nowhere to run. But I had never felt freer in all my life.

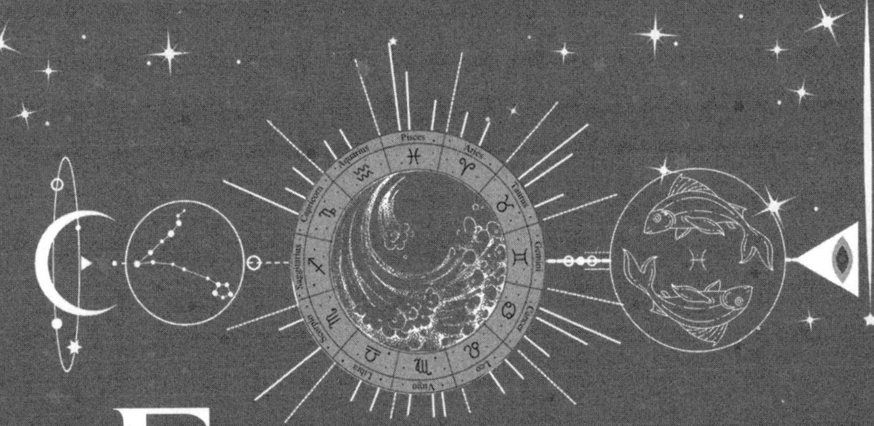

EVEREST

CHAPTER TWENTY NINE

When the canal met with the river and it became too wild and dangerous to traverse, I propelled me, Kaiser and Ransom out onto the riverbank and dragged the Avanis captives after us.

They crawled through the mud spluttering and gasping in relief as they clung to the damp soil. I'd kept the water away from their faces as best I could while travelling at speed through the canal but it had been damn difficult and I clearly hadn't done the best job.

I helped one of the women to her feet and she gasped as something pained her. Her red hair was plastered to her body and I realised she was the one Father had attacked as she lifted her eyes to meet mine. The gash on her cheek was shallow at least. It would heal.

"Have you broken something?"

"No," she said firmly, but her movements were stiff, like each step was agonising as I drew her up the bank. Our fingers remained clasped together as I looked to the other Stonebreakers.

There were nine of them in total and they'd all made it, so at least I'd kept them alive.

The woman's fingers knotted tighter around mine, her soaked dress now clean of mud and clearly speaking of her wealth.

"Thank you," she gasped, her green eyes wide and full of uncertainties.

I nodded stiffly, having no answer, unsure what I could possibly say about what I'd done. She'd witnessed firsthand the treasonous act I'd committed against my people. I didn't know where I'd end up now, only that I had to run and keep running until I could catch my breath enough to think.

"Why did you do that?" she pushed.

"I think… there is war and there is savagery. I won't stand for the latter," I explained.

"So you betrayed your own people for your morals?" she asked in confusion. "They'll never let you live for that."

"I know," I said tightly. "But I'd rather be standing here facing death at my people's hands than to have idly stood by letting my father and his warriors take pleasure in torturing Fae who had surrendered to us after the battle was won."

She gazed at me with something akin to admiration and I didn't feel at all deserving of it. I'd let this go on too long. I'd stood at my father's side. I'd helped him. It was my fault they'd been captured in the first place.

"But you're the Void," the woman breathed and I glanced at her people, wondering if they might make some move to seize me even in their desperate state.

"I am," I agreed, a warning in my tone that dared her or any of the

Stonebreakers to try something. They would hardly get far without magic or their Orders though.

"Some Fae can afford to make choices and run away, but you're the key to ending the war. You're the most important Fae in The Waning Lands," she said in disbelief. "You risked everything for a handful of Stonebreakers."

I said nothing, unsure I had answers to the frantic questions in her eyes. I'd done what I'd done. That was all there was to it.

"You should go," Kaiser told the woman and her people.

I eyed the Fury with caution, distrust crawling back into my skin. But what choice did I have now other than to stick with him until we were out of this mess?

"They're coming," Ransom hissed, tugging on my arm to draw my attention back along the river where we'd come from.

A great wave had risen from the water in the distance, a hulking ship of Cascada riding it and no doubt more followed in its wake.

I could sense their desire for vengeance on the air. I'd killed the great Commander Rake. If I was caught, they'd make me suffer deeply before I was given the mercy of an execution. There was no greater crime in Cascada than treason.

"What's your name?" I asked the woman as I released her hand and touched the magic blocking cuffs on her wrists.

"Septa," she answered.

"Well, Septa…" I used the Void to gutter out the power in the cuffs and shattered them with ice so they fell from her wrists, allowing her magic to flow free. "You'd better run and not stop running."

She opened up a tunnel in the ground with nothing but a wave of her hand and her people rushed into it, calling out their thanks to me while she lingered.

"I won't forget this," she vowed then she wrapped her arms around me, squeezing me tight.

I pulled her close, our hearts beating in unison for a moment, like they were one and the same.

She released me and raced down into the tunnel, closing it behind her to disguise their passage and I felt oddly sad at her departure.

"She could have taken us with them if she was that grateful," Ransom growled. "What the hell are we going to do now?"

"There's an archway a few weeks' walk from here. We need to head east," Kaiser said and my ears pricked up at that.

"An archway? Like the ones at Never Keep?" I asked in suspicion.

"Yes. It can get us far away from the Cascadian army," he said. "Let's move."

"We're not going anywhere with you, Flamebringer," Ransom spat. "I don't know what you mean by an archway, but I'm certainly not fool enough to follow you to my death."

"It's the best plan we have, pishalé. Take it or leave it but I'm not staying here to die." I stepped closer to Kaiser, touching the magic blocking cuffs on his wrists and cutting off their power before shattering them with ice. He stared at me with an intensity that made me shiver and I stepped back to put more distance between us.

"Take us there," I gestured for Kaiser to lead the way on and he ran straight for the trees at the top of the riverbank.

I sprinted after him, leaving Ransom to decide his own fate but not even a second passed before I heard him hounding my footsteps.

"Are you sure about this?" he hissed as he fell into step with me.

"Never been more unsure about anything in my life," I tossed back. "But do you have a better plan?"

He fell silent and that was the only answer I needed.

"Good. So just keep moving and cast some concealment spells while you're at it."

Ransom obeyed me – perhaps for the first time in his life. I felt Calcifiend crawl out from the damp curls of my hair, having lost track of him amidst the chaos. I was relieved to feel his little feet creeping along my shoulder despite what a traitor he'd turned out to be. Twice. I really had to stop trusting the sneaky little lizard.

Kaiser cast a silencing shield around us as Ransom and I moved close at his back and I tried not to consider the possibility that he was leading us into a trap. Even if he was telling the truth about the archway, what was to say a hoard of Flamebringers weren't waiting to capture us the moment we walked through it?

I just had to keep moving for now and deal with that when it was time to face it. The most urgent task was to get as far away from the Cascadian fleet as possible.

As the cold began to grip my bones, I wielded the water soaking our clothes and dragged it from the material, casting it the ground and leaving the three of us dry. Ransom grunted a thanks but Kaiser said nothing, running tirelessly on through the trees like he'd been gifted the energy of the stars. I had to be grateful for all those years Ransom had hunted me around Castelorain because this rocky terrain and steep incline would have slowed me down if not for all the practise I'd had in the past. Ransom lost pace with me but he didn't stop running, the heavy padding of his footfalls falling into rhythm with our breaths.

None of us spoke again.

Ransom and I ran and ran, following our enemy into the dark and I prayed the moon remained hidden within the clouds to aid our cover. There wasn't time to conceal our tracks beyond the odd blast of water Ransom shot behind us to try and turn the soil to mud. All we could do was hope we made it to the archway before the Cascadian warriors caught up. But a few weeks was a long time to remain hidden and I knew the army wouldn't stop hunting me. I would be the priority above all else.

A rumble of thunder behind us made the hairs rise on my arms, but the sound didn't dissipate. It grew louder, making the earth tremble beneath our feet and I realised my mistake in believing it was thunder.

"Hooves," I gasped, glancing over my shoulder but not seeing anything between the trees behind us.

"The cavalry's coming," Ransom said in fear, running faster to keep beside me once more.

"Don't stop," Kaiser commanded.

"I wasn't planning on it, asshole," Ransom barked.

We pushed on as the pounding hooves grew ever closer and I could feel the rumbling of their movements shaking the foundations of my soul.

"How close are they, fiend?" Kaiser called and Calcifiend took off from my shoulder, darting away up into the sky.

A beat of silence passed where I knew Kaiser was connecting to the Sayer Dragon to see through his eyes, then he yelled, "Faster!" just as an arrow of pure white ice sliced through the air and slammed into a tree to our right.

I glanced back in alarm, sending my Void out into the darkness between the trees, catching sight of glinting armour and the bright whites of horses' eyes. A cry went up among the warriors on our tail as I shut off their magic but that didn't stop them from gaining on us.

The trees ahead of us thinned and harsh brush scratched against my arms as we shoved our way through it. We'd made it to the top of a hill where a village clung to its side with a large belltower at its peak, but it was too exposed. There was nowhere to hide.

Kaiser turned and cast a wall of fire at our backs, the sheer height of it making my lips part. The heat washed over me and a series of startled neighs sounded as the Cascadians were forced to a halt beyond it.

Kaiser caught my wrist even though I never slowed, dragging me toward the village with Ransom on our heels. One look down into the valley beyond made my gut knot in horror.

Cascada had flooded it and the ships were dotted all between the hills toward the horizon, hunting for us. There was no way forward. No way back. And I could only blindly follow Kaiser as he tugged me past the belltower toward a ramshackle building that didn't look as though it had been lived in for over a century.

We hurried through a doorway that had no door to stop us and we all looked around in frantic dismay at the cold stone room beyond.

"Why would you lead us in here?" Ransom snarled, lunging at Kaiser like he might swing for him.

"There!" I cried as I spotted a hatch in the roof, barely visible in the darkness of the dank ruin. Kaiser leapt up, catching hold of it and tugging it open to reveal a small crawl space beyond.

"It's the best we've got," I hissed and Kaiser grabbed hold of my waist, lifting me up and half shoving me through the hatch with hardly any effort at all. I scrambled around on the dank boards beyond, casting an ice ladder from the hatch down to the floor and Ransom shouldered past Kaiser to climb up it first.

He barged his way into the small space and Kaiser entered last, his bulk barely fitting as he forced his way in beside me and we all laid down in tense silence. I melted the ice ladder and Kaiser swung the hatch shut just as the horses made it to the village.

With a shaky breath, I kept my Void power in check, not wanting it to pinpoint me here in this building. And in the dark, with Kaiser's silencing shield spreading out to encase the loft, I wondered how we would ever escape.

VESPER

CHAPTER THIRTY

The days were tense inside Wrathbane castle and I had more focus on me than ever before as I stalked its corridors.

Even training with my Sinfair Legion drew a crowd now, Fae sizing me up, passing judgements and either trying to win my favour or satisfy themselves that I wasn't worthy of it everywhere I went. I couldn't blame them. There was a twenty-five percent chance that I might end up their queen now.

The funniest thing was that I didn't even mind their stares. In fact, they made no difference to me whatsoever. Aside from making it impossible for my movements to go unnoticed. Which meant hiding my connection to Bastian was more and more difficult.

I found his gaze across the room when I sat at Evard's side for meals. Our hands brushed against one another if we passed each other in the corridors. They were tiny interactions but they had become the highlights of my days.

I was hopelessly corrupted by him now. And the truth of that filled me with both longing and fear.

Had it been so long since I'd fallen for this kind of trap that my bruised heart had forgotten all about what it had cost me the last time?

I wasn't his. I'd told him so plainly after waking in his bed that morning. But I wasn't anyone else's either. Defiantly so. My tolerance for flirtation or insinuations had always been flexible. Sometimes I'd even coveted the admiration I gained and made good use of the Fae who offered their bodies up to worship mine. But now I bit and sniped at any who dared so much as compliment me aloud.

There were whispers about it. The court believed me committed to my new husband and I allowed those rumours to flourish. But it wasn't for his sake that I now guarded my virtue like a pious little virgin. I wanted no eyes on me but those shot through with silver. I wanted no declarations from any lips but those which had worshipped between my thighs and left an ache there which refused to be banished.

I'd resisted the urge to return to his chambers since that night. But I hadn't once managed to resist thinking about him while I lay alone in the dark, silk sheets kissing my peaked nipples. My hands roaming wildly between my thighs, my orgasms all accompanied by the lingering memory of him.

Denying myself his touch was torture and I wasn't certain how much longer I could endure it. But I couldn't offer him what he wanted from me either.

Once again, I strode into the ballroom, walking between the towering statues of Gemini, Aquarius and Libra, my skin prickling as if those great stone monoliths might actually be watching me.

The king surprised me with his presence, though he sagged low in his throne at the royal table now, his breaths coming slowly, his eyes the only part of him which still seemed filled with vitality.

My gaze moved over the royal table, taking in those seated at it. Laurena, Alexandrius and Roarson were in their places. Evard and Dragor were not.

The thought of enduring Laurena's company for longer than absolutely necessary had me turning aside before I could approach the table. I was hungry, but I'd sooner starve than choose to subject myself to her barbed comments. It wasn't that her words bothered me. It was the fact that I couldn't be certain I wouldn't accidentally spear her eyeball with a fork at any given moment.

I found my eyes on Libra's statue as I turned away from the table and continued straight for it as if it had always been my destination.

For centuries, Fae had brushed their fingers along the base of the statues in this great room, begging for blessings from the stars and smoothing out the stone with a million loving caresses.

Behind the statues gifts were presented to the zodiac symbols too. Auras, tokens, notes, all heaped up and collected occasionally by the Reapers who used anything of value to maintain the astral sanctuaries and such.

I hadn't meant to actually ask anything of Libra, but as I approached the giant scales and assessed its balanced sides, I found myself scowling.

"If you are the deity who controls fairness, then how do you explain taking them and leaving me here?" I muttered, reaching out to scrape my fingers over the stone. Not in a caress, but a strike filled with accusation. "Where is the balance in that?"

No whisper came in reply to my scorn and for a moment I thought of the two comet pieces Bastian and I had stolen. Would I really be able to converse with the stars if I wielded mine? And what would I ask of them if I could?

Not that it mattered. Dragor had seized Bastian's pack and everything of worth within it when he'd captured him, so I doubted I'd ever lay eyes on those comet pieces again.

I made to turn away from Libra, my contempt at the symbol making it hard to stomach standing within its shadow, but as I lifted my head, movement beyond it caught my eye.

A dagger found its way to my palm in seconds and I rounded the statue, moving into the darkened space beyond it where the offerings were heaped up, awaiting the Reapers to collect them.

Long tapestries lined the walls back there, forgotten in the shadows and depicting battles long since won.

I stepped towards them, narrowing my eyes as I hunted for the source of the movement I'd seen.

The hairs on the nape of my neck stood on end. A low growl sent a shiver right through me.

I should have been shouting a warning to those who filled the great room behind me, but I said nothing, only moved closer to the danger which had my heart rate climbing beat by beat.

The distant flickering of a flame in one of the sconces near the dining tables illuminated the wall momentarily and I spotted a servant's passage hidden within the shadows between tapestries.

Nothing else was revealed by the fleeting light but instinct had me moving closer to that passageway.

Still my pulse climbed, still no warning sprung from me.

With my free hand, I took a sprig of rosemary from my pocket, the tip of my dagger grazing my thumb so that I could smear a drop of blood onto the herb.

Ether rushed through me as I opened myself to its current, the soft cry of my name reminding me that I still had work to do in service to this well of immense power.

"It isn't wise to stalk me in the darkness," I called softly so that only the creature lurking in that passageway would hear me. "But if you're keen to play with me, I'll just warn you that I bite…"

I crept between the tapestries, stepping into the dark passage, a wicked smile spreading on my lips. I did so love the hunt.

A growl called me on into the dark and anyone more foolhardy would have taken that warning to run, cry for help, alert the guards… but not me.

The passage turned a sharp corner ahead of me and I burst into a sprint as I ran for it, meaning to take my prey by surprise, to startle whatever beastie dared to tempt me into the dark. But as I sped around the corner, dagger in hand and ether pooling at my feet, an arm snapped out of the darkness and banded around my waist.

I was thrown against the wall, my attacker's hand managing to snare my wrist as I swung my dagger. He slammed my hand against the bricks above my head, caught my knee with his other hand as I aimed it at his manhood and pinned me to the wall in a move so fluid I couldn't counter it fast enough.

I swung my fist at his jaw, rosemary and blood crushed between my fingers as I sought to make him bleed and claim his body with the dark magic which was burning through my blood.

My fist connected with his jaw and his head snapped aside at the impact, a dark and familiar chuckle escaping him before his mouth took mine hostage and he let me taste the blood I'd drawn from his bottom lip.

"Bastian?" I gasped into his mouth and his laugh only deepened, his hold on my wrist tightening above my head until I released my grip on my dagger.

It clattered to the floor and I broke our kiss, turning to look back towards the ballroom, my heart thundering at how foolish this was.

"If we're caught–" I hissed but his hand was already beneath my skirt, his fingers pushing my undergarments aside.

"I'd stop if you weren't so wet, spectre. But it seems like cruelty to leave you wanting like this–" He sank his fingers into me with those words and I barely stifled a cry at how perfectly they filled me, how ruinously the heel of his hand grazed my clit.

I made a noise which should have been a protest but instead became a moan, my fingers fisting in the sleeve of his shirt as I felt the flex of his bicep in synchronicity with the motion of his fingers inside me. Rosemary tumbled to the floor, my blood stained linen, the ether spilled from my grip.

"My husband will be looking for me at breakfast," I panted, trying to remind us both of the folly of this. Evard might not care if I took lovers, but if we were caught in this position before his father died, so soon after the wedding–

"Don't call him that," Bastian snarled, taking his fingers out of me before thrusting them in again roughly. It was punishment and worship all in one.

"Silencing shield," I panted, biting back a cry.

"No," he replied with a dark laugh. "I want to watch as you try to stifle your cries. I want to watch you shatter for me in the shadows. I can't take another wanting look across the room, I can't spend another night knowing you ache for me like this and are going unfulfilled. Bite me like you warned you would if you can't contain the noise any other way."

"How do you know I'm aching for you at night?" I gasped as he twisted his fingers within me then used my own wetness to massage my clit expertly.

I bit down on my tongue while he watched me fight the pleasure he was giving me, my cries barely contained, too many people too close by for me to allow them out.

"You don't know your own power, do you? You've been sending me dreams, spectre. Filthy fucking dreams which make it very hard for me to keep to the vow I made you."

"Then don't," I hissed between my teeth, my fingers finding his solid cock through his trousers and caressing it with need. If he'd been sharing in my dreams then he knew how much I ached for him, so why was he so insistent upon denying me?

"I will," he replied, taking his fingers out of me so that he could catch my hand and stop my exploration of his dick. He grinned at me in the dim light as I fought against a whimper and he raised my arm so that it could join with the other, pinned above my head in one of his hands. "You're still not ready for me, love. But I won't let you suffer while I wait for you."

My spine arched against the wall as he took his sweet time running his hand back down my arm, along my jaw, down my neck, over my breast, my navel, the bunched fabric of my skirt, until–

"Fuck," I hissed as he pushed three fingers into me with aching slowness, his thumb finding my clit while he stretched me wide.

Bastian dropped his mouth to my throat, licking, kissing, his stubble a rough delight on my sensitive skin while his fingers fought each other for the right to be the one to destroy me.

My whole body was trembling with need, desire rushing from me so potently I knew the Fae in the ballroom would feel it. There would be a fucking orgy breaking out by the time we returned if I wasn't careful but– *fucking hell.*

I bucked against him, surging forward as he rubbed my clit in rough circles, the friction of his callouses bringing me to ruin far too quickly and yet not fast enough.

A cry built in my throat and I turned my head, giving in to what he'd demanded of me, my teeth sinking into his shoulder, my cry of pleasure buried against his skin.

I came in a flood of pleasure, my cunt clamping tight around his fingers, his wicked growl of triumph at my destruction making the ecstasy surge on for longer.

Bastian withdrew his fingers and I sagged against the wall, a heady smile on my lips which he kissed right off of them.

"Feel better?" he asked, releasing his hold on my wrists and gently tugging my undergarments back into place. They were soaked in my pleasure and would no doubt be a reminder of him throughout this entire meal and beyond.

"So you plan on luring me into dark corners and simply–"

My words cut off as a horrified shriek filled the air and we both jerked around to look back towards the ballroom.

More cries rang out, panic echoing from the walls and I shoved Bastian back a step before breaking into a run and sprinting towards the sounds of alarm.

Power buzzed around me, a shield of air magic springing from my fingertips to cover both Bastian and myself just as we burst from the concealed passageway and into the room filled with panicking courtiers.

"The king!" someone wailed and I used a blast of magic to force a path through the crowd so that I could approach the royal table where King Aquila lay slumped over the disturbed cutlery.

His arm was outstretched and a long, thin box was clasped in his weathered fist.

A Reaper was hunting for a pulse but I could tell with one sweep of my gifts that he wouldn't find one. The king held no desires in his heart anymore for me to take a taste of but the echo of his final wish lingered like a foul taste in the air.

My eyes fell to the box in his grasp. His choice lay within that carved wooden trinket, only to be revealed upon his death…

Bastian moved close behind me, the heat of him enveloping me as he pressed my dagger against my side in offering. I'd forgotten I'd even dropped the damn thing and my fingers curled around it gratefully.

My gaze flicked to Prince Dragor who stood at the end of the royal table, his eyes burning into me despite the scene which was unfolding before us.

I turned my focus back to the dead king, inching away from Bastian but holding my ground while many courtiers began to back up, edging toward the exit. They wanted to hear which of the king's children had been chosen for his heir – but they wanted to flee before the fallout of that decision struck.

Evard appeared through the crowd, striding towards the royal table just as Roarson moved to pluck the box from his father's dead hand.

On instinct I caught my husband's arm before he could pass me, jerking him to a halt and expanding the protection of my air shield so that it included him.

"What are you–" he began, tugging to free his arm but I only dug my fingernails in to hold him in place.

"Wait," I hissed in warning.

"This cannot be serious!" Roarson bellowed and my gaze snapped to the small scroll he'd taken from the box. Clearly the king hadn't selected him.

Dragor smiled darkly, moving to pluck the scroll from his brother's fist but Laurena got there first, a wild laugh escaping her as she read the name upon it and thrust the scrap of curling parchment aloft.

"The king is dead," she cried. "Long live the queen!"

The crowd broke out into excited chatter, some dropping to their knees and calling out praise to the new queen, others cursing and fighting to race for the exit.

"Laurena?" Evard growled, yanking on his arm in an attempt to free it from my hold but I snarled at him and tightened the air shield that surrounded us so that he couldn't pass through it.

"My first decree–" Laurena's gaze narrowed on me but whatever vile proclamation she'd been planning ended before it could so much as grace her lips, the bloody length of a sword appearing through her chest as Dragor struck like a viper from the grass.

Screams filled the air, the courtiers either ran or drew blades, battle breaking out as Roarson commanded his supporters into action to fight for the crown on his behalf. Dragor's warriors met them with sharpened steel and the clang of metal colliding echoed from the vaulted ceiling with horrendous sharpness.

"We need to leave," I commanded Evard, shoving him around and forcing him toward the door.

"I need to fight for my–"

I punched him in the jaw to shake the bloodlust from his gaze. "Your brothers are better warriors than you," I snarled. "But you are the better tactician. So tell me – what move should you make in this battle if you wish to see another day?"

Dragor bellowed a command for Bastian to join the fighting and I cursed as I shoved Evard away from my terrifying lover mere moments before he shifted, his oath to the prince compelling him into action.

Fae screamed louder as Dragon fire billowed above their heads, the statue of Gemini cracking down one side as Bastian's tail struck it.

"Retreat," Evard spat. "And let these two battle themselves towards death."

"Good," I hissed, my shield rattling as some bastard threw his magic at us in attempt to strike me or Evard from the game. "Then stay behind me and run when I tell you to run."

Evard cursed but did as I'd commanded, letting me take the lead so that I could carve us a bloody path to the exit before Dragor could turn his wrath and ambition upon us next.

Blood flew, Fae died, a Dragon bellowed fire throughout the ballroom and through the midst of it all, I cut a blood-drenched retreat for the man I'd never wanted for a husband. Because my fate had become bound to his. For better or worse.

SEPTA

CHAPTER THIRTY ONE

The pain in my joints was unbearable, far worse than any I'd endured before now. Somehow I'd found myself as the leader of our ramshackle group of escapees and that only added to the burden of our flight from the Cascadians.

We'd been beneath the ground for hours, the lack of light a trickster which had us all disagreeing on the time, or how long we'd been running for.

We hadn't slept, hadn't eaten, hadn't dared rest for more than a few moments at a time.

I'd bound my legs with vines and was using earth magic to propel myself along more than my own muscles because the stars knew I'd have never been able to keep up without doing so.

"A little further," I urged, my mind half occupied with the tale one of the warriors was telling me. He was recounting his training in the use of a bow in great detail so that I could study his instructions.

I was the only one among us able to regenerate my magic in our current situation thanks to my Order form.

As a Sphynx I needed to gain knowledge to recharge my power. Usually I made use of books to do so but I could do it while listening too. So long as I was learning, I was producing power.

Which meant that I was the only reason we were able to keep tunnelling our way to freedom beneath the ground. And I was the only thing keeping us alive.

"Avanis is too far to reach on foot," Tessa gasped, her hand pressed to the wound at her side which still hadn't fully stopped bleeding. She wouldn't complain of the pain she was in but I knew she was struggling to keep going.

She needed medical attention. We all did.

"We aren't headed for Avanis," I admitted, finally giving up the secret I'd been keeping from them all.

"What?" Tyrese bellowed, whirling on me angrily. "Then where the fuck are we going?"

"Back to Cinder Vale," I said, raising my chin. "Our army was decimated in the fighting there. I've deduced that it is more than likely that some underbeasts will have been abandoned in the tunnels we forged beneath the city. I plan to find one so that we can use it to return home."

"And if there isn't one to find?" Tyrese demanded, fury sparking in his eyes, an angry moo following his words and betraying his Minotaur nature.

"Then we are as dead as we would have been if we'd tried to walk the whole way back home regardless. It wasn't ever going to be possible for us to make it on foot," I said firmly.

"But you swore you could get us home!"

"I did. And I am. There will be an underbeast waiting for us to use. I bet my life upon it."

Tyrese spat at my feet and whirled away, the rebellious mutters of the other warriors joining with him as they gathered close together.

I knew they weren't glad to have me in charge of them. But I was the highest-ranking member of the court among us and the only one able to recharge my power. Besides, no matter their doubts, I knew my plan was the only one which gave us any hope of ever making it home.

"It's not much further," I assured Tessa, the only one to have stayed close to me following my revelation.

"Then lead on, my lady. I trust you."

That made one at least.

I nodded firmly, sending out a quick prayer to Taurus in hopes that my stubborn resolution to stick to this plan would work in our favour then continued the work of burrowing our way north.

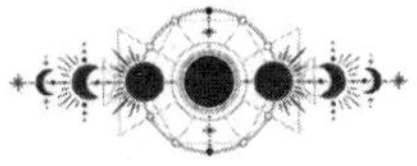

It took another hour for us to reach our destination and I had Tessa to thank for her faith in me as she'd stoically walked alongside me and recited the history of her family's mining business back home to keep my magic replenished.

I felt the shape of the underbeast in the ground ahead of us a few minutes before I managed to unveil it with my magic and a sob broke from my chest.

"It's there!" I cried, throwing my power out to draw the dirt and rocks away from the machine which had brought our warriors to this foreign land and receiving a cheer from the survivors as they spotted it too.

We all forgot our quarrelling as we hurried to clamber into the magically-powered transporter and Tyrese even took my arm to help heave me on board.

"We need magic to power this up," Amari called as she started inspecting the controls.

I moved closer to her, frowning at the series of levers and knobs which sat before the driver's seat, my mind whirring with all I knew about runes and their use in powering this kind of technology.

It wasn't something I'd ever studied in great detail but I did understand the basics of it.

"The runes should already be holding the magic the underbeast needs," I said, reaching out hesitantly towards the closest lever, my rudimentary understanding of the runes making me believe it was the one we needed.

As my hand curled around the metal, I felt a surge of energy awaken beneath my palm and with the slightest spark of my own magic, to urge it along, the underbeast growled itself to life.

Faelights flickered on overhead, a low rumbling sounding as the drills began to turn.

"Now what?" I asked, glancing at the others, hoping against hope that one of them might know something about how to drive one of these things. But all I got in reply were shrugs and blank looks.

"Now you get us home," Tessa said hopefully as she sagged against the wall, still clutching at her bleeding wound and the others murmured their agreement.

"Right," I breathed, my cheeks flaming as the weight of their belief in me settled like a blanket around my shoulders. It felt good. But it would have felt a whole lot better if I actually knew what I was doing.

I lowered myself into the seat intended for the driver while the other escapees took hold of rails and straps which hung from the ceiling. There were no plush seats in this contraption as there had been in the one I'd arrived at Cinder Vale in. This underbeast was meant for transporting our army, with as many bodies packed into it as possible.

My eyes roamed over the unfamiliar controls, my pulse thumping harder and harder with each passing second. But as panic threatened to rise up and devour me, I forced myself to close my eyes and focus.

The magic imbued within the rune which now glowed beneath my fist was potent and hungry, eager to…

I sucked in a sharp breath as I realised that the magic within it had already been cast with its purpose in mind. All I had to do was concentrate on it and I could feel the tug of its desire. This lever powered the drills…so that meant…

My hands flew from lever to knob, my magic connecting to the power held dormant within the controls as I untangled the mystery of their purposes one by one, instructions forming in my mind, understanding dawning on me piece by piece until finally–

A smile pulled my lips tight as I took hold of the lever which powered the drills and pressed it down firmly.

The underbeast snarled as it followed my command and we dove into the dirt with one destination firmly in mind.

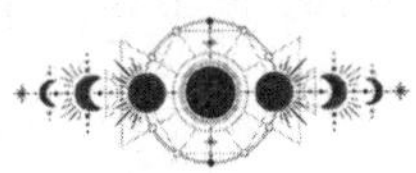

We burst from the ground at the foothills beneath Stone Castle and a sob tore from my throat as I took in the sea of endless greenery which was our homeland.

Every piece of my body ached, my wounds burning anew as if I'd put off feeling the pain of them until I could be certain we were safe.

I stumbled after the others as we clambered out of the underbeast, Tyrese carrying Tessa who was growing weaker and weaker from blood loss.

Warriors surged around us, hailing our return as a miracle, praising Taurus for our determination, Virgo for our fortune, Capricorn for our discipline.

We were bundled into carriages forged of vines and transported at speed back to the Stone Castle to make our reports and receive whatever medical attention we required.

It felt like a dream, my aching body a secondary consideration beyond the lightness of my heart.

"He's coming," one of the guards said to me, leaning close to make sure I caught his words. "He heard of your return."

My heart pounded at those words, anticipation filling me as I forced myself to sit up, hunting the path ahead of us for any sign of him, though it seemed like folly to do so. Would he really come so eagerly to see me? Had he been concerned for my fate? Was he–

"Alestro!" the guard called as we reached the huge, stone doors which barred our entrance to the castle. "Here she is!"

My heart sank at the use of my husband's name, reality crashing in on me as I realised who the guard had been referring to. Of course he'd meant Alestro. I was a fool to have thought he meant anyone else. Of course our Earl wouldn't have come rushing to greet me at the gate. I was no one. Just a voice in his court, a body to fill a seat. I may have earned my place at his table but he wouldn't have any greater care for me than any other member of his court.

The vines which had been cast to transport me parted and

I stumbled out, my ankle failing me and causing me to stumble.

Alestro caught my wrist before I could hit the floor, hauling me upright with a jerk that made my shoulder bark in pain too.

"What happened to your face?" he hissed, frowning at the bloody wound which had scabbed over down the right side of my cheek.

I blinked at him, my own words stalling as I took in the pustules which coated his own face, the marks of the curse upon him plain for all to see.

"I got my wounds in battle, husband. Which is more than can be said for yours."

Alestro's face twisted with anger but before he could respond to my barb, the stone doors crashed open and our group of gathered escapees and relieved guards turned to look as our Earl strode out.

My lips parted as I took in his huge frame, his powerful body half exposed where he was shirtless, bandages of moss and healing poultices coating a savage-looking wound on his chest.

His dark hair was pushed away from his face, his green eyes piercing as they locked on me and he shoved through the crowd to approach.

"You're alive," he breathed, reaching out to cup the right side of my face in his hand, his thumb tracing a line just shy of the wound which had been carved into my flesh. "Who did this? Tell me now so that I might hunt him down." His voice was a dark and threatening thing, the violence in it casting a spell over me which should have had me retreating instead of shifting closer.

I lifted my hand to place it over his, holding him there in case he might have been thinking to release me.

"We were taken captive by Abraham Rake," I told him. "He tortured and killed many of our people. But then one of his own turned against him and freed us."

My Earl's face tightened with confusion, his other hand reaching out to brush my waist as though he meant to pull me closer then thought better of it.

"Who?"

"His daughter," I breathed, my eyes locked on his, my husband utterly forgotten beside us. "She killed him and set us free."

"Which daughter?" Earl Tarlord asked, his body tense and aura threatening, but not to me, only to those who might seek to wrong me.

"Everest Arcadia," I told him plainly. "She killed him and ran. The Void has betrayed Cascada. The war is no longer theirs to claim."

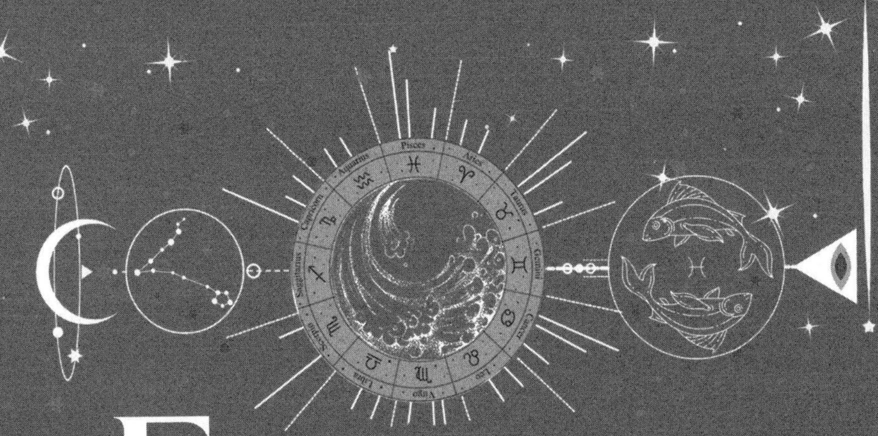

EVEREST

CHAPTER THIRTY TWO

Three torturous days had passed and my muscles felt so cramped it seemed like I was going to turn to stone at any moment. Kaiser watched the Cascadian warriors through Calcifiend's eyes for hours a day, waiting for a moment where we might make a run for it, but it never came.

The cavalry had set up camp in this very village and they'd been meticulously hunting the houses one after the other. When they'd come to this shack on the first night, we'd all held our breaths and prepared to be found but, by the luck of Delphinus, they hadn't noticed the hatch in the ceiling that we'd concealed with magic. We'd tried using Calcifiend to start a fire later that night to distract the warriors long enough for us to run, but they'd dealt with it too swiftly and we'd been nervous to attempt it again in case it confirmed our presence here.

Since then, we'd barely spoken despite our silencing shield.

We barely breathed half the time. We just waited. Perhaps to die. I didn't know anymore.

At least Ransom and I could cast water for us to drink, but our stomachs grumbled for food and the ache was growing intolerable.

Ransom was wedged hard in on my right and Kaiser was jammed in on my left, the heat of my enemy beside me always impossible to ignore, especially with the scent of oak and cinders taunting my senses. Ransom threw snarled remarks at him occasionally, threatening to throw him out there as bait to give us a chance to run. When I reminded him that his connection to Calcifiend might be our only hope of escape, he bit his tongue.

He had a point I couldn't ignore though. I wasn't throwing in with Kaiser by any means. But I did want to stay alive and right now his eyes in the sky and his promise of an archway to whisk us away from the army were our only hope.

A group of Cascadian warriors had made camp right outside the shack's door and there were three more camping close at its back too. Kaiser said little at all between his updates from Calcifiend and when he spoke again, all I felt was more resounding disappointment.

"No movement."

"There must be some change?" Ransom hissed. "Why aren't they patrolling? Or hunting us down in the woods for fuck's sake?"

"They're starving us out," Kaiser said darkly.

"How could they possibly know we're still here?" I whispered in frustration.

"They don't," Kaiser answered. "But enough of them have been stationed here to test that theory while the rest of them hunt the area. I've kept Calcifiend close to their new commander. Someone named Lisbeth Regal."

"I know her," I said grimly. "She's ruthless and damn persistent too. Kaské, how are we ever going to get away?"

Kaiser had no answer to that, but Ransom groaned.

"We're going to die in this fucking loft," my brother snarled, clearly running on fumes at this point. "I need a piss."

"Again?" I cursed. "You only went an hour ago."

"Alright I don't need a piss. I need a shit. And I've been holding it for three days so I'm pretty sure I'm gonna rupture my fucking spleen or something if I don't go."

Kaiser released a low growl in his throat, his anger evident and shifting the atmosphere around us.

"You got something to say, Flamebringer?" Ransom snapped, and I had to be glad of our silencing shield as his voice rose.

"Only that I am not going to die because some Cascadian bastard left a festering trail of turds right to our hiding place," Kaiser snarled.

"Well, we can't all start a fire in our ass and burn up our shits like you, asshole," Ransom hurled back.

"Can you really do that?" I whispered in surprise.

"Of course not," Kaiser growled back.

Ransom stopped the conversation dead by swinging the hatch open and drawing in concealment spells around him.

It was a relief to get some fresh air and a bit of sunlight from the doorway but my heart rioted as Ransom cast an ice ladder to the floor and descended. He kept to the shadows at the far side of the room and we lost sight of him.

While we waited, I melted the ice ladder and pulled the hatch shut, ensuring we were hidden if someone came into the shack.

"I thought you despised your brother," Kaiser said coldly, as if angry at me for changing my mind on that. I mean, I hadn't exactly gotten over all the shit Ransom had put me through in the past but I had found something of a kinship with him in recent weeks. I certainly wouldn't call him a friend. But the fact that he'd come with me, turned his back on Cascada alongside me, that had to change something between us, didn't it?

"I have many reasons to hate Ransom but he isn't the clone of my father that I thought he was. He cares – more than he'd like to admit. He was as sickened by my father's unnecessary violence as I was. Besides, what's it matter to you how I feel about him?"

"It causes me rage but I don't know why." Kaiser shifted beside me, all too close, his muscular body jammed tight against mine. There was no avoiding touching him in this space, the more I wriggled, the more I seemed to entwine myself with him so I'd given up trying to escape his all-consuming presence.

"Why did you come for me, hollow man?" I whispered, airing the confusion of my mind, all the questions I'd tried to avoid thinking about in this dank place finally bursting free.

"Mirelle suspected the Reapers of great atrocities some time ago. Now she knows her suspicions are correct and that they're bringing a monster to this world to destroy us all, she will stop at nothing to expose the Reapers for what they truly are and to annihilate that monster before it gets its teeth into The Waning Lands. But she could use the assistance of the Void."

"So she wanted you to kidnap me. Again," I said coldly, though I couldn't deny how The Matriarch's wants aligned with my own.

"No, this was my idea not hers. I told her I would come to you and ask for your help. Nothing more."

"And you thought I'd just run off into the sunset with you?" I scoffed.

"I seem to have gotten you running with me one way or the other," he said, a dry taunt to his voice. "Tell me, silka la vin, why have you come this far with me?"

"You know where an archway is," I said quickly. "You're my key to escape, that's all. That doesn't mean I'll go anywhere with you once we get out of this mess."

"So where will you go? You're the Void and now you're a traitor to your land. Every other nation will know of it soon enough and they will come hunting for you with even more vigour than before. You have no protection now."

"Yeah, I realise that, pishalé," I snapped, his declaration of my dire fucking circumstances not exactly helpful to hear.

"Don't you wish for the monster to be destroyed? Don't you want the Reapers to be served justice?"

"Is that what you want?" I deflected. "Or are you still Mirelle's puppet despite the fact that you're not under a spell anymore?"

"Since my emotions have been returned to me, I have wanted nothing more than I wanted to find you, silka la vin," he said, his voice full of grit.

A dark kind of desire rose in me. I recalled laying on top of him on the deck of the White Mare, how close our mouths had been, how fiercely my heart had beat at finding him alive.

He continued while I remained silent. "So perhaps I don't care much for monsters and Reapers while you are still at the crux of my mind."

"You said back on the ship that you didn't know whether you wanted to kill me or kiss me." I felt foolish for repeating it, but how could I not think of those maddened words he'd spoken to me?

"Your mouth is a want I'd commit treason for," he growled.

"Your death is what I hungered for in penance for your father's crimes. That's the logic of it. That's all I understand."

"But now he's dead," I pointed out, my skin prickling as a storm brewed between us. He was volatile and I had no idea how his emotions might swing next.

"Mm," he grunted but I didn't know what that meant.

I shifted away from him even though there was nowhere to go, a sense of danger shivering through my skin. Kaiser Brimtheon had no clue who he was anymore and he was torn between desiring me and hurting me. I hated to confess to myself that the feeling was mutual.

"Where does the archway go, Kaiser?" I asked in a low tone. I hadn't asked, sure I knew the answer anyway but I didn't want to hear the truth.

"It will take us to Mirelle and where all of Pyros is hidden."

I nodded thoughtfully, having expected that answer. "You'd trust me to wander into your stronghold alongside my brother? No chains? No cages?"

"Yes."

I believed him. I shouldn't have, but this plan of his to lead me to them would only be worth trying if he was telling the truth. Otherwise, he would have just captured me and taken me to them straight away.

"How is there an archway to your hidden place? Don't the Reapers know of it?" I questioned suspiciously.

"Mirelle has wedded Lazarus Astrophel and allied with the Vampires. They know how to build the archways."

"Hia Kaské," I cursed in shock. "I thought she refused his offer?"

"It's a strategic move. The Vampires are a fierce force. They will strengthen Pyros greatly."

"Eské," I swore again, thinking on how hugely this would shift the dynamic in the war.

"So what will you do?" he pushed.

I let that question hang in the air while I thought over my answer. Mirelle wanted the monster gone. I needed a strong force to get into Never Keep on the night of the blood moon. I couldn't let Harlon down, he was counting on me. Who really knew if Mavus would show up now? I hadn't seen him since the battle and the trader was hardly the most loyal Fae in The Waning Lands. But this decision meant placing my trust in the hands of my enemies. With time ticking down to the blood moon, the whole of Cascada hunting for me and few Fae to rely on, what choice did I have but to follow this path?

"I'll come with you," I answered firmly.

"Good," he said, his voice suddenly cold, like some new emotional turmoil had him in its grip again.

Before I could question what rogue feeling had taken hold of the Fury now, a familiar voice made my head snap up.

"Oh bother," Galomp lamented. "Please, I don't want to sleep in there. I do not. No, no."

A loud thump sounded below us and I heard someone scrambling around on the floor in the shack.

"Your traitor bitch isn't here to protect you now," a man laughed beyond the doorway. "Make camp in there or I'll tie you to a tree and let you sleep with the forest creatures."

The sound of their footfalls padded away and I reached for the hatch, meaning to yank it open but Kaiser grabbed my wrist.

"Don't be a fool," he snarled.

"He's my friend," I hissed back. "He can help us."

"You trust him implicitly?"

I paused, realising that yes, I did. Somewhere along the line I'd come to trust Galomp with my whole heart and honestly, what choice did we even have now? We needed help and there wasn't anyone better to offer it.

I tugged the hatch open, gazing down at my friend on the floor, finding him looking up at me from his back.

"Miss Everest?" he rasped and I extended our silencing shield around him fast.

"Yes, Galomp. It's me. Will you help us get out of here?" I asked, desperation laced to every one of those words. I trusted him, I really did. I would have thrown people to the wolves to get a taste of glory, but Galomp wasn't like me. Not even close.

Galomp threw a cautious glance toward the open doorway then nodded several times. "Oh boy, an adventure. A secret. Yes, indeed. I will help you, my friend."

Ransom appeared behind him, wielding a saucepan and swinging it for Galomp's head.

"No!" I gasped, casting ice over Ransom's arm and freezing it into stillness so he couldn't land the blow.

"He's going to rat us out," Ransom barked at me.

"Oh, *you* are here," Galomp said, turning to Ransom with a frown. "I do not like you. No I do not. Not at all."

"Well the sentiment's shared," Ransom sneered.

"He's our chance of getting out of here," I tossed at Ransom. "Be nice to him or we'll leave your ass behind."

My half-brother pursed his lips, looking like he definitely wanted to hurl abuse back at me, but somehow he managed to stay silent.

"Galomp, can you cause a distraction?" I implored. "Give us a chance to run."

Galomp nodded several times. "Oh boy, yes indeed I can. Give me five minutes that is all I will need. Yes it is." He bustled out of the shack, seeming excited as hell and I hoped to the stars he realised what this meant for him if he got caught. I didn't want to get him in trouble and I'd do anything I could to protect him, but we were star damned desperate here.

I cast an ice ladder beneath me and hurried down it, moaning in relief at being able to move my limbs again.

Kaiser followed me down and shot Ransom a cold look. "Done shitting?"

"Yes and I hid it under a flower pot in that little room over there if you must know," Ransom said, pointing to the rotting door that led into the only other part of this shack as if that was something to gloat about.

"Just focus," I demanded, moving into the shadows beside the doorway and listening for Galomp. "Kaiser, is Calcifiend close?"

He closed his eyes for a moment. "I'm directing him to Galomp now. Ah he's… okay, fuck, get ready to run."

A commotion sounded outside, the sound of many horses neighing then the wild thundering of hooves. Shouts sounded as some sort of chaos broke out.

"The warriors around the shack are moving," Kaiser said, moving right beside me next to the door. "Ten seconds. Nine, eight, seven–"

"Where will we go?" Ransom demanded in alarm.

"Just follow me," Kaiser snarled. "Three, two – go!" His hand latched around mine without warning and he dragged me out of the shack with Ransom chasing us.

Galomp was running towards us, the reins of three horses grasped in his hands including his horse Lalakin, my father's black war horse Karkinos and Ransom's beautiful white stallion Bay.

Behind them a herd of Cascadian horses had been untethered and were running, bucking and rearing up in fright from the swarm of ice flies that Galomp must have cast around them. The warriors were all rushing in to try and calm them down, leaving us unnoticed as we raced for freedom.

I grabbed Karkinos's reins, leaping onto his back as Ransom climbed onto Bay.

"Get away, vile Fury!" Galomp cried as Kaiser lunged for his mare and my friend elbowed him aside and climbed up himself. "I am coming! Ride Miss Everest! Leave this fire cretin to his fate!"

"No," I refused in shock. He couldn't be a part of this. He couldn't become a runaway because of me.

"I am coming and that is that," he said simply and there was no time to argue as a shout went up from a warrior close by as he spotted us.

Fuck.

I met Kaiser's gaze, having no chance to explain anything to Galomp as I offered the Fury my hand and he grabbed it, hauling himself up onto Karkinos's back behind me. His arms banded around my waist as I kicked Karkinos into a gallop and led the charge downhill beyond the shack, leaving the village behind us as we followed the treeline to the flooded valley below.

Ransom and Galomp's horses weren't quite as fast as Karkinos and they raced to keep up as we took the lead.

Another bellow carried from the village and I saw a man pointing at us from the hilltop. "The traitors are escaping down the northern slope!" He amplified his voice with magic and I cursed, willing Karkinos to go even faster.

We made it to the water's edge below and I froze it with a wave of my good hand, thickening the ice as we charged across it toward a forest on the other side of the valley.

Galomp and Ransom bolted after us but they were still ten paces behind and a cry of horror left my lips as two giant whips of water snared them both around their waists and yanked them clean off their horses.

"No!" I screamed, meaning to turn Karkinos back but Kaiser snatched the reins from my hands and kicked Karkinos hard in the sides.

I sent my Void out behind us, reaching for the warriors who were sprinting down the hill toward Galomp and Ransom, reeling them in. I managed to cut off their magic but it was too late as ten warriors fell on my brother and my friend. A scream left me, my fear for them palpable.

I was sure they were about to die, but it was a mercy when I spotted them being dragged away up the hill just as we met the other side of the flood and were swallowed by the trees. Lalakin and Bay continued running after us, bolting into the woods with us.

"We have to go back," I demanded.

"Forget them," Kaiser commanded.

"I'll die before I leave them." I turned my head to meet his gaze and his eyes flared with the red gleam of his Fury.

"You are the only thing that matters!" he yelled back.

"Fuck you. I'll Void you and leave you here to rot if you try and stop me from going back for them," I swore. Galomp didn't deserve this. He shouldn't have been wrapped up in my shit. He was in trouble because of me, and I'd be damned if I'd leave Ransom to his fate too after he'd given up everything to follow me.

Kaiser's jaw ticked as he considered that then he grunted in agreement, realising he had no choice. "Fine, but we find a refuge to hide the horses first and make a proper plan. Then we'll return."

"We might not have much time. They'll execute them," I said in terror and I had no doubt the Fury could feel every drop of my fear.

"They'll torture them beforehand. I've spied on your kind long enough to know that," Kaiser said grimly. "We have hours, maybe days. I'll send Calcifiend to watch over them."

I nodded, relenting to the fact that we needed a plan. And with the Sayer Dragon watching them, we'd find a way to return. Because I would not leave them behind.

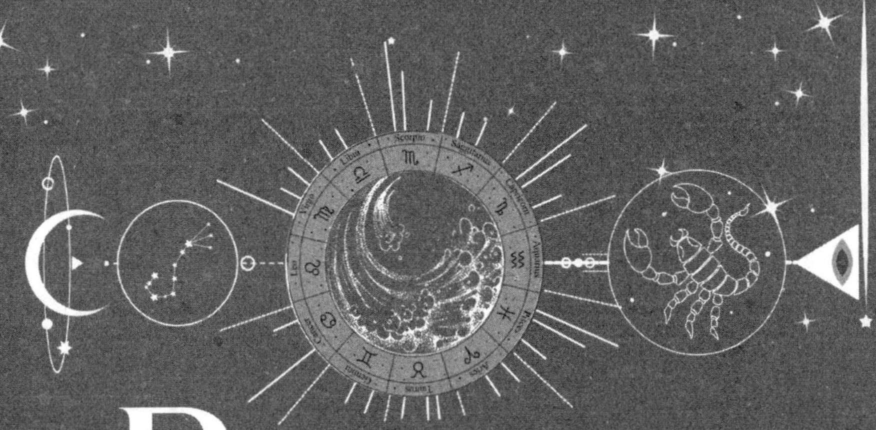

RANSOM

CHAPTER THIRTY THREE

I was tied to Galomp, back-to-back, magical blocking cuffs digging into my wrists and the promise of our deaths on the wind. A couple of warriors had force-fed us one of Father's Order suppressant powders that he'd often bought from Wandershire, the potion strong enough to suppress our Orders for several hours.

We'd been placed in the village square near a water fountain with a statue of a flaming Phoenix in the centre while we awaited our execution. But there was a lot of debate going on around how we should be dealt with. It seemed like a shambles in all honesty.

Lisbeth Regal, the new commander, was standing with a group of high-ranking warriors around her, all arguing loudly. It seemed her rise to power was not going smoothly, none of them taking too well to her rule. She'd likely asserted herself during the chaos but the usual proceedings involved a vote among the generals when a commander died in battle. That vote evidently hadn't taken place and now Lisbeth was struggling to maintain order.

Some cried out for our immediate execution while others pleaded the case for a long torture, while the last few tried to demand we were used as bait to trap the Void. My sister was a prime topic too. Many called for her capture but others were adamant she be killed. It was clear there was a divide here, some still hoping to placate Everest and earn her trust once more, while others wished to wield her as an unwilling prisoner. But so long as they couldn't decide, Galomp and I remained breathing and that was about all I could hope for to buy us time to escape.

"Stop wriggling," Galomp huffed. "You are twisting and turning and rubbing my elbows."

"We need to get out of here, you great wildebeest," I hissed at him. "We're down to our final hours, maybe minutes if one of these assholes decides to take this decision into their own hands."

"Yes, it is quite the bother. I am no fool, I am not. But wriggling will do us no good. We must cut our binds. That broken stone on the fountain's base looks sharp, yes it does."

I followed his gaze to the stone and cursed beneath my breath. He was right. The imbecile had more braincells than I'd counted on.

"Well get shuffling then, oaf," I growled.

"Oh bother, I do not like being called an oaf. And I do not like being bossed around either. You have a foul mouth and a fouler tongue. My uncle says men like you are just boys with bad tempers. I think he is right, I do."

"Move or I'll make you," I snarled trying to drag him but the bastard was too damn heavy even for me to lift.

"You are a very angry man. And I do not know why you ran with Miss Everest. Are you not sad your father is dead? I thought you were his favourite son, I did. You were his lap dog, why aren't you pining?"

I gritted my teeth, shoving my feet against the cobblestones to try and force him to move but he wouldn't budge. I let out a huff and answered him, figuring it was the only way I was going to get him to move.

"I'm no lap dog, oaf. Maybe I was once, but I didn't know what my father was truly like. I didn't see this coming any more than you did. I tried to give him the benefit of the doubt, but I saw too much."

"Oh," he said thoughtfully. "So you are not sad?"

"No," I hissed, but that wasn't entirely true. I'd felt a lot of things watching Everest kill my father alongside a fucking Flamebringer. Part of me had wanted to cry out and yell at her to stop, but another, darker part that I didn't understand had won out. It had told me to remain quiet, to wait and watch and let it happen.

So I had. And as he'd died, I'd felt both horrified by my inaction, pained at what I'd once shared with my father, but most of all, liberated by his death. He had never loved me, not really. Not in the way I'd thought. I'd seen his interest shift from me to Everest with such severity that he'd never even glanced back.

All the years of being his favourite, his doted-on prodigy, and he'd dismissed me the moment he'd seen something more useful in another child. I'd worked my whole life to please him. I'd tried to become all he'd wanted me to be but when I'd found myself on a battlefield, facing the reality of war, I'd flinched.

I still hadn't killed in battle. I'd avoided every strike, feigned kills by following the footsteps of other, braver souls. I was disgustingly cowardly when it came to war. And I would never say it out loud but I was damn relieved Father had never realised it.

And now he never would.

But I'd gone rogue, followed Everest and run from everything I'd ever known. What path would she lead me on if I could return to her? What place in this world did I belong to now that I'd turned my back on my entire nation?

No, I couldn't think of those things. I could only try and live one more day. Then I'd work out the rest. As long as I didn't have to run into battle again, I would be content.

"I am not sad either. He was mean and I did not like him. I do not like what the people of our nation are saying about Everest now either. I do not believe she is a traitor. But if she is, then I will be one with her," Galomp said proudly then he started shuffling toward the wall, dragging me along with him. Our ankles were tied so we couldn't move with any swiftness, but we managed to get to the wall and angle our wrists against it.

"Ok, they're not looking. Hurry," I hissed, gazing over at the arguing generals as we started rubbing the rope against the sharp rock.

"I will hurry, yes I will," Galomp assured me. "But if we get out of here, you will not call me oaf again, Ransom Rake."

"Deal," I muttered, wincing as the rock slipped and nicked my skin. "But you will in turn not name me Rake again. I renounce that name."

"What will I call you instead?"

I paused then answered smoothly. "Ransom Arcadia."

"That is not your name to take. Your mother was not her mother," he scolded.

"She's my sister. Fuck being a Rake. Arcadia has a nice ring to it. Why should she get to claim it alone? And my own mother's name was Squidly. So fuck that."

“Miss Everest will not like that, no she will not.”

“Too bad,” I smirked. “I’ve taken a liking to it.”

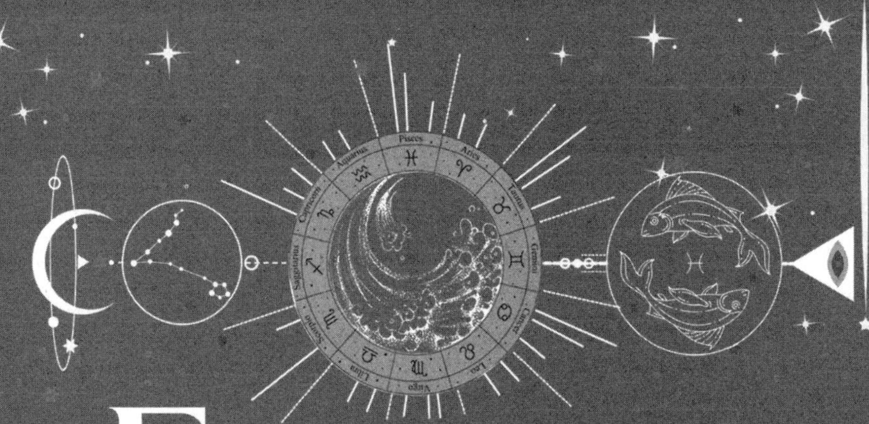

EVEREST

CHAPTER THIRTY FOUR

We'd left Karkinos, Bay and Lalakin deep in the forest in a concealed cave awaiting our return and had cautiously made our way to the edge of the flooded valley once again with a tenuous plan in mind.

We'd hurried along the water's edge for over half a mile until we reached a good viewpoint of the village perched upon the hill ahead. I gazed out between a gap in two trees which had wound themselves together as they grew toward the sky. The newly made river was busy with boats near to where we'd escaped into the forest earlier and the sound of warriors hunting us in the woodland made my heart race.

Kaiser and I had barely spoken since we'd formed our plan to rescue Ransom and Galomp but he'd silently followed me since, hounding my footsteps in a brooding mood.

I could feel his ire seeping from him but he didn't try to force me from this path again. I wasn't going to leave them behind and that was that. He could assist me or run and save his own ass. It was up to him.

"Can you see a good target, silka la vin?" Kaiser muttered in my ear, the sound of his voice after the unending silence making my pulse skip. I couldn't ignore the heat of him as he pressed close to my side and peered through the gap between the two intertwined boughs. His cheek brushed mine, fresh stubble like grit against my skin. The sensation drew a breath between my lips, the nearness of my enemy feeling like a sin against the stars. But I didn't draw away.

Whatever shaky alliance we'd formed was holding firm in the face of our joint endeavour. Besides, for reasons better left unexplored, I didn't currently have the desire to plunge my dagger into his heart anyway.

My gaze fixed on two warriors guiding a rowing boat across the water to our left, using their magic to drive it fast toward the forest's edge.

"There," I whispered, my eyes never leaving the pair as they met the riverbank and disembarked twenty feet away.

I felt Kaiser draw more concealment spells around us, tugging the shadows of the trees over us like a cloak.

"Stay here," he commanded, then strode off in the direction of the warriors, keeping his approach quiet with a silencing shield.

I cursed and chased after him, ignoring his order and hurrying along in his wake. "I can handle a couple of warriors, hollow man." I went to elbow my way to the lead, but he caught the crook of my arm and his fingers locked tight. His touch was unyielding, the kind that left no room for questions. But I wasn't his to command anymore.

"You're the most valuable asset in The Waning Lands. They will stop at nothing to capture or kill you," he warned. "I will handle this."

"I'm no one's asset," I said venomously. "And there's a reason I'm wanted." I turned and sent the Void tearing out ahead of me, finding the two warriors within the trees.

Kaiser hurtled forward as they let out gasps of alarm and I raced after him, rounding a large oak to find both warriors dropping to their knees before him. Kaiser's eyes were darkest red, gleaming bright as he caught both men with his possession.

"Strip," he ordered them and they did so, pulling off their clothes and laying them at the Fury's feet. "Now sleep." They lowered to the ground, falling into sleep and quickly curling in on themselves, shaking with terror.

Kaiser stepped toward them, releasing a low breath as he fed on the fear caused by whatever nightmare he'd trapped them in. I couldn't tear my gaze from his face, the way his eyes lit with their terrors, the closest thing to elation I'd ever witnessed from him. He was a master of horrors, wielding the deepest, darkest terrors of his foes and feeding them the worst visions he could conjure for them. Kaiser Brimtheon was a formidable creature, a monster even. And with the fears of others bringing him satisfaction, I wondered what he'd become now he was able to feel so much more than that one, harrowing emotion. Would he dwell in the darkest delights of war like my father had? Or would he learn empathy for those he tortured?

I picked up the standard Cascadian armour that the smaller man had been wearing, pulling my own off and replacing it with the drab metal that held none of the lustre mine did. I tied my hair back with a ribbon, keeping my curls contained and hoping it would pass as enough of a disguise to let me reach my brother and Galomp. Then I carefully hid my armour in a hollow beneath a leaning elm while Kaiser pulled on the Cascadian uniform of the other warrior. He was too large for it, the armour not fitting him well at all, so I moved forward to adjust it for him, loosening the leather straps that held the plates in place until they fit him well enough.

"You'll pass for a Cascadian," I said, studying him with a frown. "So long as no one examines you too closely. It doesn't look like you've seen the sun for months."

"That's not too far off the truth," he muttered and my frown deepened.

"Where has Pyros been hiding exactly?"

"You'll see soon enough. Get moving," he growled, jerking his chin at the rowing boat that had been pulled onto shore.

"You'd better watch your tone with me, hollow man," I warned. "I'm not your Fearsire anymore. This is my plan so I'm leading it."

I shoved past him and in a flash he whirled toward me and raised his sword to point at my throat. To make it worse, I realised it was my mother's blade in his grip, the shining steel perfectly crafted, gleaming with strength. She'd hammered that blade into shape, she'd crafted that hilt with her own fingers, and he dared wield it against me.

Kaiser's teeth were bared, a wild madness coursing through his eyes which slowly ebbed away as his gaze bored into mine. His lips twitched as he realised I'd unsheathed my own dagger and had jabbed it right against his cock.

"Are we working together or against each other?" I demanded. "Because I'm happy to de-cock you here and now if it's the latter."

He lowered the sword, carving a hand over his face with a grunt then jamming the heel of his palm to his forehead in frustration. "It was just a reaction," he snarled, seeming no less angry than before.

"A big fucking reaction," I accused with a sneer, lowering my dagger cautiously.

"I can't control it. Not yet. North says I need to learn to breathe more, but what the fuck does breathing have to do with it?" He jammed the heel of his palm against his head again and I regarded him, hating the way my chest panged at his struggle. I moved forward, one step then two, catching his wrist and lowering it for him so he didn't strike himself again.

He met my gaze, a harsh rage lining his features like he was a wild animal that had been baited and beaten. He looked… broken.

"North has a point – and do not ever tell him I said that," I warned. "That feeling…it's here, right?" I hesitantly loosened the straps of his breast plate and drew it off of him, tossing it to the ground. He eyed me closely as I placed my palm on his chest, feeling the furious pumping of his heart beneath my fingers.

He nodded stiffly.

"Breathe into it," I instructed and he sucked in a breath, following my instruction.

I lowered my hand to his stomach, feeling his muscles firm as my fingers sailed lower. "And here," I whispered, my voice coming out soft instead of hard.

He did so, his obsidian eyes still pinned on me. So harsh and unyielding was his stare that I couldn't help but meet it, unblinking and drowning in those molten black eyes.

"Better?" I asked, my voice nothing but a whisper on the wind.

"Much," he exhaled and the tension rolled out of the taut muscles that were knotted beneath my hand.

I withdrew but he caught my wrist, reeling me in, keeping me there a moment too long. A moment in which it felt like the stars had paused all of their great dealings to observe it.

"Wait," he growled, his gaze heated, still riveted to mine. "I've never seen your eyes without hatred in them." He stepped closer, invading my personal space like he belonged there, his thumb pressing to my temple and circling my right eye.

I pulled away, breaking the connection between us as panic rose in my chest and welded the gates shut between us. "There is never anything but hatred in my eyes when I look at you," I snarled then I picked up his breast plate and hurled it at him.

He caught it, pulling it on and tightening the straps as I turned and made for the boat, trying to ignore the erratic tune of my pulse in my ears.

I climbed into the boat, not looking back as I felt Kaiser climb in behind me. Then I placed my hand in the water and guided the little vessel forward, leading us across the flooded valley toward the base of the hill.

Kaiser dispelled the concealments around us, unveiling us for all to see as we made it to the other side and disembarked.

I walked with him up the hill, not too fast, not too slow, heads down.

We made it into the village without notice and headed toward the town square where Calcifiend had been keeping an eye on Ransom and Galomp. A ruckus reached us as we walked along an alley between two stone houses and we found a group of generals arguing loudly over what to do with their prisoners.

My hand curled around the hilt of my dagger at my hip and I drew in a deep breath. We were only going to get one shot at this and that time was now.

Galomp and Ransom were wedged up against a fountain at the heart of the square and as we started toward them, they broke apart, their hands coming free of the tethers which had bound their wrists together.

"Get them and run." Kaiser pushed me toward the fountain, giving me no room to argue as he went striding over to the generals like he could take on all ten of them at once.

I had no choice but to obey as he was about three seconds from giving us away so I ran straight for my brother and friend, taking out my dagger and slashing through the tethers that secured their ankles in place.

"Miss Everest, you came back for us," Galomp said with a bright smile as I dragged him to his feet.

"You're an idiot, runt," Ransom added as he jumped up.

A scream came from behind me and I turned to find Kaiser had caught Lisbeth Regal with his possession along with half the other generals. For a moment I feared he'd ignore my instruction and start killing them all, but relief filled me as he directed them to grab hold of their comrades and force them to the ground. The confusion caused by their own people turning on each other gave us long enough to run.

"Go." I shoved Galomp, pointing for an alley across the square and we sprinted for it just as Calcifiend came darting down from the sky to guide the way forward. He clicked his teeth in encouragement, flying ahead of us toward a street and leading the way across it, checking if the path was clear.

I glanced back, finding Kaiser tearing after us. I hated the relief I felt at finding him there, sure I should have been wishing for his death. But I supposed I needed him for now.

Calcifiend led us out of the village, ensuring we didn't cross paths with any more warriors. When we made it to the water's edge, I Voided the magic-blocking cuffs on Galomp and Ransom's hands, then shattered them to pieces with ice.

"Thank you, Miss Everest." Galomp beamed, then he shoved Ransom headfirst into the water.

"You bastard," Ransom spluttered as he came up for air.

"Oh do not be a boring Bob." Galomp dove in after him, and they wielded their element, letting the river swallow them so that they could sail across it undetected.

I snatched Kaiser's hand, tugging him after me into the water and he waded in with his fingers knotting around mine.

"I can't promise I won't get the urge to drown you," I taunted. "But I guess you'll find out one way or the other."

"I hardly have a choice then, do I?" he said with a dark look and I yanked him under the water, wielding the cold grasp of the river like a hand and dragging us away into the abyss.

BASTIAN

CHAPTER THIRTY FIVE

A cold wind raced across my scales as I stood tall and menacing in my Dragon form, a reminder of the power the new king commanded.

Dragor won the crown of Stormfell, though some might have claimed I'd won it for him when I'd burned his brother Roarson alive moments before his sword could carve through Dragor's neck.

The ballroom had been plastered in blood. One of the two Gemini statues had been reduced to a heap of rubble and the charred remains of the royal table had been disposed of almost as quickly as the corpses of three of the royal bloodline. Laurena, Roarson and Dragor's wife Alexandrius had all met with their ends in the wake of the old king's death. Only Evard had escaped and I knew that was entirely in thanks to one woman. My spectre.

Though where they'd run to, no one was certain.

A cold wind blew through the mountains and swept over my scales as I stood in my shifted form, a growl upon my lips while I looked at the kneeling members of the court of the kingdom of air.

King Dragor sat before his subjects wearing his newly-claimed crown and lording it over them in a tall throne, raised up on a wooden stage to make certain all could see him. His pet Cyclops Merika was moving through the amassed warriors and courtiers, politicians and war generals. I watched as she took the trembling hands of one Fae after another, her single, bulbous eye peering into their faces as she stole her way through their minds and sought out their loyalty.

This was the third day I'd been forced to endure this. Luckily, most of those Fae who had harboured secret thoughts of rebellion had quickly changed their minds on the idea when forced to watch me burn their co-conspirators one by one.

Dragor wouldn't stop this witch hunt until he'd had Merika test every one of the court's most powerful subjects. Their loyalty to him would be assured either through devotion or fear. He didn't seem to care much for which it was.

The cobbles of the courtyard that had once been a uniform and pale grey were now blackened with soot, forever stained to remind anyone foolish enough to plot against him of what fate would await them if they tried.

Vesper and her…*husband* were gone.

I knew she had saved him for the sake of her own vengeance, needing to maintain their alliance so that he could deliver his part of their bargain and give her the information she needed to find the man she hunted. But that didn't make me any more comfortable with the knowledge that the two of them were secreted away somewhere together.

She may have assured me that their union was nothing but political but that didn't make me trust it. He was using her just as she was using him. But I was certain that hers was the worse side of their bargain. Now she was in hiding with the most wanted man in the kingdom. Who knew when any of us would see her again?

The thought alone had kept me in a foul mood for days, the memory of her mouth against mine little comfort when I was forced to listen to the howls of Dragor's guards searching the city for her throughout the night. I knew better than to fear for her life, but I did fear for her freedom. If she had any sense she would have fled already, but my gut told me she'd done no such thing.

The light was dimming as the sun sank toward the horizon and my mind wandered while I waited for the last dozen Fae to have their fates decided.

Thankfully, Merika found no more traitors among them and I was spared the role of executioner at least.

"All hail King Dragor!" one of the faithful servants of the new king cried and the call was taken up quickly, the voices in the courtyard joined by those of the ranks of warriors who were amassed in the barracks beyond it.

For better or worse, the crown of Stormfell now rested upon a new head.

Dragor looked out over the crowd with enough smugness to tempt me toward the thought of roasting him alive. Not that I could do so while our deal and this damn collar bound us, but it was a pretty thought. I could almost hear the rattle his bones would make as they hit the cobblestones if I concentrated hard enough.

Just as the cries of his new subjects started to dim, an arrow speared through the sky and struck the wooden stage a few feet before Dragor's boots.

My head snapped up from the quivering arrow and the note tied to it as the scent of her caught in my nostrils. My spectre was haunting this gathering.

My lips pulled back to reveal my teeth. It probably looked like a snarl, but it was a grin in Dragon form.

Dragor stooped to snatch the note from the arrow and I leaned down over him so that I might read it too.

There was only a single word written in her curling hand – *'parlay?'*

A rumble of amusement rolled through my chest. Vesper was toying with him.

"Show yourself then," Dragor called and the sound of steadily paced footsteps came in reply a moment later.

I saw her over the heads of the crowd even before they parted to let her by.

Vesper was dressed in the style of the Sages of the mountains, a group of twenty or so of them following her into the courtyard, their eyes wild and the stench of dark magic clinging to them.

The seasoned warriors and bloodstained soldiers of Stormfell recoiled, many of them bowing their heads or dropping to their knees, muttering prayers to the stars to spare them.

But the Sages only had eyes for the king.

"The crown suits you well," Vesper purred, and I couldn't stifle the growl that escaped me as I noted the seductive tone her voice carried, the weight of her gifts spilling from her like poison. And every bastard watching wanted a taste of it.

She'd shifted. Her beauty in her full Order form was so captivating that it took me far too long to realise that she was holding the warriors back with air magic, keeping them from hurling themselves at her feet while they begged for the blessing of her attention. She'd muted them too, their desperate cries hidden within a silencing shield so that it was almost possible to imagine the only people standing in that courtyard were her, the king and the Sages. And I supposed they'd all taken note of the Dragon looming over them too.

"What is this?" Dragor ground out, his feet shifting forward a few inches and I could tell he was fighting with all he had to resist her allure.

"An offer. Evard will bend the knee if you keep him as your right hand and offer your word that you will make no attempt to take his life the way you took your other siblings'."

"And why might I do that?"

Vesper smiled and I was hit by her beauty like a bolt to my chest, my clawed feet striking the ground either side of Dragor's stage as I found myself fighting against the spell of her too. Though I would have gladly given in to it under any other circumstance.

"Because Evard is valuable…and so am I. You'd be far better off with us as your allies," Vesper said, her voice almost teasing like she was playing with this man who had named himself king.

She didn't state plainly that she included the Sages in that 'us' but the way ether rolled out from them to touch the stones of the castle walls made the threat plain. I knew too little of blood magic to fully understand what those devoted to its call were capable of, but I wasn't fool enough to want to risk finding out. This was an offer and a threat in one.

A growl slipped from me unbidden and Vesper turned those storm grey eyes on me at last.

"Down boy," she teased and I growled again.

Dragor seemed to be weighing his options, his eyes scanning the crowd who had been so easily cowed by the powerful creature before him. I wondered if she was doing the right thing by making this offer at all. It seemed to me she might just be able to claim the crown herself if she chose to fight for it in that moment. Though I supposed the cost of that decision would be paid in brutality and bloodshed.

"Deal," Dragor spat, his boot stamping against the wooden platform as he fought the urge to step closer to her once more. "Evard will be my heir until I produce another. He will swear not to harm me as I shall him, and there will be no quarrel between us. I love him, after all, as any good brother should."

Vesper's smile called him a liar as plainly as if she had shouted the word. But with a single nod she shifted back into her Fae form, and the Sages called the tendrils of dark magic they'd been wielding back to them too.

I released a deep breath, watching as it knocked the long curls of pale pink hair away from her face and tilting my head at her as she gave me a knowing smile.

I'd spent days fearing for her life should she be discovered, plotting ways to steal her away from here and making the decision to damn myself by turning on my captor if I had to for her sake.

And all the while she'd been ready to play this hand and save herself.

But of course she had. Vesper Crossborn was never going to be a creature in need of rescuing. She'd learned the hard way to always be her own knight in shining armour and of course she wouldn't ever wait on someone else to save her. She was formidable, terrifying and utterly unstoppable, like a force of nature given flesh.

And that was precisely why I was so endlessly enraptured with her.

VESPER

CHAPTER THIRTY SIX

"This feels foolish to say the least," Evard muttered as he moved to stand at the entrance of the room I'd selected for my own among his chambers.

I looked up at him over the knife I was sharpening, my eyebrow arching as I took him in. His return to the palace had gone surprisingly smoothly. Merika had rummaged through his thoughts of course to make certain he had no nefarious plans in mind to overthrow Dragor, but Evard wasn't the kind for rash and foolish plots based on nothing more than prideful ambition.

I had no doubt that he still harboured the desire to become king one day, but he wasn't going to end up dead trying to snatch a crown he couldn't be certain to win.

"What does?" I asked.

Evard hesitated for the briefest of moments then stepped into the room, offering me the ledger he'd been filling with information on my hunt for the bastard I still thought of as Cayde Avior.

I dropped my knife onto the desk and reached for the journal, flipping it open hungrily, the vial of blood at my throat warming as if they too knew that this mattered.

I flicked aside the pages I'd already read and stilled as I found both a written report and a hand drawn map awaiting me.

"He is being kept safely in the heart of Stone Castle," Evard said while my eyes drank in the detailed report one of his spies had managed to fill out for him on this matter. "They say he is cursed, foul to behold and covered in boils which were placed upon him by the Sky Witch."

A cruel smile lifted the corners of my lips.

"He's been trying to talk," I said and Evard nodded.

"They have tried everything they can think of to break the curse and unseal his lips so that he might be able to speak of the secrets trapped within his mind but nothing has worked."

"Only death can free him," I taunted.

"That is the assumption they've come to," he agreed. "And as such, there is quite the price placed upon your head."

I barked a laugh. "Good. Let them come for me. I'd welcome a fight after all these weeks stowed away in this castle, hiding like rodents in a trap, waiting for the Void to come for us."

"Don't tempt fate by speaking of that," Evard muttered. "Besides, we have it on good authority that the Void has returned to Cascada."

"Has she indeed?" My thoughts fell to Everest and I couldn't help but wonder if she was happy now that fate had gifted her all she'd ever desired. I couldn't say I was particularly satisfied now that fate had served me up my wishes.

"She has. Which has gone some way into helping me make peace with the fact that you'll be leaving to seek out your vengeance."

"I will," I agreed but as my thoughts turned to Avanis and the beginnings of a plot to break into the Stone Castle, a voice whispered my name. A voice I'd been trying to ignore for what felt like an eternity.

"Vesper..."

Cayde wasn't the only thing awaiting me in the land of earth magic. The ether had been calling me there for weeks now. And I knew I would be seeking out yet another corrupted ley line while partaking in the hunt.

"The map details the safest route I can provide you with for your journey. Though of course the Stonebreakers are known to change their terrain at whim. But they aren't expecting you and won't be looking for two Fae on foot."

"Two?" I asked with a frown and Evard gave me the knowing grin I'd come to understand meant that he was pleased with himself for some snippet of information he'd gleaned or cunning plan he was implementing.

"I've decided to send the Dragon with you."

"How?" I demanded. "And why?"

"The why should be obvious, shouldn't it? Do you think I haven't noticed the way you look at one another? I promised you could take your pick of lovers and I meant it – but I think we both know that this moment of political turmoil isn't the moment in which to have anyone questioning the strength of our union. So I would prefer it not to become common knowledge that the two of you are...entangled just yet. But Dragor is away for several days and left me in charge. So I get to make the call on what the Dragon does. Think of it as a gift."

"For what?" I blurted.

"For saving my life the night the king died. Don't think I'm unaware that I only draw breath thanks to you. And I am a man who always pays his debts."

I stared at this prince of Stormfell, a creature who should have been nothing but ruthless and cruel just as his siblings had become in their bid to seize the crown of this land. And in his eyes I found a tendril of compassion and understanding which I'd experienced all too infrequently throughout my savage life. He wanted me to seek out the vengeance I was owed and I may have been imagining it, but I had the feeling he wanted me to try and claim something more than that too, even if I wasn't ready to admit to myself that I might ache for such a thing.

"Thank you," I said and it may have been one of the only times I'd ever spoken those words and meant them with my whole heart.

"Make it hurt," he replied with a dark smile before turning and leaving me to prepare for my departure.

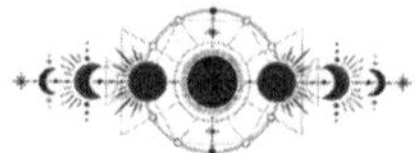

The flight to the Avanis border had been exhilarating to say the least. Bastian had transformed into his Dragon form and I'd ridden him across the snow-capped mountains of Stormfell and beyond.

We'd taken a route south which avoided all major cities and towns, adding several days to the flight in our attempt to go unnoticed across the skies of my people. But I hadn't complained about the extra time spent in his company or the nights we'd stolen to curl up together in a single bed within our tent.

Though I had found the time spent curled in his arms as torturous as it was satisfying.

Bastian still refused to bed me, his silver shot eyes drinking me in as he stole kisses from my willing lips, his mouth and hands venturing down my body to offer me a heady release of tension too – but he wouldn't allow me to reciprocate. And despite me loudly voicing my frustration at his stoic refusal to let me deliver him pleasure in turn, he still wouldn't change his stance.

"You know it makes no sense to deny yourself," I growled at him as he licked the taste of me from his lips, my body a trembling mess of destruction beneath him. "If you won't fuck me then at least let me taste you in turn. I want to feel you come apart for me, I want to swallow every inch of your solid–"

Bastian pressed a calloused hand down over my lips to silence them.

"I'm already yours in every way you want me, love," he said, his voice rough with desire, his cock driving against my clit through the rough fabric of his trousers as he settled himself between my parted thighs.

I whimpered at the closeness of him, my body aching for the fullness of his cock, my want for him a need which had a plea forming on my tongue. But he didn't want me to beg for his body, he wanted me to wrap my lips around words far heavier than those. And despite the feeling of them crawling up the back of my throat, I found myself unable to let them escape.

Bastian released a low curse, taking his hand from my mouth so that he could press a kiss to my lips in its place.

He rolled off of me and tugged my trousers back up with a sharp movement which had me growling at him in frustration.

"Do it yourself then," I urged, taking his hand and guiding it towards his throbbing cock. "If you won't let me do it then let me watch you. I promise I won't touch unless you ask me to…"

Bastian huffed out a laugh then turned his hand in mine, knotting our fingers together and stopping their descent towards his dick.

"No, spectre," he said, though I could tell he was tempted to give in at last. "Not yet."

"But–"

He took hold of me and rolled me onto my side, tucking me in against him so that my back pressed to his bare chest, his arm becoming my pillow while his lips pressed down on my neck.

"Tell me about another one of your adventures," he said, firmly ignoring the way I was pressing my ass against his solid cock.

It would have been so simple for him to just tug these damn clothes out of the way and sink inside me…but no. He was as adamant as ever to deny my body what it so desperately craved.

I wanted to convince myself that it was because he didn't want me ruining him. I'd looked into the facts of that rumour since returning to Stormfell and knew it was only meant to be true for Fae foolish enough to have feelings for the succubus they bedded. Bastian claimed to have such feelings so it made sense for him to fear bringing about his own ruin at my hands. But the more I tried to tell myself that was all it was, the less I managed to believe it.

Why keep asking me to tell him stories of my past then? Why share so many stories of his own with me? I'd told him many tales of the things I'd gotten up to with Dalia and Moraine by my side and I knew just as much about the friends and family he'd left behind two hundred years ago when the Reapers had taken him captive.

And every tale he told me only gave me more questions, every piece of grief or pain we shared only made me ache for the feeling of his body claiming mine all the more. But still, he wouldn't relent, wouldn't have me, wouldn't so much as let me release the need in his flesh with my hands.

It was driving me to insanity. And I knew the answer to my frustration, I knew how to claim exactly what it was I so wanted. I just couldn't make myself do it. I couldn't confess to feeling anything for him beyond lust because anything more than that would be too fucking pathetic, too fucking real.

I'd made that mistake already. I refused to do so for a second time.

But as I lay in the dark, recounting tales of when I'd been the closest to happy and listening to stories about his own losses and loves in turn, I found myself considering the words he wanted to hear from me more and more.

They simply remained caught in my throat.

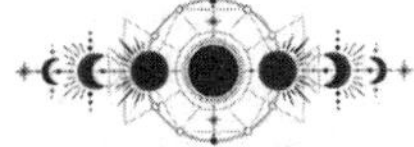

Crossing the border into Avanis had been the final marker for our journey by air, the clouds wrapping around us as we flew so high that Bastian's wings clipped the magical barrier which kept our continent isolated from the rest of the world. By doing so we managed to pass over the crackling boundary which parted Avanis from Stormfell but the air was thin at such altitude and even my shield wasn't enough to keep the worst of the cold from biting at me.

Bastian landed quickly after that, dropping down into a valley in the heart of the Ramdale mountains to shift back into his Fae form and avoid the eyes of any Stonebreaker sentinels who would be watching the sky for signs of an attack from Stormfell.

It was night and the land was so dark around us that my eyes could hardly pick out the gaps between the trees but I didn't dare risk a Faelight.

"Are you good?" I asked Bastian while he dressed in the dark clothing of his people, brown leather covering his huge frame and a fur-trimmed cloak wrapping over it once he'd finished lacing his boots.

My attire matched his, the Stonebreaker style fitting me in an unfamiliar embrace. We hoped to pass for citizens of this land if we were spotted and as such I'd once again dyed my hair – this time a pale blonde which Bastian had joked made me appear more approachable, less harsh. But anyone testing that theory would quickly be corrected on the false assumption.

"Yes," he replied. "Better than usual. It's good to be home."

"Home," I echoed, glancing around at the dark shadows of the forest. We couldn't see much but the scent of earth and greenery was far richer here than in Stormfell. "Did you live near Stone Castle?" I asked, wondering if I'd ever felt the same sense of belonging in my homeland as he clearly did here. The snow and the cold were familiar to me, comforting even, safe. But…I'd never called it 'home' with the same devotion he offered this place.

"Yes and no. I travelled a lot when I joined the army and spent a fair amount of time close to this mountain range. But my family hailed from Hallow Heath which is west of here. The mountains there aren't so tall but are far more beautiful. I'll take you one day."

"Promise?" I asked, wishing I could snatch the word back out of the air the moment it escaped my lips. But it was already gone and even in the dark I could tell he was grinning at me.

"Cross my heart and hope to die," he swore, painting an X over his chest.

I reached out to halt the movement, flattening his palm over the steady tempo of his heart.

"Not that," I said. "You're immortal, after all." I reached up to brush my fingers over the collar at his throat and he sighed.

"The moment I can rid myself of this thing I'll gladly do it," Bastian said. "I have no wish to linger in immortality. I only want to live a single lifetime. I'm just waiting for you to take me up on the offer of making it utterly unforgettable."

"You don't need me to provide you that," I scoffed, turning away but he caught my chin and leaned in to brush the faintest hint of a kiss across my lips.

"But I want it, spectre. I want it so very much that I can hardly breathe for wanting it."

I swallowed the words which knotted on my tongue and he withdrew a heartbeat later, stepping aside and looking out into the darkness.

I pressed my lips together, cursing my heart for racing so forcefully and curling my palms into fists to stop them for reaching out to pull him back to me.

I cleared my throat, focusing on the task at hand. "We need to move, put some distance between us and this place before dawn in case we were spotted in the sky or our arrival triggered some alarm," I said.

Bastian shouldered his pack then dropped down to place his palm against the dirt. I still wasn't used to that. Watching him wield his earth magic sent a tingle racing across my skin.

It should have been abhorrent.

It wasn't.

"Fate may be favouring us at last," Bastian remarked as he stood. "There are trails ahead frequented by some fairly large animals – bears if I had to guess. We can follow one to the foothills and avoid tangling our boots in the undergrowth and leaving a trail which might be found."

I nodded, moving closer to him and letting him lead the way on.

Bastian found the path easily, the trail left by animals wide enough for us to walk side by side and though we moved in silence, my hand brushed against his, sending a jolt to my pathetic heart.

I pulled my hand back but he caught hold of it, binding my fingers within his and smirking at the path ahead when I made a half-assed attempt to retrieve it.

"Really?" I taunted.

"Oh stop pretending you don't like it. There's no one here to judge you but me and I've already made up my mind about you anyway, spectre."

"Is that so?"

"You know it is."

"I don't think I can recall. Why don't you tell me again?" I pushed.

"You want me to tell you that I think you're the most captivating creature I've come across in over two-hundred years?" he teased.

"Let's not forget that you were trapped in an underground cavern for the vast majority of that time, Bastian. I doubt there was anything captivating for you to lay your eyes upon beneath the dirt."

"You're a harsh woman."

"I'm an honest one."

"You're also impossible to compliment. You deflect and dismiss, you throw words like missiles and barbs, aiming to hurt in anticipation of any which might be aimed your way in reply. It's exhausting."

"If you're looking to be exhausted by me, Bastian, I can think of far more entertaining ways to use up your energy."

Bastian released a low chuckle. "Not yet."

I sighed audibly. "You realise I never asked you to care about me, don't you?"

"You realise you are worth caring for, don't you?" he threw back in reply, his silver shot eyes fixing on mine. "Because I don't think you do."

"Everyone who has ever–"

"That's just another wall you've constructed to hide behind, Vesper," he growled, drawing me to a halt and stepping closer to me. "But I can see you. You know I can."

I peered up at him in the dim light, my stomach knotting under the intensity of his scrutiny. I didn't like it when he made me study my own bullshit that way. I didn't want to admit to the truth of his claims. Because if I did then I would have to admit that I might have someone to care about again. Someone who mattered to me. Someone to lose. And I couldn't afford for that to be true.

I almost bit back at him, almost cursed and baited him into an argument to escape the intensity of his expression. But as my eyes met with the silver in his I found I didn't want to fight for what might have been the first time in my entire life. I was so very tired of fighting all the time.

"Bastian," I breathed, shifting a little closer to him, my heart a riot of fear, uncertainty and expectation in my chest. "I–"

"I was told the Sky Witch would be hard to capture," a cold voice jeered from behind me and I jerked around, magic flaring in my palms.

But before I could so much as attempt to strike the Fae at my back, he shot towards me in a blur of motion, a syringe in his fist driving straight for my throat.

I jerked aside, the needle grazing my skin, air magic exploding from me and hurling the Vampire back.

Bastian released a Dragon's roar behind me and I spared a single second looking to him in panic. My eyes locked on the needle that another of the Vampires had managed to drive into his arm, whatever concoction lay within it now surging into his veins.

That moment cost me whatever chance I might have had to escape, the Vampires surging around me so fast that I barely even felt the stab of the needle as one of them drove it into my skin.

I threw my fist out, catching my attacker in the jaw and sending him stumbling away but more of them rushed me at once.

Blood flew as I swung my sword, curses coming from a Vampire to my right but as I tried to turn towards him to continue my attack, my knees buckled and the floor swept up to greet me.

Bastian was fighting furiously behind me, the pained cries that came from his combatants confirming it, but I couldn't so much as turn my head to look.

One of the Vampires knelt down beside me as I lost all sense of feeling in my limbs, his cold fingers sweeping blonde hair out of my eyes so that he could look down at me with a cunning interest.

"Kaiser Brimtheon sends his regards," he said, making my thoughts twist in nonsensical patterns because why the fuck would that bastard have anything to do with this?

"The Fury sent you? Why?" I growled, the words slurring as I forced them from my throat.

The sound of Bastian collapsing to the floor had my heart constricting in my chest.

"He believes you might be interested in a proposal we have for you," the Vampire supplied.

"Then he truly is cracked in the head," I sneered, fighting to tighten my grip on my blade but darkness was closing in around me and I could no longer feel the hilt in my fist.

"We'll see."

I parted my lips on a demand for them to leave Bastian out of this but the darkness swept in to consume me before I could manage it, my consciousness stealing away and my fate once again left up to chance.

VESPER

CHAPTER THIRTY SEVEN

"She's smaller than I remember," a woman said.

"She packs a wicked punch regardless of her size," a man replied roughly.

"Is he truly a Dragon?" she asked.

"We haven't seen him shifted but he fits the descriptions our spies in Stormfell gave. Can't say I've seen a bastard as big as him before either."

"Quite the pair…" she mused, footsteps moving toward me.

I knew that voice.

I was bound with my hands at the base of my spine and my ankles tethered too but the chair I sat in was plush and comfortable. The heat of a fire washed over me from my left and there was no echo to either the words of the Fae who were here with me, nor their movements, so I assumed the room we were in was fairly small.

I kept my eyes shut, letting my mind wake up while I took note of what I could about my surroundings.

"I will admit I have my doubts about this. Not to mention what the rest of my people will think when it comes to light…"

Mirelle Brimtheon. That was who was speaking, though I didn't recognise the man she spoke with.

That was right – the Vampires had mentioned Kaiser when they'd drugged me so I supposed he was a part of this too.

I tested the strength of the ropes binding my hands, cursing internally as they caught against a pair of cuffs which were stopping my magic in its tracks. Unsurprisingly I was tied tightly and I knew within moments that I wasn't going to be able to free myself without them noticing.

They didn't seem inclined to speak much more so I gave in to the inevitable and opened my eyes, straightening in my seat as I did so and fixing Mirelle Brimtheon with a dark glare. She was dressed in black with a magpie perched on her shoulder that scrutinised me closely.

"Your eyes are the colour of my tormented soul," a voice blurted from my right and I cut my attention that way, taking in the Wolf who so often hung around Kaiser. But there was no sign of the Fury in the room despite the Vampire having mentioned him. Everest had told me she'd killed him so perhaps the order to grab me had been given before that. But that made no sense. The last I'd seen of the Fury had been when I was a captor of Pyros before. He wouldn't have had any need to capture me then…so had Everest been mistaken in thinking she'd killed him?

"North," Mirelle growled. "I warned you that you will not be permitted to stay if you cannot hold your tongue around her."

I ignored them, my eyes roaming over the lavishly furnished room as I took in the copper-haired Vampire who stood a little behind

Mirelle, his predatory gaze locked on me. What was all this then? Had Pyros made an alliance with the Vampires?

We appeared to be in a cavern despite the fireplace and plush furnishings. There were no windows in the room but the walls were hewn from stone much like the caves where Moya and the other Sages dwelt in the Cavern of Lost Souls. This place didn't possess the same taint of death as those caverns did though. It was homely, lived in, *nice.*

I wondered if this was the secret hiding place those Flamebringer children had inadvertently told me about when I'd saved their lives back in Cinder Vale. I supposed secreting themselves away below ground made sense. So long as no one knew where to look.

Bastian was slumped in a chair beside mine, the two a matching pair of red velvet and thick cushions. He was still unconscious but his brow was furrowed as though his dreams tormented him.

I relaxed a little as I took in the steady rhythm of his breaths, though I didn't let my concern for him show in so much as a flicker across my features. This wasn't my first time playing captive. Though most who had gotten me in this position before had met with death rather swiftly and no doubt spent their final breaths lamenting ever chaining me at all.

I was a monster which would only be halted by death itself. The fools in this room would learn that soon enough.

"You appear to be quite easy to capture, Sky Witch," Mirelle observed, moving to drop into a chair beside the Vampire – yet another matching piece to the set I sat in. The Vampire followed her lead and sat too, his hand taking hold of hers in just the right way so as to aim her wedding ring at me.

I grinned. "And you appear to have sold Pyros to the Vampires, Lady of the Flames," I taunted in reply.

"Our union comes with equal benefit to both parties," she replied coldly.

"If you call buying the protection of the bloodsuckers by parting your thighs and handing over the keys to your empire then yes, I'm sure you can convince yourself that it is equally beneficial to both you and him. I suppose fear of the Void pushed you to such desperate measures?"

Ice fell over the Matriarch's features as she took the brunt of my insult but she managed to bite her tongue against firing a return shot my way. The same could not be said for the mutt.

"Don't you speak about my mother like that, you beautiful bitch woman," the Wolf hissed, taking a step towards me then falling still as I cut him a look, my allure working its magic on him again.

He opened and closed his mouth three times over, clearly fighting the desire to spout some kind of desperate compliment my way.

Mirelle huffed in irritation, shooting a spark of flame at his ear to snap him out of it.

The Wolf yipped in pain, slapping a hand over the small burn before dropping down into a chair of his own and glaring at the wall.

"I'm certain I'm not the only one of us in this room who has secured a bargain by parting their thighs," Mirelle said, drawing my focus back to her. "I hear you are given your pick of the prisoners of war to use for your own sexual deviancies before you kill them."

"At least they die with a smile on their faces. Which is more than can be said for most of the Fae I kill," I replied, not bothering to correct her on that rumour. There were so many tales told about me that I'd long ago given up trying to defend myself against them. If people wanted to believe I fucked Fae to death then what did I care? It only added to the fear attached to my name.

"Though perhaps that isn't the truth any longer?" the Vampire asked, tilting his head as he inspected me. "I heard a whisper just this morning which suggested we might not be the only newly-weds in this room."

I said nothing. I was hardly going to admit to being a part of the Aquila royal family. It would only make the price on my head all the higher.

"Why isn't he awake?" I asked, jerking my head towards Bastian.

"We had to dose him five times over to put him down," the Vampire said dismissively. "I'm sure he will awaken soon enough. But it is you we wish to speak with most urgently."

"Oh?"

Here we were, at the point of this rendezvous and I was still no closer to being free. But if Bastian woke he might be able to rip his bonds apart with brute strength, so it served me to keep this conversation going for as long as possible.

"Do you know who I am?" the Vampire asked.

I made a show of looking him over, taking in all his long, copper hair which was brushed to a shine and the carefully cut suit, tailored perfectly to his frame before I shrugged.

"Some asshole in an expensive suit. But you weren't born to money and it shows."

The Vampire barked a laugh. "Spoken like a woman who knows the feeling well. But where I come from, we earn our place so it doesn't much matter if I am used to the wealth it brings or not."

"Of course," I agreed. "Well, that's what they *say* anyway."

The Vampire gave me a knowing smile and I almost felt myself warming to him. He certainly was good at putting on the charm.

"Go on then, tell me who you are," I said.

"I am Lazarus Astrophel. Ruler of Effelridge. You won't have heard of it but we know all about you and your warring nations."

"So the Vampires don't simply roam the wastelands preying on those foolish enough to wander into their paths then?" I asked, drinking in that information. For too long the world beyond The Waning Lands had been a mystery to me. And though this Effelridge place wasn't technically outside of our lands, it was beyond the borders of the four nations I knew and had explored through spy-work and warring. The idea of there being somewhere new for me to visit was intriguing indeed.

"Though we are of course well able to defend ourselves, we are in fact a place of peace and prosperity. Our land flourishes while the divided nations remain trapped in the dark shackles of war. Where I come from, we do not care what element you are born to, nor what Zodiac sign our people claimed at birth. All signs and elements, orders and bloodlines are appreciated and celebrated equally. And in so doing we all prosper through mutual respect and allegiance."

"Sounds…" I searched for the word and Mirelle supplied it for me.

"Wonderful," she breathed, gazing at her bloodsucking husband with what I could have been fooled into believing was true affection.

"I was going to say that it sounds like bullshit. But sure, let's meet in the middle and call it wonderful bullshit," I said with a sweet smile.

Bastian groaned beside me and I stilled, working to keep my emotions in check as I allowed myself a glance in his direction.

"Funny that you should be so disparaging of the idea of unity while conspiring with a Cascadian and travelling with a Stonebreaker," Lazarus purred.

My attention shot back to him, my eyes narrowing. "What are you talking about?" I sneered.

"The Dragon beside you used earth magic while attempting to fight us off. And we know all about your secret meetings with the Void – Everest is her name. Isn't it?"

Any amusement I may have found in this conversation died away at that accusation. A chill slipped through my bones as his words wound their way around me and painted me out to be something I refused with all my soul, mostly because I knew it was becoming a little too true to deny.

Traitor.

"You don't know what the fuck you're talking about," I spat, lurching forward and baring my teeth at him in warning. I may not have been able to free my hands or use my magic, but they didn't know I could shift.

The change tore through me in a flash, the Wolf crying out in wonder as my features transformed, my allure shifting from a flickering flame to a blaze of undeniable desire in less than a second.

Mirelle sucked in a sharp breath and Lazarus clutched the arms of his chair.

"Release me and hand me a weapon," I purred, my voice pure seduction, my words a command none could deny.

They all surged towards me, the magic of what I was captivating them as words of praise and devotion slipped from their tongues.

But just as I was certain they would do as I bid, the Wolf turned, snarling at the others, staking his claim on me and lunging for them with vicious intent.

His fist struck Lazarus in the jaw and the pain of the blow was enough to shatter my hold on the Vampire just long enough for him to grab a glass of wine from the table and throw the liquid in Mirelle's face to break my hold on her. The magpie cawed in alarm, fluttering away from her to perch on the mantlepiece where it ruffled its feathers to shake droplets of wine free of them.

The Wolf howled as the Vampire shot around the room but he couldn't get between us in time to stop the bloodsucker from reaching me and forcing a measure of Order suppressant down my throat.

I bit down on his fingers and spat in his face but by the time he managed to fight his way free of me, I'd swallowed enough of the foul powder to return me to my Fae form.

"What the fuck was that?" Mirelle panted, clutching at her chest and backing away from me with a look of horror written over her features.

"That was my spectre," Bastian growled from beside me, clearly having seen enough of the show. "And you're all fucking fools if you think that's even close to the worst of her."

"By the stars," Mirelle hissed, stalking back to her chair and grabbing a cloth to wipe her face clean while I fell back in my seat and laughed at them. "This is madness. I knew it would never work. Kaiser doesn't understand people like her. She is hateful and rotten right down to her core. Of course she isn't looking to end the war – why I ever allowed him to convince me that she was is beyond me. Kill her, North. We have no use for her after all."

Bastian released a deadly growl but it was the Wolf who spoke up in defiance of her order.

"Kai isn't wrong about this. He doesn't get this shit wrong and you know it. You haven't even told her what you want to do, so how can you make a judgement on her answer? Of course she's trying to escape, she's a fucking captive. So just tell her why she's here. You know we need her."

My laughter fell away as I listened to his plea on my behalf.

He wasn't even under my spell, yet he was begging her to let me live. That meant they really did need something from me.

"You speak of the Fury as if he still lives. But the way I heard it, he was killed at Cinder Vale," I said.

"Left for dead," the Wolf growled. "But not dead enough. I found him and saved him. Now he's stronger than ever."

"Is that so?" I asked, wondering what my kitty cat would think about that.

"Why do you need her?" Bastian demanded, bringing the conversation back to its point.

"Wait…I know you, Dragon," the Werewolf interrupted. "You were fighting in the ring for us at Cinder Vale – you were dressed as one of us then!"

Mirelle's gaze snapped to Bastian and narrowed. "I remember that too," she said, pointing at Bastian who only shrugged.

"What of it?" he asked.

"What were you doing in Cinder Vale pretending to be fire-born?" the Wolf demanded.

"I came for her, obviously," Bastian drawled, his focus flicking to me and the corners of my lips lifted in amusement at their outrage over having been fooled by him at the time. "But none of that answers my question. Why do you need her?" Bastian pushed, returning focus to the matter at hand.

"Because she is the only Fae we know of who is capable of freeing the keystones from the dark magic which binds them," Lazarus supplied.

That got my attention.

"How do you know about the keystones?" I demanded, my skin prickling at how many of my secrets they kept revealing. I'd told no one but Bastian and Everest about those. Moya and the Sages spoke to no one and they didn't know the full extent of what I'd been doing with the keystones regardless. Everest was as likely to align herself with these Flamebringer assholes as I was and Bastian… I shot Bastian a look, my gut souring at the thought.

"Don't you fucking look at me like that," he growled. "I'm not him and you know it."

"Not *who?*" the Vampire asked and I snapped back around to scowl at him.

"I'm surprised there are any of my secrets you *don't* know, parasite," I hissed.

"I'm a man who is always on the hunt for more information. But if you don't wish to discuss that, then what of our offer?"

"What offer?" I demanded.

Mirelle sighed, dropping back into her seat and waving a hand at Lazarus, presumably giving him permission to go on without her. She beckoned the magpie back to her but it cawed irritably, narrowing its eyes at Lazarus as if holding a grudge.

I could feel Bastian's gaze on me but I didn't turn my head to acknowledge him. I knew it was shitty of me to suspect him, but what was I supposed to think? He was the only person who knew the full truth of all I'd done with the keystones.

Behind my back, I dug my thumbnail into the pad of my finger to draw a drop of blood. I was done playing the part of a prisoner.

"There is a threat lurking beneath our continent. A monster born of dark magic and fed with bloodshed. You know of the creature I refer to," Lazarus said while Mirelle snapped her fingers in a firm command to her bird and the magpie reluctantly flew back to sit on her shoulder.

I said nothing but clearly he took my silence as confirmation and he went on.

"It has no name for there has never been another like it but we call it the eschaton star. Though it is not a star at all, but its power shall soon rival those of the deities of the skies if we do not make haste in stopping it."

Ether curled around me in answer to the small offering I'd made with my blood but I held it at bay as his words sank in. This was what I'd been working against, it was what I knew to be true but still had so many questions about. Even now I could hear the ether whispering my name, guiding me towards the other two corrupted keystones so that the flow of power through the ley lines could be returned to its true course.

"What will happen if that thing gets free?" I asked because I'd already seen the destruction it was able to cause when slipping through the cracks at Never Keep and devouring the sacrifices the Reapers laid out for it. I didn't want that thing ever gaining free reign to roam the four lands.

"The Reapers believe it will bring about a new age, punishing the wicked and removing them from this earthly plane. Leaving only the pious and worthy alive after it is done feasting – rebuilding The Waning Lands anew."

"And how exactly does it decide on who is worthy?" Bastian asked.

"It doesn't," Lazarus said sharply. "The creature is cunning and sentient – it knows that their worship of it is linked to that foolish belief and so plays along with their games, picking and choosing which Fae to devour in their ceremonies. But if it was free its appetite would never again be stifled. It is hunger, greed, gluttony. It will feast until nothing is left of this world at all. My people have spent years spying on the Reapers and researching what this creature is. Old prophecies warned of it but of course they take every Seer and make them their own, so there is no way the rest of you can learn the truth."

"Well that sounds fittingly horrific. But it still doesn't tell me what you want from me," I drawled, though his words were ringing throughout my skull, taunting me with the truth of them which I'd already suspected and was now confirmed.

"This problem is bigger than any war," Lazarus stated. "Bigger than any prejudice or hatred. It will be the end of us all if we do not unite ourselves against it. And even then, I will admit that I fear we may already be too late."

"Unite?" I sneered, my eyes moving from him to Mirelle, the effective queen of Pyros, ruler of my enemies. "You do know who I am, don't you? I can't even count how many of her people I have killed in battle. Not to mention the fact that my hatred for *your* kind is second only to that of the man I am currently hunting."

"My kind?" Lazurus asked. "What have the people of Effelridge ever done to you?"

"The Vampires attacked Never Keep and forced me and my sisters into battle–"

"A battle in which *you* killed one of my people. Not the other way around. And you hurled the rest of them through the hallowed archways. So why hold such a grudge over a fight you won when I am willing to forgive the fact that you murdered my kinsman?"

"That fight caused a distraction which ended in the death of the only people who have ever loved me!" I roared, all of the pain, heartache and anguish I'd kept buried for so long bursting from me in a fit of pure rage. "They died at the hands of a traitor who only managed to outmanoeuvre them because they'd been focused on dealing with the bloodsuckers. And for what? Why were your people there that night?

Just looking to cause bloodshed and feed their sordid desires."

My hold on the ether sharpened with my fury and I squeezed the cut on my fingertip, offering my blood to the potent power of all that was so that it would aid me in my moment of desperate need.

Power surged through my limbs and I ripped the ropes at my back apart, lunging from my seat and throwing my fist into the face of the startled Vampire before he could so much as think to shoot out of range.

Flames sprung up between us before I could further my attack, the ropes at my ankles tripping me so that I stumbled backwards.

Bastian bellowed my name but all I could hear were my sisters in their dying moments.

I bent to rip the ropes from my ankles but before I could complete the task, vines shot at me through the flames, coiling me in their hold and hurling me back down into the chair.

The flames fell away and Lazarus shot forward, baring his fangs at me in warning.

Mirelle cursed me, demanding once again that they just take my head but Lazarus held a hand out to her so that he might speak.

"We were there to seek out the eschaton star and try to destroy it," he snarled. "You and your sisters stood between us and it. At that time we had no alliance with any people of The Waning Lands and our desperate need to end this threat to us all led to an act which was foolish in hindsight. We hadn't learned of the ley lines being redirected then, we hadn't realised the folly of trying to vanquish it while that power still fed it. We know better now."

He swiped a hand over his face, banishing his own anger far more quickly than I was able to banish mine.

"But if it means anything to you then I am sorry," he said earnestly. "We were only there for the eschaton star. And now that we have learned of the ley lines' power being redirected and what you have been doing to repair that damage, we understand what needs to be done next."

"And what is that?" Bastian asked.

"Firstly, we want to offer you our assistance in reaching the remaining keystones. We understand that they need to be repaired but no one in Effelridge practices the dark arts beyond simple runes. We are not learned in ether and cannot replicate what you have done with the other keystones to repair whatever foul work has been done upon them to feed the power of those fallen in battle to the eschaton star instead of allowing it to return to the land as it should. To put it simply; we need you."

"So that's all, is it? You want me to ally myself with Vampires and the people of Pyros, betraying my homeland and making myself a traitor in the process simply because you asked nicely?" I sneered.

"It is because the world is in peril. Are you so spoiled from your life of pampering in Stormfell that you can't think of anything beyond your own desires?" Mirelle asked icily and my gaze fixed on her once more.

"Spoiled?" The word came out as a bitter laugh. "If you think me spoiled then you really do know nothing about me."

"We know you made friends with the Void because of this threat. Because both of you wanted to figure out what the Reapers were up to and wanted the monster gone," the Wolf piped up, drawing my gaze to him where he lurked in the corner. "Why is an alliance with a Cascadian acceptable to you in aid of this but not Pyros?"

My upper lip curled back as I tasted the bitter truth of that accusation. "We worked towards a common goal together. It was a cease fire. Not an alliance."

"You liked her," he accused, pointing at me. "Kai told me. He watched you with her. Calcifiend showed him everything. You captured her on the battlefield and let her go again. Maybe you can convince yourself that working with her to uncover the secrets at Never Keep wasn't treason but you know full well that allowing the Void to walk free definitely was."

"Fuck you," I spat, bravado spilling from me in waves but inside my heart was caught in a vice. The fucking Sayer Dragon. That little blue bastard had reported my treachery straight to my enemies. I was done. When this information made it back to Stormfell they would butcher me for it. And the worst thing was that it was the truth. I'd held the Void in my grasp and let her go. I *was* a traitor.

"I think what my spectre means to ask is what's in it for her?" Bastian said before they could respond to my outburst.

Lazarus glanced at Mirelle who hesitated a moment before nodding her agreement to whatever offer was simmering in his mind.

"Freedom," he said simply and I couldn't help but look to Bastian as that word hung in the air between all of us. It was his one and only desire after all. True freedom. "You will be welcome in Effelridge. You will be free of all obligation to Stormfell and Avanis. Free of obligation to any of the warring lands, in fact. You will be given a large house and the option to become whatever your heart desires – so long as you agree to live peacefully within our city and abide by the laws which unite us."

"For both of us?" I clarified because I may have had little to no desire to make any kind of bargain for my wretched life, but maybe this was something I could secure for Bastian. He deserved to be free of Dragor and captivity, even if I didn't.

"Yes," Lazarus said without hesitation. "The offer is for both of you, of course."

"Why?" I demanded. "You have explained plainly why you need me. I am the only Fae you know of who is both somewhat sympathetic to your cause and able to wield ether sufficiently to repair the keystones. But what is it you want from *him*?"

Again Mirelle and Lazarus shared a look, though this time it seemed they came to the decision to be less forthcoming.

"That is something we cannot tell you yet. But I assure you, we do not want you to fight or make war on our behalf. Our offer of freedom is genuine but there is a task a Dragon could perform for us *if* you were willing to do so. I can say that *only* a Dragon can do it. And we would not obligate you to agree. The offer of freedom is there regardless, we simply hope you would consider our request when the time comes for us to make it of you."

I looked to Bastian whose silver-shot eyes were as filled with suspicion as mine but what choice did we have? They held us captive and could do so indefinitely. I might be able to break free of this place but I had no idea where we even were. It certainly didn't seem like we were in Avanis anymore. How long had we been unconscious?

"I planned to restore the keystones either way," I said eventually, looking back to our captors, my distrust for them clear in my expression. "But if you want to grant us a place in your wonderous Effelridge for something I was already going to do anyway, then fine. Who am I to turn down payment for simply going about my day?"

"Good," Lazarus said, the relief in the room palpable. "Then you can set off at once. You will deal with the Cascadian keystone first."

"I have business in Avanis," I growled. "I won't be deterred from it."

"Don't worry, little Sky Witch." The Vampire smiled wickedly. "We won't delay you from your murderous intentions. You'll find yourself at Stone Castle far faster than you would have managed on foot, so long as you keep your promise to us."

"How?" I asked in disbelief.

"I can show you. Assuming I have your word you won't attempt violence if I release you?" Lazarus asked, eyeing me shrewdly.

"I swear it on every piece of kindness inside my empty heart," I replied, my lips lifting in a taunt. But clearly that was good enough for him because he banished the vines which had bound me and cut Bastian free too.

"Follow us," he commanded, taking Mirelle's hand and leading us from the room.

The Wolf followed at our backs and I gave him a dark smile as I looked over my shoulder. "If you plan on stabbing me in the back, I suggest you make sure your aim is good, mutt," I said. "Because I'll spill your guts across the dirt before you can so much as attempt a second strike."

"We're allies now," he replied, lifting his chin. "Don't forget it."

I snorted dismissively and focused on following Lazarus and Mirelle down a long, stone passageway.

The magpie on Mirelle's shoulder was scowling at me every step of the way. It seemed ridiculous to think such a thing of a bird but it was even ruffling its feathers as if in judgement of my every move.

Bastian prowled along at my side, ducking his head where the roof of the passage proved too low for him. His hand brushed against mine, fingers curling around my palm in a brief squeeze before releasing me again.

I'm here, that squeeze said.

Me too, my own grip replied.

We exchanged a brief glance then looked ahead once more.

Whatever awaited us, we would face it together.

Lazarus led us past a cluster of guards who all kept their faces turned from me stoically, making certain they wouldn't be struck by my allure.

I couldn't help but let my eyes roam over every detail I could glean of this place, taking note of everything even though I doubted I would ever speak a word of it to those I'd sworn my allegiance to. The passages we walked through were nothing but bare rock, the only thing to note about them the reddish quality of the stone so I supposed there would be little I could report regardless.

Finally, Lazarus opened an iron door which had been set into the stone itself, both he and Mirelle using their magic to unlock it.

We stepped into a wide chamber with nothing at all inside it besides three tall, stone archways which made my heart skip a beat in recognition. But how the leader of Pyros had come by any of them was beyond me. And if she had access to them then why hadn't they made use of them to wage war yet?

"How long have you had these at your disposal?" I demanded.

"What are they?" Bastian asked, frowning.

"These are the archways I told you of – the same kind I found hidden beneath Never Keep. Including the one which led me to you, defying the laws of time and space," I hissed and Bastian released a low growl.

"You intend to use these for war?" he asked.

"No. I told you, the war isn't our focus. Lazarus built them here after our marriage. We use these for travel only. And they happen to be able to deliver you to the keystones in both Cascada and Avanis," Lazarus said. "So you see, no one from Stormfell will ever know you deviated from your intended path if you choose to return to them.

You can help us defy the eschaton star and never let another soul know of what you did. Or you can accept our offer of a new life. The choice is yours."

"And if we refuse?" I mused, my distrust of those archways making the hairs on the back of my neck stand on end.

No one replied and I exchanged a loaded look with Bastian. This was no offer. It was an ultimatum. Not that either of us was surprised.

"I see," I muttered.

"So, Sky Witch," Lazarus purred confidently. "Are you ready to accept our terms and prove yourself in Cascada?"

I exchanged a loaded look with Bastian before replying, but really, it wasn't like I had much choice.

"Apparently I am," I said. "But you know what they say about making bargains with witches, don't you?"

"Enlighten me."

"You should be careful what you wish for."

"Oh I know that, believe me. But difficult times call for hard choices. I am hoping this one will pay off for all of us," Lazarus said. "Come, eat, sleep. We can leave in the morning when you're rested. And you'll be needing fresh clothes – can't have you heading into Cascada looking like Stonebreakers now, can we?"

I looked to Bastian again, protests rising to my tongue then falling away before I sighed, accepting the fact that I had no choice in the way this would play out.

"Fine. But we stay together," I said.

"Of course. Are you wanting separate beds or…" Lazarus looked between the two of us expectantly and I narrowed my eyes.

"If you are trying to imply something, just say it," I demanded.

"You are a Succubus," Mirelle noted.

"Is that an observation or an offer? Because you don't really look like you could handle me – no offence."

"I could," the Wolf blurted before slapping his hands over his mouth.

I scoffed but Bastian's booming laughter broke over us all. "No pup, you really couldn't," he said, stepping closer to me in what felt a lot like a claim from the biggest dog in the room.

I gave my Dragon a scathing look but I couldn't quite hide my amusement from him all the same.

"We have rooms prepared. But you'll understand that we ask you not to leave them while you're here. This place is a well-kept secret and we can't have you discovering more about it than entirely necessary. At least not until we trust you a whole lot more," Mirelle said. "And I have a feeling that day won't ever come."

"Of course," I agreed easily, but we both knew she'd already shown me far too much. I'd have been a fool to believe she didn't have eight different plans in place to kill me after this was done. But if she was brazen enough to attempt my assassination she'd soon live to regret her mistake.

We headed back out of the room which held the archways and Lazarus and Mirelle diligently locked the door behind us before leading the way deeper into the passages carved through reddish coloured rock.

They guided us through turns designed to confuse and disorient us but I kept count of each one, noting them in my mind the way I'd been trained to.

"It's her," a girl whispered and I turned to look as a small child peered out at me from a doorway we passed, an older woman hurrying to take her hand and haul her back inside. "She's the one who saved us, grandmama."

My heart skipped a beat as recognition struck me, two more little faces appearing from behind the woman who was still trying to pull the first child back into the room.

"Stars bless you, lady," the woman breathed, bowing her head to me and pressing a hand over her heart before she managed to tug the children inside and snap the door closed between us.

"Told you she was nice!" one of the girls yelled and Bastian chuckled in amusement.

"I know what you did for those children," Mirelle said softly, not looking back at me as she continued to lead the way on but her magpie still watched me closely. "And I thank you for your mercy."

Mercy? Was that what it had been? I knew Dragor never would have named it such.

A barb rose to the tip of my tongue, a dismissal, a deflection, but before I could speak it, Bastian knocked his elbow against my arm and I cleared my throat before forcing different words past my lips.

"You're welcome."

Silence followed us until we reached our destination but there was a softness to it which hadn't been present before.

Finally Lazarus opened the door to a suite of rooms which had already been laid out with food on a wooden table set for two, a fire blazing in the grate to warm the space despite it being beneath the ground. The walls were bare, reddish rock but there were beds in two of the rooms which led from the central space, both dressed with warm, fluffy blankets in red and brown tones. To the side of the space, someone had hung two sets of Cascadian clothes from a rail in preparation for the following day.

"Someone was confident we'd agree to their terms," I said as I wandered into the space, the eyes of my enemies following me.

Bastian turned to Lazarus and held out his wrists. "Will you be taking these cuffs off us?" he asked.

"Not tonight," the Vampire replied. "But we will remove them before you travel in the morning. And we'll return your weapons to you then as well. The Order suppressant should wear off by then too, though it will keep your beastly forms subdued tonight."

"What about the rest of our belongings?" Bastian asked.

"Your bags have been searched and will be kept safe."

"I need my things," I said, not turning to look at them while I moved through the suite they'd given us to rest in. "The herbs, specifically–"

"Tomorrow," Lazarus promised. "But we won't be providing you with the tools of your craft while you're sleeping in our home, Sky Witch."

"Fine. But if I don't have what I need then I won't be able to do anything with the keystone. So don't fuck with my stuff and make sure it's all accounted for."

"Of course." Lazarus made to leave with the others but Bastian called after them.

"I need my tarot cards tonight," he said. "I need to replenish my magic and they're the most valuable thing I own. No offence, but your rugs and pillows won't suffice."

"North," Mirelle commanded and the Wolf nodded before turning and hurrying away. "He will deliver them to you. After that, this door will not reopen until the morning. There will be guards posted beyond it all night and the lock will only open at my magical signature."

"Don't worry. We have no interest in getting our heads cut off for the sake of exploring," I said dismissively.

The Wolf returned at a sprint, almost falling over his own feet as he stumbled to a halt in the doorway and tossed Bastian his tarot deck. The same deck I'd hurled at him in anger. The one I'd spent days picking out in the antiquities sector of Wrathbane, hunting for the most valuable set I could find so that he would never have to draw magic from mundane items again.

"Sleep well," Lazarus said in parting and the doors closed heavily behind them as they retreated.

A lock sounded and then we were alone at last.

"Well this is…unexpected," Bastian said, taking the tarot cards I'd given him out of their protective tin and shuffling them while he moved around the space they'd given us.

"It is," I agreed, moving to the small table and taking my place at it before loading my plate with food.

"You're not going to try and break out of here tonight then?" Bastian asked, taking a bread roll from my plate and ripping into it with his teeth before I could manage so much as a bite.

"I figure I may as well keep my word to them," I said, selecting a roll for myself and chewing thoughtfully. "Besides, they know all of my secrets. It seems like I have little choice."

"Come now, spectre, there isn't a Fae alive who is capable of backing you into a corner unless you want to be there," he taunted.

"True," I agreed. "Their wants and mine happen to be in alignment. So it makes sense for me to make use of their help in achieving them."

"The ether still calls your name?"

"Constantly," I agreed, the sound of it louder as I allowed myself to think of it. Drowning it out with my own thoughts had become a habit.

"Vesper…"

"And when they send us after the keystone in Avanis they'll be delivering me back to Cayde. If we run from here now, we'll only be faced with a much longer journey to the same destination."

"That's probably true," Bastian agreed and I gave him a cunning smile.

I was using them of course. And they were using me. I didn't like it but it seemed fate was always conspiring to keep me in these types of quandaries, my freedom as out of reach as his.

We ate quietly, both of us no doubt considering all of the implications of the arrangement we found ourselves in. My eyes roamed to the collar still fixed around Bastian's throat. Evard had given me leave to hunt Cayde and we could push the time that took to a point but we couldn't remain absent from Stormfell indefinitely without rousing suspicion. Not to mention what would happen if Bastian broke the deal he'd made with Dragor and was punished by the stars for it.

This freedom would be fleeting at best if I couldn't come up with an answer to that problem. Lazarus may have been willing to give us a fresh start in Effelridge but we weren't free to simply take him up on that offer.

"You're forever frowning, Vesper," Bastian teased.

"There is always something to frown about," I countered, pushing my empty plate aside.

"We should do something about that." He offered me the tarot deck he'd been shuffling and I indulged him by drawing a card.

The Tower, of course.

Bastian smiled and got to his feet, unclasping the fur lined cape he was wearing and tossing it aside before tugging his shirt over his head with one hand and dropping it to the floor next.

"Too easy," he remarked, reclaiming the tarot deck from the table and shuffling it again.

"Easy?" I questioned, my eyes moving over his powerful body, the lines of his tattoos almost seeming to dance in the light from the flickering fire.

Bastian turned so that his back was to me and pointed to the tattoo which depicted the card I'd drawn.

"Next," he commanded, holding the deck out for me again and my lips pulled up as I selected another.

The Strength card presented itself to me and I looked up from the depiction of a woman stroking a lion to find Bastian's eyes darkening.

"Control and surrender," he said.

"What?"

"This is my deck, love. And I'm doing the reading. There is strength in allowing yourself to submit control to another. So are you going to play along for me? I promise the reward you claim will be worth it."

I swallowed, my own nature demanding control at all times, but his words sent heat prickling over my flesh, my gaze roaming down his bare chest as I considered what fully surrendering myself to him might entail.

"We're in the home of our enemies," I said.

"I'm asking for your answer, not your excuses, love. So are we playing or not?"

I bit down on my bottom lip, glancing at the door before dragging my eyes over him once more and nodding.

"I surrender," I said, a teasing note to my voice.

"Good girl. Now take yourself to the bed and strip for me."

"Never in my fucking life has anyone called me a good girl," I growled, pushing to my feet, my fingers releasing the clasp of my own cloak before I let it drop to the chair I'd been sitting in.

"That's because you don't know how to *be* good, Vesper. But don't worry – I'm a damn good teacher."

A thousand words sprang to my lips in defiance of his commands but when my eyes fell on the Strength card once more I shut them down, wanting to play this game with him, wondering if I could follow the rules.

I turned and strode towards the bed, dropping items of clothing as I went, tossing them aside piece by piece until I was entirely naked.

I slowly turned back to face Bastian and lowered myself to sit on the edge of the bed.

Bastian took the two cards I'd already drawn and tossed them onto the heaped blankets behind me before leaning down to place one hand on the mattress beside me, placing his face in line with mine as he offered me the deck once more.

I drew without breaking eye contact and held it up between us for him to see.

"The Seven of Swords," he said. "That's hidden desires, love. Am I making you feel like you need to hide what you want from me? Because you're not doing the best job of it if I'm being honest."

Bastian tossed the deck down beside us then placed his hand on my knee and slowly tugged it aside, parting my thighs for him while keeping his gaze pinned on mine. I watched the way his pupils dilated as his fingers trailed up the inside of my thigh, my breath hitching as he closed in on my core.

My nipples hardened at his touch, my hands knotting in the blankets either side of me as I held myself still.

"Wider," Bastian growled as his knuckles brushed the inside of my other thigh and I obediently parted my legs further for him, the reward of his fingers stroking across my slick entrance coming a heartbeat later.

He growled lustfully as he ran his fingers over my clit, wetting them in my arousal for several seconds before withdrawing his hand

and licking his fingers clean.

I bit down on a curse as he held the deck out for me again, then snatched a card from the top of it.

"The Empress," Bastian said with a wicked grin. "That's loving yourself, isn't it? So go on then, spectre, show me how much you love yourself."

My chest was heaving with expectation, my body aching with need already and despite my desperate want for him to be the one to destroy me, I gave in to his command and moved my own hand between my thighs in place of his.

Bastian stepped back, his gaze burning into me as he watched the way I stroked my clit, my other hand toying with my breast as a heady moan escaped my lips.

I continued to rub and tease myself, my fingers bringing a rush of pleasure closer and closer and–

Bastian caught my wrist and tugged my hand aside. "Draw," he growled, his muscles rigid with tension, the cards fisted in his hand between us.

"You're not playing fair," I panted, tugging a card from the deck anyway, but in my haste, two came free at once, the pair of them falling to the bed beside me.

We both looked down at The Lovers and The Devil.

Bastian grinned like a heathen.

"Good girl," he taunted again, but before I could protest his ridiculous assessment of me, his mouth was on mine and he was hauling me into his arms.

Bastian's teeth dug into my bottom lip as he bit me hard enough to draw blood before breaking away and flipping me over on the bed beneath him.

I landed on my forearms and he caught my hips, heaving me up onto my knees before widening my thighs and pressing his mouth to my cunt from behind.

I cried out as he devoured me, his mouth moving lower to worship my clit, his fingers finding their way inside me.

He gripped my hip, hauling me backwards, driving his tongue inside me, lapping and sucking, forcing me further and further towards the edge.

I pushed back against him, my gasps of pleasure punctuated by curses of his name as he feasted greedily. My head spun, my arms trembling where they held me up and the persistent pressure of his tongue across my clit.

"Yes," I gasped, driving back against him, trying to hold off on what I knew was inevitable.

He lapped at me again, feasting like he was starved for me and my fingers knotted in the sheets before one final rake of his tongue sent me crashing into an orgasm which stole all thoughts and sense of reality from my mind.

I collapsed onto the bed beneath him, and he slapped my ass before flipping me over and looking down at me with heady lust burning bright in his expression.

He was like a god lording over his land as he took in the way he'd destroyed me, but as I tried to reach for his belt, he only shook his head and knocked my hands away from the huge bulge in his trousers.

"Not yet, spectre," he panted, swiping a hand down his face before turning and striding away.

"Where are you going?"

"To dunk my head in a pail of cold water," he replied, striding towards the small bathroom and leaving me aching for more on the bed. "Most likely followed by my cock."

I growled audibly, shifting further up the bed and moving beneath the blankets. There was a Tarot card stuck to my ass, and I tugged it free while cursing him for his stubbornness.

The Tower.

Ruination at its finest.

I huffed in frustration, unable to even be fully pissed off at him because my body was still floating on a cloud of ecstasy in his wake. But I wanted to leave him feeling the same. I wanted my name to tumble from his lips in a moment of blissful release.

By the time Bastian climbed into bed and wound his arms around me, I was already on the verges of sleep. Cold droplets of water spilled onto my bare shoulder as he pressed a kiss to my neck beneath my ear and I smiled as he wound his arms around me and hauled me back against his chest.

"Goodnight, Bastian," I murmured into the crook of his arm.

"Goodnight, love," he breathed in reply.

As I drifted off, wrapped in the embrace of his powerful arms, for the first time since I'd lost the only people I loved in this world, I didn't feel the pain in my heart at all.

BASTIAN

CHAPTER THIRTY EIGHT

Our hosts delivered breakfast at what I assumed was dawn, though of course in our chamber beneath the ground there was no real way to be certain. We ate and dressed in Cascadian garb while Vesper muttered irritably about wanting to get on with her task in Avanis. But we knew the fastest way to get to Stone Castle was to do as they wished of us in Cascada first.

Lazarus led us back to the chamber which held the three archways and I looked over the Fae who had been selected to join us in this task.

A group of six Vampires, led by Lazarus and accompanied by the Werewolf North all looked back at us with more than a little distrust written into their features.

"Cuffs," Vesper said sweetly, holding her wrists high so that Lazarus could remove them for her. I said nothing as he did the same for me, but I sighed as I was reconnected to my magic at last.

We took our packs and weapons back from them next and the

Werewolf shifted uneasily beside us.

"How does this work then?" I asked, staring at the stone archways and wondering how something so innocuous was supposed to transport us across The Waning Lands.

"Like this." Lazarus took a pouch from his pocket and poured a measure of glittering black dust into his hand. He took a step towards the archway but I lurched forward, snaring his wrist in my grasp and peering down at the substance he held.

"Where did you get that?" I snarled, a Dragon's growl rolling up the back of my throat with the words.

"It was a gift," Lazarus said hesitantly. "Do you recognise it?"

"The Fae who held me against my will forced me to create that. They dragged comets into the cave where I was chained and made me blast them with Dragon fire. This glimmering dust was the result of that. They gathered it up greedily and I know no more of its use or value than that. But it was the reason my life was stolen from me, the only purpose my captivity served."

Lazarus pressed his free hand to my bicep, his brow furrowing as he peered up at me with sorrow in his expression.

"That is how stardust is created," he said. "And without Dragons it cannot be done. The world's supplies of it are limited indeed. But I am so very sorry that you had to suffer so much for it to be created."

Accusations rose to my lips but the Fae who'd captured me had been Reapers. This man was actively working against their kind and he was a Vampire no less. I certainly hadn't seen any of his Order during the years I'd spent locked beneath the ground. He couldn't have had anything to do with my captivity. But that didn't make me feel any better about seeing the substance which I had suffered so much in pursuit of.

I released his wrist and he stepped back, moving to place the stardust into a shallow depression at the foot of the archway.

Vesper watched as the stardust raced up and over the outline of the archway, illuminating it in a bright, golden glimmer through which I thought I caught glimpses of something beyond this place.

Her hand knocked against mine, her fingers brushing my palm for the briefest moment. An acknowledgment of my suffering.

I gritted my jaw, meeting her eye for a moment before the two of us strode forward as one, diving straight into that glimmering light and letting it sweep us away in a rush of motion that had my head spinning while whispers pressed against my ears like we were being watched.

We stepped out of the archway, leaving it at our backs as bright sunlight blazed down on us and stole my ability to see much beyond my own boots.

Our entourage for this expedition followed closely behind us. Supposedly here to help us, though we both knew they were here to watch us too. Neither I nor Vesper required any help and they knew it.

I turned to frown back at the glimmering archway as the vortex of stars at its heart faded away and it was left empty. Only Lazarus held the stardust used to re-open it and without him we'd be returning to Stormfell on foot.

Sand shifted beneath my boots and I frowned down at it while the glimmering blue of the ocean lit the world in pale tones warmed by the sun in a way I hadn't felt in over two hundred years.

"If this is madness then I am happy to lose my mind to it," I murmured, tilting my head back and welcoming the warmth onto my face.

Vesper moved closer beside me, her fingers brushing against my waist, a poorly concealed smile on her lips as I looked down at her.

"What?" I asked.

"Poor Bastian," she teased, her fingers tiptoeing up my chest. "I didn't know you were such a sucker for the sunshine. Have you been suffering in the mountains of Stormfell all this time, hating the cold and the snow?"

"I gladly endured the torment because my reward for it was your company," I replied, causing her smile to widen a little more. The bright blue dress she wore to blend in with the Cascadians suited her well, the thin fabric meant for this climate and allowing me a look at far more of her flesh than the leathers she favoured in her home country.

"Are you two a…thing?" North blurted, reminding me forcefully that we had not come here alone.

"No," Vesper snapped while I replied with a firm, "Yes."

She scowled at me and I scowled in turn.

"Now he knows to use you against me if he has to," she chided.

"Not the other way around?" I asked, catching her hand as she made to withdraw it and pressing it flat against my chest above the pounding of my heart. "Feel how it beats for you alone, spectre. Tell me yours doesn't match its rhythm."

She swallowed back her reply, finding herself captivated by me for several long seconds before she snatched her hand away and turned to face the Wolf. He'd been sent with us by Mirelle as a test – if he didn't return with news of our success and in good health then we would be held to account for his demise.

"So which is it?" North asked expectantly and Vesper sighed, tugging her hand free of my hold and rounding on him.

"Ignore the Dragon. I have him in my thrall. I can place you under it too, if you like?" she suggested.

I growled, fixing my darkening gaze upon the Wolf who quickly shook his head.

"No thanks. I wouldn't fall for that shit anyway. That's an issue for weak minded Fae. So you're all his or he's all yours or whatever but I'm just here to watch… I don't mean to watch you fucking, just to watch you do this keystone thing. Unless option A is on the table and I might be persuaded – in a totally non-thralled kind of way."

I growled again, Dragon fire burning the back of my throat but Vesper only snorted dismissively and strode away from us both, heading along the beach and away from the rocks which concealed the archway.

North held my gaze for longer than most Fae would have managed but as I took a step toward him he ducked his head and strode after my spectre.

Pity. I wouldn't have minded wringing his neck.

Vesper hadn't so much as slowed her stride to wait for us and I stalked along at her back, watching the wind as it blew her dress around her legs, revealing the daggers strapped to her thighs. Blonde hair tangled in the breeze too and I found myself lost to the idea of her being able to simply stop and enjoy a single moment of peace.

I remembered then that this was the land she truly hailed from. She'd been born for the sun, her bloodline that of this place, not of the frozen expanse of Stormfell. I knew she couldn't have any memory of ever having been here but she'd taken her first breaths in this land, first opened her eyes to the warmth of this sunlight and felt the kiss of it upon her skin. My gut knotted at the thought of her never having had a say in whether she'd wanted to leave Cascada.

The Vampires passed me to follow her and all thoughts of stealing a moment with her in this beautiful place vanished. We weren't alone and our task here couldn't wait.

"We know that the keystone is somewhere in this region," Lazarus said, taking a map from his pocket and unfolding it. "We've been researching old records and have managed to dismiss some leads but–"

"I don't need a map," Vesper replied, not even bothering to look back him. "It's calling my name."

"What's calling her name?" North asked.

"Something far more powerful than anything you've ever so much as dreamed of, pup," I said, striding past him and the confused-looking group of Vampires so that I could follow Vesper along the coastline.

The sandy beach was beautiful but inland cliffs rose up behind it, all manner of caves and formations decorating their faces.

"Is it far?" I asked her in a low tone.

"No," she replied, taking my hand in hers and dropping the barrier to her magic in offering. The moment I let my shields down too, the roar of her name filled my head with so much force that I released her hand at once.

"VESPER!"

She gave me a knowing grin then turned abruptly toward the cliffs.

"Are you going to explain what you meant by that?" Lazarus asked, appearing on Vesper's other side in a flash of movement that had a snarl pulling back my upper lip.

"Maintain your distance," I warned him and he sighed but obligingly took a few steps to the side so that he wasn't walking so close to her.

"You might as well just wait out here," Vesper said. "Unless one of you wishes to volunteer yourself in sacrifice?"

"Sacrifice?" North barked. "Who said anything about a sacrifice?"

"It's not necessary, but the ether is always willing to accept fresh blood. And it might even save me a measure of pain if I offer up a willing victim for it."

"If it isn't necessary then let us go without it," Lazarus said firmly.

"Pity," Vesper sighed and I released a low chuckle because I knew she meant that.

We led the way into the caves, the walls closing in around us quickly and the scent of salt clinging to the walls from when the tide came in. I threw a look back over my shoulder at the short stretch of beach behind us, eyeing the waves as they reached across the sand before retreating again.

"The tide is coming in," I commented.

"We'd better hurry then," Vesper replied.

"Or wait," North suggested, falling still at the entrance to the cave. "I don't really wanna end up drowning in some fucking cave."

"What's the matter, mutt? Are you scared?" Vesper taunted while the Vampires exchanged concerned mutterings too. "Feel free to wait out here."

Vesper strode away into the cave but Lazarus caught my arm as I made to follow. "How long does this usually take?"

"Depends on how long it takes us to find the keystone. The others were buried deep beneath the dirt." I shrugged him off and headed after my spectre.

"We'll wait here and keep an eye on the tide then," Lazarus called, and I had to wonder if that was precisely what Vesper had been hoping for when she'd decided to put a time limit on this hunt.

"I'm coming," North said just as I thought we were going to be gifted some time alone at last. "I'm not afraid of the tide."

"Oh good," I muttered.

The dark swallowed us but I sent a Faelight out to illuminate the way on. The cave was twisting and narrow just as the others had been but Vesper didn't so much as hesitate in choosing the path ahead.

"How come you and her are working together anyway?" North asked, sidling up to walk beside me despite the passage not being wide enough to do so comfortably, his voice echoing in the tight space.

"She is all I have," I replied which seemed to throw him off for a moment but he didn't let the silence stretch.

"You're from Avanis though, right? And she's from Stormfell, so how did you even meet–"

"I am bound in service to her king," I replied, not feeling inclined to offer him more than the bones of my situation. Though I could admit that I had begun to wonder about my connection to the woman I'd vowed to walk beside in all things, whether we might be more than two Fae who had found each other in the dark, whether she might be destined to become my mate… If only I still had the piece of comet we'd stolen in Pyros, I could have asked the stars the truth of it. But Dragor had stolen them along with everything else I owned when he'd captured me and I doubted I'd ever lay eyes on them again.

"Oooh, so you're his captive – that explains the collar. Do you do tricks on command too?" I ignored North's question but that didn't deter him from filling the silence with more drivel. "My brother Kaiser had the Void as his captive once so I know how it works. She hated him for it, obviously. I guess you hate old Dragor then too, eh? Which we have in common because he killed my brother Diego, and that left me with lingering regrets because Diego always wore this dumb hat everywhere and do you know the last thing I ever said to him?"

"No."

"I said 'Diego, that hat is dumb'. Fucking haunts me it does. In the dead of night. Like, sometimes it's all the war stuff that haunts me but that comment was harsh. True…but harsh. He loved that dumb hat but it had tassels and a bell and it was just *so* ugly. Apparently it was still on his head even after Dragor chopped it off. Well, I say it was Dragor, but I guess it could have been any fucker in his army really. Maybe it was the Sky Witch – do you think she did it?"

He peered at Vesper's back and she cut him a scathing look for talking about her as if she couldn't hear him. "How would I remember even if it was?"

"Harsh. Decent folk keep count of their murders, you know? The fact that you don't says a lot about your moral fibre. It's very telling."

"And yet you keep blathering on and tempting me to add yours to the list of names and faces I've already forgotten in death," she replied.

"Anyway… back to the point. Do you hate Dragor? I bet he's fucking insufferable now that he's king. I mean, I don't know him personally and I only really saw him up close that one time and it wasn't really a studying his face kind of moment. But the paintings I've seen make him appear unbearable – real turned-up-nose-thinks-he's-better-than-everyone type. Am I right?" North asked.

"Yes," Vesper replied and I snorted a laugh.

"He is," I agreed.

"So you gonna try and kill him like the Void tried to kill Kai?"

I said nothing. And I supposed that was telling enough.

"You said you found him on the battlefield and rescued him?" Vesper asked, her attention seemingly piqued by that claim.

"Err, yeah. She stabbed him good but I got to him, carried him to safety, nursed him back to health. It was pretty heroic of me actually, thanks for noticing."

"But his hold on her shattered regardless?" Vesper pressed.

"Umm, yeah – wait, how do you know about the bond he'd put on her?"

Vesper fell still suddenly and we were forced to a halt too.

"Wait here," she commanded, ignoring the Wolf's question as something stole her focus from their discussion.

"Last time–" I began, reaching for her.

"Last time *you* almost lost yourself in the flow of ether and were spotted by the monster at its heart for good measure. I don't want to draw its focus again and it is likely expecting me now. So this time stay away unless the silence stretches so long as you have no choice but to approach. And don't for the love of the stars open your magic to mine while I'm caught in it either. I know how to pull myself free but if you can't wake me then just get me out of there and when we're at a safe distance, burn this in my right fist."

She handed me a scrap of fabric decorated in runes and tied tightly around a bundle of herbs, her gaze meeting mine and locking there.

"Promise me, Bastian. Do as I say or I'll send you away and entrust my survival to the mutt instead."

"Me?" North asked in surprise but we both ignored him.

"Fine," I growled, shoving the bundled herbs into my pocket. "But I'm not waiting on some lingering silence. You have five minutes and no longer. Tell me where I need to go."

"Turn right at the fork and follow the passage to its base. The keystone is there," she said, turning away.

"Vesper," I called, barely managing to restrain myself as I fought the urge to catch her hand and refuse this mad plan.

Water trickled over the stones and bumped into our boots as we locked eyes with one another and I couldn't help but look down at it. "Be careful," I said. "And hurry."

She made to turn away then stopped, stepping toward me instead and catching hold of the front of my shirt to yank me down and press a hard kiss to my lips.

It didn't last for more than a heartbeat and I fought the urge to drag her into my arms for a proper goodbye as she turned and swept away along the passage, leaving me to dwell upon thoughts of what might be awaiting her there.

"Wow," North said as she stalked away. "Are you her enemy? I heard she likes to fuck her enemies to death and the two of you seem kind of like you're fucking, so…"

"Don't speak about her like that if you value your life," I growled.

"Okay man," he said, raising his hands in surrender. "Just figured maybe you didn't know and needed a warning. But I guess it's a better way to go than most if it is true so…oh right, yeah, shutting up."

I gained a full three seconds of silence during which another wave washed into the caves, my pulse ticking a little faster as I considered how long it had taken us to make it down here. Would we be able to get out before we found ourselves submerged?

I placed a hand on the rock, my magic leaking into it as I picked out a path of weaker stone in case I ended up having to tunnel us out of here.

"Vesper," North said thoughtfully. "Ves-per. Vesssperrr. Nope. Doesn't suit her. Kinda weird that she has an actual name really. I don't like it."

"You thought she was given the name 'Sky Witch' upon birth?" I drawled.

"Naw. Well…not birth. I figured she kind of popped out of the ground one day, pre-witchy bitchy, you know?"

"No. That is idiocy."

"And you're fucking rude. And grumpy. Lucky for you, I'm used to hanging out with Kai and he was always grumpy…well no, not grumpy. More like void of any feeling whatsoever."

"That sounds about right," I muttered. A tremor resounded through the cavern which surrounded us and my eyes followed the path Vesper had taken. She was with the keystone. It had begun.

"How so?" North pushed, either not noticing or not wishing to comment on what I'd just felt in the stone that surrounded us.

"Because you said that the two of you spent a lot of time together. And you seem like the kind of person who saps the emotional energy from everyone around them," I deadpanned.

"There you go being fucking rude again. You Stonebreakers are no fun. That's what it is. It's all 'dig, dig, dig' with you bastards. And you know what they say – all dirt and no play makes for a boring, grumpy motherfucker at the end of the day."

The next wave of water ran over the toes of my boots and did not recede.

"No one says that. And my people grow things with our magic, we create life. All your kind do is burn and destroy," I said.

"And fuck – we have a lot of orgies."

I breathed a laugh but turned away from him. The water rushed over our ankles. Vesper's time was almost up either way.

"I don't wanna make a fuss or anything, but is she almost done?" North asked, lifting a boot out of the water and giving it a shake before resigning himself to the fact that he had no choice other than to submerge it again.

"She has forty-seven seconds remaining before my oath to her is fulfilled."

"How have you kept count that accurately while we've been talking?"

"This conversation is less than riveting."

"You accused me of burning everything around me but look at

you setting fire to our friendship before it can even begin."

The corner of my lips rose in amusement despite myself.

"Who puts a keystone in a fucking sea cave anyway?" North asked as a rush of water brought the level up to our knees.

"I am not certain anyone put them anywhere. They just…are. Fae may have visited and worshipped them, carved idols onto their faces, but they are the cornerstones of the continent we live upon. They sit within the ground because they are a part of the earth and so remain connected to it."

"Still seems kind of odd to me. Kind of like my sister Kayla's hiding place for her nipple clamps. She thinks we don't all know about them but one time–"

I strode away from him without a word. Vesper's five minutes were up.

Water sloshed around my thighs as I took the path she'd instructed me to follow, my heart pounding in my ears.

"Vesper?" I called into the darkness ahead, the echo of her name mocking me in reply.

Another rush of water sent the level up to my waist and North let out a bark of alarm as he waded after me.

"You walked off while I was in the middle of telling you all about–"

"Hush," I commanded and he somehow managed to silence himself for once, though he grumbled as he did so.

"Vesper!" I called again, wading deeper into the cave, the glimmering light of her Faelight urging me closer.

But before I could reach her or the keystone she'd come here to fix, she burst into the tunnel and started running for me as fast as she could through the rising water.

She was far shorter than both me and the Wolf, a wave washing over her shoulders as it crested my chest. Blood stained the water around her as she ran for me and I could make out deep cuts along both of her arms.

"What happened?" I demanded, reaching for her and pulling her to me.

"I had to use runes to break free of the ether," she panted. "I'll explain later if we get out of this but it's done. The keystone is restored."

I hauled her into my arms and I could tell she was utterly exhausted by the way she let me, her head falling against my shoulder.

"Take my hand," I barked at North, holding it out to him as more water rushed into the caves.

"What?"

"Now or never," I growled, tugging Vesper closer to me and lashing her body against mine with vines.

North opened his mouth to say something else and took a slap from a final wave of sea water instead as it rushed in to steal the last remaining space within the cave.

His hand caught mine a moment before I abandoned him to his fate instead, my other palm striking the cave roof above us as I urged the stone to mould itself to my will.

Rock was harder to manipulate than soil, taking far more effort to do so, but I poured my power into it, holding my breath while I forced a path into place which hadn't been there before.

Water rushed into the opening almost as fast as I could climb into it, North coughing and spluttering as I hauled him up behind us.

The rocks groaned as I forced them to part further above our heads but the water was rushing in quicker than we were going to be able to climb into the passage.

Vesper cursed, flicking water from her face before turning to North and grabbing his arm too.

"I need magic," Vesper growled at North. "Give me yours."

"What? I can't. I hardly even know you, let alone trust you enough to power share," he spluttered as the water once again rose to our chests.

"Then I'll do it the old fashioned way." Vesper shifted, her body hardening where it was lashed against mine, her features sharpening into the ethereal level of beauty which was hard to behold.

It took every piece of will I possessed to turn my gaze from her and focus on opening the way above. But North was overwhelmed by her allure instantly.

"Let me brush your hair," he breathed, grabbing at the hand she still held him by and closing in on us so tightly that I growled in warning. "You're the most beautiful thing I've ever–"

His words were cut off by a wave slapping him in the face but Vesper had clearly stolen enough of his power through his desires for what she needed and a moment later a ball of air magic closed around us tightly, forcing the water out at speed, its walls as solid as stone.

North fell to his knees at the air ball's base and I leaned against its wall as the water continued to fill the tunnel I'd carved for us to escape through. We rose like a cork atop the rising sea level and Vesper's face pinched with effort as she fought to maintain her hold on her power.

I gritted my teeth as I stretched my magic to its limit, carving a route for us right to the peak of the cliff and releasing a curse of effort when I finally felt the rock crack apart to reveal open air above.

"We're almost there, love," I told her, banishing the vines and lifting her into my arms instead.

Her gaze was shuttered, her jaw clenched as she fought to hold the bubble around us, the space shrinking inch by inch until I was forced to drop to my knees beside North.

He was muttering prayers to Aries, Sagittarius and Leo, urging them to see us to safety, listing all the great things about himself that the world would miss out on if he died. He was certainly very confident of his own self-worth.

I was almost spent but I placed my hand against Vesper's cheek, opening the floodgates to what remained of my magic and pouring it into her so that she could keep the bubble in place.

Daylight loomed above us.

"Thirty more feet," I growled.

"Bastian…" she panted and I dropped my gaze back to her, my brow furrowing as I took in the runes she'd carved into her own arms.

"What have you done to yourself, love?" I growled.

"I did what I had to," she hissed. "To…return…to you…"

I saw the moment she lost her battle with oblivion before I felt the water closing around us.

North yelled in alarm as our air was stolen and the water crashed into the space it had defiantly been claiming for us. But we were still being propelled skyward by the current and I crushed Vesper to my chest as we sped the remaining distance to the surface.

My lungs burned and head spun but all the time I held her fate in my arms, I knew I wouldn't succumb to the water. I kicked as hard as I could, propelling us higher and higher until finally we breached the surface in a spray of salt water.

Hands grabbed hold of us as the Vampires shot to meet us with their unnatural speed, the three of us dumped on the ground to cough and splutter.

"Here," one of the Vampires rushed forward, wielding water

magic and coaxing what we'd inhaled back out of our lungs.

I wouldn't let him help me until he'd assisted Vesper and by the time I was able to breathe easily again, my mind was filled with nothing but fear for what repairing that keystone had cost her.

Each of these corrupted ley lines had been harder to restore than the last and I could only imagine what it might demand from her to repair the final one which awaited us in Avanis.

"She did it," Lazarus said in wonder but I only scoffed at his awe.

"Perhaps you know less about her than you think you do, Vampire," I said. "Because there isn't a thing in this world that that woman can't do when she sets her mind to it."

"She's insane," North muttered, shaking his head like a dog to remove the water from his hair.

"No. She's fucking unstoppable. And you'd all do well to remember it."

I took her hand in mine and curled her fingers around the bundled herbs she'd given me.

"Fire," I barked, my glare finding North as he failed to do as I'd commanded.

"What?" he asked, frowning at me in confusion.

"Set this alight," I said, pointing at the bundle in Vesper's fist.

He looked ready to protest again but at my snarl he sent a shot of flame onto the sodden package of herbs and runes.

They blazed a bright green as they burst alight and the Vampires retreated, muttering curses about dark magic.

Vesper's fist snapped shut, snuffing out the flames just as I began to fear they'd burn her. She sucked in a sharp breath as her eyes flew open and I dropped down, pressing my forehead to hers in relief and drawing her further into my arms.

"Did you doubt me, Dragon?" she teased, her voice still weaker than I would have liked.

"Never," I replied. "But that doesn't mean I have to like the lengths you go to."

"Stop fussing."

"Never," I repeated and the breath of laughter that escaped her had my pounding heart slowing at last.

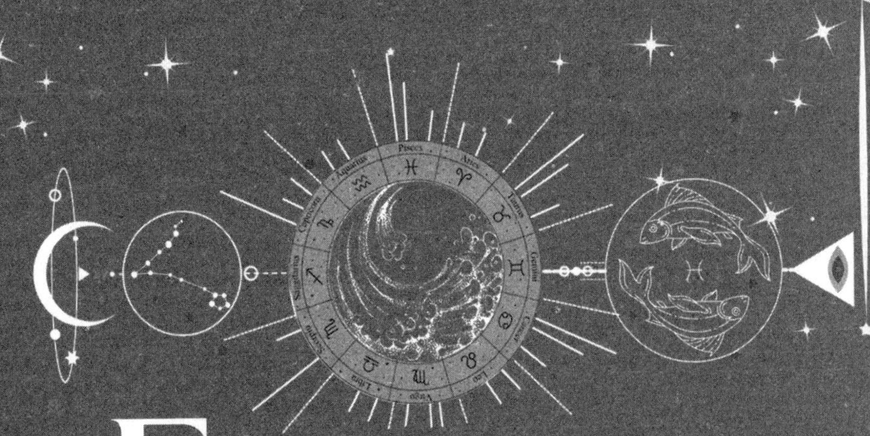

Everest

CHAPTER THIRTY NINE

The ride had been long, arduous and a fucking pain in the ass. But we'd made it. Somehow, for reasons beyond my understanding, the stars were looking out for us. Three Cascadian traitors and a Flamebringer who had risen from the damn dead.

We'd finally reached the cavern set into a mossy hillside where Kaiser promised a magical archway awaited us and despite Ransom and Galomp's questions about such a thing, they had placed their trust in me that this magic would lead us far away from the Cascadian army.

It had been an awkward ride, Kaiser leading the way on Ransom's stallion Bay while my brother rode with Galomp on his mare Lalakin – much to his disgruntlement. But every time he tried to raise it with Kaiser, the Fury possessed him and forced agreement from his lips.

Kaiser had kept his distance for the most part while Ransom, Galomp and I remained close together.

Sometimes I'd wake to find Kaiser pacing outside whatever cave or shelter we'd taken for the night. On several nights he'd drawn his sword, struck at trees until exhaustion took him and I'd silently taken watch in his place when he passed out. We rarely spoke. But our eyes met more often than I liked. There were unvoiced words between us, like we'd broken the rules of fate and were sharing a twisted secret. But I wouldn't put a name to it. I only looked at him and he looked back. Then we carried on riding toward freedom.

Apart from one close call with a cavalry squadron, we'd managed to avoid the hunting Cascadians. Whenever we met a town, we stole through it in the night, taking what supplies we could from the abandoned houses and moving on toward our destination.

Despite Ransom's complaints, we never chanced sleeping in the towns. They were too obvious a place to look for us. Perfectly comfortable hideouts. So we roughed it instead, making the three week long trip all the more difficult. But if I was honest with myself, it had been a long time since I'd felt this alive. Living as a pampered creature hadn't suited me. I much preferred roaming these lands with purpose, even if that purpose went against my own people. Or at least that was how they saw it. I was focused on the monster now, a being who would destroy all the beauty of this world and every Cascadian in it. So perhaps they'd thank me one day, but that day was certainly not today.

I dismounted Karkinos, following suit as Kaiser climbed down from Bay and both Galomp and Ransom dismounted too.

"Come, we're here," the Fury clipped at us, his eyes lingering on me again. It always felt as though he could see beneath my flesh, like any guise I wanted to wear could be melted by that look alone.

I nodded to Ransom and Galomp in encouragement then led Karkinos into the cave, sending a Faelight out ahead of me to light the dark passage. My skin prickled as I thought over what was to come. Kaiser could be leading us all to our imminent capture, I'd considered that possibility night after night. But something in my gut was telling me to place my faith in this plan. Not him. But this promise of an alliance. I had no care in my heart for Mirelle Brimtheon or her Flamebringer nation but if she wanted the monster dealt with then she needed me. And I needed an army if I was going to survive another trip to Never Keep. Still… working alongside my enemies felt utterly wrong. It went against everything I was.

Kaiser tugged on Bay's reins, drawing him alongside Karkinos, his arm brushing mine and sending a tremor through my body. Calcifiend trilled excitedly to me from his shoulder like he'd sensed my reaction and I scowled at the little beastie. "Mirelle will welcome you. You need not fear her."

"I'm not afraid," I muttered.

"You are a little," he answered and I clenched my teeth, irritated that he could read that emotion from me with his Order gifts. And that he was using it to bolster his own magic.

"Well I have nothing but blind faith and a gut feeling to guide me forward, hollow man. Great warriors have died for following their instincts. They're not always right. Perhaps the stars want me dead and they're luring me into your net. Or perhaps you have some plot to make me your prisoner again."

"Perhaps," he agreed darkly. "But would I really have come alone if that was my intention? I could have brought many warriors and I could have stolen you from your bed when I had the chance. But here we are…"

"I've considered that," I admitted. "Which is why I'm willing to take the risk."

We rounded into a dark cavern where a stone archway stood, unassuming yet the hairs on the back of my neck lifted to attention. There was no stone bowl here full of black powder to ignite the magic within it, but Kaiser moved to a wall, reached into a concealed hole and pulled out a handful of it.

I glanced back at Galomp and Ransom, their eyes reflecting the glow of my Faelight.

"Are you sure you want to walk through the archway? I can't promise safety lies beyond it," I said. "This is your last chance to run. I've decided I'm walking through. I told you of the monster and what it will do to this world, so I'm going to do whatever it takes to stop it. But you don't have to take on that burden too."

"I go where you go, Miss Everest. I am your Sentinel," Galomp said confidently.

I took a step toward him with a tug in my gut. "You understand how dangerous this is, don't you? I can't promise I can protect you."

Galomp nodded. "I have never had such a good friend as you. I will face a monster at your side. I will be there. That's what friends do for each other." He lifted his chin and my heart squeezed with warmth for him.

"Thank you." I looked to my half-brother and the hard frown on his face.

"I'm coming," he grunted.

"That's it?" I pushed. "No doubts?"

He shrugged and I narrowed my eyes at him until he sighed and gave me more of an answer. "Yes, I have doubts. Fucking thousands of them. But the only path that feels right to me now is following you. You're my runt sister and I've hated you for as long as I can remember, but you're the only family I have left that I actually respect.

And maybe you're not as much of a runt as you used to be. So I'm coming. And whatever Galomp just called himself – your Sentinel? I'm that too now. So just keep walking and I'll follow."

"What about the monster? The end of the world? The fight we're going to have to face to stop it?" I demanded. "You can't just blindly follow me to your death."

He pressed his lips into a tight line, thinking over that before responding. "My eyes are wide open. I'm coming. Stop yapping."

"There's your answer," Kaiser said firmly. "No more time wasting." He threw a handful into a hollow at the side of the archway and the portal lit up in a shimmering glow, making Ransom and Galomp gasp in awe.

"I wasn't sure I believed you about these archways until right now," Ransom admitted. "Will it really transport us somewhere if we walk through it?"

"Yes," I breathed excitedly, feeling like I was headed on the path I'd been destined for at long last. Perhaps the greatness I was meant to claim had never been among the army of Cascada. Maybe it was awaiting me right beyond that gleaming light.

"Are you ready, silka la vin?" Kaiser asked in a low voice.

I stared at my enemy, thinking of my mama as doubts clawed through my chest. But I'd made my choice, and there was no turning from it now.

"I am." I took the lead and guided Karkinos after me into the glittering archway. It enveloped me like the hand of the sun, warming me through and guiding me from this place to another. I stepped out on the other side and found an empty stone chamber awaiting me where two other archways stood empty.

How had the Flamebringers come to possess these?

Karkinos nudged me with his nose, pushing me aside as if he wanted to see the chamber for himself. He assessed the room with a bland look then let out a snort which sounded disapproving.

"Ever the grumpy pony." I petted his nose, leading him aside as Kaiser came through leading Bay, then Galomp and Ransom appeared with Lalakin.

"Oh boy," Galomp exhaled. "That was something. Really something."

Ransom looked at his hands, patting himself down as if fearing he might have left a body part behind. "What the fuck kind of magic is that?"

"The kind the Reapers like to keep secret," Kaiser answered. "But they're not the only ones. The Vampires know of it too. They've been sharing their knowledge with us since Mirelle allied with them."

I didn't have any time to process that because another archway lit up beside us and the damn Sky Witch walked through it accompanied by that big bastard Bastian she'd been keeping company with the last time I'd seen her on the battlefield at Cinder Vale.

They were followed by a horrified-looking North Brimtheon, the imposing form of Lazarus Astrophel and a group of six more Fae in their wake.

"Vesper?" I gasped.

"Kitty-cat?" she questioned in shock and I noticed she was bleeding, pale, and looking like she'd been dragged through a gutter lined with broken glass.

"What are you doing here?" I asked, confounded.

"Kai!" North howled, shouldering past Vesper and pulling Kaiser into a fierce hug. "You won't believe what we just did!"

"We?" Vesper questioned dryly.

"Are you working with them?" I demanded of her and her eyes snapped back to me.

"I wouldn't put it that way. But they're of use to me. For now."

"You must be the Void." Lazarus swept forward keenly and I rested a hand on my dagger's hilt, a snarl rolling up my throat, warning him to keep his distance. "Ah, it seems you're not so fond of my kind either."

"Not so much," I agreed.

"Understandable," he said thoughtfully. "But as you are here, I assume this means you're agreeing to work alongside your enemies?"

"For now," I said, lowering my hand from my dagger.

"I have too, I have," Galomp piped up. "I am Miss Everest's Sentinel and I will protect her at all costs, I will." He gave Lazarus a menacing glare – well, it wasn't as menacing as he probably thought it was. But I appreciated the sentiment.

"I'm also her Sentinel," Ransom added. "I'm Ransom Arcadia and–"

"What?" I blurted, rounding on my brother. "That's *my* surname."

"And now it's mine too," he said in that goading way of his. I glared at him and he glared back, but as we were in a room full of our adversaries, I decided now was not the time to push the subject.

Bastian moved closer to Vesper, subtly bracing her as she staggered back a step. She looked terrible. Her arms were marked with bloody runes and her face was as white as snow.

"What happened to you?" I pressed.

"The eschaton star's been stealing power through corrupted ley lines," Lazarus began answering for her in a voice that dripped power.

"What's that?" I frowned.

"It's what they call the monster," Vesper explained. "I just broke its connection to the third ley line and repaired another corrupted keystone. Ether is required and it always demands a price."

"You look half dead," I said in horror at what she'd given to complete the task.

"Better than fully dead, I suppose," she drawled.

I smiled and she smiled back, and I felt all eyes falling on us.

"We'll take a few days to recover," Lazarus instructed. "Then we will go after the final keystone and put together a plot to take down the eschaton star. We will need a month or more to prepare–"

"We don't have that long," I cut in fiercely and Lazarus frowned at me.

"What is that supposed to mean?"

"I received a letter from my friend Harlon Brook," I started explaining. "He's a Reaper working at Never Keep, but he's seen what they are. He's witnessed the atrocities they've committed and he knows of the monster. So he's been working in secret to undermine them and he sent me a letter in which he told me of a plot to summon the eschaton star into this world on the night of the blood moon. He spoke of tomes and prophesies that confirmed that the moon has the power to open gateways between realms and–"

"Yes," Lazarus cut in, looking horrified. "I have discovered such knowledge myself, but I never thought…"

"That wasn't all he'd learned," I continued as everyone hung on my words. "He discovered that my power, the Void could potentially be strong enough to thwart the moon's magic and so in turn, stop the eschaton star from crossing the boundary into our world."

Lazarus nodded. "Yes that could work. My people have been studying prophesies about the Void power and I believe it might be possible."

"Fuck a duck. All the ducks," North exhaled and I noticed Ransom looking at him with a sneer.

"Well you know what they say," Galomp piped up. "A pot of different fish makes the tastiest dish. So together we will find a way to save the day."

"Well I'm not a fish like you are," North muttered.

"I think you look more like a peacock," Ransom sneered.

"We all need to be on the same page for this mission," Kaiser said in a hard tone before North could snap back at him. "The fate of every life in The Waning Lands depends on it."

"It's settled then," Vesper said with a smirk. "We'll smuggle kitty-cat to the eschaton star on the night of the blood moon."

I nodded. "There's someone else who will assist us too. Mavus Angelico–"

"The trader of Wandershire?" North frowned. "Why does he want anything to do with this?"

"He's a friend," I said. "He was the one who delivered me the letter from Harlon."

"Does anyone else know about this?" Lazarus's brow lowered and I shook my head. "Good, let's keep it that way."

"Harlon said he'll meet us at the ten towers on the isle of Never Keep on the night of the blood moon and lead us to where the ceremony is taking place," I added.

"Then that's what we'll do," Lazarus confirmed. "We only have a week. Let's rest and lay our plans swiftly."

He made to leave but Mirelle Brimtheon entered the chamber, eyes bright as they landed on North then Kaiser. "My loves, you have returned. And you bring gifts." She looked to me with a hungry smile and I tensed.

"I'm here of my own free will. Try to capture me and I will Void you all until you are so desperate for a lick of magic, you beg me to free you," I snarled.

"Vicious little thing, aren't you?" Mirelle purred. "You are no longer my prisoner. As you say, you're here of your own accord, are you not? I hear you killed your own father. A bloody death too." She smiled wickedly, looking to Kaiser. "I'm pleased to hear of such news."

"He suffered well," Kaiser said. "Everest ensured it."

"Good. Then we are allies," Mirelle announced. "You will have warm beds and hot food tonight."

"This is temporary," I warned as Galomp and Ransom gathered close at my back.

"Of course," Mirelle purred. "All alliances in The Waning Lands usually are. North, take their horses to the stables and Kaiser, show them to their rooms."

Everyone moved to obey as Mirelle swept toward me, her dark eyes brimming with emotion. "Everest Arcadia," she whispered. "You freed my son from a spell I couldn't break. I can never thank you enough for what you did for him." She stepped closer, lowering her voice even more, so it was a deadly whisper. "But if you ever try to kill him again, I will make you suffer. And you do not want to suffer at the hands of a mother whose child you hurt, I assure you of that."

"He killed my mother," I said, my voice breaking on those words. "She didn't get a chance to defend her child, so I did it for her."

Her face softened, her eyes searching mine. "I pray the pain you caused Kaiser was enough to sate you." She nodded to me then walked over to Lazarus. He grabbed her waist, placing a kiss on her lips that marked the truth of their union. She really had allied with the Vampires. How wildly insane did she have to be to do that? Or perhaps clever…

Kaiser was the only one who had waited for me by the exit to the chamber and Calcifiend flew from his shoulder to land on mine.

He clicked his tongue in encouragement and I walked toward the Fury who watched me like a hawk. Then he turned and led me away into the Pyros stronghold.

"Welcome to Ravensview," Kaiser murmured.

As I followed him into his den of heathens, surrounded by my enemies, declared a traitor to my own people, doubts crawled into my skin.

I shot a silent prayer to Pisces to guide me along this uncharted path and hoped I didn't one day regret my choice in coming here.

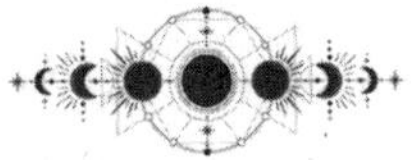

I'd been given a room in Ravensview which was larger than the house I'd grown up in and far more luxurious in every way. Ransom and Galomp had been housed in the same corridor, but we'd all been strictly instructed to remain in our quarters and I didn't like the way that made me feel like a prisoner.

A full day had passed and the only Fae I'd seen since we'd arrived here were the ones delivering food and drink to my room. I'd been caught up in a storm of thoughts about the blood moon and Harlon. My friend could be in danger. What if the Reapers discovered he'd been spying on them? It didn't bear thinking about and all I could do was pray to the stars that Pisces, Scorpio and Cancer would watch over him. And when we were finally reunited, I'd be able to get him away from that island and hide him from the Reapers.

I'd had one more thing to deliberate too. Lazarus had come to me with an offer. That if I cooperated with my enemies for this mission, he would ensure there was a safe haven for me in a place he named Effelridge. What he described of that place sounded like a pretty dream and my first thought had been to refute it as a lie. But I'd come this far without his offer to tempt me here. I'd known nothing of any reward I might get for participating in this task. He didn't need to bribe me, yet he was still willing to ensure my protection after the matter. It made me want to warm to him, even though he was a bloodsucker.

Just as I was close to breaking point, desperately needing to talk to someone and get out of this room to seek out my brother and Galomp, a knock came at my door.

"Mother's organised a dinner for us all to lay plans for the blood moon," North called to me. "Come and join us, whelk."

He flung the door open so it banged against the wall, walking away and giving me no time to decide if I was going to follow. I huffed and raced after him, finding Galomp and Ransom already there in the stone corridor waiting for me. They were dressed in the casual attire of the Flamebringers just as I was, though it looked like they'd struggled to find something in Galomp's size because his long-sleeved shirt was fit to bursting.

"Hello Miss Everest," he greeted me brightly. "I am hungry, the food here is nice, isn't it? Nicer than I thought it would be."

"It's soot," Ransom drawled, offering North a cold glare.

"Must taste familiar then," North tossed back. "Didn't Pyros burn all of the Cascadian crops last year? I bet you enjoyed nibbling on your charred tomatoes when it was all you had to eat." He turned away to lead us down the passage and Ransom sneered at his back.

"Don't rise to it," I muttered.

"What's that, whelk?" North called over his shoulder and that name set my blood boiling.

"I said you're a flaming fart-fucker with a shrivelled cinder cock!" I shouted and North's lips popped open at the outburst.

"What was that about not rising to it?" Ransom jibed, raising his eyebrow at me.

"I take it back." I glowered at North and he glowered at me, nearly walking into a wall as the corridor veered left. He cursed and swerved it, focusing on the way ahead as Ransom and I openly jeered him and Galomp guffawed.

North led us down a spiralling stairway and we soon arrived in a grand stone chamber where a long table was set out for us, filled to the brim with a feast.

Mirelle and Lazarus sat at each end of the table as if both showing they were equally deserving of the position and neither wishing to back down on the matter.

Along the length of the table sat the rest of our band of unlikely allies, Kaiser sitting near the middle while Vesper and Bastian sat opposite him. No one was speaking and I felt the awkwardness in the air as they all turned to note our arrival.

Calcifiend flew up from the back of Kaiser's chair, whizzing over to whirl around me and lick me on the cheek. I couldn't help a smile as he landed on my hand and demanded tickles by nuzzling my thumb. "Hello little lizard," I murmured, giving into his desires. He was too damn cute not to forgive for betraying me again and I knew I was a sucker for his game.

"Do join us," Mirelle said, pointing to the empty seats.

North bounded over to sit beside Kaiser and I took a seat next to Vesper while Ransom went Rogue and sat on Bastian's right so he was facing North. Galomp took the chair to my left and I found myself staring across the table at Kaiser over a bounty of bread and cheese.

His dark hair was swept to one side and he wore a black shirt that matched the sins in his eyes. His gaze dipped from my eyes to my lips and my body hummed with the feel of his unwavering attention.

I cleared my throat and looked to Vesper. "How are you feeling?"

"Perfect," she said, though there were dark circles under her eyes and I got the feeling she wasn't being entirely truthful.

Galomp tucked into the food even though no one was really eating, not seeming to notice the tension in the room.

"Oh, so crunchy." He tested a bread roll in his fist. "This is fine bread, it is."

"Thank you er– what's your name again?" Mirelle asked.

"People call me Galomp, Miss Matriarch," he said then placed a lump of cheese on the roll and took a big bite out of it. "I have heard lots of things about you, yes I have. I heard that you feast on the bones of your dead children, yes I have. Is that true, Miss Matriarch?"

"No, it is not," she clipped, but Galomp didn't seem to pick up on her tone, turning casually to Lazarus and addressing him instead.

"I heard your kind eat babies, yes I did. Is that true, Mr Lazarus?"

Lazarus only laughed, a dark drawling kind of laugh that only made the feast feel even more awkward.

"He is laughing now, Miss Everest," Galomp whispered to me. "Does he find the baby eating amusing? I do hope not."

"Just be careful, Galomp," I whispered back.

"Well, baby eating aside," North said with a smirk. "I'm famished." He placed some food onto his plate and both he and Galomp proceeded to eat like there was no reason not to.

"Look at the peacock eating with his dainty knife and fork. Do you need your food cut up for you so you don't choke on it, pup?" Ransom jeered at North.

I noticed he'd cut his food into perfect pieces and was eating them one by one.

"There's nothing wrong with the way I eat," North growled.

"He likes his food a certain way." Mirelle patted his arm and North pursed his lips, not liking the way she was mothering him.

Ransom grabbed a bread roll and took a savage bite of it, letting crumbs spill freely down onto his plate.

North's left eye twitched like that infuriated him. "At least I don't eat like a starved hog."

Bastian sighed. "I find the bickering weary."

"As do I," Kaiser agreed and they shared a curious look with each other.

"So, are we going to make a plan? Or are we here to rip each other's throats out?" Vesper asked. "I'm fine with either, I'd just rather be clear."

"My coven and the others will cause a distraction at Never Keep," Lazarus said.

"I'll join you," Mirelle added, then looked to Vesper. "We have a task for you in mind, Sky Witch."

"Delightful. What is it?" Vesper asked dryly.

"Everest will likely need time to exert her Void magic on the blood moon. I doubt it will be a simple task," Mirelle said. "Lazarus has done great research on the eschaton star and the possibilities of where its origins lie."

"I believe mere elemental magic will not be enough to hold it back," Lazarus said. "Its power is immense, unimaginable. There is only one magic in this world I can think of that may have a chance at affecting it."

"Ether," Vesper finished for him. "So you want me to use dark magic to tether it while Everest works on the moon? Sounds simple enough."

"You nearly died breaking its connection to the ley lines," Bastian growled. "We don't know what this thing is capable of. It could kill you."

"We're all willing to die for this," Vesper answered coldly, looking around the table. "Or we wouldn't be sitting at this table, betraying our lands. Does anyone disagree?"

I looked to my brother, wondering if he might speak. If the gravity of this situation might finally scare him off, but he didn't say anything. So I turned my gaze to Galomp, wishing he'd never gotten caught up in this but even he stayed silent, his jaw set.

"Vesper's right," I said. "Death is the most likely outcome of this plan. There are too many ways in which it could go wrong. But there's just one way it could go right."

"It will only go right if we are all in alignment," Kaiser said, cutting a look at North then to Ransom. "We must put our hatred aside."

"We must ensure Everest and…Vesper reach the eschaton star," Mirelle said with a firm nod. "That is our only focus now."

"Oh good, now everyone knows my name," Vesper drawled, cutting me an irritated look and I shrugged innocently.

"You can't seriously want everyone here to just keep calling you 'Sky Witch'," I said.

"Can't I?" she asked curiously. "You know the last time my name became widely known I had to enact a massacre to hide it again," she said and I flattened my lips against a laugh at her tone.

North laughed loudly then stopped. "That was a joke…right?"

"Was it?" Vesper asked him and Bastian grinned like he thought it was funny whether it was true or not.

"Well as enthralling as the subject of your name is, I think we should get back to our plans for defying the eschaton star," Mirelle reminded us and Vesper nodded.

"After the final keystone is dealt with," Vesper reminded her.

"You will go tomorrow," Mirelle decided.

"I don't want anyone with me this time," Vesper said firmly and I glanced at her sensing she was hiding something. "Bastian and I will go alone."

"I can help," I offered. "My Void will keep us safe from attack if we're discovered."

"Can't say I can remember a time when I needed someone to keep me safe, kitty-cat but I suppose I can allow for you to join us. But no more. I have business in Stone Castle which I will see done before the keystone is dealt with and I won't have my presence there discovered before I have completed it," Vesper said firmly.

"You cannot seriously expect us to just let you go there alone? Everything relies on the final keystone being repaired," Lazarus burst out. "Nothing else you may intend to do there matters beyond–"

Bastian slammed his fist down on the table so hard that plates leapt, cutlery juddered and several glasses of wine fell to stain the tablecloth.

"I don't think you're listening to her. She has business to take care of in Stone Castle and won't be dealing with the keystone until it is done. That isn't a question or a point of discussion. It is a fact. And if you don't like it then you can find another Fae who is both practiced in the dark arts and sympathetic to your cause. But you may wish to hurry – as you know, time is already running short."

Silence stretched, each person at the table seeming as likely to snap as the next, though as I glanced at Vesper I found amusement sparking in her grey eyes.

"North and Kaiser will assist you too," Mirelle demanded finally.

Vesper's jaw ticked as she stared down The Matriarch and Mirelle stared back.

"Fine," she conceded. "But that's it." She pushed out of her seat and strode for the door.

I got up before Bastian could and ran after her, chasing her into the passage beyond the door.

"Vesper," I called and she turned back with a darkness in her eyes. "You're not telling me something."

Vesper hesitated then drew closer to me, casting a silencing shield around us. "Cayde Avior is in Avanis at Stone Castle. I'll be paying him a visit before we deal with the keystone and I don't want The Matriarch breathing down my neck or Lazarus's coven spying on me."

I moved closer to her, seeing the pain in her eyes over the death of her friends. Cayde had caused her unimaginable pain. I knew that ache and seeing her agony laid bare made me want to soothe it.

"I'll do everything I can to ensure you have your revenge," I swore.

She assessed me, like she was surprised by my offer, but there was no point denying what we were to each other anymore. I cared for Vesper and I was pretty sure she cared for me in return.

"What about your own revenge plot?" She nodded to the door behind me. "You don't seem so eager to kill Kaiser as the last time I saw you this close to him."

My throat thickened and I couldn't find the words to reply with. It was shameful that I hadn't finished the job for my mother's sake. I was so torn when it came to him and I despised myself for it.

Why was there even a doubt in my mind?

“We have to work together for now. That’s all. Just until the eschaton star is dealt with,” I said, though the lie burned my tongue.

She narrowed her eyes at me. “There’s more to it than that.”

“Maybe,” I admitted in a whisper. “I still despise him. The problem is…I guess I know too much now. About his past. About the spell that kept his emotions subdued.”

“Those sound like excuses, kitty cat. You either want him dead or you don’t, so which is it?”

Bastian opened the door behind us and Vesper shattered the silencing shield, looking to him.

“You need to rest,” Bastian urged. He’d gathered up some food on a plate for her and she looked at it in surprise.

“Come on then. If you’re so desperate to coddle me, so be it,” she taunted, but there was a slight blush on her cheeks as Bastian took her arm and led her away.

I was left with Vesper’s question tearing me in two and no answer to give, except a silent apology to my mama. Because the fact Kaiser Brimtheon was still breathing was a strike against her. And that felt far worse than turning my back on my nation.

VESPER

CHAPTER FORTY

Stone Castle was a lot greener than I'd expected. The Stonebreakers had done a good job of camouflaging the sprawling building where it nestled between two mountains, taking up the entire space which must have once been a valley.

Windows were shrouded by leaves and the turrets of the castle towers were not built in a unform shape but some were larger than others and all were coated in greenery. No doubt they could have passed for just another piece of the forest when looked at from a distance.

"Do you know what you're all doing?" I asked, not bothering to look at my rag-tag squadron. They did not follow orders in the way my Sinfair Legion did, with haste and without argument and I was already growing frustrated with the amount of questions I received.

"You know you're not actually the one giving orders here, don't you?" North sniped.

"Actually, I am," I replied. "Because I'm the only one of us who this mission cannot be completed without. I am the one who must kill Cayde and I am the one who must seek out and repair the keystone. Bitch about it all you want, mutt, but you're just the pretty distraction."

"Pretty? Did you all hear that? She said I'm pretty."

"It wasn't a compliment," Bastian replied.

"How wasn't it? Pretty is only ever a compliment, isn't it Kai?"

I glanced at the Fury as he considered that question.

"Pretty is one of the words which is usually used as a compliment, but her tone and delivery suggests it was intended as an insult. If I were to guess I would say that she is implying you are only good to look at – but not in a way that infers sexual attractiveness, as in this situation she means more that you will make for appealing prey to draw the focus of the Stonebreakers. A bit like a partridge or a duck."

"A duck?" North spluttered. "You did not just call me a duck!"

"He did," Everest said with a snort of amusement. "And I agree. You make a fine duck to tempt the hunters from their caves."

"The Fury is correct in his interpretation," I said and Bastian laughed in amusement.

"I can't believe you would call me a duck, Kai," North hissed.

"Vesper called you a duck. I just helped you decipher her meaning."

"You can't just start calling the fucking Sky Witch 'Vesper', Kai – we've spoken about this," North said angrily. "Don't let her fool you into forgetting her witchy nature. She's not a person. She's a…a…"

"Careful now," Bastian warned.

North huffed irritably and the corners of my lips lifted in amusement. "Looks like the big, bad Wolf is afraid of the Dragon," I taunted.

"I'm not afraid of anything," North growled.

"Apart from snakes," Kaiser said. "And quicksand. And drowning. And commitment. And–"

"You shut your damn mouth, Kai, those were secrets I told you in confidence."

"You never told me they were secrets."

"It was *implied.*"

"Oh."

"So are we gonna storm the castle then?" Everest asked with a wicked gleam in her eyes.

"As much as I'd enjoy watching them all shit themselves at the sight of the Void, I have to believe our party of five probably isn't sufficient to take out their entire stronghold."

"I guess," she sighed and I had to admire her bravery.

"Can you make us a back door, Bastian?" I asked.

"I'd say so."

"And the Flamebringers can go light some fires to distract the watchmen," I said, pointing across the valley in a clear command.

North growled angrily. "But you can't tell us what to–"

"Let's go," Kaiser caught his arm and hauled him up, shoving him into the bushes to our left where his grumbling faded away.

The Fury paused before he followed, taking the little blue Sayer Dragon from his pocket and placing it on Everest's shoulder.

"If you need me, he'll summon me to your side," he said before turning to stride away.

"Kaiser–" Everest said quickly, causing him to turn back. "I… won't need you." She flicked her gaze back towards the castle and I arched a brow as I felt the warring mixture of desires coming from her.

Kaiser hesitated another moment then turned and strode off after North to focus on the task I'd set them.

"Don't," Everest warned me, her finger swinging up to point in my face. "Do not say a single word or I will Void you while you're flying through the air and laugh as you go splat on a pointy rock."

I scoffed lightly. "I wasn't going to say anything."

"Liar," she muttered.

"Come on," I said.

Bastian moved ahead of us as we crept towards our destination, anticipation building within me as the weight of what I was about to finally achieve coiled around my heart.

I took the vial of blood in my fist and squeezed. "I'll make it hurt," I swore to my lost sisters and for a moment I could have sworn I heard their dark laughter echoing between the trees.

A tear slipped down my cheek but I ignored it, letting it fall to the dirt while focusing on our destination.

"The keystone is close," I said while trying to ignore the rampant cries of the ether.

"Good," Everest replied but Bastian cut me a dark look.

"It will be fine," I told him.

"It won't," he disagreed. "But I'll be there with you."

We crept closer to the castle with Bastian using his earth magic to seek out the perfect spot for our entrance.

The wild greenery of this place was disconcerting in its beauty. The forest surrounded us on all sides, its density intimidating. A girl could get lost in a place like this. And wouldn't that be its own kind of wonderful?

"Here," Bastian announced and I focussed on him as he dropped to one knee and pressed his hand to the ground. "Ready?"

"Always," I replied.

"For what?" Everest asked.

The ground opened up beneath our feet and we plummeted down into it at speed.

I let us fall freely for several seconds, enjoying the panicked yell which burst from Everest's throat before I caught us in a net of air and lowered us more slowly.

The light was snatched away as Bastian closed the hole over again above our heads, concealing any sign of our passage, and a few moments later we dropped down into a dimly lit chamber beneath the dirt.

"Vesper, Vesper, Vesper!" the ether was chanting my name on repeat but I forced the sound of it from my ears. I would answer its call. But not yet. I had something to finish first.

"A bit of warning would have been nice," Everest muttered.

"Next time," I promised, painting a cross over my heart but she just rolled her eyes at me, knowing I revelled in the carnage too much to ever give warning of its arrival.

Bastian sealed the stone roof above our heads and we all looked around at the small room we found ourselves in with interest. Luckily it was unoccupied, a bedchamber, presumably for a low-ranking member of Earl Tarlord's court.

I moved to the door, reaching out to see if I could taste the desires of anyone beyond it but there was no one there.

"Come on," I said.

"How exactly do you expect to find Cayde in this place?" Everest asked as we slipped through the door.

"Why? Are you offering?" I took a dagger from my belt and held it out to her but she scrunched her nose in refusal.

"No."

"Spoilsport."

I took a scrap of parchment and a sprig of mugwort from my pocket then cut the tip of my finger with the blade and gave myself to the ether. I focused on Cayde's hateful features and painted the runes Ansuz for insight and Kanaz for learning in blood. If he was here then I should be close enough for this to work. "Find him," I breathed before crushing the herbs and parchment in my fist and letting it all fall to the floor.

"I don't like it when she does that," Everest muttered to Bastian.

"Really?" he mused. "I find it utterly captivating."

"Yeah, captivating…and creepy. You have to admit it's creepy."

"Come on," I said, my voice rough with the dark magic that was rolling through me.

"That's not the word I'd use," Bastian replied to Everest.

The balled-up parchment tumbled across the floor ahead of us, leading the way on and we took chase.

We were dressed like Stonebreakers but I wasn't certain if we'd be recognised as strangers by anyone we passed or not. Stone Castle was vast and housed hundreds of people so I was hoping we would be able to slip through unchallenged. But I kept my hand close to my daggers just in case and my hair was now dyed an inky black.

Our first test came as we reached a wide staircase and two Fae passed us on their way down it.

They neither spared us a glance nor noticed the little piece of parchment which tumbled up the steps ahead of us, the two of them focused on the conversation they were having.

"Flamebringers?" one of them gasped. "How did they make it so deep into the valley?"

"They'll be dead soon enough and perhaps we'll get that answer," the other replied.

Everest paused in her ascent, looking back after the two Fae as they disappeared out of sight.

"Everest?" I said, drawing her focus back to me. "You can run off out there if you're worried? I…won't need you," I teased, repeating the words she'd spoken to Kaiser as they parted and her jaw tightened.

"I *don't* need him so that was an accurate statement. And I have no interest in heading out there, so let's just get this over with."

Calcifiend chirped from his spot on her shoulder like he was taunting her too.

"Very accurate," I agreed.

"Sometimes I forget how irritating you can be," Everest accused.

"Glad to offer up the reminder," I replied.

"The parchment has moved out of sight," Bastian commented and I muttered a curse before hurrying up the stairs to catch it.

The ether was screaming my name so loudly that it was hard to focus on bending it to the task of hunting Cayde but as we made it up to the next floor, the scrap of parchment fluttered out of the staircase and down a wide corridor.

The stone walls were a pale grey, images carved into them between doorways, though I had no time to pause and study any of them. The floor was dressed with a dark brown runner and green vines adorned with fruit and flowers climbed over doorways to decorate the ceiling and patches of bare wall. The Stonebreakers certainly knew how to flaunt their magic.

We followed the parchment past groups of Fae who were running towards the stairs but they paid us little attention and we made an effort to get out of their way.

The corridor turned, growing narrower as we passed into what appeared to be more living quarters until finally, the parchment tumbled over itself and struck a door before sticking there.

Adrenaline rushed through me in a wave, my fingers moving to the vial of blood at my throat as I took a moment to close my eyes and send a prayer out to my lost sisters.

"Sorry I'm late, but this took a bit of doing," I breathed.

I could have sworn I felt their hands pressing down on my shoulders as I stalked for the door, uttering a single command to Everest and Bastian as I finally made this move to claim my fate. I cast a silencing shield over myself and expelled a heavy breath.

"Stay here. I need to do this alone."

Neither of them complained, the two taking up position either side of the door while I reached for the handle…and turned it.

I held my breath as I eased the heavy wood open, my pulse pounding so hard it echoed through my limbs.

The room I found myself in was a grand living chamber, two doors leading off of it to other rooms, this one lavishly furnished with comfortable chairs around a fireplace and a table which could seat six for meals. It was unoccupied, so I beckoned the others inside but warned them not to follow me as I moved closer to my prey.

The spelled parchment slipped across the room and fluttered through the door to the right of the space which stood ajar in welcome to me. Beyond it, a man groaned in pain.

I crept across the room as silent as a shadow, a dagger finding its way into my grip as if it had only ever been destined to live there.

A foul scent struck me as I reached the door, a mixture of potent herbs and barely concealed rot beneath.

I slipped through the door and finally found myself looking at the man I'd been hunting all this time. His back was to me and he was shirtless, revealing the reams of oozing sores and wounds which my curse had placed upon his body.

He appeared to be smoothing the crushed herbs over more of the wounds on his chest, his head lowered, his frame tense. My fingers trembled as anticipation and relief knotted inside me and I curled them into a fist as I forced myself to calm.

I could end it now.

My knife could have been lodged in his heart before he even knew I had come for him.

But where was the fun in that?

"Hello, lover," I purred. "Remember me?"

Cayde whirled around and though I knew that wasn't truly his name, I could call him by no other. The lie suited him too well. The falseness of it matching to every other piece of his duplicitous soul.

"You," he gasped. "How? Guards!"

That last word was a yell, but of course I'd already wrapped him in my silencing shield. Our play date had barely begun and I wasn't going to let it end so quickly.

"Tut-tut, betrayer of mine. Did you think I'd allow this rendezvous to include anyone but us? We have unfinished business you and I. And I won't let anyone rush us."

Cayde blanched, backing up, his hand grasping wildly for the sword which stood in a rack at the rear of the room but I'd already placed a wall of air magic between him and it.

I cocked my head at him as he shook his head, still backing away.

"How did you get in here?"

"Haven't you heard? I'm a witch. Only a fucking fool with a death wish would ever cross me."

I threw my dagger so fast he couldn't dodge it in time, the blade striking him in the shin and sticking in bone, drawing a ragged scream from his lips.

"Crossborn bitch," he cursed, casting a wooden spear and throwing it straight for me, but his throw was sloppy as rage and pain clouded his actions.

I knocked it aside with the sweep of my hand and a gust of tempestuous wind. It hit the wall with a clatter and I laughed.

"It's Aquila now, actually. I'm second in line for the crown – isn't that a wild turn of events?"

I threw another dagger, but he managed to place a shield of air between us in time to deflect it.

"Pity your husband can't fuck you," he spat, his eyes bugging out. Had I ever truly found his foul face alluring?

"He can't?" I asked in confusion. "What do you think you know of my life?"

"I know you ruined us both with your fucking succubus magic. Does your cunt close up when he attempts the act, the way my cock refuses to harden anymore?" he snarled.

"Us?" I released a mocking laugh. *"I'm* not ruined. But if you are…you really must have fallen for me – and there I was thinking nothing could give me joy in this situation barring your extended agony and eventual demise. But I have never ruined any other Fae I've taken to my bed because they didn't feel anything for me aside from lust. You do know that's how it works, don't you?"

I taunted him with those words even though I'd never put much stock in them before. But I'd read about my Order form and knew it was rumoured to be the truth. 'Fall in love with a succubus and you will forever be ruined for all others.'

"That's all I ever felt for you too. It's all you're good for," he hissed, trying to rip the dagger from his shin but giving up in a cry of agony.

"Liar," I hissed, my fingers flicking and air magic slamming into his shield with so much force that I shattered it before hurling him back into the wall. His head cracked against stone and he stumbled as he fell to his feet, his fingers touching the back of his skull and coming away bloody.

I reached for his desires and there it was, buried beneath the hatred and desperate need to kill me – *yearning*. It was too fucking pathetic. And too fucking poetic as well.

I barked a wicked laugh.

"All this time I've been hunting you with nothing more than the desire to make you pay for taking the lives of those I loved. And here you've been, screaming in agony at the mere attempt to spill your secrets, your body a ruined echo of the foulness within you. Taking a wife who you couldn't even fuck, and no doubt has had to endure your pathetic attempts to do so, while deep down inside you *pined* for me too. Well here I am, *lover*. Your wish has come true. So why don't you come get me?"

Cayde bellowed furiously, taking the bait and running for me. I let him come, placing no magic between us and simply focusing on dodging his attack at the last moment. I swung around behind him, my fist striking the back of his head hard enough to send him sprawling to the ground.

He threw a shield of air up between us once more but it didn't matter. I had what I needed.

His blood stained my knuckles and with it, I let myself fall into the depths of the ether.

"Gotcha," I said with a dark and menacing grin.

He lurched for me then stopped as my power bore into him, his screams coming like sweet music as I made his blood burn and boil.

His magic shattered as his ability to focus on it fell to nothing and I took another dagger from my belt, weighing it in my grasp while approaching him slowly.

"Now," I said, the blood magic I was using to contain him making my throat raw and my words rougher than usual. "Let me show you a few tricks I picked up in the Cavern of Lost Souls. You'll be surprised how much a Fae can suffer before death. But I plan on letting you find out exactly how agonising it can be."

KAISER

CHAPTER FORTY ONE

"Feels good to dance the demon's dance with you again, freyin!" North howled to me as he blasted a hole in a tree and the baying of Avanis warriors chased after us.

"What is this feeling?" I demanded as a manic smile stitched itself onto my mouth.

We climbed a rocky ridge then sprinted along its length, blasting fire in every direction to cause as much noise and destruction as we could.

"Elation, invigoration, exhilaration!" he shouted to me, blasting fire from his hands with every word.

Arrows and spears were launched at us but I burnt them up in the heat of our flames before they could ever come close to touching us.

North leapt from the ridge to a treetop ahead of me and I jumped after him, the foliage slipping through my grip as I started to fall, but he caught my arm and yanked me up, grinning from ear to ear.

"You feel it now, don't you? All these years you lived our wildest moments with your emotions muted. Do you adore it as I always knew you would?" he asked.

"This is fucking everything." I turned sharply as the whistle of something metallic came shooting after us.

I unsheathed my sword and knocked the silver arrow off course so it embedded itself in the tree trunk. A few more silver arrows tore our way, but it would take the Stonebreakers longer to cast them than wood and that stole us a moment to run while they made more. We climbed down from the tree then sprinted away from them, thud, thud, thud of the arrows hitting the trees at our backs sending another bolt of adrenaline through me.

I leapt over a fallen log and crouched behind it with North. He grabbed my face, squeezing it tight. "This is called having fun."

"We must do this every day," I said and he laughed before running toward a row of supply carts parked ahead of us, climbing on top of one and setting them all on fire. Then he back flipped off of the cart and landed on his feet. We'd found this supply train close to Stone Castle and had caused enough havoc to cause the distraction Vesper had wanted.

"You'll have to teach me that," I demanded as I ran to his side and shoved him out the way of a flying arrow.

"That's a promise I intend to keep." He clapped me on the arm then pointed to a large wagon filled with barrels of whiskey further down the track that wound through the forest.

"Yes," North growled keenly.

"Fuck yes," I added as we stalked closer, hands raised and hellfire tearing from our fingertips. The whiskey was consumed in the blaze and North caught my wrist, dragging me away into the trees with a yell to move fast. The explosion that resounded set my heart racing and laughter fell from my lungs as I sprinted from the chaos alongside my brother.

A line of Avanis warriors came into view ahead, cutting us off with swords in hand. One of them blasted tiny splinters of wood at us, hundreds of them shooting this way and I cast fire with North to burn them. A few made it through, slicing into my arms and legs, but I could hardly feel the pain at all. If anything, it only spurred me on with my blood spilled and the promise of violence on the air.

I shoved North between two trees to our right and he cried out as he fell out of sight.

I barrelled after him, righting him and realising we'd just stumbled across an old supply tunnel. The steps dropped steeply below ground, but it didn't look like the tunnel had been in use recently from the amount of cobwebs that covered our path.

An arrow pinged off the stone doorway above us and I shoved North into a run.

"Arghh," North snarled as he charged ahead of me, taking the brunt of all the cobwebs as I cast a ball of fire in my hand to guide the way. He was soon coated in white fibres as he spat to try and get them out of his mouth.

"Stars be damned! There's a fucking black widow in my ear!" he bayed.

I snatched the spider in question from his ear, the thing definitely not a black widow which weren't even found this far north and tossed it to the ground.

"I thought you were afraid of snakes, not spiders," I commented.

"I have a reason to be scared of snakes as you know very well. It takes a traumatic event to cause a phobia and if this isn't a traumatic event then I don't know what is." He clawed at his hair and I saw many little legs running over his hand but decided not to mention it.

The tunnel began to tremble around us and I realised our mistake in heading below ground as dust crumbled from the ceiling onto my shoulders.

"North, go faster," I urged.

He put on a spurt of speed, so many more spider webs covering him that he was blinded, waving his hands out and a doggish whine leaving him.

"I can't see," he cursed and I grabbed a fist of his clothes, wielding him like a battering ram to take down all the cobwebs in my path and force him into a sprint.

"You bastard!" he yelled but I could see steps up ahead. A way out so close as clumps of dirt and rock started crashing to the floor around us.

"They're going to cave it in," I growled and North gave up any resistance as I shoved him ever faster, keeping him upright when his feet stumbled onto the steps.

"*Go*," I demanded as huge rocks smashed down into the tunnel behind me.

Somehow we made it up the steps to a hatch and I blasted it clean off its hinges with a fireball. We stumbled into a forest glade just as the whole tunnel caved in behind us.

North turned to me, his face mummified by spider webs, just the vague shape of his features visible beneath it. I laughed, a roaring belly laugh that made him growl at me then I swiped the worst of it from his face and shook them free.

"You owe me," he hissed then reached for his hair in horror. "Tell me straight, are there many spiders on me?"

I looked him over, seeing a lot. More than a hundred probably. I remembered what he'd told me about it being okay to lie to people sometimes if it would make them feel better and lifted my chin in pride as I answered. "None at all."

"That was the worst lie I've ever heard," he grouched then he looked to a small stream close by, ran over and launched himself into it. He came out shivering with plenty of spiders still clinging to him, but the worst of the cobwebs had gone. I tried out one of the gestures he'd taught me to use when I didn't have the right response to a situation.

I gave him a thumbs up.

He scowled at me. "You're useless."

"Did I do it wrong?" I looked at my thumb but a roar of shouts carried from the trees behind us and we took off running again.

I shut my eyes to steal a look at Everest through Calcifiend's eyes and found her bickering with Bastian where they stood inside a lavishly furnished room. She seemed well enough so I returned my focus to the forest ahead and the game of drawing the Stonebreakers' attention away from our allies.

VESPER

CHAPTER FORTY TWO

I was bloodstained and out of breath, my grasp on the ether filling my mind with dark deeds and drawing me closer to the edge than I'd ever come before. But I couldn't stop. His screams were a balm to the ache of loss inside me, and I knew I was past the point of needing them to stop, I just couldn't bring myself to do it.

It wasn't enough.

It could never be enough.

A cry of alarm from a woman in the room outside drew a small measure of my focus but I couldn't summon the energy I needed to release my hold on the dark magic and investigate it.

I understood now why Moya had warned me against this level of their dark practices but it was too late for me to stop. I didn't *want* to stop anyway. I could hear my sisters' laughter in accompaniment to every piece of pain I dealt the man who had stolen their lives from them.

This was the least they deserved. It was the least *I* deserved. And it was all I had left to me now.

The ether tempted me deeper and I could distantly feel my lips curling in a wicked smile, the slickness of blood on my hands, the fatigue in my limbs. I was going to let it sweep me away.

And then I'd be gone and this pain I existed within would be no more.

But…something nagged at me as I tried to let myself slip into the darkness and drift away upon a tide of it. Like a hand grasping the edge of a doorframe and trying to haul me back through it. But why would any piece of me cling to that life of endless disappointment, pain and suffering? What reason would any part of me have to cling on?

Every time I grew close to figuring it out, the ether beckoned me back again. It still screamed my name, though I knew I wouldn't be able to do what it wanted if I let it have me. But what did that matter? What did anything matter?

I'd caught up to my prey and he was suffering on the verges of death. He only lingered this side of The Veil because my dark hooks were sunk so deep within him that he couldn't fall through it.

If I let go, he would fall too. Down, down, down into the dark where he could be judged and punished forever more for his crimes.

Perhaps I'd be right there beside him in that place of torment and judgement. I'd certainly earned that fate. There had to be countless Fae who had dreamed of enacting vengeance upon me just as I was upon Cayde. And they deserved their pound of flesh.

I only hoped I might be able to sneak a glimpse beyond the bars of my cage of torment and see my sisters there, free and at peace in the place beyond. Just once. I didn't deserve more than that, but if I could be assured that they were at peace then that would be enough for me. It would all have been worth it.

A door crashed open and panicked yells echoed in the distance like raindrops settling at the base of a well.

I was going to leave it all behind anyway. Every single piece of it. At least I would whenever I figured out how to stop myself from clinging on.

Hands grasped my face and pulled me around so that I found myself blinking stupidly up at the features of my one good thing. My secret respite from my pain.

Bastian was saying something. Yelling something. His fingers dug into my skin and I frowned through the haze of dark magic.

My vision began to clear as I looked at him, my eyes aching to see the silver which shot through his irises.

This was what I'd been holding on for, what I hadn't so easily been able to let go.

Him.

I sucked in a ragged breath as reality flooded back in on me, my hold on the ether shattering and my body sagging with relief. I fell against him and he wrapped me in his arms while I fought to simply stay on my feet.

My body felt as though it had been crushed beneath a giant weight, my veins seared with hellfire, my skin raw and tender.

A sob broke from my chest before I could contain it and he only held me more tightly.

"It's not enough," Bastian murmured and all I could do was shake my head as the weight of disappointment soured in my gut.

"He shouldn't just get to die," I said. "He shouldn't just get to take them and then go on living, but death…death is too fucking easy."

"Easy?" a horrified voice gasped and I stiffened as I failed to recognise the source of it.

"We have a problem," Bastian growled.

"Someone might have heard her scream," Everest said and I turned my head, forcing myself to step back just enough to be able to see her where she stood, restraining a woman in a sheer, pale green gown, Everest's knife tip pressed to her throat.

I knew that woman. I'd studied her portrait.

"You're her…" I said, my eyes roaming over the red-head who was staring at me in utter horror. "The one he betrayed first."

"F-first?" she stammered, her eyes on the bloody wreck of her husband's body.

Cayde was still breathing…just. A low groan of pain wheezed out of his lips but he couldn't speak. He had no tongue after all.

"We need to go," Bastian said darkly.

"And the problem?" I asked.

"I won't let you kill this woman," Everest said firmly. "I saved her life when I fled Cascada. I won't let her die here now."

"You're the one with a knife to her throat," I pointed out. "And I didn't come here to murder civilians. Tie her up and let her people find her when we're gone if you care for her so much."

"I curse you," Septa Thorngrove spat at me, her eyes wet with unshed tears. "I curse you as you did him. I will see you dead for this, Sky Witch. I will–"

"Doesn't work like that," I sneered but there was little bite to my tone and I was almost certain I was only still standing because Bastian was holding me upright.

"Finish it, spectre. We need to leave," he urged, taking his sword from his scabbard and pressing it into my grip. I'd lost track of my own blades, though as I looked down at the bastard who had earned the worst of my wrath I found them all lodged in him at various points.

"He did a terrible thing to earn this fate," Everest was saying to Septa, though why she cared enough to try and do so, I had no idea. "He murdered two warriors who trusted him. He killed them in cold blood. Stabbed them in the back. I know there is a lot of death in the world and I know there are a lot of Fae seeking revenge but if it brings you any comfort at all to know that he earned it then…" she trailed off when Septa failed to reply.

"Why are you bothering to explain this?" I snapped, my head ringing with the after-effects of so much dark magic, her words driving into my skull and making it ache. "Who cares why I did it? They're all the same anyway. Any one of them would have done what he–"

"How can you say that while standing in the arms of a Stonebreaker?" Everest growled. "You're a fucking fool to say that and a damn liar too. Didn't you make a deal to escape this place and live away from war? Will you still preach that prejudice shit about every other element than yours then? You were born in Cascada for the stars' sake!"

A hollow laugh fell from my lips and she fell quiet as she took in the hopeless, emptiness of me.

"Don't you get it, kitty-cat? I'm done. The moment I run this motherfucker through I am out of reasons to keep doing anything at all. I only kept moving all this time to see him ended in payment for their deaths. And that's it."

Bastian's grip on me tightened and a growl rippled through him.

"You're full of shit, Vesper," he snarled. "You know you have far more than that to live for now if you choose it – but that's the fucking problem, isn't it? You refuse to choose it. To choose *me.*"

"It isn't you that's the problem," I snarled, shoving free of him and stumbling back, the world spinning as dizziness struck me, but I clung onto my anger, my disappointment, my pain, and I let it sustain me so that I didn't fall. "It's me. Look at me, Bastian. Really look. This is what I am. And it is not deserving of any of the things you try to claim it is. You'll see that clearly soon. You'll see that the only reason you think you want me is because I'm the only thing you have. But it won't be enough. *I* can't be enough."

"It isn't *can't* Vesper. It's *won't!"* he yelled, the booming roar of a Dragon echoing in his tone, his anger, his hurt.

I'd done that. And I couldn't make myself undo it either.

The silence dragged and was only breached by Cayde's agonised groans. I couldn't make my tongue bend around the words I should have. I couldn't bear to do it. And I knew that Bastian could see that, see me, bloodstained and wounded, inside and out.

"We shouldn't be doing this here," he snarled, swiping a hand over his face and turning his back on me. "Finish this in whatever way you want. I can't stand by and watch you choose to destroy yourself anymore." He strode up to the wall and slammed his fist into it, the rock shattering beneath his strike, a spiderweb of damage falling apart before he turned and headed back out of the door.

"That's it?" Everest asked in a low voice as the sound of Bastian's footsteps faded and I found the hurt in my heart only sharpening.

"What?" I muttered.

"You said you have nothing to live for beyond Cayde's death. But what about the promises you made? What about the other reason we had for coming here? You know we can't do this without you. You know the whole world is at stake. Are you really so damn selfish that you plan to die before completing that task?"

"Yes," I said simply, because I was. Coming here had reminded me of that. Finding Cayde, fulfilling my promise, all of it had only brought my grief right back to the forefront of my mind. The corruption in my heart blinded me to everything else as I found myself right back where I'd been when I'd found myself coated in their blood, their bodies broken on the ground beside me.

"The world?" Septa whimpered. "What are you talking about?

"We're looking for a keystone," Everest told her. "Do you know what that is? It's tall and carved with the three faces of Taurus, Virgo and Capricorn. Something has–"

"Why are you telling her any of this?" I asked hollowly, my fingers cold where they gripped Bastian's sword.

I should have called out to him, gone after him…but he was better off that I hadn't.

"Because you're done, aren't you? So be done. I'm not giving up though. My word means something," Everest spat, taking her blade from Septa's throat and letting her step away so that she was no longer in immediate danger of death.

Septa blinked back the terrified tears which still pooled in her eyes, her hand touching her throat as though to make certain it hadn't been cut.

"Look…I know this is fucking horrible from your point of view," Everest said, waving a hand in the vague direction of Septa's mutilated husband. "But…umm…he deserved it. And we didn't come here to hurt anyone else. There really is a threat to all of us which we are trying to end. If you know anything that could help me find the keystone–"

"You won't be able to do shit to it even if you can find it," I muttered.

"Then stop being a selfish cunt and come with me," she replied forcefully.

The vial of blood which still hung from my neck heated sharply, making me hiss in pain as I snatched it away from my skin, the haze I'd been losing myself to clearing a little.

I frowned at the necklace. Were they mad at me too? Did they want me to keep my word?

"There's something wrong with it – the keystone," Septa said, forcing my focus to move to her and I frowned.

"You know of it?" I asked, my fingers tight around the vial which was cooling as rapidly as it had warmed.

She flinched at the question as though a mere word from my lips was as good as a strike. But she answered all the same. "It's a place of worship in the deepest part of the castle but…I don't know how to describe it. I've never liked going there. Something about it isn't right."

"We came here to fix it. It's important that we do that – for you as well as us, even if I can't explain it to you now. Can you show us where it is?" Everest asked.

Septa's lips opened and closed, her eyes moving from me to Cayde who still clung to the last tendrils of life at my feet.

"If I take you to it, then you must swear not to kill a single Stonebreaker while you are here. You see the keystone and you leave," she said.

"Are you including your…um…husband in that?" Everest asked. "Because yeah, we won't hurt anyone else, but I don't think he's going to make it either way–"

"I can petition the Reapers," Septa said in a shaky voice. "I will beg them to–"

"If you're that desperate to fuck him, I can assure you it is not worth the anticipation," I sneered. "Besides, I already rendered him incapable of the act in a far more permanent way than any fucking 'ruin' might have managed. So you're out of luck."

"Gross," Everest muttered, glancing at the bloody stains surrounding the dagger embedded in Cayde's groin.

Septa looked like she was going to vomit as she forced herself to look at the man who clung to life at my feet, then back to Everest who was definitely the safest choice for her focus.

"It isn't his body I want. He…"

"Oh," I said, realisation striking me as I caught the flavour of her desires. "It's those secrets he has locked up inside his head, isn't it? You've all been desperately trying to bypass my curse and loosen his lips, and it doesn't even fucking matter anymore. You want his secret? Fine. He was with me and my sisters when we entered a chamber filled with archways secreted away below Never Keep," I said, weighing the sword in my grip as I prepared for what I knew I needed to do. It was too simple, too easy, but I wanted it over. I *needed* it over. "He saw these archways being activated – it was utterly incredible magic and insanely dangerous in the wrong hands. When activated, the archways could be used to step from one land to another in a matter of seconds. We could travel from the Keep to Stormfell or Pyros or Avanis in less than a heartbeat."

"But…if that is true, then whoever knows of these archways would be able to send armies across the world in seconds. They would be able to wage war without any chance of the opposing nation being able to prepare or–"

"Which is why Prince Dragor destroyed every last one of them. So Cayde's secrets are fucking useless to you anyway. And any other little titbits he might have tucked away in his mind about Stormfell are likely useless to you too. Dragor is king now. Everything has changed in the months since this bastard killed the only people I ever loved over a worthless secret. We all know he's a traitor too, so any knowledge he had of the movements of our armies or anything else has been altered so that the information he holds is now worthless. He doesn't know anything of use to you anymore. And even if he did… you'll never find out."

I drove my sword straight into Cayde's heart as I finished it, his eyes flying open as a final cry escaped him, accusation and hatred burning through his gaze as it locked with mine.

Septa stifled a cry, staggering back against the wall, terror clinging to her, but I had no interest in taking her life too.

Relief found me in the moment of his death, and I dropped to my knees as the last of my energy failed me, tears sliding down my cheeks freely as I wept for all I'd lost.

It was done. He was gone, vengeance sought and claimed. But it didn't bring them back.

My grief closed in on me so potently that I felt like I was being crushed beneath the weight of it. I'd only kept moving to complete this task for them and gain this vengeance. It had become all I was, all that I lived for. And now that it was done, I felt so fucking empty that it was a burden to even drag air down into my wretched lungs.

"It should have been me," I told them, tears scalding my cheeks.

They were worth a thousand of me, yet they'd offered themselves up in my place, stepped between me and death and taken the only goodness in me with them. I didn't know how to go on without them, I didn't know how to be worthy of any kind of existence at all. I'd pushed away the man who had offered me something else because I knew I didn't deserve his affection. I didn't deserve *him*. And he and everyone else would be better off if I just let death have me now the way I'd intended.

I thought of the vow I'd given Bastian, of the promise I'd made to let him end my life. I'd dreamed of the sweet release I might feel as his hands tightened around my throat, of how my death would be well deserved. But now I knew in my heart that he would never claim it from me. He saw something in me which I didn't believe existed. And in payment for the spark of hope and joy he'd gifted me I'd sent him running from me too.

I was alone. Just as I always should have been. And the pain of that was going to tear me in two no matter how much I wished it wouldn't.

I pulled Bastian's sword free of Cayde's broken body and turned it in my grip so that the point rested against my heart, relief spilling into me at the thought of simply letting myself fall onto it now, letting it all end.

A hand landed on my shoulder as the seconds dragged on, and I forced my eyes up to meet with Everest's as I found some small measure of my pain in her expression too.

"They wouldn't want you to die, Vesper," she breathed, and the vial of blood I still clung to warmed in my fist again. I ached for the release of death but still I lingered on the wrong side of it, looking into the eyes of a woman who should have been my enemy while some fractured piece of my soul clung to the hope that she might give me a reason to keep going. "But I bet they'd fucking love it if you saved the whole damn world in their honour."

"They hated this fucking world," I said with a laugh which was half a sob, Bastian's sword falling from my hands to clatter against the stone. Perhaps death wasn't ready for me yet, or perhaps I needed to admit that *I* wasn't ready for *it*. "But fine, you win, kitty-cat. I'll do my best to save it anyway."

"She sees sense at last," a low voice rumbled, and my gaze snapped beyond Everest to Bastian as he stepped back into the room, his expression shuttered and jaw tight.

"Bastian," I breathed, the relief of seeing him helping to patch up some of the bleeding hurt in my soul. "I'm sorry…I–"

"There isn't time for this now," he said, offering me his hand, and I let him pull me to my feet. "I'm just glad you finally realised what you are."

"And what's that?" I asked, my eyes moving to the mutilated corpse of the bastard who had wronged me.

Bastian caught my chin and returned my gaze to his.

"Entirely unstoppable."

EVEREST

CHAPTER FORTY THREE

We walked in silence behind Septa with Vesper beside me and Bastian at our backs, and I took comfort in the feeling of Calcifiend's little feet on my neck where he hid under my hair. My fingers brushed the Sky Witch's arm and she looked to me with a frown that questioned all I was and why I walked at her side. I didn't have the answer to the questions in her eyes but they seemed to be answered when she laid her hand on mine. Just for a moment, our fingers brushing, telling me she felt this connection between us even if she didn't want to admit it out loud either. I'd silently cleaned Cayde's blood from her with my elemental magic, letting the water wash it away and leaving her clean. But she didn't look any less broken.

We were two souls born of this ruinous world, torn apart by war, lines drawn between us by Fae who had lived long ago. Too long ago to care for us now. Everything I'd been taught had fractured, like a sword had struck cracks in me over and over again until it had revealed something real beneath the layers of falsehood.

I didn't know who that made me now, but I was starting to trust my instincts more than anything else, praying Pisces had always intended for me to walk this path. I wasn't sure why the company of my enemies felt this way. Perhaps if we managed to destroy the eschaton star, this feeling would go away. But I wasn't certain I wanted it to.

Septa led us deep beneath the castle, down winding stairways and through doors that were veiled in shadow. She glanced back at us uncertainly and I feared she might change her mind on helping us if I didn't reassure her.

"Look, I know this seems bad…" I started.

"Bad?" Septa breathed, shooting a glare at Vesper. "She's a monster."

"Your husband killed her sisters," I tried.

Septa's lips twitched. "I thought you were better than Fae like her."

"Watch your mouth," Bastian warned, but Vesper didn't seem to care.

"That man took away the only people she loved in the world," I said. "He made Vesper think he loved her when no one else ever had."

Septa frowned, staring at Vesper then turning away and continuing on.

A shiver tracked over my skin as we neared the stone Septa had spoken of. It was a familiar feeling, one which made me think of the dark voice of the eschaton star in the hole Kaiser and I had jumped into back at Never Keep.

I knew without any need for confirmation at all that we were on the right path to the ley line. Vesper had assured me these dark tethers fed the eschaton star through the bloodshed of war, some horrid magic forged of death giving it strength. If she could repair this last keystone and free the ley line from its corruption, the eschaton star would be weakened. It would no longer be able to draw power from our world and then we might just be able to destroy it on the night of the blood moon. So I'd vowed to assist her in whatever way possible.

Septa led us through one final door, unlocking it with a large, brass key and leading us inside. I inhaled sharply at the roiling power that trickled over me, the bite of cold tempered by some unholy magic.

Sconces lit the chamber in an amber glow, revealing a large, triangular pillar of pale stone jutting from the ground at the end of the long room. Three faces were carved into its sides, a bull's head for Taurus, a sea-goat for Capricorn and a beautiful maiden for Virgo.

An iron spike speared the brow of the bull, cracks splintering away from it which seemed to hold nothing but darkness within them.

Vesper strode toward it and I followed in her stead, my hand resting against the hilt of my dagger. Though it was nothing but a fool's assurance. No blade could counter magic such as this.

My steps faltered as a knot of tension rolled through me, the hairs on the back of my neck lifting with discomfort and a warning that something foul was at play here.

"Fae worship this?" I asked Septa, wrinkling my nose as I fought the urge to turn and walk away from the unpleasant sourness which seemed to seep from that thing.

"I told you there was a…wrongness to the feeling of this place. But some believe it is the discomfort caused by standing closer to the stars – they think the earth deities can hear them more clearly if they whisper to them here."

I took in the room which I supposed must have been carved around the monolith using earth magic. It was grand, the ceiling high and painted with depictions of the earthen zodiac symbols among fields of green grass and blossoming flowers.

The stone floor was polished and gleamed a pale white, the walls hung with flowering vines which had no business surviving beneath the ground at all, the magic in them clear.

Above the monolith hung a chandelier with a Faelight trapped inside it, the metal cylinders which contained the light punctured with thousands of tiny holes so that dots of illumination escaped and patterned everything they fell upon like stars in a distant sky.

"Were the other keystones celebrated this way?" I asked, though Vesper seemed not to be listening to anything any of us said.

"No. They were in lost and forgotten places, caverns, dank and mouldering," Bastian muttered, his posture tense and gaze fixed on Vesper who lifted a hand as she reached the stone pillar. "Brace yourself," he added.

"For wha–" I gasped as the ground beneath my feet rocked violently, a shockwave resounding out through the walls, the roof, the entire castle and mountains beyond it as Vesper placed her palm against the stone.

Septa cried out in alarm, stumbling back against the wall and I caught her arm to steady her, my brows pinching as my fingers tangled in a vine which was concealed beneath her sleeve.

"What have you done?" I cursed, my head snapping around as I spotted the thin vine which snaked out from beneath her dress and hugged the edges of the room before slithering out beneath the door we'd used to get here.

"For fuck's sake," Bastian snarled, a strike of his hand severing the vine while another shot from him and wrapped itself around

Septa's throat, hoisting her off of her feet and into the air. "Who did you just summon?"

"Don't kill her!" I demanded, stepping closer to him as the sound of thundering footsteps raced towards us from beyond the door.

Bastian seemed inclined to ignore me, Septa's feet kicking wildly as she clawed at the vine which was choking her. I threw my arm up, the Void tearing from me, snatching his magic away and causing the vine to disappear, leaving Septa to crash down to the floor with a cry.

A scream tore from Vesper's throat and we snapped around to look at her, horror lancing through me as I took in the way she grasped the iron spike which had speared the heart of the keystone. Her head was thrown back, her eyes staring unseeingly upward, that scream ripping from her throat and echoing around the chamber like the haunting cry of something utterly unworldly.

Her screams broke and became words, the weight of them striking me like fists to my chest, their meaning unknown but dripping with ancient power that had my mind spinning.

Footsteps beyond the chamber were accompanied by a battle cry and Bastian whirled for the door, throwing his hands towards it and encasing it in stone to block the way into the room.

I exchanged a look with him, both of us knowing that the Stonebreakers would be able to break through that in moments.

"I'll hold them off," Bastian said fiercely, his hand flicking towards Septa as she scrambled to her feet, vines binding tightly around her and flattening her palms against her sides so that she was immobilised.

She fell back with a cry and Bastian unfastened the fur-trimmed cloak he wore before hoisting his shirt over his head, revealing a body painted in scars and ink.

"You're going to shift?" I asked, my gaze moving to the wide space around us and wondering if a Dragon would actually fit in it or not. It was going to be damn tight if he did.

"Yes. They might be able to break through a wall, but I'd like to see them cut through Dragon fire."

"You swore not to hurt anyone!" Septa cried. "And you have the power of our people – aren't you one of us? How can you turn on your own kind?"

A growl rumbled from Bastian as he unfastened his belt, tossing his sword on top of his clothes, still in its scabbard.

"I can do it," I said, stepping forward and throwing my Void power out towards the blocked door, cutting off the magic of the Fae who had arrived beyond it.

Their yells echoed through the stone as they began to pound on it, curses carrying to us through it as they found themselves unable to unblock their way.

"Septa!" a powerful voice roared from outside and my blood chilled at the threat in the way the man bellowed her name.

"Who is that?" I demanded, looking to Septa who had pushed herself to sit upright.

"My Earl," she breathed, fear in her eyes. "You made me a promise."

"And we'll keep it," I swore despite knowing it was madness to do so. "What we're doing here, what Vesper is doing – it matters. You know that, right? There's something wrong in The Waning Lands. There's a monster called the eschaton star stealing power from the ley lines, fighting to break through into our world so that it can devour *everything*. This is bigger than the war. It's important. We didn't come here to kill anyone besides Cayde and that was personal."

"This creature is more important than the war?" Septa breathed, her gaze jumping between the wall where her Earl and his warriors pounded fiercely to gain entry and Vesper who was still caught in the grasp of the ether, fighting to save us all.

"It is," I said firmly. "I can't explain everything now but I swear to you that this matters more than anything else."

A huge, growling roar of energy cut our words off and I looked at the blocked door in alarm as it began to quake violently despite the power I still extended over it.

"What is that?" Bastian demanded.

"An underbeast," Septa breathed, her eyes wide as she stared at the wall where the stone was trembling and cracking.

"I can't Void it," I cursed, backing up. "Is it powered with magic stored in runes?"

Septa nodded and I exchanged a look with Bastian who turned and blasted a hole in the opposite wall, carving a tunnel into it with his earth magic.

"How long do you need, Vesper?" he called but she didn't answer, the words of ancient power still falling from her tongue, her body stiff with tension while she fought to pull the iron spike from the heart of the keystone.

"You're going to do whatever it takes to help her," Bastian told me, taking a bundle of herbs wrapped in a piece of parchment from his pocket and shoving it into my hand. "Burn that in her fist if you can't wake her. And climb onto my back with her when the moment for our escape comes."

"You're mad," I hissed, backing up as he dropped his trousers.

"Probably." He shifted in the blink of an eye and Septa screamed as an iron grey Dragon burst from his flesh, its enormous size filling the space around us and forcing me to back up hurriedly.

My heart raced as I took in the majestic beauty of his Order form, his spiked tail swinging a breath away from me as he lunged for the huge, metallic contraption which burst through the blocked doorway a moment later.

Bastian roared, Dragon fire blasting the Stonebreakers' machine before he collided with it, teeth and claws digging into the metal and forcing it to a halt.

He was so big that I could barely see anything of the fight he was engaged in, his sides crashing into the walls, spines striking the ceiling while he kept his powerful wings tucked tight to his body.

Septa screamed in fear and I snared her in a whip of water, hauling her away from the carnage before she could be crushed.

"He won't hurt them," I swore to her just as a lump of roof came crashing down onto the metallic contraption she'd named an underbeast. "Or…he won't kill them at least."

I hoped there was truth to that claim, but there was little I could do to aid in his fight, so I turned my focus to Vesper instead, moving closer to her as she spat words laced with power from her tongue and wept tears of agony from unseeing eyes.

She must have known the cost of doing this. She'd done it before. But she'd still come here, still walked straight up to this thing and exerted her power over it without so much as flinching.

"Vesper?" I called. "We're running out of–"

I felt the moment Vesper shattered the dark magic tainting the keystone, the vile power abandoning the stone and severing its connection to the eschaton star for good.

With a tremendous crash, she tore the spike free of the stone monolith, an explosion of power bursting from the hole it had carved into Taurus's brow and sending her flying backwards.

The power knocked Septa and me to the ground too, the force of it stealing the breath from my lungs and pinning me in place for several agonising seconds while the rumble of stone told of the cracks and damage to the keystone healing over at last.

I rolled onto my side as the rush of power ebbed then fell away, scrambling toward Vesper and cursing as I took in the ruined flesh of her hands where the magic had burned her right down to the bone.

I reeled at the sight of the wounds but before I could so much as consider how to help her, the skin began to knit over, her spine arching and eyes flying wide as every wound the act of repairing the keystone had caused her was healed away by some divine gift.

Vesper's body tensed then fell limp, her unseeing eyes still staring aloft as Bastian's tail swung over our heads and knocked a lump of stone from the walls.

She took a knife from her belt and dug it into her arm before I could stop her, her hand moving in swift and precise motions like a pen across parchment instead of a blade over flesh, leaving runes behind which bled in their wake.

Blood tarnished her skin as I threw myself toward her, capturing her wrist to try and stop her. She smacked me away but I grabbed her again, taking the bundled herbs Bastian had given me and forcing them between her fingers. She'd told me this might happen, that she might become lost in the flow of the ether and need help breaking free of it.

She started to shake and convulse before me, still cutting into her own arm, a curse falling from my lips as I ripped my pack free of my back and hunted inside it for a flint to light a fire.

"Hold on," I commanded, shoving provisions and weapons aside until I found what I was searching for and tugged it free.

The magic which held her in its grip built to a terrible crescendo, her body jerking violently beneath me, blood running from the corners of her eyes, her ears, her nose. A song lingered on the edge of my comprehension which sounded like the chorus of death itself and I had no doubt Vesper was going to die if she couldn't break out of it.

I wrapped my arms around her as she cut into herself and screamed a wretched scream.

"Vesper Crossborn!" I yelled at her. "It's not your time to die!"

The Void poured from me, the power lashing out at whatever dark magic had hold of the Sky Witch. It connected to it, dragging me in too and I cried out at the agony contained within it, like it was built of purest death. It was an echo of all that had happened in The Waning Lands, every battle waged in Avanis, every mother's tears who'd wept for their lost child in battle, every broken heart, every abrupt loss.

It was a pain like no other, a wound in The Waning Lands itself. I'd felt this very anguish before, when I'd somehow connected to this roiling power in the earth of a battlefield in Pyros with Mavus watching over me. I'd only managed to break free then because of the battle stims he'd given me, but there was no hope of that this time. I pushed back against it, controlling the Void far better than I had when I'd felt this very anguish before.

But there was no way of forcing this power to answer to me, the claws it had hooked into us made of magic so different to that which my Void knew how to banish that I found myself powerless against it.

We were both lost to it now, both trapped in the confines of this hell which both terrified and called to me.

A flare of burning pain against my fingers snapped me out of the turmoil of dark magic with a violent crash which left me panting and blinking on the stone floor of the chamber with Septa backing away from us, my flint falling from her hand.

I looked to the scraps of burnt herbs and parchment which were crushed between mine and Vesper's fists.

"I heard what the Dragon said about burning that," Septa said, backing away from us, the vines which had been wrapped around her now heaped at her feet where she'd broken free of them. "Consider my life debt repaid to you, Everest."

Vesper groaned as she fell back into reality too, her eyes unfocused as she blinked between me and the Stonebreaker who had just saved our lives.

"Thank you," I said.

"I did it for The Waning Lands," Septa replied. "And so that you'll leave here before the Dragon hurts anyone else."

"We will," I swore, the bellows of Bastian's fight with the underbeast still echoing around the room.

I pulled Vesper close and she leaned into me, panting and bloodied. I held her as my heart began to slow, relief consuming me. I'd almost lost her. She had come so very close to death, perhaps she'd tasted it.

"Vesper?" I whispered and she lifted her head, blood red tears falling from her eyes and staining her cheeks crimson. I wiped them away, my chest tight, but no more fell.

"I almost gave in to it," she admitted.

"There's no point in dying until you're either a hero or a villain who'll be remembered for the rest of time," I taunted and she cracked a smile.

"How about we try being both? Save the world but kill a lot of bastards along the way."

"Sounds like the perfect way to live to me." I shared her dark smile, then hauled her to her feet, yelling Bastian's name so that he knew our task here was done.

"That was…" Septa spoke, looking horrified by what she'd witnessed. "It's true, what you said. This place was wicked. But you've fixed it. Whatever foul magic was here, it was a taint on the earth, I felt it as though it whispered its horrors in my ears. But you shattered it." She stared at Vesper, eyes bright with confusion.

Vesper made to answer her but instead crumpled to her knees and I barely managed to catch her before she could hit the ground.

A potent blast of Dragon fire heated the space around us as Bastian turned, more flames bursting from his open jaws and down the new tunnel he'd blasted into the walls.

I didn't waste any time and called on my water magic, a whip of it wrapping around both me and Vesper, hauling us into the air and launching us up and onto Bastian's back where we landed heavily in the joint between his tightly tucked wings.

He broke into a run at once, wooden and metal spears hurtling towards us as we made our escape and Earl Tarlord and his warriors burst from the belly of the broken underbeast to chase us.

I threw a wall of ice up at our backs to shield us from attack, holding Vesper tightly as she teetered on the edge of consciousness before me.

Bastian blasted the wall of dirt ahead of us with more Dragon fire and I sucked in a sharp breath as it broke apart revealing the bright sky beyond as we burst free of the side of the mountain.

Bastian's wings snapped wide as he leapt from the tunnel and we were launched into the air, my heart racing furiously as I found myself tearing into the sky on the back of a beast of legend.

A roar broke from Bastian's lungs as we made our escape and I whooped in victory, my head turning left to right as I took in the stunning landscape which spread out beneath us.

Calcifiend crawled out of my hair, chirping loudly in my ear and a flash of fire caught my attention to the south. I yelled to draw Bastian's focus to it too, my stomach knotting with concern that I refused to accept I felt.

"Kaiser is over there!"

My stomach swooped as Bastian dipped his wing and we turned hard, air whipping my hair from my face while I clung on to Vesper so she wouldn't fall.

Another flash of flames burst into the sky above the tip of a towering pine tree and I caught sight of two figures clambering upward through its branches.

A group of Stonebreakers bellowed and threw magic at them from the ground. I threw my hand out to place a shield of ice between the Flamebringers and the warriors who hunted them.

Kaiser made it to the top of the tree, hauling North up behind him while we closed in fast.

Bastian dipped low, talons outstretched and I held my breath as the two of them leapt from the tree, nothing but blind faith and hope guiding their movements.

Bastian's powerful body lurched beneath me as he snatched them from the sky and North howled in victory while Kaiser released a booming laugh filled with adrenaline and the thrill of the dance he'd just taken with death.

The knot in my stomach loosened and a breath of laughter fell from me too while Calcifiend licked my cheek to display his own happiness.

Bastian beat a path straight for the clouds above, taking us higher and higher. The endless greenery of Avanis spread out to the horizon, the view so beautiful it stole my breath.

Vesper fell slack in my arms, my heart lurching as she threatened to tumble right off of Bastian's back, causing me to cast ice to fix her in place.

"Hurry!" I shouted to Bastian, unable to do anything to help her from here and he replied in a growl which let his concern for her be known.

We turned west sharply and I sent a silent prayer to Delphinus to grant us the luck we needed to make it back to Mirelle's stronghold without incident, the miles speeding past at a ferocious pace as he raced for the archway which would deliver us to Ravensview once more.

"Just hold on, Sky Witch. You haven't finished painting your fate yet."

SEPTA

CHAPTER FORTY FOUR

Earl Tarlord dropped to his knees before me, leaving the pursuit of the Dragon and those riding it to his warriors as he cupped my face in his hands and lifted my chin so that he could meet my eyes.

"Are you hurt?" he demanded, a wildness in his expression that should have had me recoiling in fear but instead had the terrified thrashing of my heart calming at last.

"No," I breathed. "Not physically."

"You're bleeding," he said in disagreement, dropping a hand to the bloodstained hem of my dress and fisting the material as he lifted it to reveal my leg beneath.

"That isn't my blood," I said, swallowing back the bile which threatened to rise as I was reminded of what had happened to my husband. "Alestro is…"

"Which of the other warlords did this? I'll have their Earl's head by morning," he snarled, his hand lifting to the remainder of the vines which had bound me and were left knotted around my chest, tugging sharply as he broke apart the magic in them.

The jolt of motion jerked me forward before they had entirely shattered and I found myself breathing in his air, the stubble lining his jaw almost grazing the softness of my cheek.

His other hand still cupped my jaw and our eyes locked as we found ourselves altogether too close.

The want which I'd fought so hard to stifle in his presence reared its head again, the ache I felt when I looked at him all too present with his powerful aura dominating mine.

My lips parted, the words I'd been choking on for so long begging to be free. But then my mind snapped back to the brutalised corpse of my husband which still lay warm in our bed chambers.

I jerked back, scrambling to right myself, locking my jaw as a bite of pain shot through my hip.

Earl Tarlord stood as well, the disbalance in our heights becoming all the clearer as he towered over me.

"It wasn't one of the other warlords," I said, focusing on what mattered. "The Dragon had earth magic but he was allied with…"

I trailed off, the truth of what I'd just witnessed seeming too unlikely to be real. The three people who I'd just witnessed working together in this chamber had all been from warring nations, each of them born on opposing sides of The Waning Lands.

"What happened with the Flamebringers?" I asked, forcing myself to meet my Earl's eye despite the heat it brought to my cheeks. "The ones who were launching an attack in the forest?"

"I sent out a legion but…" his words cut off with a frown.

"What?" I pressed.

"It is strange," he said. "We took up position in the outlook to take stock of their numbers and assess the threat. There was no army. The flames were certainly cast with magic but they were sporadic and localised. It appeared there were only a handful of them out there."

"A distraction," I breathed, my eyes moving to the keystone which now stood whole once more. The foul stench of power which I'd always associated with this place was gone too. "Pyros, Stormfell, Avanis and Cascada…" My hand met with the stone and I closed my eyes as I put the pieces together. Members from every nation had been here, all of them working toward this common goal.

"What is it?" Earl Tarlord asked, moving up behind me like a wraith. "Are you well, Lady Septa? I wish to see you somewhere safe before I join in the pursuit of the Dragon–"

"The Dragon will be long gone by the time you join the hunt," I told him plainly, everything making sense to me even if I didn't want it to. "They didn't come here to fight."

"Did you hit your head when they attacked you?" Tarlord asked softly, his fingers brushing a knotted tendril of my hair aside, the skim of his hand on my neck sending a shiver through me.

I choked out a strangled sound which might have been a laugh or might have been the beginnings of hysteria.

"I would bet my soul that no Fae beyond Alestro have met with death at the hands of those intruders today," I said, turning to my Earl, the truth of that statement sounding as insane to me as it clearly did to him. But it made sense. In a way which only madness allowed… or in a way which demanded I accept the truth of all they'd said to me.

"What reason would they have to come here beyond warfare?" Tarlord asked. "And if that wasn't their purpose then why would only your husband have fallen prey to their wrath?"

"Because with him it was personal," I choked out, my mind once again landing on the memory of Alestro's bloody corpse, of the way he'd clung to life despite the torture he'd been through. Of the way her sword had finally run him through and I'd been able to do nothing at all but watch as it happened. "The Sky Witch was among them."

"Stormfell?" Tarlord demanded. "Are you certain? Stormfell are upon us too?" he turned as if meaning to raise the alarm once more, his agitation clear but I snatched his hand and forced him to turn and look at me.

"No," I said firmly. "Not Stormfell. Only her. The Sky Witch, the Dragon, and…"

"And?" he pushed, his fingers banding around mine in a firm assurance that he was here with me, locked in and listening, needing to understand this just as I was slotting every piece of it into place.

"The Void," I finished.

"The…" His brow furrowed in confusion, his eyes piercing me to my soul. There wasn't doubt in his gaze but there was a hungry need for understanding which I knew all too well. I'd spent my life seeking to understand everything to its fullest, unveiling facts and figures, analysing, assessing, adjusting my take on things because I didn't ever want to dismiss the truth in favour of blind faith or prejudice. "Septa, how can that be?" my Earl demanded.

"They came because this was corrupted. They came together because they have united for a greater cause. I think… There is something happening in The Waning Lands which is bigger than the war and far more dangerous than it too."

Tarlord moved closer to me, the stillness in his powerful body proving how much he valued my word. He wasn't going to dismiss or deny this. He was listening. And I let every drop of what I knew, suspected, and feared spill from me as I told him the truth.

VESPER

CHAPTER FORTY FIVE

I cursed as the world came rolling back to me on a slow and violent wave. The pain hit first, the echoes of agony which I'd been certain would shatter my body. It wasn't as intense as it had been but it was still there, my flesh on fire with it, my bones aching from its grip on me.

"I don't trust him," a deep, familiar voice growled to my right, heat enveloping my hand as the person holding it tightened their grip.

"You don't need to," another male voice clipped. "You need to trust that we have him under our control."

Bastian growled in that low, possessive way of his, and then a different, colder, clammier hand was taking hold of my left.

"If you so much as attempt to disturb a single hair on her head, I will rip you limb from limb in this very room," Bastian snarled in warning.

"I-I-I–" the owner of the clammy-handed voice stammered

before the other man in the room interrupted.

"She will die without this help. Is that what you would choose for her, Dragon?"

"She's too fucking stubborn to die in any way she didn't choose for herself," Bastian replied.

"But she did choose it, didn't she? She chose to risk everything to fulfil the bargain she'd made with us and give us a fighting chance against the eschaton star. But it isn't over yet and regardless of what she may have been willing to sacrifice, we still need her. There are no others with her capabilities. There are none who can fill her role in all of this but her."

"You speak of her as if she is a tool for you to wield," Bastian spat, chair legs screeching across a wooden floor as he stood, my hand falling heavily out of his, the loss of his warmth making my wounds throb all the worse.

A groan escaped my lips and the arguments in the room fell silent at last.

"I speak of her as a warrior set to play a crucial role in a war far more important than any other that has been waged upon this continent in hundreds of years," Lazarus said firmly, his voice aligning with a name at last.

"She's in pain," Everest said in a low voice and I felt the brush of her fingers across my brow. "Just let him heal her. I'm here. If he tries anything then I can Void him in the blink of an eye and you can roast him in Dragon fire. But she's hurting, Bastian. Whatever else is going on, don't you want to see her out of pain?"

It appeared there was an entire party taking place around my death bed.

Bastian didn't reply but the clammy hand still grasping mine tightened its grip on me and I was dimly aware of magic brushing against my skin.

I'd experienced this before and tensed as I felt the rush of power closing in on me, the healing magic tearing through my limbs in a way that was terrifyingly euphoric.

It stole across my skin and dove beneath it, seeking out my wounds, the injuries I'd taken internally and even the fatigue in my muscles and miraculously repairing it all.

Or perhaps…not all. There was no improvement to the constant pain of my grief. And there was still a burning ache on the flesh of my arms which seemed to be at war with the magic he was using on me.

"Why isn't it working?" Bastian demanded. "What are you doing to her?"

"It *is* working," the man holding my hand gasped. "But these injuries…I don't understand them…I can't–"

"Dark magic comes at a cost," I muttered, tugging my hand free of his and wiping it clean on the sheets of my bed.

I blinked at the people surrounding me, trying to take in where I was and what was going on while my eyes fought to adapt to the light provided by flaming sconces on the walls.

We were beneath the ground, the walls made of rock. But the room I was situated in was well furnished, and clearly had been made use of plenty of times before.

"Ravensview?" I asked.

"Yeah," Everest replied. "You kinda lost your shit in the dark magic stuff and there was a whole massive, terrifying situation which really made me think you'd died for a minute there. But then Septa rescued us from the ether by burning those herbs in our fists and I managed to get you out and Bastian saved our asses and got us away from there and...well, long story short, we're back here. You did it. Oh and that's a Reaper who is being held captive and just used healing magic on you – I didn't catch his name."

"It's Pedro Pantalini Poozwin," the Reaper said, bobbing his head at me.

I looked him over as I pushed myself up on my pillows. He was dishevelled, his golden cape torn and smeared with dirt, his eyes full of fear and his desires all centring around the desperate hope to survive.

"Bastian shifted where everyone could see him?" My eyes moved to the Dragon who now stood with his arms folded at the foot of my bed, Lazarus at his side.

He knew the word of that would spread. But I supposed Evard had known we were heading to Avanis, he wouldn't be surprised by that much. Though I doubted he or Dragor would be pleased to have the fact known widely.

Kaiser, North and Mirelle were also in the room though they'd all chosen to remain on the far side of it by the fire, watching us, but saying nothing.

"Why aren't your arms healed?" Bastian asked, his gaze dark and focused on the wounds he was referring to.

I looked at the runes I'd carved into my skin, a lump forming in my throat at how far I'd gone to repair the keystone. The wounds were bloody and stung in the warm air, the taint of ether still simmering within them a little.

"I told you, the price of that kind of magic is high. I suggested offering up a sacrifice but none of you seemed keen on the idea so I refrained from cutting the throat of the Stonebreaker who witnessed our actions."

"Without her we'd be dead," Everest added and I frowned at that.

"Then more fool her I suppose." I looked to Bastian again. "I used what I did to Cayde as an offering but it wasn't enough. So I worked with what I had."

"Damn the consequences, right?" Bastian said coldly.

I felt I should have had some answer to that which might have banished the anger in his expression but I couldn't apologise for what I was. He was the one who'd told me to stop doing so after all. Clearly he expected more from me though. The trouble was, I didn't think there was any more I could offer.

"I've fought and won battles with far worse wounds than these. They won't slow me down," I said finally.

Bastian tensed while Lazarus and Mirelle expressed satisfaction at my reply and began talking about the next stage of their plans. Striking at the beast itself on the night of the blood moon.

"Then you're no longer lingering at death's threshold?" Bastian asked.

I shook my head, my eyes on his as the truth of that struck him and for a moment it seemed like all the tension in his powerful body fell away.

"Good," Bastian said finally and something seemed to burst into bloom within my chest, stirring my senses, giving me a reason to be glad to have awoken still living and breathing in my own flesh. Or at least it did until he continued, making it clear his anger with me was far from banished. "Your death is mine, after all spectre. I won't see it fall into the hands of another."

Bastian turned and strode from the room, the door thumping shut at his back, whatever small spark had been stirring within my chest snuffed out with the strike of the latch.

My fingers fisted in the sheets at my lap and I fought to swallow down a lump in my throat.

"*Out*," Everest barked suddenly, rounding the bed so that she could stand between me and the others in the room. "You can go talk tactics somewhere else. Vesper needs to bathe and stitch her remaining wounds. And she doesn't need anyone lurking in here while she does it."

Lazarus bowed his head to me, murmuring a few words of thanks for what I'd achieved before taking hold of the terrified Reaper and shooting from the room.

Kaiser and North followed, though Everest had to shoo the Fury out of the door rather forcefully. I could feel his desire to protect her from me coiling around my chest. I supposed I could have reassured him but I only offered him a dark smile instead.

Mirelle paused before following them, her gaze roaming over me thoughtfully.

"You aren't entirely what you seem, are you Sky Witch?" she mused.

"Is anyone?" I replied.

Her lips twitched with the faintest hint of amusement and then she was gone too, leaving me alone with my kitty-cat.

"I thought everyone was leaving?" I asked.

"Obviously I don't count," she replied, moving to the large, copper tub in the corner of the room and casting steaming water into it from her palm.

"Obviously," I replied slowly, my eyes remaining on her as she pulled open drawers and cupboards, rummaging through their contents as if she owned the place.

"You need to bathe in salt water," she said, tossing a handful of salt into the steaming tub. "And I was hoping to find a sprig or two of lavender to help you relax–"

"I need ginger and turmeric," I replied. "To ward off infection. Relaxing is something other people worry about."

"Yes…I can see that stick of tension is rammed firmly up your ass. We'd need a whole lavender field to even begin to rectify that. I'll go ask if they've got any ginger."

She headed for the door and my gut tightened. Everyone else had left me already. *He'd* left me. I found I didn't want her to do so too.

"There should be some in my pack," I said quickly. "If it's here somewhere?"

"It is," Everest agreed, shooting me a look which said she'd noticed how I'd spoken to stop her from leaving.

I pursed my lips and got to my feet while she started rummaging through my belongings.

"Is this a sex thing?" she asked, waving a coil of rope in the air and I rolled my eyes.

"It's to bind my captives with."

"So…yes then?" she teased and I snorted in amusement.

I peeled off the filthy Stonebreaker clothes I'd been dressed in and stepped into the tub, releasing a low groan as the hot water enveloped my skin and I sank low beneath it.

I held my breath beneath the surface for a count of ten then emerged, leaning my head back against the tub and staring up at the whorls and scars which marked the cavern roof above me.

"Ginger," Everest announced, almost taking my damn eye out as she threw the entire root at me.

I caught it with my air magic before it could bludgeon me and gave her a cutting look.

"You don't hurl a whole root into the water. You grate a measure of it and–"

"I don't know anything about your hocus pocus shit, Ves," she said. "And I don't know what the fuck turmeric looks like either. Is this it?"

"That's a rock you found on the floor."

"Yeah. But it has turmeric vibes, don't you think?"

I snorted a laugh and she grinned at me before striding over and handing me both a turmeric root, a dagger and the rock.

I took them all with a roll of my eyes and she dragged a chair across the room to sit beside me while I bathed.

I placed my rock down on the side of the tub then proceeded to shave a small amount of the turmeric and ginger into the water with my blade.

"He's just mad because he cares, you know?" Everest said, leaning back in her seat and kicking her feet up to rest on the end of my bath. "And you frightened him with the whole, blood-covered corpse look you had going on."

I tossed the ginger and turmeric back towards my bag and turned the dagger in my grip so that I could start picking blood and muck out from beneath my fingernails with it. It distracted me from both the sting of the runes cut into my arms and the twisting knot in my stomach which seemed determined to draw my focus.

"He's a fool to care about me," I said finally.

"Yeah," Everest agreed. "You're the worst. But…you're kind of addictive too. Being around you is a bit like having a really angry pit-bull for a pet. It has a sore paw and is really fucking hungry. And because it's so empty inside it's snappy as shit and occasionally tries to kill you. But it's also weirdly sweet when you don't expect it to be and because you're in its pack it actually defends you against the nasty old world out there when push comes to shove. You don't really *like* it because it's grumpy as shit but…you find yourself trying to tempt it with treats in the hopes it might forget to be an asshole for a little while. 'Cause when it does it's actually kinda nice to be around."

"Gee thanks," I drawled and she smiled widely.

"You're welcome. And don't worry – Bastian has a thing for strays too. He won't be able to stay mad at you for long."

"He'd be better off if he did," I muttered, looking away from her and into the fire.

"Probably. But we don't really get much say in those kinds of things, do we? And if I were you, I'd probably stop trying to sabotage one of the few good things you've got."

"I have a few?"

"Well yeah, obviously – I don't just run baths for anybody, you know."

"Oh, so I'm special?" I asked.

Everest cut me a look which said I was pushing my luck with her but then she sighed heavily and agreed. "Okay fine, you're special. I'm the great and powerful Void after-all. So you'd have to be, to be able to call me your friend."

I didn't say anything in reply to that claim but as I leaned back against the edge of the tub, I wrapped my fingers around the vial of blood which remained hanging from my throat and I could have sworn it warmed against my skin once more.

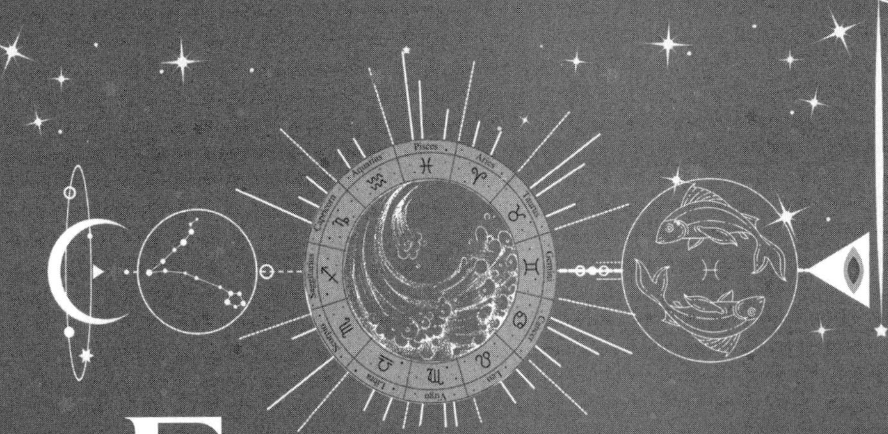

EVEREST

CHAPTER FORTY SIX

I pulled on my armour in the quarters I'd been offered here at Ravensview. It was far grander than I'd expected to be given by my enemies, and I didn't like to spend too long thinking about why they were kissing my ass so much.

They needed me as I currently needed them. But this alliance had a deadline and once this night was over, if we managed to stop the eschaton star breaking through into this world, then this fragile union could shatter fast and violently. I may have been offered a place in Effelridge as we all had, but I wasn't convinced that we were all going to play happy families once this was done. There were too many years of hatred stacked against us. How could the four elements really co-exist long term?

I decided not to dwell on it too much now that the blood moon was almost upon us. The chances were, none of us would survive this night. So if I made it to tomorrow morning with breath still in my lungs, I'd figure out what fate had in store for me then.

I adjusted the emerald green breast plate onto my chest and sheathed my sword at my hip while hitching my dagger to the other. I'd made a few alterations seeing as Mirelle had done me the service of placing a fire in my room. One I had swiftly made into a forge.

I'd added new engravings to the metal, the Pisces constellation running down the plate at my back and a sea serpent subtly curved around the cuff on my right forearm. I held a cluster of metal flowers in my hand, all intricately forged with swirling patterns and twirling tips on each petal. They were made in the image of deathless primroses, a flower that grew in all parts of The Waning Lands, and no matter what destruction happened to its habitat, it always grew back. It was a beautiful flower, white and pure with dark black tips to the petals that tapered to subtle magenta twirls. I'd made them as a symbol of this night of alliance, thinking if we all wore a pin of the same emblem, we might work as one unit. It was foolish, but forging always calmed my soul and I'd made them now so I may as well offer them out.

A knock came at the door, a hard firm rap that could only belong to one person. My fingers clasped tight around the metal flowers in my grip, tight enough to imprint them onto my scarred palm.

"Come in," I called and Kaiser entered my room, dressed in his usual black casual wear. I supposed his Order offered armour on his skin whenever he needed it so he didn't need to dress for war tonight.

His head tilted as he kicked the door shut behind him and my breaths came unevenly. We were alone. Something we hadn't been in Ravensview. And it felt strangely forbidden.

"This night will change the fate of The Waning Lands," he mused as he looked me up and down in that penetrating way of his.

"I'm aware," I clipped.

"Always so touchy," he commented, walking forward, leaving me to decide whether I was going to retreat. But I stood firm. "I've been thinking…"

"Makes a change," I drawled.

"A joke?" he guessed.

"Clever boy."

He didn't smile.

"What have you been thinking then, hollow man?" I prompted.

"I've been thinking about the tomorrow we're not promised," he said darkly, walking over to my forge to examine the dagger I'd been working on. It wasn't anywhere near ready. I hadn't even finished hammering it into shape yet, but I supposed it had comforted me to leave something unfinished in the face of tonight. The stars just might let me come back and complete it.

He crouched down, rifling through the forging tools I'd talked North into gifting me. Kaiser touched them like he owned them and I scowled at his back.

"I see getting your emotions back hasn't made you any less rude," I muttered.

He glanced at me over his shoulder, my half-forged blade in his hand. "I can never decipher what classifies as rude to you." He tossed my blade back by the fire with a clatter and stood up, turning to me with a glare. "Do you have any idea how difficult it is to decipher you? You are not consistent. You touch me softly one moment then strike me the next."

I knew he was referring to how I'd helped calm his breathing back in the forest and something about that made my cheeks heat.

"Says the man who threatens me one moment and gets hard for

me the next," I scoffed. "You're the enigma here, not me. I know my own mind."

"Do you?" he growled.

"Yes," I hurled back. "Do you understand the madness of you desiring anything from me beyond my death?"

"Enemies. Lines. Lands. I'm well versed in our history. I may have had no emotions but I've not been blind and deaf all these years, silka la vin."

"Stop calling me that damn nickname. I'm not your killer, am I? I failed."

"So far, yes. But something tells me we'll come to blows again," he said grimly. "That hatred in your eyes never dulls."

"You saw me as nothing but a weak runt when we first met. Why give me that name?"

"You scarred me. No one had ever done that before your father," he said and the mention of him sent a shudder through me. "I saw the venom in your eyes. Even as a man with no feelings, I knew the power of revenge. I killed your mother, of course you would come after me."

I winced at the reminder, turning from him, looking down at the cluster of metal flowers clutched in my scarred palm. If she could see me now, would she be ashamed of me?

"I cannot make up for what I did," Kaiser said, his voice heavy. "It was an act of war. I'm not excusing it. It was who I was. Who I am, I suppose. I follow orders; I kill, I make moves which swing the war in Pyros's favour. I'm a tool for a victory that may never come. Aren't we all? We're honed and hammered like this blade of yours. This half-made thing reminds me of myself. Not quite anything yet but still battered into a shape of someone else's design."

"I wasn't raised like you," I said coldly, still refusing to look at him and be reminded of the day he'd seen to my mother's death. I pocketed the metal flowers, eyeing the marks they'd left on my palm. "No one wanted to hone me. I was the scrap of steel that didn't make the cut. So I forged myself. I've always been different. Always stood out. Because I looked at weapons like you and saw the hollowness of being just like every other warrior in this world. But you're right, Kaiser. We're all tools. How pathetic of me to try and be different because all I really wanted deep down was to fit in." I laughed bitterly. "I still walked the path our rulers wanted. Still ended up on battlefields risking my neck for the 'greater cause'." I turned to him. "But you know what I learned by being the great and powerful Void? The revered creature who is prophesied to end the war?"

He stepped closer to me, a frown creasing his brow. "What?"

"That being a warrior means nothing if your heart isn't aligned with the cause. Because I don't think the war was ever really for the greater good. It was for the greater evil to prevail. The land that could swing the biggest axe, kill the most of their enemies. Destroy, annihilate, conquer. There's no peace beyond that. I watched my father kill Avanis warriors who had surrendered to him without mercy and I realised that it didn't matter if it was Cascada that won the war or Avanis or Pyros or Stormfell. Whoever wins will have no mercy. They aren't going to accept the other lands they defeat, they're going to punish them for all the atrocities they blame them for while ignoring the fact that they are guilty of the very same crimes. They'll destroy them or enslave them. And that's where the most taboo truth lies. Because I think there can only be death in The Waning Lands until we accept each other. Air, fire, earth and water united." I breathed a humourless laugh, knowing how ludicrous it sounded, even balking against the mere suggestion of it myself. But when only logic was considered and all hatred was put aside, that was the answer to this war.

"I agree," Kaiser said, surprising me. "I've weighed all other options in my mind too, and this is the sole conclusion that equals true peace. But you know as well as I do how farfetched that possibility is. Look at us, for example. How could you ever live alongside a Fae who hurt your family? How could your hatred ever be doused? There are countless stories like ours, perhaps less personal in many ways but hatred is stitched into the soul, it's not so easily unpicked."

"You're right," I breathed. "We could never be true allies, let alone friends."

He regarded me with scrutiny, seeming confused by something. "North says people lie to protect themselves. I'm working on detecting such lies and I think I may have just caught you in one."

"You're wrong," I snarled, heat rising in my skin. "There's no lie in those words. We could never be friends."

"That I do agree with," he said darkly, prowling closer to me like a wolf with its sights set on a meal. His eyes flashed red and I was caught unprepared as he possessed me with the power of his Fury, snaring me in a net I'd wished never to be trapped in again. "Speak the truth," he commanded and it slipped from my tongue before I could stop it.

"Sometimes I want you. I despise myself for that desire. But I think of you and I feel hunger."

The Void tore from me, shutting off the power of his Order form and he closed in on me, capturing the back of my neck with his hand and lowering his mouth to mine.

"Finally, the sweet truth," he growled, his mouth brushing mine. "I believe it's possible to feel two opposing things at once, Everest.

Hate and want. A need to claim your death and the conflicting desire to claim your mouth, your body, to bend you to my will and sink my teeth into you. Given the night will likely end us both, why don't we live out our final hours without regret?"

"It's wrong," I said breathily, but my fingers knotted in his shirt, yanking him closer so his body was flush to mine and the scent of cinder and oak surrounded me. "You're my nightmare. You're threaded into every hate-filled thought I've ever had. My body is tainted by you."

"You're the burden I cannot rid myself of," he snarled and then we kissed. It was filled with venom and liquid fire. His tongue pressed against mine as he shoved me back against a bookcase, the force of his weight pinning me there. His fingers fisted in my hair, pulling to make me tilt my head and kiss him with more ferocity. The sound of my gasp was swallowed by our mouths connecting again and I despised myself for giving in to this maddening desire. He forced my legs apart, hitching one of mine over his hip and the hard ridge of his large cock rode against my clit through the fabric of our clothes.

"No," I hissed but what I really meant was *yes* as he ground against me and pleasure rolled through me. He made to pull away in answer to my refusal but I grabbed his neck and dragged him near again, his dark laughter polluting the air around us.

He lowered his hand between us, finding my clit and toying with it through the material of my trousers, his kiss punishing and demanding at once as he swallowed my moans.

My armour felt all too cumbersome as it kept the distance between our bodies and I decided I wanted it off as Kaiser growled in my ear, "This won't end until we've had our fill of each other. Perhaps the lunacy will cease if we give into this. Then if we live another day beyond this one, I will offer you a duel. You against me. We don't stop until one of us is dead. Then both of our wants will be fulfilled. How's that for a deal?"

"One that sates me now and sates me later," I growled. "It sounds like a win-win."

"We don't have much time," he said, starting to unclasp my armour. "I want you on your knees for me on your bed. Ass up, silka la vin."

"I'm not one of your scorched submissives," I spat. "You don't get to order me around. You can have me your way but only once I've had you mine."

"You bargain so prettily," he taunted then he whirled me around and tossed me onto the bed. "But I decline. Now get undressed," he barked.

"You only know one way to do this, don't you?" I laughed icily as he strode toward me with intention.

I unsheathed my dagger, rising onto my knees and pressing the tip to his neck as he stopped in front of me. He caught my wrist, grinning like a demon as he forced my fingers to release the steel and he eyed his name upon its hilt.

"I can learn other ways." He unclasped my breast plate, tossing it on the bed then flipping me over onto my knees. I gasped as he dragged my trousers and undergarments down, sliding his hand between my legs and finding me soaking wet for him.

"Bastard," I growled then he pushed the hilt of my own dagger inside me, making me cry out in surprise.

"Ride my name where you etched it on the hilt," he commanded and I could do nothing but obey as he held it there for me to push back against. His fingers rode my clit and I was reduced to a moaning creature of purest pleasure as he guided my hips with his free hand, forcing me to fuck my own blade for his amusement.

"You tried to destroy me with this dagger, it's only fair I return the favour," he taunted.

I cursed as I fisted my hands in the sheets, so close to coming already that it was all I could do to hold off. His fingers heated against my clit, a tiny flash of fire making me burn all the way through.

I tried to hold back, the pleasure too much, but it was tangling with how wrong this was. He was the man I should have wanted dead. I shouldn't have hungered for him like this. I shouldn't have let him touch me let alone roll his fingers over my clit like he was doing.

"Can you feel my name between your thighs?" he asked in a rough voice, the sound rolling through me and sending me into mania.

I came like a heathen as Kaiser buried the hilt of my dagger inside me then pumped it as I clenched around it. It was ecstasy, the darkest, most sinful kind and I hated him for claiming it from me so easily. The pleasure rolled on as he fucked me with the hilt and teased my clit, drawing out my orgasm. It was too good, but so fucking bad.

He sank his teeth into my ass cheek before I was quite done, marking me with his mouth before drawing the hilt out of me.

"I've never been so fucking hard," he muttered as I rolled over, finding him squeezing the impressive length of his cock through his trousers. Shame coloured my cheeks as I stared up at my enemy and he saw the hesitation in my eyes. But hell, I wanted him. He was the tormentor of my soul and perhaps he was right, this madness would stop if we could only sate it.

I shuffled to the edge of the bed and pushed his hand away from his cock, taking its place with my own and rubbing him in firm strokes. He gripped my hair with a low growl in his throat, urging me closer.

"This happens once," I warned. "Then never again."

"Fine by me," he said with grit.

The door clicked as someone walked in and Kaiser shoved me with force onto the floor to the side of the bed.

I ducked low, stifling my curse and peering under the bed to find a set of boots walking into the room.

"Oh," North's voice came in surprise. "I was told to fetch Everest. We're about to leave. What are you doing in here and why… oh fucking hell. Are you jerking off over her dagger?"

A pause came from Kaiser then he grunted, "Yes."

"What is wrong with you?" North hissed. "This is enemy territory. Are you into her or something? You do remember the rules?"

"No fucking the enemy," Kaiser confirmed. "And it's not her, it's…" he trailed off, struggling with the lie but North finished it for him.

"It's the close shave with death, isn't it?" he said knowingly. "That dagger nearly put you down and now you get hard for it. I get it. I felt the exact same way about an arrow that grazed my left ass cheek. I kept it in my bed for a couple of months and me and her got real friendly a couple of times. It's okay, freyin. It's totallllly normal."

"Right," Kaiser muttered. "So can you buy me some time then? An hour maybe."

"An hour?" North balked. "What are you gonna do with that thing for a full hour?"

Kaiser's answer was silence and North sighed.

"Look, we've gotta go. Mirelle's rounding up the Vampires. The blood moon's about to rise. We don't have a minute, let alone an hour. I'll give you thirty seconds to say goodbye to your dagger friend, then we're out of here."

North left the room and I stood up, feeling regretful of this whole idea now that I'd had a minute to think about it. I was still naked from the waist down and my cheeks burned as I looked to the dagger on the bed, knowing what he'd done to me with it.

"Hot for the dagger, huh?" I tried out a taunt but he just gave me a sinful look.

"You're the one who came all over it, silka la vin," he said dryly and I shoved him away, snatching my weapon and wiping it off on the sheets before sliding it into its holster.

"Yon eskindo pishalé," I cursed him. "This was a bad idea." I tugged on my trousers and fixed my armour back into place, refusing to look at the Fae who had just had his hands all over me. I could still feel the bite mark on my ass burning hotly.

Kaiser said nothing but I felt his eyes on me and I finally turned to him when I was dressed to leave, trying to face what had just happened between us. What had I been thinking? He was a monster. A fiend. How idiotic did I have to be to give into the allure of him?

"North's waiting," he muttered.

"Spin him a nice old tale about how you shoved my dagger up your ass, won't you?" I purred and his eyes narrowed on me.

He caught me by the throat, yanking me close and kissing me firmly on the lips. I shoved him away with a snarl. "What are you doing?"

"Kissing you goodbye," he snarled with equal vehemence then he strode for the door and I quickly hid behind the bed again as he threw it open and stalked out.

My pulse roared in my ears as the door swung shut and I took in a deep breath, expelling it hard to try and calm the manic beating of my heart. By the ocean, I'd just let my enemy fuck me with my own dagger. A dagger that had been forged to kill him, that had his fucking name etched onto the hilt.

Stars, what is the matter with me?

I swept a hand over my face and pushed to my feet, giving North and Kaiser a minute's head start before I exited the room. This was shame in its truest form. I felt leaden as I walked down the winding stone passages to the chamber with the archways.

I could never tell anyone what had happened between us. And if I survived this night, I'd never be fool enough to fall into his trap again. He'd promised me a duel, and I was going to damn well hold him to that if we got the chance.

Everyone was gathered in the chamber, Vesper and Bastian were dressed for war, standing a measured step away from Ransom and Galomp who were wearing their armour with swords on their hips.

North and Kaiser were gathered with Mirelle and Lazarus, and the divide between us all was pretty damn evident.

Vampires started filing in behind me, no armour in sight, just glinting fangs in their mouths and a couple of blades strapped to their hips. More and more of them queued out beyond the chamber, ready to attack.

"Does everyone understand their role tonight?" Mirelle called out. "I will lead the Vampires alongside Lazarus, the rest of you will use the distraction we cause to reach the eschaton star. The Sky Witch and the Void must make it there at all costs, do you understand?"

"Oh boy, yes I do understand," Galomp was the only one to answer, everyone else sharing distrustful glowers.

"Are you sure his help is necessary?" North jerked his chin at Ransom. "He looks like a dolphin fiddler to me. Definitely can't be trusted. How can I be sure he won't jab a blade in my back when I'm not looking?"

"Because I'm here for the same reason you are, you damn peacock," Ransom snarled. "And it has nothing to do with you or your big brown eyes."

"You've noticed my beautiful eyes then?" North taunted.

"Just shut your fucking mouth," Ransom snapped.

"Why? Because you want to kiss it?" North jeered.

"I'd sooner cut my tongue out and shove it up my own ass than lay my mouth on you, Flamebringer," Ransom spat.

"Kinky," North mocked, then he turned to Mirelle. "I vote the ass-licker stays behind."

"He's named himself as a sentinel to the Void, so it is up to her whether he stays or goes," Mirelle said, looking at me.

"Come on whelk," North said to me. "I think we can manage without this one. He's a bit slow. Must be all the whale sperm clogging up his brain."

Ransom lunged for North but Kaiser got between them, shouldering Random so hard he hit the floor.

"We do this together or not at all," Kaiser boomed as Ransom got to his feet with a curse.

"Careful, the Fury's about to lose his marbles," Vesper taunted, turning to me then she frowned like she could read something from me. By the stars, she couldn't tell what I'd been doing with her sex magic, could she? I tried to scroll through all the things I knew about Succubuses to figure it out but I came up short. She didn't know. She couldn't know. Definitely not.

Vesper glanced at Kaiser then winked at me.

For fuck's sake, she knew.

"Can we just leave already?" I demanded. "Ransom, you're coming."

Ransom lifted his chin and nodded at my command. "Of course. I love battles. And fighting. And death. All that stuff."

"Oh boy, he does. He is quite horrible," Galomp said brightly. "He is the son of Abraham Rake. A terrible, terrible man. Now he is dead though, so that is good."

"I'm not a Rake anymore," Ransom hissed as North growled at him, his Wolf Order form gleaming through his eyes.

"Can we just leave?" Bastian stepped forward. "I'm tired of this squabble. I ache for the swing of my sword and a lack of inane bickering."

"Ditto," Vesper agreed, leading the way to the archway that Mirelle was awakening with the black powder.

"Oh, wait," I said, taking the metal flowers from my pocket. "Here." I moved between everyone, pinning one onto their clothes, some tucked beneath their armour, others on display. Vesper eyed hers in confusion, touching the flower I'd pinned to her sleeve. "A deathless primrose," she said. "Why?"

"It's a mark of resilience," I explained. "Death can't take us this night."

"Oh boy, I do like it," Galomp gushed. "I will treasure it forever, Miss Everest."

"These used to grow in the garden of my family home," Bastian muttered. "They were seen as a sign of prosperity and fortune."

"Then the stars will protect us while we wear them," I said and he nodded to me.

When the heart of the archway was glittering and I could almost smell the icy air of the sea at Never Keep beyond it, we all headed through.

On the other side, the cold chilled the breath in my lungs as we arrived in a dark cave then moved out onto a plain of snow. I moved to Vesper's side, nodding to her as we gazed across the barren landscape toward the imposing shadow of Never Keep.

The blood moon shone down from above, highlighting the gothic walls of the Keep in a deep crimson.

I looked behind us to the pillars of the ten towers in the distance, thinking of Harlon with a squeeze of my heart. He was so close.

"This way," I called.

"Take them there," Lazarus ordered and the Vampires swept toward us. I was scooped up alongside the others and my gut lurched as the Vampire carrying me put on a burst of speed. He moved like the wind, faster possibly, tearing through the snow and depositing me right beside the towers in less than a few seconds.

I muttered a thanks to him as he moved away and met Vesper's eye, the face of the Sky Witch fixed in a scowl as she pushed the female Vampire away who'd carried her.

"Everest!" I turned at the voice, finding Mavus running out of one of the towers, letting a hood fall from his head to reveal himself. Part of me was surprised he'd shown up. He'd actually kept his word.

His eyes roamed over our group, the Vampires not yet here but there were far more of us than he'd been expecting. And we were all from varying lands.

"Well I'll be," he purred. "This is a surprise." He looked to me. "Is this your doing, lass?"

"You said we needed reinforcements. Here they are." I looked around for Harlon but couldn't spot him. Surely he should be here by now?

"You've allied with your enemies," Mavus said with intrigue. "And many of them. The Sky Witch herself, and even The Matriarch… well, well, lass, you've surprised even a weathered trader who's seen more of this world than you can imagine."

"You look familiar to me." Bastian stepped forward with a frown.

Mavus regarded him with narrowed eyes. "I can't say the same about you. But I've traded with half of The Waning Lands, so we've likely struck a deal once or twice."

"No. That's not it," Bastian grunted dismissively but didn't stop scrutinising Mavus.

"You made a plot with the Void." Mirelle walked toward Mavus. "We are here to assist in it. So perhaps we should stop wagging our tongues and get moving while the night is young?"

Mavus looked her over with keen interest, glancing at Lazarus behind her and frowning. "And who might this be?"

"A king of death," he said wickedly then he turned to his Vampires, directing them toward Never Keep. "Go friends!" he called. "Do as we planned!"

"Vampires," Mavus gasped, retreating warily as they went sweeping across the snow at high speed, a blur of shadows marking their path toward the Keep's gates.

"Good luck, loves." Mirelle squeezed North's arm and Kaiser's then let Lazarus lift her off her feet and carry her away after the Vampires in a blur of motion.

"They're our distraction," I told Mavus plainly.

"Lovely," he answered.

"Do you know where they're summoning the eschaton star?" Vesper asked the trader.

"I do, yes, but…" Mavus gripped my arm. "Lass, they've got your boyfriend, Harlon. Your sweet lover boy has been taken to the northern tower in the Vault of Frost to be tortured and executed. There isn't much time to save him, but you need to come with me to the monster. You're needed there more than anywhere else. Perhaps these fine fellows can save your lover boy?"

Terror ripped through me at that news. That the Reapers had caught him. Had they discovered him spying on them? Had he been close to their ceremony tonight, perhaps attempting to thwart them with a plan of his own? My mind reeled and I felt Vesper drawing near to me, her hand brushing mine.

"I have to go to him," I said in desperation.

"No," Mavus insisted. "This is our one chance to stop the monster. You must lay your trust in these other Fae. They look strong enough to handle a couple of Reapers. But if you don't get to the beast before the blood moon reaches its apex then all of us will be lost."

Kaiser growled deep in his throat as he glared at Mavus. "I will not be leaving Everest's side."

I whirled to him. "Harlon's in danger. I won't abandon him," I said fiercely, certain he could feel my fear over the matter and his jaw flexed.

"I will go, Miss Everest," Galomp offered, puffing up his chest. "You can count on me to rescue your dear Harlon. I swear it."

"Then I'll go too," Ransom offered. "And you might as well come as well, peacock." He looked to North whose brows arched.

"Yeah, nah, I'm good," North drawled.

"Go with them," Kaiser ordered and North pouted.

"But–"

"We don't have time for buts," Kaiser growled. "We must stop the eschaton star and Everest will not go if she is not certain her friend will be safe."

"*Boy*friend," Vesper corrected then laughed as Kaiser shot her a hard glare and I gave her a dry look.

"Fine," North sighed. "I'll go. But I'd better find you again before the fun's over or I'll be pissed."

"You'd better hurry then," Kaiser said and North howled before taking off with Galomp and Ransom across the snow.

"And then there were five," Mavus purred, glancing between us all. "Come then. The monster is being summoned beneath the Keep and I know precisely where to go. The blood moon is upon us and only the Void can save us now."

"No pressure or anything," I muttered, watching Ransom and Galomp race across the snow and praying to Delphinus that they would rescue Harlon swiftly. I despised not being able to go myself, but what choice did I really have?

"You only have to Void the magic of the moon herself, lass," Mavus laughed darkly. "Nothing you can't handle. I've seen your power. This is your moment, Everest Arcadia."

Vesper took my hand, her fingers squeezing mine and I found all the strength I needed in her eyes.

"You can do it, kitty cat. I know you can."

And that was all I needed to start running across the snow with the watchful eye of the moon upon us and the sense of her unyielding power filling the air. If I could stop the magic of a celestial being, it would be a damn miracle. But I'd sure as hell try.

BASTIAN

CHAPTER FORTY SEVEN

"It's colder than a polar bear's ball sack in this water," I grumbled as we swam through the darkness of the ice cavern.

"I would have made you a suit to help combat the cold but I didn't have enough time," Everest said, a note of apology in her voice. But she'd had enough time to create one for Vesper.

"Can't you just use Dragon fire to keep yourself warm?" Kaiser questioned and I shot him an irritable look.

"That isn't the point."

"Once I saw a gastrin shark hunting in these waters," Mavus said thoughtfully. "Nasty way to go, that is."

"Nice of you to warn us before we got in the water," Vesper muttered.

"Well…I figured it'd be a thrilling surprise if one showed up."

"I get the feeling your surprises are never the fun kind, Mavus,"

Everest said uneasily, glancing back over her shoulder into the midnight depths of the ocean.

If there was anything hunting us down there, we weren't going to know anything about it until it struck.

"There's something ahead of us," Vesper said urgently. "I can feel it like a tug in my gut."

"Dark omens," Mavus murmured. "Something foul is stirring in the air."

"Then we should–" My words cut off as I was yanked beneath the surface by something which wound its way around my ankle, hauling me into the depths of the sea.

I kicked and fought, the image of a sea monster lunging from the dark dominating my thoughts for several moments before I realised there was no cut of teeth driving through flesh. Just a tether pulled tight around my foot.

Bubbles spilled from my throat as I fought to take hold of my ankle and release it from whatever held me, water rushing all around me as I was hauled away from the cavern we'd been swimming through into a darker, narrower tunnel.

My fingers locked around a rope built of water as I grasped my ankle and I cursed the magic which had captured me.

My own power rose to my fingertips and I cut through the rope of water with a slice from a stone dagger I forged in my fist.

It fell apart and I managed to breach the surface, dragging down a breath in the few inches of air I found between the waves and a rocky roof above me before another tether bound around my waist and yanked me down again.

The water magic was forcing me away from the others, pulling me down a passage which grew narrower and narrower by the second.

I threw my hands out with a powerful blast of magic, vines shooting from my palms and spearing back the way I'd come. The vines burst from the water and wrapped themselves around the rocks they found there, jerking me to a halt.

I threw more power into the cast, the vines knotting around my wrists and hauling me in the opposite direction to the current.

The tension around my waist tightened until I feared it might rip me in two before releasing me but finally, it shattered.

My vines hauled me away from the foul water magic, tugging me back out of the narrow cave so fast I could only hold my breath and hope to the stars I didn't strike the rocks I passed.

I was yanked from the water and fell panting and cursing onto a rocky outcrop, the vines I'd cast slackening and dropping to the ground beside me as I fought to catch my breath.

Vesper slammed into me as I got to my feet, propelling herself above the water with air magic and fisting her hands in my shirt as she forced me to look at her.

"I thought a fucking shark had gotten you," she hissed, fury sparking in her grey eyes and almost concealing the fear there. "Don't do that again. It wasn't funny."

"Someone attacked me," I said, pushing wet strands of hair from my face and glaring back down at the water as Everest, Kaiser and Mavus swam into view. "Was it you?" I barked at the Cascadian and she blinked up at me in confusion while clambering out of the water.

"Was what me?" Everest demanded.

"Someone attacked me with water magic and you're the only one here who can wield it," I said, pointing at her.

But instead of denying it or putting up a fight, she spun away from me, drawing a blade.

"That wasn't me," she hissed and my eyes followed hers as she looked back out into the water. "So someone else must know we're here."

Vesper moved to stand alongside her, frowning at the water, her head tilted at an angle. Flames illuminated in Kaiser's fist as he peered around us too.

"I sense no desires but those coming from this group. If someone was trying to kill me, I'd know," Vesper said.

I scowled between the members of our group with suspicion roiling in my chest, my eyes landing once again on Everest.

"She didn't do it," Vesper said sharply. "Everest can't hide her desires from me well enough to be able to cover it if she had. She's a terrible liar. And even if she wasn't – I trust her."

"You do?" Everest blurted, a smile biting into her cheeks even though she was clearly trying to hide it.

"Yes," Vesper said, turning her focus onto me. "So that means you do too," she added smacking my arm with the back of her hand to chastise me for my accusations. "Now come on, we have work to do."

Everest gave me a shrug, her hand twisting as she drew the waterout of my clothes and leaving me dry before doing the same for the others. "You can apologise later," she said before striding away after Vesper.

"Someone attacked me," I said in reply, my eyes moving over the shadows which filled the space around us. Because if it wasn't her and none of the others here could have done it then someone else was lurking close at hand.

"Trust is a funny thing," Mavus muttered as he followed along at the back of the group. "Can't buy it. Gotta earn it. Easy to break it. Even easier to fake it."

"Shut up," I snapped but he only shrugged.

"Truth is truth," he said, picking his way across the rocks past me so that he could walk with Everest.

"I don't like him," I muttered to Kaiser as he came to stand at my side.

"I don't think you have to like him to get this done," he replied, his gaze moving from the roguish trader to meet with mine. "But if it helps, I don't like him either."

"Good." I jerked my chin at the path ahead and we strode on into the dimly-lit passageway side by side.

We concealed ourselves with various magics and silencing spells, clambering from jagged rocks onto smooth paths clearly trodden by many feet. The sound of low chanting soon beckoned us on as we walked and our group shifted closer together as we kept moving steadily towards it.

"Reapers," Mavus purred.

"Well I didn't think it was a flock of sheep," I grunted.

Kaiser barked a laugh so loudly that the sound of it echoed off of the walls around us, his amusement flaring to laughter quickly then dying away as he found us all staring at him in surprise.

"That was funny," he said and I grinned.

"It was," I agreed.

The corners of Everest's lips twitched and Vesper rolled her eyes before continuing to lead the way. Because of course she was in the lead, charging head first into danger as always. I knew she had to do it, knew she couldn't bear to allow anyone to ever face danger or death in her place again after what had happened to her sisters. So I said nothing. But I haunted her steps, determined to make certain she wouldn't be the one to pay the price if we found ourselves under attack. No matter her own thoughts on the subject.

We reached a door and I drew my sword as Vesper glanced around at us to confirm we were ready before opening it.

We all nodded our assent and she pushed it open slowly, creeping through into the darkness beyond and leading us into a chamber where the roof opened up above our heads and the sound of the Reapers' chanting echoed on endlessly into the air.

We crept onto a small stone platform which ran around an upper level of the chamber, a flood of golden-cloaked Reapers gathered in the wide space beneath us. Something dark and ominous was roiling in the shadows beyond them, lurking within a large chasm which split the ground apart at the farthest edge of the cavern. Above it was a round hole in the ceiling that must have been carved right up to the surface of the isle because the crimson light of the blood moon poured through it.

My heart skipped a beat as I peered into the dark abyss in the chasm, shadows shifting at its edges to reveal towering green objects obscured within them.

My fingers pressed to the gemstone embedded in the collar around my throat, recognition buzzing through me.

Magic built around me as the others all called it into their grasp, the four of them drawing weapons and preparing for our moment to strike.

"C'mon Lazarus," Everest muttered under her breath.

From our vantage point we couldn't see all of the Reapers but we could hear them, at least a hundred voices raised in a haunting chorus.

A single figure stood closer to the darkness, his arms raised as he encouraged the others to keep up their eery chanting.

"That's the Grand Maester," Vesper said in a low voice as she looked at him.

"So where is the Cardinal Reaper?" Kaiser asked, but no one had an answer for him.

"Those crystals," I murmured to Vesper and her eyes flicked to the collar I wore for a second before she nodded.

"I know," she said roughly.

I parted my lips to say something more but before I could, Lazarus and the others finally fulfilled their end of this plot and an echoing boom shook the walls, knocking the Reapers from their feet and making the rocks quake around us.

I pressed my hand to the closest wall, strengthening it to shield us from the destruction. But many of the Reapers weren't prepared and failed to shield themselves from the great lumps of rock and stalactites which crashed down on them from above.

Screams filled the air in place of chanting and whatever they were rousing from the abyss on the far side of the chamber bellowed in fury.

The Reaper who had been stood before them all yelled instructions for those who had survived to find out what was happening, and we waited in the shadows as more than half of them raced from the chamber.

"Ready, kitty cat?" Vesper purred, holding her hand out for Everest as she prepared to leap from the platform with her air magic.

"Always," Everest replied, taking her hand and the two of them leapt from the edge without another word, leaving the rest of us to chase them into the dark.

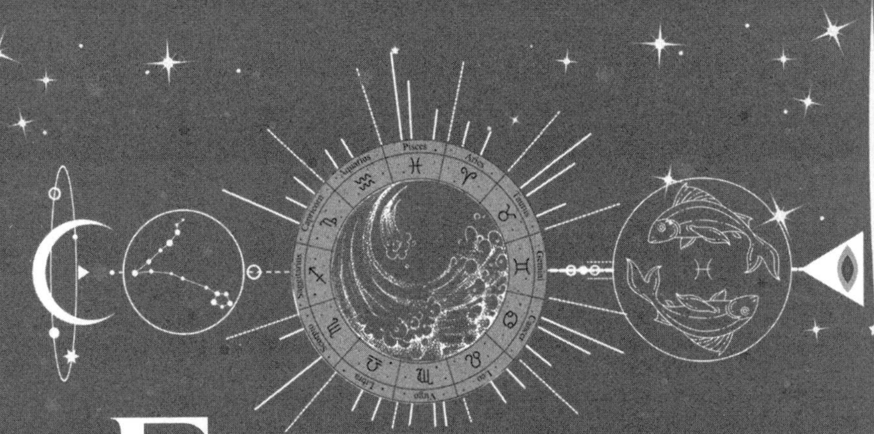

EVEREST

CHAPTER FORTY EIGHT

I raced into the cavern with the Sky Witch at my side and my gaze fixed on the shadowy abyss beyond the scrambling Reapers and lumps of fallen rock.

I knew that hole, the terrible place Kaiser and I had leapt into now torn wider by magic. This chamber must have been forged around it with earth magic, the great opening in the roof above cutting right through the rock, up, up, up toward the snowy plain beyond where the blood moon shone down on us.

Crimson light flooded that terrible abyss where the eschaton star surely lurked, but it couldn't penetrate the darkness within, only illuminating the hulking green crystals which stood in jagged formation around its edges.

Vesper broke from me, swinging her sword with perfect precision and slicing open the neck of the closest Reaper. Before they could even think to cast magic at either of us, I let the Void tear from me in an unstoppable wave. I cut off their power and they cried out in anguish, gold cloaks swishing as they scrambled to react but they had no blades to fight us with.

Vesper shoved me on and I leapt over the bloody man she'd cut down and set my gaze on the chasm.

"Void the power of the moon, lass!" Mavus shouted to me, even though I already knew that was my task.

Vesper swung her sword in a wide arc, making the Reapers stagger away from the abyss and the thing that lurked within it.

She herded them like cattle, swinging her sword in a threat of death while I focused the Void on the moonlight pouring down over the chasm where that beastly thing was fighting to break out into our world.

Large green crystals pulsed with energy around the hole, climbing the walls, scattered on the floor of the chamber, spreading out everywhere around me.

I gasped as my Void met with the power of the moon, the magic unlike anything I'd felt before. It was relentless, this pure, unquenchable power that fell down over everything it touched like a waterfall hitting rock. How could I stop such magic? How could I ever Void it?

I could no longer hold off the Reapers' magic, having to use every ounce of power I'd been gifted to try and halt the force of the moon. It was all I could give my attention to.

A horrible growling came from within the pit and I glanced down with a cry of effort as I desperately tried to Void the moon's magic. Two burning eyes glared at me from the chasm, lashes of shadow and claw tearing at the walls as the blood moon beckoned it into our world from the place of horrors where it belonged.

Magic clashed in the air and I heard Kaiser, Bastian and Mavus join the fray as the Reapers fought back.

I gritted my teeth, throwing all of my energy into unleashing the Void upon the power contained within the moonlight.

Mavus raced to the edge of the pit, casting earth magic and pouring soil and rocks down on top of the monster to try and hold it back.

Large green crystals erupted from that hole, somehow created by the monster and shooting through the ground around Mavus's feet. He pocketed a handful with a laugh, thinking of greed even now.

"That's it!" he cried to me. "Look at ya now, a real legend in the flesh."

Warmth poured through me at his praise, this man who had come to be something of a friend to me. Even if he was an unpredictable madman, the fact that he'd shown up tonight to put his neck on the line for the sake of the world had to count for something.

His foot slipped on the edge and he yelped in alarm as he nearly went tumbling into the hole. My heart lurched wildly, but he caught himself at the last second. Mavus glanced back at me with a shaky laugh and continued blasting stones down onto the eschaton star.

"Don't go dying on me," I called and he shot me a wink.

"Not today, girl," he smiled wide, a feral glint in his eyes.

My feet skidded across stone as the moon's magic pushed me back and I threw my palms out, the Void ripping from me in a torrent as I fought to stay in place.

The eschaton star didn't seem to be climbing any higher, so it had to be working. I just had to use every drop of power I possessed, show every damn Fae in this world what I was made of and hold back the moon itself. I could do this. The Waning Lands would shatter if I failed and I wasn't done living yet.

The eschaton star managed to claw its way higher and I screamed in defiance, digging my heels into the stone and shoving back against the moon once more. Its light was guiding this creature of death and chaos into our world whether the moon desired this or not. It was a beacon of power and no one could undo it but me. The weight of that responsibility fell on me now. The entire world was relying on me to manage this and if I failed all would be lost.

Vesper kicked a Reaper to the ground at the edge of the pit, slashing his throat with her dagger and calling the power of ether into her grasp as she offered up his death in sacrifice. Her eyes darkened, head snapping back as she fell to her knees and painted a rune across the stones in his blood.

"Stay back!" she ordered the beast through gritted teeth as if she could command it herself.

"You do not belong here!" I roared at that terrible monster reaching up through the chasm, letting the Void tear from me in a potent wave.

The moonlight flickered with the atrocity of my power, but its magic hardly waned. Pain splintered through my body at the effort it took to keep fighting it. But I wouldn't stop, not unless I turned to ash and bone beneath the moon's might. And even then I might battle for this world with the Sky Witch at my side.

It may have been a ruinous place of bloodshed, but it was our home. And I was going to give all I had fighting for it.

KAISER

CHAPTER FORTY NINE

Fire raced from my hands in a tornado of death, ripping through two Reapers and casting them to ash. A third came at me with air and fire twisting from his palms, a blast of sheer magic aimed at me. But before he could release it, Bastian stabbed him in the neck with a sharp blade, tearing it out with savagery and letting the Reaper fall dead at his feet.

I nodded to him, the Dragon bastard having saved my life. As a Reaper came up behind him, shooting an arrow of ice for his head, I sent a blast of heat out that melted both his weapon and his head. Bastian glanced back with his eyebrows raised, nodding to me in return.

I smiled. He smiled. And then we ran at three Reapers together, the Dragon snaring one in a net who I then burned to a crisp. Bastian ran through the second with a blade he cast with his element and the third we took hold of together. He snared his limbs with chains, ripping him apart while I heated up the metal so it burned like hellfire as the Reaper died.

Bastian smirked. I smirked. Then he wielded those chains of heated metal, whipping them at two more Reapers and shredding their golden cloaks.

"Nice," I commented, flipping my sword over and catching the hilt before hurling it at a Reaper's chest so it sliced through flesh and bone.

Calcifiend was playing a game of his own, causing the Reapers to run in circles trying to blast him from the air, all the while stealing their focus so Bastian and I could destroy them.

Fiend landed on a woman's shoulder and blasted her with his ferocious power, her hair setting alight and a wail cutting the air apart.

I glanced at Everest where she was fighting her own battle, her Void tearing through moonlight itself. She was all too distracting in her majesty and a sharp silver blade whistled past my cheek, slicing the skin open.

I growled, turning on the man who had thrown it and summoning my Fury hounds to me. They dove on the Reaper, ripping him apart with savage bites and Bastian watched with raised brows as he reeled in the chains, the metal clinking as they slid over the golden cloak of a Reaper he'd just felled.

I stepped to his side, letting my hounds run riot through the chamber and herd more Reapers our way.

"They've drawn my blood," I muttered.

"We can't have that," Bastian said darkly, sharing a murderous look with me.

My heart thumped with the thrill of the carnage and I was fairly sure the Dragon shared the sentiment.

I set my gaze on the closest Reaper, snaring his mind with my possession and making him pirouette his way toward Bastian's heated chains. The Dragon cut him down with great swipes of the metal and I sent more Reapers dancing and cartwheeling his way.

Their screams were pretty music to my ears as I handed them their deaths by Bastian's hand and he laughed a roaring laugh as they twirled into his lashing chains.

"This is child's play," Bastian called to me.

"The most villainous game I know," I agreed, looking to Everest again and luring all of our enemies away from her.

This chamber would be ours before long and I would buy her all the time she needed to Void the power of the moon and keep that vile eschaton star at bay.

Mavus and Vesper fought to hold the beast off together, the Sky Witch drawing on power gifted to her from the blood she'd spilled and summoning the ether to her, using the corruption of dark magic to thwart the monster below.

We all had a role to play here and there was no denying we were each doing our duty. *There might be a tomorrow for us yet.*

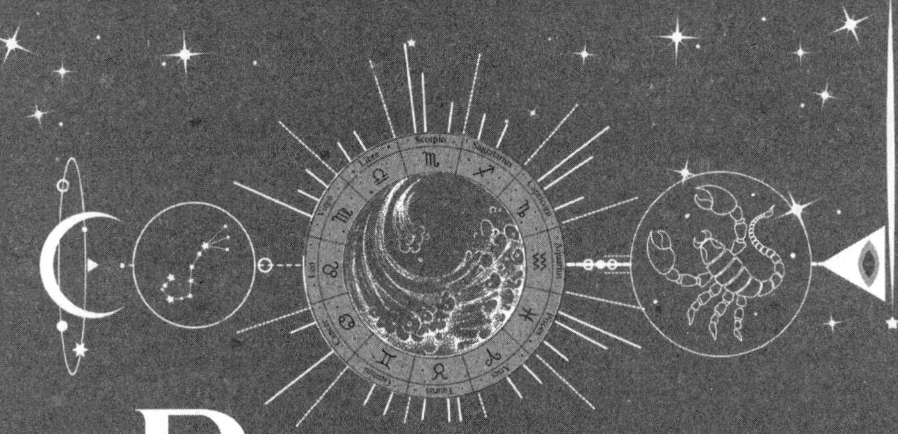

RANSOM

CHAPTER FIFTY

Galomp was damn fast for a giant. He sprinted up the steps in front of me and the Wolf asshole, taking them two at a time as we raced for the top.

The stairway narrowed until North was shoulder to shoulder with me, his elbow jamming into my side more than once and I shoved him back in kind.

"Fucking smoke stain," I spat. "Get out of my way."

"Shut your fish-filled mouth, you cod licking, tuna humper," North snarled back.

"You are both most creative, but we must press on. We must be united for this night. Even if it is a bother," Galomp called. "I do not like the flame flapper any more than you do, Ransom Rake."

"Arcadia," I hissed.

"No, no I do not believe Miss Everest has agreed to that," Galomp answered and I scowled at his back.

We made it to the top of the steps in the northern tower in the Vault of Frost and he threw a door open, wielding his sword with a battle cry.

I muscled through the door with North as he tried to get ahead of me, releasing the spines of my Order form along my arms so he yelped like an un-weaned pup. I smirked at him as I made it past, rounding into the large chamber where Mavus had told us Harlon Brook was being held.

I'd always hated that pompous, puffed up peacock, but I'd been glad of a task that didn't involve a battle. I could assist in a rescue mission easy enough and North and Galomp could do the killing part if necessary. I didn't need to dirty my hands. I was content with my role. But this large bedchamber was empty. Not a Reaper, nor a Harlon in sight.

"Oh bother," Galomp exhaled. "We've been bamboozled."

"Mavus," I hissed. "He lied to us."

"Or he was wrong," North muttered. "This is bullshit. I should have stayed with my brother. Now I'm missing all the fun."

I looked to the Wolf who was apparently keen for a fight and a flash of irritation crossed through me at the realisation that he had no qualms sticking his sword in someone. I was the one lacking in that department.

"What now then?" I looked to Galomp to see if he might have some ideas but North answered instead.

"Now, I'm going to find Kaiser. You can stay here and stick your dick in a narwhal if you like, or whatever Raincarvers like to do with their free time." North turned for the door but my fist connected with his face before he could make it.

"Shut your damn mouth, Wolf."

He turned on me with a vicious snarl, lunging like an animal and knocking me backwards onto the large bed. He pinned me down, choking me and I punched him in the kidney, sending him flying onto his back. It was my time to get on top of him, my hand knotting in his hair while my other slapped him like the little bitch he was.

"Hey!" he barked and I slapped him again.

He reared up, yanking his hair free of my fingers so some dark hairs came loose in my grip before he headbutted me right in the forehead. I lurched backwards with a yell, swinging for him again but he dodged it, pushing me off of him and jerking his knee into my balls as he went.

I cursed, curling in on myself as nausea hit me, hating that fucking Werewolf perhaps more than anyone else in this world.

North sprang off the bed with a taunting laugh and raced out the door. "Bye whale fuckers!"

"Oh bother," Galomp sighed. "Did he crush your danglers?"

I released a groan in response.

"You are probably owed that for being a big bully all these years. I will wait until you are ready to go. Then we will leave together." He sat on the edge of the bed, his weight making it creak as he waited for me to recover. He patted me on the shoulder while I muttered curses. "There, there. Karma is a bother but it will be over soon."

VESPER

CHAPTER FIFTY ONE

Dark magic burned its way through my veins, my eyes watering and muscles cramping as I fought to hold the monster back. I knew I wouldn't be able to keep it at bay much longer but if I could only buy Everest enough time to do what she had to then that was all I needed.

A Reaper managed to get past Bastian, his yell of warning the only thing that saved me from taking a dagger to the back.

I threw myself at the gold-cloaked bastard, my fist colliding with his jaw and boot striking the side of his knee.

He crumpled with a wail of agony and my dagger cut his throat open a heartbeat later, the ether roaring potently in thanks for the sacrifice I'd offered it. But no matter how much death I fed it, the power I could channel wasn't enough to hold back the thing which was rising from the depths of that abyss.

I shoved the body down in front of me, dropping to my knees to use his blood to paint runes against the stone surrounding the chasm where the eschaton star fought to break free. My fingertips were raw from how many times I'd done it, the runes painted over the top of one another time and again.

My ears were ringing, my fingers trembling as I pushed my hold on the dark magic to its limits. Ether roared in my ears, burning out of me, and I knew I was summoning too much of it. A drop was all Moya had taught me to command. But I was calling on a flood and I knew I wasn't going to be able to withstand the force of holding onto it for much longer.

I blinked as bloodied tears slipped from my eyes, painting twin paths down my cheeks. The sound of fighting and the bellows of the eschaton star seemed further away with each strike of my pulse.

The sacrifice I'd given the ether would buy Everest a few more minutes at best. After that, I wasn't sure what would become of me.

"You can do this, Everest!" I yelled, my voice a rasp that warned of my oncoming demise and how little time I had left. Time wasn't on our side and the thing in that hole was going to burst free at any moment.

Metal rang against metal, the iron tang of blood coated my tongue and it was all I could do to maintain my grip on the ether for a few moments longer.

The rest was up to her.

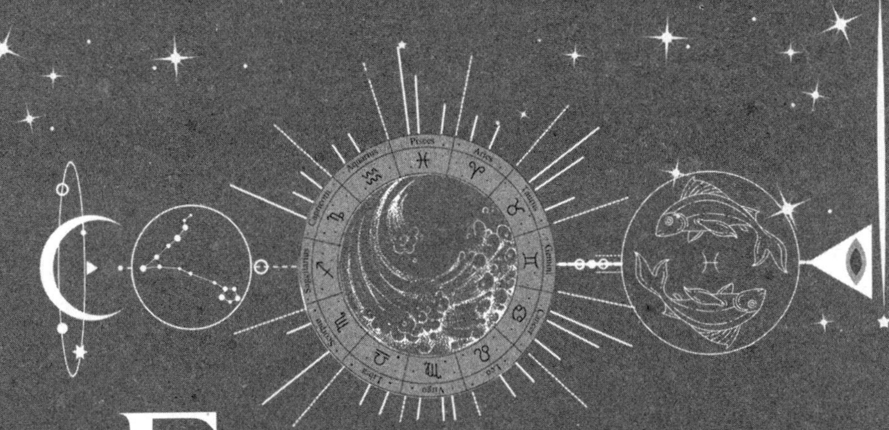

EVEREST

CHAPTER FIFTY TWO

The moon's power thrashed against me with all the impossible strength of the heavens. Sweat slid down the back of my neck, my teeth clenched together as I tried to hold it at bay. The Void was like a dark shield that was the only thing slowing the moon's magic as it was sucked into the abyss below, but it wasn't enough.

My knees hit the floor as another frightful wave of the moon's power clashed with the force of the Void and I screamed with the effort of fighting it back.

"I am Everest Arcadia!" I roared. "I am born of Cascada, a runt, a nothing creature of this battle-torn world. But I made myself into something. I will not be denied! I will be seen! My power will be answered!"

The crimson light flickered, the room shuddered, the violence of the Void somehow grew to a crescendo.

Mavus worked desperately to fill the hole with stone and soil while Vesper stained the rocks with blood magic in desperation to buy me more time. They were pouring everything into this endeavour while Kaiser and Bastian sliced through the Reapers who wished to thwart us.

We were giving all we had, each of us worn to the bone as we offered out our power in refusal of this fate. This monster would not rise. I wouldn't allow it. None of us would.

The eschaton star bucked against the mound of rock and soil, blasting it out of the hole. It started climbing again and terror speared through my chest. I had to stop it. I couldn't let it get through.

"I am the Void!" I bellowed and power tore from me that was built of the fabric of destruction itself.

The green crystals in the room shattered with the inescapable force sweeping from me in a deluge. The moonlight faded as if somehow I'd weakened its power, dulling the magic of a celestial being.

I gasped as I gazed up through the hole in the roof towards the moon in muted shock, a great ripple of magic daggering through the sky as the Void poured from me in a torrent and connected with the immense boundary that domed over The Waning Lands. It was a tear that became a crack that became a fissure which crossed the entire heavens.

Vesper moved closer to watch it too, her grey eyes wide and unblinking as they reflected the glittering rainbow-shot ribbons of magic that were shivering out of existence in the sky.

"The barrier that keeps us closed off from the rest of the world… it's falling," Vesper breathed.

"By the stars," I rasped, unable to believe what I was seeing as that unholy boundary of unspeakable magic began to fall.

It had been cast so long ago, by who even knew. Perhaps the instigators of the war, perhaps the Reapers themselves.

The sky shuddered with its fall, the isle of Never Keep trembling violently and Vesper caught my arm to pull me away from the edge of the chasm.

The chamber shuddered so hard that we stumbled and Mavus went tumbling into the hole with a cry of fear.

I yelled out in horror, lunging for him, but the fabric of his shirt slipped through my fingertips. He crashed down into the shadowy grasp of the eschaton star and Vesper steadied me as I reached for him, sending a chain of ice down into it for him to grab hold of. But he was caught under some dark spell, jerking and writhing as the shadowy grasp of the monster held him tight, its claws gouging into his flesh. The beast itself was cloaked in shade, its features indistinguishable outside of two hellish eyes and its slashing talons.

"Mavus!" I screamed in fear, trying to reach him with magic as he wailed in horror, but then his face began to change, confounding me beyond all reason. He was no longer Mavus but Solomon Imai, the Cardinal Reaper himself yelling out to me instead.

"Everest!" he yelled. "Pull me out!"

I shook my head in confusion, Vesper and I drawing back another step but the ground shook and threw us to the floor at the chasm's precipice. So all we could do was hold onto each other and watch.

VESPER

CHAPTER FIFTY THREE

"What is this?" I gasped, my fingers pressing to the bloody wound on the back of my head, shards of green crystal piercing my skin.

The man who had been Mavus jerked and thrashed, his face changing from Solomon Imai to some unknown Fae, then again and again, his body rippling as muscles shrank and expanded, wings burst from his spine then rippled away to be replaced by a spiked tail.

He began to rise out of the abyss, tendrils of darkness puncturing his spine, lifting him higher like some freakish mannequin hoisted up on a stage where only we were the audience.

The Reapers were dead, Kaiser and Bastian calling out our names as the ground continued to tremor beneath us and we fought to scramble away from the gaping edge of that terrifying chasm.

I fought to get to my feet and Bastian caught my arm, hauling me back as Mavus's face turned pale, his body lengthening, his hair becoming white.

Kaiser had hauled Everest upright too, the four of us huddled together before the grotesquely-transforming body, more limbs and claws formed of darkness driving into his body and making him scream.

His face changed again, becoming familiar, hauling a lifetime of memories to the forefront of my mind.

"Dragor?" I breathed, staring into the hard lines of my prince's face in utter confusion.

It wasn't possible to cast magic like that – any Fae worth their salt knew how to protect their image from magical impersonation and there was no Fae alive who would be able to make their face appear as that of the king of Stormfell. But there was no denying who I was staring at.

Dragor yelled in pain, his height lowering a fraction but muscles expanding, and I shook my head in dismay as he became Earl Tarlord, then Mavus again, then a bald man of advanced years whose harsh expression stirred memories in the corners of my mind.

"That's the Cardinal Reaper," Everest croaked, her voice hoarse where she slumped against Kaiser who held her in his arms.

The man's face and body shifted again and again and again, a roar escaping him which could only belong to the monster we'd fought so hard to deny entry into our world, the thing which was driving itself beneath his flesh, forcing its way inside him.

He jerked and screamed as those slick tendrils of darkness forced their way inside him and I leaned back against Bastian who held his sword out before us defiantly.

The man's face and body kept shifting though the scream on his lips and horror in his eyes never changed, only rising in pitch and fear until every piece of darkness from within the abyss had forced its way inside him.

They'd become one somehow, that beast and this man – but I still didn't understand how Mavus now wore the faces of so many others.

"We have to leave," Bastian snarled, hauling on my arm and pushing me behind him so that I could retreat, his sword still raised between us and that…thing. "Come on," he barked at Kaiser who tugged Everest into his arms and hurried to join us.

I wanted to argue, wanted to keep fighting. But my limbs shook with fatigue, every scrap of magic gone from my grasp, even the ether fleeing my call as if it ran from this place too, knowing something which I hadn't quite managed to figure out yet.

But as we scrambled back towards the door, rocks slammed down from the roof and sealed us in.

"You can't leave, lass," Mavus called and we whirled to look back at him as he took a slow step towards us, his feet landing on the edge of the abyss, his eyes locked on Everest as they gleamed a bright yellow.

He appeared the same as he had done before plunging into that abyss but there was a darkness that clung to him now, a hidden power which haunted his steps like a lost shadow.

"What are you?" Everest breathed, pushing herself free of Kaiser's hold so that she could stand tall in the heart of our group. "What have you done to my friend?"

Mavus grinned widely, his cheeks stretching abnormally and far too many teeth appearing at once.

"We *were* friends, weren't we?" he purred, taking another step towards us and though his foot landed lightly on the stone, I felt a ripple of power pulsing through the rocks beneath our feet at his advance. "And friends help each other out of a bind."

"A bind?" Everest asked. "Is that what you're in?"

I eased my last dagger from my belt, my pulse settling at the feel of steel against my palm even if I had the feeling it would do me no good.

"That I am. You tried to help me but–" His words cut off in a haunting scream, his knees slamming to the floor as the bellow of a monster burst impossibly from his lungs, his eyes flashing that bright and haunting yellow again as he jerked his head back up to glare at us.

"You betrayed me!" he howled in a booming, unnatural voice which didn't seem to be his own at all.

"I wanted to stop it from escaping!" Mavus howled at Everest, his voice his own again though it was raw and filled with pain now. "But there was never much chance of that."

"We need to get the fuck out of here," Kaiser hissed as Mavus began to jerk and thrash again, black, reptilian wings bursting from his spine.

"I'm out of magic," I replied, my eyes darting around the room in hunt of some point of escape.

"We all are," Kaiser breathed.

"There." Bastian jerked his chin towards a dark passageway on the far side of the chamber where some of the Reapers had escaped earlier. But it was right across the echoing space, past the creature and whatever was left of Mavus now that it had forced its way inside him.

We tensed, all of us ready to run, Kaiser's hand coiling around Everest's in the shadows.

I turned the dagger in my grip, met Bastian's roiling gaze for half a second, then threw it.

The monster screamed so loudly that rocks broke from the roof above us as we ran, its fury hounding our steps while we sprinted for the exit.

I led the way, Kaiser keeping Everest close behind me while Bastian guarded our backs.

The passageway was close, closer–

A wave of power slammed into us so forcefully that we were all thrown from our feet and hurled across the ground, broken shards of crystal cutting any piece of exposed skin they could find.

We landed in a heap, and I fought to scramble upright. If I was going to die here, then I would do so on my feet.

I whirled towards Mavus and flinched when I found Dragor scowling back at me, those black wings still protruding from his spine. But that wasn't right. Dragor was a Harpy; his wings had feathers and were white.

"How are you doing that? How are you wearing his face?" I demanded furiously, my own anger at this situation all I had left because it had come to nothing! I'd given all I was to this plan, to this fool's hope that I might be able to do something *good* with my life after rotting in the bad for so long. And this was what it came to? Us dying in this frozen hole while that monstrous thing escaped anyway and carried out its plans regardless of all we'd done to thwart it.

Dragor laughed, that cold, haunting chuckle I knew so well.

"I'm not wearing anything, little witch," he purred, his voice, his expression, all of it so precisely *him.* "I own this face just like all the others. I earned it and took it and made it my own."

"What the fuck are you talking about?" I spat.

"He's an Incubus," Bastian breathed, his arm brushing mine as he stood beside me, his silver shot eyes bright with haunted understanding.

"Ah – I see those extra few hundred years of life I gifted you weren't for nothing then, my sweet Dragon. At least one of you can see the beauty of my truth."

"An Incubus?" Everest hissed. "I thought they just shifted for sex – made themselves look like your most desperate desire so they could steal your magic and–"

"And what?" Dragor asked, except he wasn't Dragor anymore, his face was changing again, his hair and complexion darkening, his eyes flashing red until Kaiser stared back at us, a grin on his lips.

The real Kaiser released a low growl of warning beside me, his grip on Everest's arm tightening as if he thought she might launch herself at the Incubus.

"Thank you for this face by the way, Everest Arcadia," the fake Kaiser said, offering her a smirk. "It will make it all the easier for me to get closer to the Matriarch."

The real Kaiser broke from our group, raising his sword as he ran at the Incubus with a furious bellow but he didn't get within ten feet of him before he was blasted back by the wild force of energy which seemed to surround Mavus – or whoever the fuck he really was.

Kaiser collided with our group and we were all knocked to the ground once more, his sword skittering away across the stone while Bastian's arms wrapped around me protectively.

The Incubus swiped a hand over his face and as he dropped it, he was Mavus once more.

"I am sorry, lass," he said with a voice that was at once his but also laced with the growl of the monster. "We tried, didn't we? But this is what it is now. And I can't have you coming back to try and stop me again."

Power built in the chamber, the walls cracking as a howling wind blasted through the space and the Fae who had been Mavus advanced on us once more, his eyes blazing yellow as a beast peered out from the depths of his soul.

Bastian held me tighter and my heart raced in panic as I felt the wings of death flying straight towards us. We were going to die. *He* was going to die. And all he'd ever had from me were half-truths and chains to bind him so that he could never fully claim the freedom he so longed for.

I looked up at him with tears burning in my eyes, my hand gripping his face so that I could peer directly into his soul and nowhere else.

"I love you," I told him, shattering every wall I'd placed between us with the admission I'd fought for so long. "And I won't let this be your end."

I took hold of the vial of blood around my neck, the heat of it burning me as I ripped it free of the necklace it hung from. I threw my consciousness towards the ether, offering that which was most precious to me so that I might save the only people I had left in this world to care about.

Everest was yelling something, Kaiser still crumpled on the ground by her feet, his blood staining the stone.

I dove into the vast power of the dark magic which had raised me more thoroughly than any mother and smashed the vial of my sisters' blood in front of us, using the weight of their sacrifice to buy me enough power to shield us from the wrath of a monster.

The Incubus howled as its power collided with mine and the ether tore its way through my veins until they stood out, dark and livid against my skin.

Bastian grabbed my arm, trying to haul me back as I sank further and further into the depths of the ether, throwing everything I could summon at the endless force of power which was exploding from the eschaton star.

I cried out as the terrible weight of its power surrounded us, far too much of it for me to stand against for long. Shadows pooled in the corners of my eyes and within them I felt the gaze of two lost souls staring back at me, the weight of their hands pressing down on my shoulders as they gifted me whatever power they still held from beyond the grave.

My grief at their loss struck me with force and the pain of it ignited a fierce determination in me as I lashed myself to the power I was calling upon and refused to let it fail me. I wouldn't lose him as well. I couldn't.

Bastian yelled my name, his arms banding around me from behind as he pressed his cheek against mine and opened himself up to the ether too, offering me whatever power I could wield via him. But I wouldn't take it. I refused to drag him down with me. I refused to fall into death with him at my side.

"Let me help you," he demanded.

But I was lost to the ether, unable to pull back, unwilling to attempt it even if I could. There were wounds on my arms and I smeared my fingers through the blood that wept from them, spitting out words to bind this power to my own lifeforce, offering myself up in payment for the protection of the Fae at my back.

"Stop!" Bastian bellowed. "You're killing yourself!"

A yell tore from my throat as I demanded more and more from the ether, refusing to back down, my boots sliding against stone, Bastian's hold on me the only thing keeping me on my feet, Everest and Kaiser shielded behind us.

The Incubus howled in fury, claiming another step towards me as my power roared and tears of blood spilled down my cheeks.

The sensation of my sisters' hands on my shoulders grew firmer, the feeling that I was with them soothing my soul as I made the decision to sacrifice myself. For him. Only him. My one good thing.

"Vesper," Bastian snarled, his grip on me tightening as he fought to summon me back to him. He knew what I was doing, he could feel it just as surely as I could feel the cloak of death creeping up behind me.

I wouldn't stop. I couldn't.

My heart struck a ragged rhythm against my ribs, its beats rushing to a crescendo I knew would end in death. But I fought for every second longer, every extra moment I could steal within his arms. Because the second I broke I knew I would be torn from him. And I would cherish each moment with him until our last.

I cried out, stumbling back against Bastian whose arms never once loosened around me, his mouth against my ear as he returned the words I'd given him, the pain I felt in the admission breaking what was left of my ravaged heart.

"I love you, Vesper. Have done since the moment I first saw you in that cave. And if I only got to make you mine in this one second then that's enough for me."

A bloodstained tear fell from my jaw to splash against his arm where he held me, the power I was forcing through my limbs cracking me open, burning me alive.

We were almost out of time and we both knew it. I couldn't win this fight. The eschaton star was too strong.

I turned my head so that Bastian would be the last thing I saw in this wretched world. But instead of my eyes landing on his face, I found myself blinded by flames of brightest red and blue.

Where death had come creeping up on me, fire now chased it away.

My hold on the ether snapped before I could complete the sacrifice and I stumbled back against Bastian, throwing my arm up to shield my eyes from the blazing flames.

It was so hot it seared the air in my lungs, dried the bloody tears against my cheeks and threatened to peel the skin from my bones. But before it could burn us all, a shield snapped up around us, a dome of glimmering, solidified air protecting us from the blaze.

I blinked at the dark-haired man who had appeared from nowhere to protect us and stood with his arms outstretched ahead of us. Black, feathered wings spread wide at his back and tattoos were scrawled across every inch of skin I could see on his bare torso.

In the blaze beyond the stranger's shield, the eschaton star was screaming, its power battling the blue and red flames which blazed all around it.

"There's a woman flying out there," Everest gasped, pointing into the depths of the fire but she was gone before I could get a proper look at her.

"Two," Bastian said and I tilted my head back to look just as two figures sped by overhead, wings made of that same, impossible fire burning at their backs. They appeared to be twins, though one had dark hair while the other's was blue.

"Gemini?" I breathed, staring at the deities who soared above us.

"The stars have come to save us," Everest exhaled.

"No," the tattooed man who was shielding us said darkly. "I just fucked up on the timing when the shield fell – we're running late."

"What?" I asked but he didn't answer me, his muscles bunching as he focused on protecting us from the blaze.

A piercing shriek burst from the eschaton star. I flinched as the cavern cracked apart beyond the flames and the shield tremored violently.

Mavus howled as his face was illuminated between flames of red and blue and then he spread those black, reptilian wings from his back and launched himself into the sky, careering away from us at a frightening speed, taking the sickening taint of his foul power with him.

The fire fell away and the twin warriors landed in the ruins of the cavern, turning to look at us as the inked man dropped his shield.

"Well?" the dark-haired twin asked, her green eyes meeting with mine, accusation burning bright within them. "Which one of you is going to tell us how the fuck that thing was unleashed?"

THE MAN OF MANY FACES

CHAPTER FIFTY FOUR

I lay panting in the snow, surrounded by nothing and no one, my flesh both freezing and unblemished.

I was no longer what I'd been. My mind no longer mine alone.

"You broke your vow to me, faceless one," Caelum growled from within the recesses of my mind.

My skin felt too tight around my bones, my mind too constricted with the monster's presence taking hold of its dark corners.

"I would kill you for your betrayal. But it seems I have use for you yet."

"What do you want?" I panted through lips known as those of Prince Dragor, though of course I'd killed the real prince many years ago before taking his place along with his face. Just as I had done with so many powerful Fae before him. My empire had been complete and none but me and this hideous creature had known of it.

But I'd always feared this day would come. I'd known making a bargain with a monster would only end in horrors.

"I want the same thing I have always craved. More souls for the reaping."

I swallowed thickly. I had lived for many hundreds of years and claimed power no other Fae had ever dared to dream of seizing. All with the aid of this beast. My part in our deal to keep the war waging so that it could feast on the magic their deaths fed it while it gave me the gemstones which bought me immortality. All with the knowledge that this day might finally arrive. It had been my creature for so long, gifting me the crystals I'd needed to extend my lifespan while I simply fed it with death and ruin as it had demanded.

But all those years of feeding it pain had made it far stronger than I'd ever wanted to believe possible. The Void had been my only hope to keep it in check, to keep my own position as master of The Waning Lands in place and stop this beast from breaking through from its own world into mine.

"You can still maintain your position as master of all," it purred from within me, the rotting stench of its power burning as it filled my nostrils. *"But in return, you will keep me fed."*

"Yes," I agreed. I had no other choice left to me regardless.

So once again I made a bargain with a monster. But this time, I feared I would not be the one in control of the destiny we wove as one.

AUTHOR NOTE

Well heyyy, are you doing okay there? I think that was actually a pretty nice cliffhanger so far as we go – no big characters getting their heads chopped off, no lovers being torn apart, not even a curse to end all curses – but I will say that twist was one of my favourites we have ever written. For so long we have had to keep track of the Man of Many Faces (or Von Blah as we affectionately call him in the writing cave) and now you finally know about him too!

I very much look forward to unveiling the full extent of his conniving ways in the next and final book in this series.

Yes – you heard me correctly, the next book will be the last!

And the crossovers shall be delicious in all the best ways. So if you haven't read Zodiac Academy yet, this may be a good time to catch up – we promise to keep spoilers to a minimum but as this series takes place after the events in Zodiac Academy there will be some revelations which we can't avoid (such as the fact that some characters did in fact manage to survive).

But that's all fun and games for next year!

As always, we want to thank you for continuing to devour our words, fall in love with our characters and risk the horror of our cliffhangers. It really means so much to us that we have been able to turn this dream into a reality and we are forever grateful to all of you for making that happen.

We love you all, and look forward to meeting you at the next heart-stopping cliffhanger.

Love, Susanne & Caroline XOXO

DISCOVER MORE FROM CAROLINE PECKHAM & SUSANNE VALENTI

To find out more, grab yourself some freebies, merchandise, and special signed editions or to join their reader group, scan the QR code below.